Praise for the novels of
New York Times **bestselling author**
Jo Beverley

The Devil's Heiress

"[A] deftly woven tale of romantic intrigue. . . . Head and shoulders above the usual Regency fare, this novel's sensitive prose, charismatic characters, and expert plotting will keep readers enthralled from first page to last."
—*Publishers Weekly*

"With her talent for writing powerful love stories and masterful plotting, Ms. Beverley cleverly brings together this dynamic duo. Her latest captivating romance . . . is easily a 'keeper'!"
—*Romantic Times* (Top Pick)

"Exciting. . . . The story line is filled with action, but it is the charming lead couple that makes the plot hum."
—Harriet Klausner

"A riveting, completely captivating blend of romance, intrigue, and suspense that enthralls from the first page to the last. Beverley is a master storyteller and this book, with its superb plot, fascinating characters, and lush prose, is a stellar example of her talent . . . a strong contender for best historical romance of the year."
—Romance Fiction Forum

Hazard

"Engaging. . . . Fans will appreciate the spicy chemistry between [Anne] and Race."
—*Publishers Weekly*

continued . . .

continued . . .

"Delightful . . . thrilling . . . with a generous touch of magic . . . an enchanting read."   —*Booklist*

"An excellent read—definitely for dreamers!"
                                              —*Rendezvous*

"Jo Beverley's style is flawless. . . . A wild ride filled with humor, suspense, love, passion, and much more."
                                              —*Gothic Journal*

Lord of Midnight

"Beverley weaves a stunning medieval romance of loss and redemption . . . sizzling."
                              —*Publishers Weekly* (starred review)

"Noted for her fast-paced, wonderfully inventive stories, excellent use of humor and language, and vividly rendered characters and situations, Beverley has created another gem that will not disappoint."   —*Library Journal*

"Jo Beverley brings the twelfth century to life in a vivid portrayal of a highly romantic story that captures the era with all its nuances, pageantry, and great passion . . . a real treat!"   —*Romantic Times*

"Extremely enjoyable . . . intriguing. . . . Jo Beverley is clearly one of the leading writers lighting up the Dark Ages."   —Painted Rock Reviews

ALSO BY JO BEVERLEY

The
Devil's Heiress

Jo Beverley

A SIGNET BOOK

SIGNET
Published by New American Library, a division of
Penguin Group (USA) Inc., 375 Hudson Street,
New York, New York 10014, USA
Penguin Group (Canada), 90 Eglinton Avenue East, Suite 700, Toronto,
Ontario M4P 2Y3, Canada (a division of Pearson Penguin Canada Inc.)
Penguin Books Ltd., 80 Strand, London WC2R 0RL, England
Penguin Ireland, 25 St. Stephen's Green, Dublin 2,
Ireland (a division of Penguin Books Ltd.)
Penguin Group (Australia), 250 Camberwell Road, Camberwell, Victoria 3124,
Australia (a division of Pearson Australia Group Pty. Ltd.)
Penguin Books India Pvt. Ltd., 11 Community Centre, Panchsheel Park,
New Delhi - 110 017, India
Penguin Group (NZ), cnr Airborne and Rosedale Roads, Albany,
Auckland 1310, New Zealand (a division of Pearson New Zealand Ltd.)
Penguin Books (South Africa) (Pty.) Ltd., 24 Sturdee Avenue,
Rosebank, Johannesburg 2196, South Africa

Penguin Books Ltd., Registered Offices:
80 Strand, London WC2R 0RL, England

First published by Signet, an imprint of New American Library,
a division of Penguin Group (USA) Inc.

First Printing, August 2001
First Printing ($4.99 Edition), January 2006
10 9 8 7 6 5 4 3 2 1

ACKNOWLEDGMENT

I had visited Brighton in the past, but I wanted up-to-date information about particular streets. On the Web I found Gail and Pete Robertson's Writers Information Registry at http://www.pacific coast.net/~gprobert/registry.html and put in a request for Brighton. Gary Crucifix replied with some help and his father took photographs and sent them to me over the Net. Isn't technology wonderful! Thanks to all.

Chapter One

～

June 1816, Sussex

Home.

It had been a word without much meaning, but today, with his village *en fête* for his friend's wedding, the contact, the bone-deep belonging, was like a cannonball for Major George Hawkinville—one slamming into earth far too close and knocking the wind out of him.

Following Van and Maria out of the church into the midst of the bouncing, cheering crowd, he felt almost dazed by the familiar—the ancient green ringed by buildings new and old, the row of ramshackle cottages down by the river, the walled and thatched house at the end of the row . . .

Hawkinville Manor, his personal hell, but now, it would seem, his essential heaven.

"Welcome home, sir!"

He pulled himself together and shook hands with beaming Aaron Hooker. And with the next man, and the next. Soon women were kissing him, not all decorously. Hawk grinned and accepted the kisses.

This was Van's wedding, but Con was introducing his bride, Susan, here, too. Clearly the villagers were making it into a return festivity for all three of them.

The Georges.

The plaguey imps.

The gallant soldiers.

The heroes.

It wasn't the time to be wry about that, so he kissed and shook hands and accepted backslaps from men used to slapping oxen. In the end, he caught up to the blushing new bride and the very recent bride, and claimed kisses of his own.

"Hawk," said Susan Amleigh, Con's wife, her eyes brilliant, "have I told you how much I love Hawk in the Vale?"

"Once or twice, I think."

She just laughed at his dry tone. "How lucky you all are to have grown up here. I don't know how you could bear to leave it."

Because a tubful of sweet posset could be soured by a spoonful of gall, but Hawk didn't let his smile twist. He'd been desperate to leave here at sixteen, and didn't regret it now, but he did regret dragging Van and Con along. Not that he'd have been able to stop them if their families couldn't. The Georges had always done nearly everything together.

What was done was done—wisdom, of a trite sort—and they'd all survived. Now, in part because of these wonderful women, Con and Van were even happy.

Happy. He rolled that in his mind like a foreign food, uncertain whether it was palatable or not. Whichever it was, it wasn't on his plate. He was hardly the type for sweethearts and orange blossoms, and he would bring no one he cared for to share Hawkinville Manor with himself and his father. He had only returned there because the squire was crippled by a seizure.

If only he'd died of it.

He put that aside and let a buxom woman drag him into a country dance. Astonishing to realize that it was shy Elsie Dadswell, Elsie Manktelow now, with three children, a boy and two girls, and no trace of shyness that he could see. She was also clearly well on the way to a new baby.

Somewhat alarmed, he asked if she should be dancing so vigorously, but she laughed, linked arms, and nearly swung him off his feet. He laughed too and ricocheted down the line off strong, working-women's arms.

His people. His to take care of, even if he had to fight his father to do it. Some of the cottages needed repairs and the riverbank needed work, but prizing money out of the squire's hands these days was like getting a corpse to release a sword.

A blushing girl missing two front teeth asked him to dance next, so he did, glad to escape mundane concerns. He'd dealt with mass army movements over mountainous terrain, through killing storms. Surely the squire and Hawk in the Vale couldn't defeat him. He flirted with the girl, disconcerted to discover that she was Will Ashbee's daughter. Will was only a year older than he was.

Will had spent his life here, growing children and working through the cycles of the seasons. Hawk had lived in the death cycle of war. Marching, waiting, squabbling, fighting, then dealing with the broken and burying the dead.

How many men had he known who were now dead? It was not a tally he wanted to make. God had been good, and he, Van, and Con were all home.

Home.

The fiddles and whistles came to the end of their piece, and he passed his partner to a red-faced lad not much older than she was.

Love. For some it seemed as natural as the birds in spring. Perhaps some birds never quite got the hang of it, either.

He saw that a cricket match had started on the quiet side of the green. That was much less likely to stir maudlin thoughts, so he strolled over to watch and applaud.

The batter said, "Want a go, Major?"

Hawk was about to say no, but then he saw the glow in many eyes. Damnable as it was, he was a hero to most of these people. He and Van and Con were all heroes. They were all veterans, but most important, they had all been at the great battle of Waterloo a year ago.

So he shrugged out of his jacket and gave it to Bill Ashbee—Will's father—to hold, then went to take the home-carved bat. It was part of his role here to take part. As son of the squire and the future squire himself, he was an important part of village life.

He wished he weren't their hero, however. Two years after taking up a cornetcy in the cavalry, he'd been seconded to the Quartermaster General's Department, and thus most of his war had been spent out of active fighting. The heroes were the men like Con and Van, who'd breathed the enemy's breath and waded through blood. Or even Lord Darius Debenham, Con's friend and an enthusiastic volunteer at Waterloo who'd died there.

But he was the major, while Con and Van had made only captain, and he knew the Duke of Wellington. Rather better than he'd wanted to at times. He took the bat and faced the bowler, who looked to be about fourteen and admirably determined to bowl him out if he could. Hawk hoped he could.

The first bowl went wide, but Hawk leaned forward and stopped it so it bumped across the rough grass into a fielder's hands. He'd played plenty of cricket during the lazy times in the army. Surely he could manage this so as to please everyone.

He hit another ball a bit harder to make one run, leaving the other batter up. The bowler bowled that man out. Disconcerting not to be able to put a name to him. After a little while, Hawk was facing the determined bowler again, and this time the ball hurtled straight for the wicket. A slight twist of the bat allowed the ball to knock the bails flying, raising a great cheer from the onlookers and a mighty whoop of triumph from the young bowler.

Hawk grinned and went over to slap him on the back, then retrieved his coat.

Ashbee helped him on with it, but then stepped back with him out of the group around the game. "How's the squire today, sir?"

"Improving. He's out watching the festivities from a chair near the manor."

Sitting in state, more likely, but Hawk kept his tone bland. The villagers didn't need to feel a spill of bile from the Hawkinville family's affairs.

"Good health to him, sir," said Ashbee, in the same tone. Folly to think that the villagers didn't know how things were, with the servants in the manor all village people except the squire's valet.

And after all, men like Bill Ashbee could remember when handsome Captain John Gaspard arrived in the village to woo Miss Sophronia Hawkinville, the old squire's only child, and wed her, agreeing to take the family name. They would also remember the lady's bitter disillusion when her father's death turned suitor into indifferent husband. After all, Hawk's mother had not suffered in silence. But she'd suffered. What choice did she have?

And now she was dead, dead more than a year ago of the influenza that had swept through this area. Hawk hoped she had found peace elsewhere, and he regretted that he could not truly grieve. She had been the wronged party, but she had also been so absorbed in her own ill-usage that she'd had no time for her one child except to occasionally fight his father over him.

He realized that Ashbee was hovering because he wanted to say something.

Ashbee cleared his throat. "I was wondering if you'd heard anything about changes down along the river, sir."

"You mean repairs." Damn the squire. "I know there's work needs doing—"

"No, sir, not that. But there was some men poking around the other day. When Granny Muggridge asked their business, they didn't seem to want to say, but she heard them mention foundations and water levels."

Hawk managed not to swear. What the devil was the squire up to now? He claimed there was no money to spare, which Hawk couldn't understand, and now he was planning some improvement to the manor?

"I don't know, Ashbee. I'll ask my father."

"Thank you, sir," the man said, but he did not look markedly satisfied. "Thing is, sir, later on Jack Smithers from the Peregrine said he saw them talking to that Slade. The men had stabled horses at the Peregrine, you see, and Slade walked them from his house to the inn."

Slade. Josiah Slade was a Birmingham iron founder who'd made a fortune casting cannons for the war. For some devil-inspired reason he'd retired here in Hawk in the Vale a year ago and become a crony of the squire's. How, Hawk couldn't imagine. The squire came from an aristocratic family and despised trade.

But somehow Slade had persuaded the squire to permit him to build a stuccoed monstrosity of a house on the west side of the green. It would not have been so out of place on the Marine Parade in Brighton, but in Hawk in the Vale it was like a tombstone in a garden. The squire had brushed off questions rather shiftily.

All was not right in Hawk in the Vale. Hawk had come home hoping never to have to dig in the dirt again, but it seemed it wasn't to be so easy.

"I'll look into it," he said, adding, "Thank you."

Ashbee nodded, mission complete.

Hawk headed back into the crowd, looking for Slade. The trouble here was that he was damnably impotent. In the army he'd had rank, authority, and the backing of his department. Here, he could do nothing without his father's consent.

By his parents' marriage contract, his father had complete control over the Hawkinville estate for life. He'd heard that his mother had been mad to have dashing Captain Gaspard, and had been the indulged apple of her father's eye, but he wished they'd fought for better terms.

It was all a pointed lesson in the folly that could come from imagining oneself in love.

He saw Van and Maria dancing together, looking as if stars shone in each other's eyes. Perhaps sometimes, for some people, love was real. He smiled at Con and Susan too, but caught Con in a contemplative mood, a somberness marking him that would have been alien a year ago, before Waterloo.

No, he'd been changed before Waterloo, changed by months at home, out of the army, thinking peace had come. That change, that gentling, was why the battle had hit him so hard. That and Lord Darius's death. Amid so many deaths one more or less shouldn't matter, but it didn't work like that. He could remember weeping on and off for days over the loss of one friend at Badajoz.

He wished he could have found Dare's body for Con. He'd done his damnedest.

He saw Susan touch Con's arm, and could tell that the dark mood fled. Con would be all right.

He spotted Slade over by a beer barrel, holding court. There were always some willing to toady to a man of wealth, though Hawk was pleased to see that not many of the villagers fell into that category. Colonel Napier was there, and the new doctor, Scott. Outsiders.

Hawk had to admit that Slade was a trim man for his age, but he fit into the village as poorly as his house did. His clothes were perfect country clothes—today, a brown jacket, buff breeches, and gleaming top boots. The trouble was that they were too perfect, too new—as real as a masquerade shepherdess.

Hawk had heard Jack Smithers commenting on the horseflesh Slade kept stabled at the Peregrine. Top-class horses, but the man was afraid of them and when he went out riding he sat like a sack of potatoes. Slade clearly wanted to exchange his money for the life of a country gentleman, but why, in the name of heaven, here?

And what new monstrosity did he have planned?

Replace the old humpbacked bridge over the river with a copy in miniature of the Westminster one?

He strolled over and accepted a tankard, and a kiss, from Bill Ashbee's wife.

"A grand affair, Major," declared Slade, smiling, though Hawk had noted before that the man's smiles to him were false. He had no idea why. Van and Con had both complained of the way Slade beamed at them, obviously trying to insinuate himself with the two local peers. A mere Hawkinville wasn't worth toadying to?

"Perhaps we should have more such fêtes," Hawk said, simply to make conversation.

"That will be for the squire to say, will it not, sir?"

Hawk ran that through his mind, wondering what it

meant. It clearly meant something more than the obvious.

"I doubt my father will object as long as he doesn't have to foot the bill."

"But he won't be squire forever," said Slade.

Hawk took a drink of ale, puzzled. And alert. He knew when people were running a subtext for their own amusement. "I won't object either, Slade, on the same terms."

"If that should arise, Major, you must apply to me for a loan. I assure you, I will always be happy to support the innocent celebrations of my rustic neighbors."

Hawk glanced at the "rustic neighbors" nearby, and saw some rolled eyes and twitching lips. Slade was a figure of fun here, but Hawk's deep, dark, well-tuned instincts were registering a very different message.

He toasted Slade with his tankard. "We rustic neighbors will always be suitably appreciative, sir!" He drained the ale, hearing a few suppressed chuckles and seeing Slade's smile become fixed.

But not truly dimmed. No, the man still thought he had a winning hand. What the devil was the game, though?

Hawk turned to work his way through the crowd to where his father sat near the manor's gates, his valet hovering. A few other people had brought out chairs to keep him company—newer village residents who doubtless saw themselves as too good to romp with their "rustic neighbors," even for a lord's wedding.

Hawk put that thought out of mind. They were harmless people. The spinsterish Misses Weatherby, whose only weapon was gossiping tongues. The vicar and his wife, who probably would prefer to be in the merriment but perhaps felt obliged by charity to sit with the invalid. That Mrs. Rowland, who claimed her husband was a distant relative of the squire's. She was a sallow, dismal woman who dressed in drooping black, but he shouldn't be uncharitable. Her husband still suffered from a Waterloo injury and she was in desperate need of charity.

The squire had given her free tenancy of some rooms

at the back part of the corn factor's, and freedom of produce from the home farm. In return, the woman was a frequent visitor, and she did seem to raise his father's spirits, heaven knows why. Perhaps they talked of past Gaspard glory.

Hawk remembered that he'd meant to look in on Lieutenant Rowland to see if anything could be done for his health. No one in the village had so much as seen him. Another duty on a long list.

At the moment he was more interested in Slade. There was something amiss there.

So badly amiss that Hawk changed his mind and turned back to the celebration. He didn't want to confront his father in public, but confront him he would, and squeeze the truth out of him if necessary. Whatever Slade was up to could be blocked. All the land in the village was owned by the manor.

He'd learned to put aside pending problems and grasp whatever pleasure the moment held, so he joined a laughing group of young men, who had once been lads of his own age to play with or fight with.

He kept an eye on the squire, however, and when his father was finally carried back into Hawkinville Manor, Hawk eased away from the revels and followed. He crossed the green and the road that circled it, and went through the tall gates that always stood open these days. Once those gates and the high encircling wall had been practical defenses. A tall stone tower still stood at one corner of the house, remnant of an even sterner medieval home of the Hawkinvilles. He was aware of a strange instinct to close the gates and man the walls.

Against Slade?

The door opened and Mrs. Rowland came out, a basket on her arm. "Good evening, Major Hawkinville," she said, as if good was an effort of optimism. She was a Belgian and spoke with an accent. "A pleasant wedding, was it not?"

"Delightful. How is your husband, Mrs. Rowland?"

She sighed. "Perhaps he grows a little stronger."

"I must come and visit him soon."

"How very kind. He has some days better than others. I hope it will be possible." She curtsied and left with a nunlike step that made him wonder how she'd produced two children.

A very strange woman.

He shook his head and crossed the courtyard, evening-full of rose perfume and bird twitter. The hounds greeted him at the door, still not entirely used to him. Only old Galahad dated from his boyhood. Hawk had named him, in fact, to his father's disgust at the romantical name.

The squire called him Gally.

Perhaps it was a miracle that his father's dogs didn't bite him on sight.

When he walked in through the oak door his boots rapped on the flagstoned corridor. Strange the things that a person remembers. When he'd returned here two weeks ago, that sound—his boots on the floor along with the slight jingle of his spurs—had been a trigger for explosive memories, both good and bad.

There were other triggers. The smell of wax polish, which this close to the door blended with the roses in the courtyard. There had always been, as now, roses in the pottery bowl on the table near the door. In the winter, it was rose potpourri.

Hawkinville's roses had perhaps been his mother's savior. Over the years she had abandoned everything to her husband except her rose garden. Wryly, he could remember being jealous of roses.

When he was young. When he was very, very young.

He had always been practical, and had soon learned to do without family fondness. Anyway, he'd had the families of his friends to fill any void.

It would be different now. Perhaps that was what had tinged the day with slight melancholy. By some miracle, the close friendship of the Georges seemed to have survived, but it could never be the same, not now that Van and Con had another special person in their lives. Soon, no doubt, there would be children.

But it was still there, the rare and precious friendship. As close as brothers. As close as triplets, perhaps.

Perhaps that was the tug of Hawk in the Vale. It was the home of his closest friends. But here, in the entrance hall of the house in which he had been born, he knew it was more than that.

The Hawkinvilles had been here far longer than the house, but even so his family had worn tracks in these flagstones for four hundred years, and doubtless cursed the damp that rose from them when heavy rain soaked the earth beneath.

Perhaps his older ancestors hadn't needed to duck beneath some of the dark oak lintels, though at least one had held the nickname Longshanks. Hawkinvilles had made marks in the paneling and woodwork, sometimes by accident and sometimes on purpose. There was a pistol ball embedded in the parlor wainscoting from an unfortunate disagreement between brothers during the Civil War.

He'd thought he didn't care. Over the years in the army, he could not remember experiencing homesickness. A fierce desire at times to be away from war, a longing for peace and England, but not homesickness for this place.

It was a shock, therefore, to be falling in love like this. No, not falling. It was as if an unrecognized love had leaped from the shadows and sunk in fangs.

Hawk in the Vale. Hawkinville Manor. He reached out to lay his hand on the oak doorjamb around the front parlor door. The wood felt warm, almost alive, beneath his hand.

My God, he could be happy here.

If not for his father.

He pulled his hand away. Bad luck to wish for a death, and he didn't actively do so. But he couldn't escape the fact that his dreams depended on stepping into a dead man's shoes. There'd be no happiness for him here as long as the squire lived.

He went up the stairs—too narrow for a gentleman, his father had always grumbled—and rapped on his father's door.

The valet, Fellows, opened it. "The squire is preparing for bed, sir."

"Nevertheless, I must have a word with him."

With a long-suffering look, Fellows let him in. God knows what the squire told his man, but Fellows had no high opinion of him.

"What now?" the squire demanded, his slightly twisted mouth still making the words clearly enough. Perhaps it was the damaged mouth that made him seem to sneer. But no, he'd sneered at Hawk all his life.

The seizure had affected his right arm and leg, too, and he still had little strength in either, but at a glance he did not appear much touched. He was still a handsome man in his late fifties, with blond hair touched with silver and the fine-boned features he'd given to Hawk. He kept to the old style, and wore his hair tied back in a queue. On formal occasions he even powdered it. He was sitting in a chair in his shirtsleeves now, however, his feet in slippers. Not particularly elegant.

Hawk was blunt. "Is Slade planning more building here?"

His father twitched, then looked away. "Why?"

Guilt, for sure.

But then the squire looked back, arrogance in place. "What business is it of yours? I still rule here, boy."

Eleven years in the army teaches self-control. A number of those years spent working close to the Duke of Wellington perfects it. "It is my inheritance, sir," Hawk said, "and thus my business. What is Slade planning, and why are you permitting it?"

"How should I know what that man intends?"

" 'That man'? You had him to dinner two nights ago."

"A politeness to a neighbor." He didn't look away again, but Hawk had questioned more skillful deceivers than his father, and he could see the lie behind it.

"I was told that there were men here who sounded like surveyors studying the area along the river and that they later spoke to Slade. What interest could Slade have down here? There is no available land."

His father glared at him, then snapped, "Brandy!"

Fellows rushed to obey, protesting all the while that brandy was not allowed. The squire took a mouthful and said, "Very well. You might as well know. Slade's planning to tear down this place, and the cottages too, and build himself a grand riverside villa."

Hawk almost laughed. "That's absurd."

Into the silence, he added, "He does not have the power to do that."

Doubt and fear stirred. His father, for all his faults, was not a fool, nor had his illness turned him mad. "What have you done?"

The squire took a sip of brandy, managing to look down his long, straight nose, even in the chair. It was posing, though. Hawk could see that. "I have gained a peerage for us."

"From *Slade*?" Hawk couldn't remember ever feeling so at a loss.

"Of course not. You are supposed to be clever, George. Use your wits! It is a title from my own family. Viscount Deveril." He rolled it off his tongue. "It was thought to be extinct when the late Lord Deveril died last year, but I proved my descent from the original viscount."

"My congratulations," Hawk said with complete indifference, but then his notoriously infallible memory threw up facts. "Deveril! By God, Father, the name's a byword for all that is evil. Why the devil would you want a title like that?"

The squire reddened. "It's a *viscountcy*, you dolt. I'll take my place in Parliament! Attend court."

"There is no court anymore. The king is mad."

Like his father?

The squire shrugged. "I am reverting to my rightful family name as well, of course. I am now John Gaspard, soon to be Viscount Deveril."

"Are you also leaving here?" Hawk asked. He kept his tone flat, but it was hard. Unlikely sunshine was breaking in. My God, was all he wanted about to drop into his hands?

But then he remembered Slade.

"What has Slade to do with this? You can't—" Words actually failed him for a moment. "You aren't allowed to sell the estate, Father."

"Of course I have not sold it," his father declared haughtily. After a moment, however, he added, "It is merely pledged."

Hawk put out a hand to the back of a nearby chair to steady himself. He knew every word of the besotted marriage settlement that had given his father power here. His father could use the estate to raise money.

It wasn't an outrageous provision, since the administrator of an estate might have need to raise money for improvements or to cover a disastrous season. His grandfather had been sensible enough to have it worded so that Hawkinville could not be staked in gambling, or used to pay off gaming debts. Not that that had ever been an issue. His father's flaws did not include gambling.

"Pledged against loans?" he asked.

"Precisely."

"I must admit, sir, that I am at a loss as to how you have sunk into debt. The estate is not rich, but it has always provided for the family adequately."

"It is quite simple, my boy," said his father almost jovially. It was a mask. "I needed money to gain the title! Research. Lawyers. You know how it is."

"Yes, I know how it is. So you borrowed from Slade. But surely if you have the title, you have property that comes with it to pay him off."

"That was my plan." The squire's face pinched. "Deveril—rot his black heart—willed most of his worth away."

"It wasn't entailed?"

"Only the estate."

"Well—"

"Which seems unproductive."

Hawk took a breath. "Let me get this clear. You have mortgaged this estate to Josiah Slade to get money to claim one that is valueless."

"It's a title! My family's title. I would have paid more."

"Borrowed more, you mean. How much?"

Over the first shock now, Hawk was beginning to arrange facts and make calculations. He had some money of his own. He could borrow elsewhere to pay off Slade.

"Twenty thousand pounds."

It was like being hit by a pistol ball. "*Twenty thousand pounds?* No one could possibly spend that much to claim a title."

The Hawkinville estate brought in only a few thousand a year.

"I have been pursuing Deveril's money as well, of course."

"Even so. Your lawyers would have to have been eating gold quills for breakfast."

"Investments," the squire muttered.

"Investments? In what?"

"All kinds of things. Slade does well off them. There was a foreigner here a while back—Celestin. He'd made a fortune at it. Then Slade turned up with some good ideas . . ."

Maria's dead husband, who had led Van's father to ruin this way. But Slade—Slade was the active villain here.

"So Slade lent you money and then lent you more to invest to earn it back?"

Twenty thousand pounds.

An impossible sum, and throttling Slade would not fix the disaster.

Hawk forced his mind to look for any possibility.

"How much did Deveril leave that was willed elsewhere?"

"Close to a hundred thousand. You see why I had to have it!"

"I see why we have to have it now. What reason do you have for thinking you can overturn the will?"

"Because it gave everything to a scheming chit he planned to marry, by a handwritten will that was certainly false."

"Then why don't you have the money?"

The squire knocked back his brandy and held the glass

out to be refilled. "Because the poxy chit has all the Deveril money to pay for lawyers, that's why! And some plaguey high-flying supporters. Her guardian's the Duke of Belcraven, no less. The Marchioness of Arden, wife to the duke's heir, stands her friend. I wouldn't be surprised if the little whore has the damned Regent in her pocket."

"It would have to be a very large pocket," Hawk remarked, his mind whirling on many levels.

Twenty thousand pounds. It couldn't be borrowed, even from friends. Especially from friends. Even if they could raise it, it would take Hawkinville a generation to pay it off, and only by squeezing the tenants hard.

His father laughed at his comment. "I have to say, you're taking this better than I expected, George."

Hawk looked at his father. "I am taking this extremely badly, sir. I despise you for your folly and self-indulgence. Did you ever give a thought to the welfare of your people here?"

"They are not *my* people!"

"You've been pleased enough to call them such for over a quarter century. Families have lived in those cottages for centuries, Father. And do you care nothing for this house?"

"Less than nothing! It's a plaguey farmhouse, for all you like to call it a manor."

Hawk wished his father was well. Perhaps then he might feel justified in hitting him. "And Slade will be squire here, since the title goes with the property. You are selling everyone here for your own petty ends."

His father reddened, but raised his chin. "I do not care! What is this place to me?"

"So what is? The Deveril estate? It's going to be a damn chilly comfort with no money to go with it, isn't it?"

His father glared, but said, "You have a point. That is why I have come up with a solution. You are not a bad-looking man, and you have a certain address. Marry the heiress."

Hawk laughed. "Marry a 'poxy chit' to rescue you? I think not."

"To rescue Hawk in the Vale, George."

It hit home, and his father knew it.

All the same, every instinct revolted. He had made one vow, many years ago—that he would not repeat his parents' mistake. He would not marry unless he was sure of harmony. He'd accepted that it meant that he would likely never marry, but that would be better for everyone than more bitterness and bile.

"I have a better idea," he said. "Do you have any cogent reasons to believe the will is false? What arguments have your lawyers made in court?"

His father glowered, but he said, "It was handwritten, and it left all his money to this girl, to come under her complete control at twenty-one."

"Absurd."

"Quite. And the heiress is one Clarissa Greystone. You may not have heard of the Greystones. Drunkards and gamblers, every one."

"And yet you failed to break it. Why, apart from better lawyers and influence in high places? Our courts are not so corrupt, I hope, that they would overrule reason."

"Because the will was in Deveril's hand and found in his locked desk with no sign of a break-in."

"Witnesses?"

"Two men in his employ, but they went missing after his murder."

"Murder?" Hawk repeated. "How did he die?"

"Stabbed in a back slum in London. His body wasn't found for some days."

"Good God. So he was murdered and this Greystone chit has all his money and no one has been able to prove she did it?" He laughed. "And you think I will marry a woman like that?"

"That, or lose Hawkinville, dear boy."

Hawk gripped the back of the chair tightly. "You're finding a kind of satisfaction in this, aren't you? Does it give you so much pleasure to see me wriggling on this hook?"

The twisted smile was definitely a sneer now. "It gives me pleasure to see you taken down a peg or two. So superior you've been, especially since returning home. You've always despised me for marrying for money, haven't you? Well, what are you going to do now the shoe's on your foot, eh?"

"What am I going to do?" *Short of throttle you?* "I'm going to prove that damn will false, and if possible see the Greystone creature hang for murder. And then, I hope, I'll see you out of here, and begin to repair the lifetime's damage that you've done."

The sneer became somewhat fixed, but his father disdained to answer.

"When does the loan come due?" Hawk asked.

His father laughed. "The first of August."

"Two months!" *Control. Control.* Hawk carefully let go of the chair. "Then I had best get on with it, hadn't I?"

It was only as he left the stuffy room that another disastrous aspect hit him. Titles were hereditary. One day he would have to be Lord Deveril.

For the first time he sincerely wished his father a long, long life.

But away from here.

At his precious Deveril estates.

Instinctively he sought his mother's rose garden, even though this mess was her fault. He'd heard that there had been solid, reliable local men courting her.

He shook his head. That was all past history. For the present and the future, the Hawk had one more hunt to fly, and as reward, a golden future tantalized.

If he could prove the will a forgery and get the money for his father, the new Lord Deveril would move away from here. After paying off Slade, of course.

Twenty thousand pounds. It was a sum that staggered him, but he put it aside. Five times that much waited if he did his job right.

Then he would have Hawkinville. His father called it a farmhouse, and he was right. It was two stories and contained only four bedchambers. The ceilings were low, the fixtures practical, the "grounds" merely the courtyard and a garden at the back.

But it was his piece of heaven. He would not let it be torn down, nor would he let Slade rip the heart out of Hawk in the Vale village.

He walked back out onto the green. A few people called to him, waving, with no idea that their world was threatened. He waved back but turned to look at the manor house and the line of cottages.

Most of the front doors were open, with children running in and out. Old people, who had lived in their cottage for most or all of their lives, sat hunched on chairs, watching their generations enjoy themselves. Mothers, babies on hip or even at the breast, chatted together as they kept an eye on their families.

None of the cottages had a straight line, and most of the thatch needed work, but that was all the responsibility of the manor, not the tenants. No roses bloomed at the front because the cottages opened right onto the road around the green and faced north, but he knew that in the long gardens running down to the river roses bloomed among the well-tended vegetables that fed these families.

He watched Slade strolling around, beaming, clearly— in his own mind at least—already the master here. Perhaps he was envisioning a tidy clearing, a modern improvement.

A pure and simple urge to murder held Hawk rigid for a moment. But no. That would not serve.

What if he couldn't prove the will false?

Then he would prove the Greystone chit a murderess. That would work just as well to throw doubt on the will. It probably wouldn't even be hard for a man like him. His work in the war had included investigations, and he'd been very good at it.

He'd hoped never to unleash the Hawk again. Those investigations had left unpleasant memories, and sometimes pushed the borders of his honor.

But this, again, was war. He made a silent vow that greed and folly would not destroy Hawk in the Vale.

Chapter Two

~

June 18, 1816, Cheltenham, Gloucestershire

Clarissa Greystone stared at Miss Mallory in shock. "You are saying I have to leave?"

Miss Mallory, neat and round, took her hand to pat it. "Now, now, dear. I am not throwing you out into the street. You have been welcome here for the past year, but that year is nearly over. And this is a school, not a home for stray ladies. I have been in communication with the duke, and with Beth Arden, and both agree that you must begin to take your place in the world."

They were in Miss Mallory's private parlor in the school, a cozy room warm with potpourri and lavender linen that had always held pleasant memories for Clarissa. Miss Mallory had an office, and that was where a girl went to be scolded for misbehavior. The parlor was for special teas and treats.

"But where am I to go? The school has been as good as a home to me since I was ten."

"That is what you must think about, dear. I'm sure Beth would be glad of your company in time."

In time, because Beth Arden was expecting her first child soon. But even in time, Clarissa didn't want to live with the Ardens. She was fond of Beth, who had been her favorite teacher here, and who had helped her last year in London, but she disliked Lord Arden. He was a terrifying brute.

"Or the duke has offered you a home at Belcraven Park."

Clarissa almost shuddered. She'd visited there once to meet the man who had taken over her guardianship from her father. The duke and duchess—especially the duchess—had been very kind, but they were strangers, and Belcraven was a place of such massive magnificence she could never imagine living there.

"I think I would prefer a small house with a companion. Perhaps here in Cheltenham."

"No." Miss Mallory's voice was the one that all girls in the school learned to heed. "Not here in Cheltenham. You must start afresh. But a house and a suitable companion is a possibility. In London, perhaps. You should rejoin society, my dear."

"Rejoin society!" Clarissa heard her voice climb too high. "Miss Mallory, I was never part of it. I was a Greystone, and Lord Deveril's betrothed. Believe me, few doors were open. No, I will live quietly. Perhaps in Bath."

It was a dismal prospect. She'd spent most of her school holidays with her grandmother in Bath. Lady Molson was dead now, but the place was doubtless as stuffy as ever.

But safe. Perhaps.

"Or in a little village," she added. That was better. There she'd be less likely to be recognized as what society called the Devil's Heiress.

A shudder passed through her at the memories the name brought back. She rose. "I will think about it, Miss Mallory. When must I leave?"

Miss Mallory rose too, and gave her a hug. "Oh, my dear, there is no great hurry. We simply want you to begin to think on it. But I advise you not to try to hide. You have your life before you, and your fortune can make it a good one. Not many young women have the choices you have. It would be a sin to waste them."

Miss Mallory was a follower of Mary Wollstonecraft,

author of *The Rights of Woman,* and she judiciously shared those beliefs with the pupils in her school, so Clarissa knew what she meant. Beth Arden was also an adherent, and had discussed these matters in more detail last year. After Deveril's death.

She should be delighted to be free.

It was all very well in theory to rage against the shackles of masculine oppression, but as Clarissa left the parlor she couldn't help thinking that it might be nice to be taken care of now and then. First a father, and then a husband—if one had a good father, not one like Sir Peter Greystone.

As for a husband, she sighed. She had little faith in the notion of a good husband. A woman put her fate so completely in his hands, and he could be a tyrant.

Like Lord Arden.

Clarissa would never forget the awful argument she had overheard, and running into the room to find Beth on the floor, clearly having been driven there by Lord Arden's blow. The next day Beth had had an awful bruise.

She'd said it was over, was a problem that had been dealt with, but it had been a lesson to Clarissa. Handsome men could be whited sepulchers. On her twenty-first birthday she would have a hundred thousand pounds or more. Folly indeed to put it into the hands of a man, and herself totally in his power.

Up the stairs and along the familiar corridor, every corner of the school was familiar. She wouldn't exactly say precious. Last year she'd been desperate to leave here and take up her life. Even though she'd known her parents didn't care for her, she'd leaped at the chance to go to London. To have a season. To attend balls, routs, parties.

She'd known she was no beauty, and would have no dowry to speak of, but she'd dreamed of suitors, of handsome men courting her, flirting with her, kissing her, and eventually, even going on their knees, begging for her hand.

Instead, there'd been Lord Deveril.

She stopped and thrust him into the darkest depths of her mind. Loathsome Lord Deveril, his foul kiss, and his bloody death. At least he didn't wait for her out in the frightening world.

She knew everyone was right. She couldn't stay here forever.

She glanced down at her clothes, the beige-and-brown uniform all the girls wore here. She had nothing else to wear other than the London gowns that lay in trunks in the attic. She would never wear them again!

But she could hardly go on like this. She bit her lip on a laugh at the thought of herself—plump and fifty— trotting around Cheltenham in brown and beige, that eccentric Miss Greystone, with a fortune in hand and nowhere else to go.

But she had nowhere else to go. She would certainly never again live with her family.

She needed someone to talk to and knocked on the door of her friend Althea Trist. Althea was the junior mistress who had come last September to take Beth Arden's position.

The door opened. Clarissa said, "I'm going to have to—"

But then she stopped. "Thea, what's the matter?"

Her friend had clearly been crying.

Althea pressed a soggy handkerchief to her eyes and tried for a smile. "It's nothing. Did you want something?"

Clarissa pushed her into a chair and sat nearby. "Don't be silly. What is it? Is there bad news from home?"

"No." Althea grimaced, then said, "It's just the day. June eighteenth. The anniversary. Waterloo."

Realization dawned. "Oh, Thea! You must feel the pain all over again." Althea's beloved betrothed, Lieutenant Gareth Waterstone, had died at the battle of Waterloo.

"It's foolish," Althea said. "Why today rather than any other day? I do grieve every day. But today . . ." She shook her head and swallowed.

Clarissa squeezed her hands. "Of course. What can I do? Would you like some tea?"

Althea smiled, and this time it seemed steadier. "No, I'm all right. In fact, I am to take the girls out soon."

"If you're sure." But then it dawned on Clarissa. "Thea, you can't. You can't go to the parade! Miss Mallory would never have asked you if she'd thought."

"She didn't. Miss Risleigh was to do it, but she wished to attend a party. She is senior to me."

"How callous! I will go and speak to Miss Mallory immediately."

She was already up and out of the door as Althea was crying, "Clarissa! Stop!"

She hurtled down the familiar stairs, back to the parlor to knock upon the door. The parade was in honor and memory of the great victory at Waterloo. Althea could not possibly be expected to go there and cheer.

The knock received no response, however. She made so bold as to peep in and found the room deserted. She ran off to the kitchen, but there found that Miss Mallory had gone out for the afternoon. There were a great many parties taking place, and the better folk of Cheltenham had been invited to choice spots from which to watch the parade.

What now?

The school was closed for the summer, and only five girls lingered, awaiting their escorts home. There were only three teachers—Miss Mallory, Althea, and the odious Miss Risleigh.

What could be done?

The girls could do without their trip to the parade, but Clarissa knew that dutiful Althea would never permit that. There was only one solution. She ran back upstairs to her room, put on the brown school cloak and the matching bonnet, and returned to Althea's room.

Althea was already dressed to go out.

"Take that off," Clarissa said. "I am going to take the girls."

Althea stared. "Clarissa, you can't. You're not a teacher! In fact, you're a paying guest."

"I was a senior girl until last year. We often helped out."

"Not as escort on a trip like this."

"But," said Clarissa, "I'm not a senior girl anymore. I'm only a few months younger than you are." A lock of hair tumbled down, and she went to Althea's mirror to tuck it back in. If she was going to do this she had better try to look mature and stern. Or at least sensible.

She pushed some more hair in and tried to straighten the bonnet.

"It is my responsibility," Althea protested, appearing behind her in the mirror.

Clarissa couldn't help wishing she hadn't done that. Althea was a rare and stunning beauty, with glossy dark hair, a rose-petal complexion, and every feature neatly arranged to please.

She, on the other hand, had unalterably sallow skin and features that while tolerable in themselves were not quite arranged to please. Her straight nose was too long, her full lips too unformed, and even her excellent teeth were a little crossed at the front. Her eyes were the dullest blue, her hair the dullest brown.

It shouldn't matter when she had a hundred thousand pounds and no need of a husband, but vanity does not follow the path of logic.

She put that aside and turned to put an arm around her friend. "There are only five girls left, Thea. Hardly a dire task. And you cannot possibly attend the Waterloo Day parade and cheer. If Miss Mallory knew, she would say the same. Now, go and lie down and don't worry. All will be fine."

She rushed out before Althea could protest anymore, but only ten minutes later, she could have laughed aloud at that prediction.

One, two, three, four—she anxiously counted the plain brown bonnets around her—*five*. Five?

She whirled around. "Lucilla, keep up!"

The dreamy ten-year-old turned from peering at a gravestone in Saint Mary's churchyard and ambled over.

Unaware, she caused one hurrying woman to stumble back to avoid running into her.

Clarissa rolled her eyes but reminded herself that a noble deed lost its luster if moaned over. "Hurry along," she said cheerfully. "We're almost there!"

At least the youngest girl was attached to her hand like a limpet. It would be nice, however, if Lady Ricarda weren't already sniveling that she was scared of the graves, she was going to be sick, and she wanted to go back to the school, *now*.

"We can't possibly go back now," Clarissa said, towing the girl out into the street. "Listen—you can hear the band." She glanced back. "Horatia, *do* stop ogling every man who walks by!"

Horatia Peel was fifteen and could be expected to be some help, but she was more interested in casting out lures. She'd pushed her bonnet back on her head to reveal more of her vivid blond curls and had surely found some way to redden her lips.

At Clarissa's command, she turned sulkily from simpering at a bunch of aspiring dandies. She was not a hard-hearted girl, however, and took Lucilla's hand to make sure she didn't wander off again.

Clarissa's other two charges, Georgina and Jane, were devoted eleven-year-old friends, arm in arm and in deep conversation. They were no trouble except for their slow pace.

Afraid to speed ahead in case someone disappeared, Clarissa gathered her flock in front and nudged them forward like an inept sheepdog. It would be wonderful to be able to nip at some dawdling heels!

What would the world think if it could see her now? The infamous Devil's Heiress, with a dubious past and a fortune, dressed in drab and in charge of a bunch of wayward sheep.

"Walk a little faster, girls. We're going to miss the soldiers. Horatia, keep going! No, Ricarda, you are not going to be crushed. Lucilla, look ahead. You can see the regimental flag."

She blew a corkscrew curl out of her eyes, reminding

herself that this was a good deed. It would be horrible for Althea to have to be here. For her part, she didn't mind some cheering and celebration. It was exactly one year ago today that loathsome Lord Deveril had died. One year since she'd been saved. Bring on the flags and drums!

She counted heads again. "Not long now. We'll find a good spot to watch our brave soldiers march by."

Her forced good cheer dried up when they popped out of the lane and into Clarence Street. People must have come in from the surrounding countryside for the festivities. The place was packed with a jostling, craning, chattering, pungent mob and all the hawkers and troublemakers that such a throng attracted.

A bump from an impatient couple behind them moved her on into the thick of the crowd with everyone around pushing for a good spot.

One, two, three, four, five.

"Let's go toward the Promenade, girls. The crowd may be thinner there."

"I want to go *home*!"

"Ricarda, you can't. Hold tight to my hand."

Hawk had a flock of schoolgirls in his sights.

After intensive investigations in London, he had come to Cheltenham in search of the heiress herself. She was clearly key, and she was being kept out of sight. He'd discovered that she wasn't living with her family, or with her guardian, the duke.

He had eventually learned that she was supposed to have spent the past year back at her very proper Cheltenham school. He had trouble imagining the Devil's Heiress at Miss Mallory's School for Ladies at any age— though he gathered her education there had been the work of her grandmother—but certainly not at nearly twenty. Surely it was a blind for some other, more lively, lodging, but it was where he had to start.

He had spent the day hovering, watching for someone willing to gossip about school matters. He'd had no luck, since the school was officially closed for the summer, though he had learned from a butcher's boy that there were some staff and a few girls still there.

Now, at last, he had possibilities. The pupils all wore a kind of uniform of beige dress, brown cloak, and plain brown bonnet, but two of the flock were within flirting age—a lively blonde and the plain young woman who seemed to be in charge.

He focused on the plain one. Plain ones were more susceptible. As he followed them into a churchyard, however, he began to think that the blonde would fall more ripely into his hand. On leaving the school, she'd begun to push her bonnet back on her head, gradually revealing more and more curls. Even with a plump child by the hand, she was lingering behind with the clear intent of flirting with any man who showed interest.

Could this actually be Miss Greystone? He'd not expected to find her in the school at all, never mind in schoolgirl clothes, but she seemed the type. Pretty, and a complete minx. She didn't look nineteen, but such things were often deceptive. Nor did she look evil, but in his experience, that meant nothing. He could certainly imagine Deveril drooling over such a tender morsel.

The girl slowed even more to dimple at a group of young would-be gallants.

Hawk moved in.

He was within five feet when the plain one turned. "Horatia, do stop ogling every man who walks by!"

"I wasn't *ogling*, Clarissa. You're so mean!" But the minx did rejoin the others.

Hawk fell back to regroup. The plain one was Clarissa Greystone? He'd had a clear look at her face when she turned, and she was definitely nothing special to look at.

As he discreetly followed, he realized that it had been an error to assume beauty. "Lord Devil" wouldn't have had much choice in brides. Few upper-class families would consider such a fate for a daughter. The Greystones were just the type that would.

They all gamed, and father and sons were drunks as well. Lady Greystone was a wanton. She was growing virtuous with age, but only because her raddled looks were ceasing to attract. When he'd struck up a conversation with her in the course of his investigations, the damn woman had propositioned him!

He'd assumed Clarissa Greystone would be like the rest of her family, but she seemed to be a cuckoo in that nest.

Or, more likely, she was brilliantly disguising her true nature.

That explained it, and it pointed right at guilt. Most people who stole gave themselves away by immediately enjoying their spoils. Not clever Miss Greystone. Perhaps she was even pretending to be in mourning.

The old excitement stirred. The excitement of challenge, of a worthy opponent. It was comforting, too. With a clever enemy, there was no need to feel squeamish about tactics.

Clever, but guilty as the devil. A week in London sifting fact from fallacy had proved his father right. That will—in fact, everything surrounding Deveril's death—stank to high heaven. Strings must have been pulled for it not to have been investigated more closely.

Lord Devil had not been accepted in society until nearly two years ago when he'd suddenly acquired a fortune. No one knew the source of it, but everyone assumed it was dirty money.

He'd been partner in a popular bordello run by a woman called Thérèse Bellaire, which was an interesting tangent. Hawk happened to know that Thérèse Bellaire had been part of Napoleon's inner circle—mainly pandering for his intimates and senior officials. She had been in England in 1814 as a French spy, working for the reinstatement of her master.

Madame Bellaire had fled before she could be arrested, presumably leaving the bordello to her partner, but its sale would not have produced a fortune. Deveril had been involved in other things, however. Gaming hells. Opium dens. White slavery.

Regardless of where the money had come from, it had gained him an entrée with the less discriminating members of fashionable society. He'd leased a handsome house in the best part of town, and not long afterward, his betrothal to Miss Greystone had been announced.

Soon after that, he'd been murdered.

It had all the marks of a cunning and cleverly executed plot, and far beyond the talents of the Greystones. He didn't yet know who was behind it, but he would.

In a mere week he had some threads in his fingers. The forger was probably too clever to reveal himself, but Hawk had found the names of the two missing witnesses on the records of a ship bound for Brazil. Strange destination for a couple of London roughs, but they'd presumably been paid off and told to make themselves scarce. It would be interesting to follow up on it, but he didn't have time now.

He'd dug up another of Deveril's henchmen. They could hardly be called servants. After a jug of gin, the gap-toothed man had remembered some prime whores Deveril had sent to the house while he'd been on duty there.

"Night of the big celebration, it was," the man had remembered. "When we heard about Waterloo and the whole of London set to celebrating. We were stuck there, and these prime titties came knocking, but then their men came and dragged 'em away. One of 'em knocked Tom Cross out with a skillet, she did! He called her Pepper, and she certainly made him sneeze."

Lazily, Hawk had asked, "Why did she do that, do you think?"

"He paddled her for being saucy. I bet her pimp paddled her harder. Seems as if they were off trying to do a bit of business of their own. Shame, though," he said, sagging lower over his drink. "Never so much as got a feel, I didn't."

"You didn't look them up later?"

"No names. Anyway, the next day they found bloody Deveril's body and that were the end of that. Duchess," he said. "Her sister called her Duchess because of her airs and graces. Wanted to drink out of a glass, she did."

For a wild moment, Hawk had thought of the Duchess of Belcraven, but she was an exquisite middle-aged

Frenchwoman. He still wondered about the role of the Duke and Duchess of Belcraven in the Deveril affair. The duke was widely known as a man of dignity and principle.

Pieces that didn't fit always told a story, however, and that one would too, in time.

Time was so damnably short.

Those whores had been a distraction for the planting of the will, however. He was sure of it. And it seemed likely that Clarissa Greystone had been one of them.

The one called Pepper and Duchess, who'd knocked a man out for daring to spank her for being saucy? It had fit.

Until now.

He contemplated the harried figure ahead of him, dragging one whining child along the crowded street, chivying the others in front of her like a demented sheepdog, rattails of hair escaping from her bonnet.

Could there be more than one Clarissa in Miss Mallory's School?

"I can't see!" Ricarda screeched, still clinging.

They were in the Promenade, a much wider street, but could still see only a solid line of backs. Clarissa was ready to admit defeat, but then the adults in front made way and a smiling countrywoman said, "Come on forward, luvs. We can see over your sweet heads."

With the music coming closer and the drums shaking the air, Ricarda transferred her clutch to Lucilla's hand and slipped forward. Georgina and Jane went too. Then the adult ranks closed between Clarissa and most of her charges.

Oh, no!

She went on tiptoe to watch the four girls. They were standing still with other children at the front, but Lucilla was capable of wandering off in any direction, and now she would probably take Ricarda with her.

Constantly checking the four brown bonnets, Clarissa was aware of the parade only as approaching drums. She glanced once and saw the lord mayor still some distance away, marching along in his robes and chain of office accompanied by his mace-bearer. Beyond, she saw the aldermen, a cart or two, and the magnificent scarlet of the local regiment.

The sight of the redcoats did catch her for a moment. So many brave men, and so many others, like Althea's Gareth, lost in the wars against the Corsican Monster. More than ten thousand dead at Waterloo alone.

How did one imagine ten thousand dead, all in one place?

She pulled her mind back to simple things, to counting her charges. *One, two, three, four—*

Five?

Horatia. Where was Horatia?

With a puff of relief, she saw her right beside her. Horatia couldn't have much of a view—she was shorter than Clarissa—but of course the minx was not interested in the mayor, or even the soldiers. She was dimpling at the handsome man by her side.

A handsome, dangerous man. Horatia was trying out her flirtatious techniques on a rake of the first stare. Clarissa was frozen, not knowing what to do.

Then the man glanced over Horatia's bonnet to meet Clarissa's eyes, his own shadowed by the tilted brim of his fashionable beaver hat. His slight smile deepened. It was an insolent, blatant challenge to her ability to protect her charges.

She seized Horatia's wrist and dragged her sideways, taking her place and then pointedly ignoring the scoundrel.

To Horatia she hissed, "Admire the soldiers. They're doubtless safer."

Much safer!

She would have liked to claim immunity to handsome rakes, but her nerves were jangling like a twanged harp. Who was he? Certainly no provincial dandy. Beautifully cut olive coat. Complex, snowy cravat. An indefinable but unignorable air. Her brief stay in London had taught her something about judging men of the *ton* and he was top of the trees.

Another quick glance confirmed her assessment. All

the gloss and arrogance of a London beau, and a handsome face as well.

He suddenly looked sideways, catching her, and that amused challenge returned to his eyes.

She jerked her eyes away, away toward the approaching parade, grateful for once for the close bonnet that would hide her blushes. She remembered to go on tiptoe and check. *One, two, three, four.*

Horatia by her side, an older couple beyond her.

Safe for the moment.

All safe.

Apart from the *something* from the man on her other side. She'd met handsome beaux and wicked rakes in London and been able to laugh at the folly of other females. That was remarkably easy when neither beaux nor rakes paid her any attention.

This rakish beau should be the same, and yet she felt a prickling awareness—as if he was studying *her*.

She would *not* look to see.

Then the sway of the crowd suddenly pushed her against him, and he put his hand on her arm to steady her. She felt it. She felt his hand, felt his whole body—arm, hip, and leg—against her for a shocking moment before she pulled away.

She suddenly felt like Ricarda, panicked and longing for the safety of the school.

Which she had to leave soon.

Very well. She would soon have to leave the school, have to venture into a world full of handsome men. She must learn to cope. After all, she had a fortune. There would be fortune hunters.

She swallowed and focused on the passing parade, on a cart carrying a portly man dressed as Napoleon, looking beaten and downcast. On another containing men dressed as the Duke of Wellington, Nelson, Sir John Moore, and other heroic leaders.

A Saint George passed in front of her in Roman armor, spear in hand, foot on the neck of a vanquished dragon that wore the French tricolor. She rather thought

Saint George was Mr. Pinkney, who ran a small circulating library and was the least martial man imaginable.

"No stop," said the man, who was still pressed by circumstances too closely beside her.

She had to turn her head. "I beg your pardon, sir?"

"His spear is a throwing spear, not a dragon-killing one. It has no crossbar. A common mistake in art. If he managed to impale a dragon, the beast would run up it and eat him. Of course, the maiden might applaud."

"What?" Clarissa was beginning to fear that the man was mad as well as bad. But, Lord, he was handsome, especially with that twinkle in his eye!

He glanced at the white-robed woman at Saint George's side, presumably the rescued maiden, but also managing to look like Britannia. "If her rescuer died in the attempt, she would be free without having to be the victor's prize."

The maiden was the mayor's pretty daughter, and she certainly wouldn't want to have to be too grateful to Mr. Pinkney. Clarissa was unwillingly beguiled by the man's nonsense—and by the effect of teasing humor on already fine features—but she firmly turned her attention back to the parade.

All around her the crowd was booing Napoleon and applauding the heroes. Then it burst into huzzahs for the real heroes, the veterans of the great battle who marched to cheerful fife and the demanding, tummy-quivering thump of the drums.

She joined in, waving her plain handkerchief.

"Clarissa! Clarissa! Did you see that? He blew me a kiss! He did! Oh, wasn't he the most handsome man you have ever seen?"

Horatia was literally bouncing up and down, her curls dancing and her cheeks bright red. Clarissa smothered a laugh. The officer in question was quite ordinary, and much older than Horatia's usual practice ground, but he was in a moment of glory and he had noticed her, and so he was an Adonis.

But then a sudden squeal sent panic shooting through her. Ricarda! She stretched on tiptoe again, but the girl seemed all right. The scream had probably been caused by a horse dropping a steaming mound on the road in front of her.

"They are all quite safe," said the rake. "I can see them easily and will tell you if anything untoward occurs."

It was most improper for two strangers to be talking like this, and yet the situation made it impossible to object. She turned to him again. "Thank you, sir."

The angle of his head moved the shadow of his brim, and she was caught by startlingly blue eyes. Cornflower blue made brighter by skin that was browner than fashion approved. That, a silly detail like that, was probably what made him seem more dangerous than the general London beau.

Or perhaps not.

She seemed trapped, and then those intent eyes crinkled slightly with humor that she was invited to share.

She hastily turned her own boring gray-blue eyes forward, but she suddenly felt completely unlike herself.

As if she might do something outrageous.

With him.

By gemini! Was he *flirting* with her?

But men didn't. Even during her horrible time in London, men hadn't flirted with her.

So what was the rake up to?

Ah. Trying to get around her to Horatia, of course. Not while she had blood in her body.

Horatia, however, craned past Clarissa. "You're very kind, sir! Little Lucilla, the plump one, daydreams so. If she took it into her head to wander in front of the horses, she'd do it."

"No, she wouldn't," Clarissa said. "Ricarda would scream the heavens down."

"Ricarda is scared of horses, sir," said irrepressible Horatia, innocently smiling in a way designed to invite a man to her bed.

"Watch the parade, Horatia," Clarissa commanded. "It's nearly over."

Horatia pulled a face, but obeyed.

After a few moments Clarissa risked a glance at the rake. He was looking ahead, not at her.

Victory! He knew his evil plans were thwarted.

She smiled to herself at sounding like a character in an overly dramatic play, but she was feeling victorious. See, it wasn't so very difficult to deal with importunate men.

One skirmish won was enough for the day, however. Thank heavens this would soon be over and she could herd her flock back to the school.

As soon as the last marchers passed and the crowd began to break up, she pulled the four younger girls into a bunch around her, making sure that Horatia stayed close too. The rake moved on without a backward look.

Folly to feel disappointment at that.

"Come along," she said briskly. "It's all over now."

Anxious to be done with this, she nudged her group into the thinning crowd. It wasn't as easy going as she'd expected. The crowd had not truly thinned out. Instead, it swirled chaotically.

When they'd hurried here everyone had been streaming in one direction, but now people went all ways at once. It was market day and many were heading there, but others wanted to get to the taverns, to homes, or to the fairground that had been set up on the outskirts of town.

The mob pushed and pulled, like a monster with a hundred hands snagging at one child or another. Ricarda began to cry again. She let go of Lucilla and clutched Clarissa's skirts. Clarissa reached out to keep Jane and Georgina close.

Then a mighty voice rang out. The town crier. "*Oyez! Oyez!* Mr. Huxtable, landlord of the Duke of Wellington, is rolling out three casks of free ale so all can toast our noble heroes!"

Oh, no! As the crowd's mood changed, Clarissa was already gathering her flock close. Lucilla, her butterfly attention caught by something, swirled off between an enormous man and two elbowing lads. Clarissa just managed to seize the back of the girl's cloak and haul her close—at some risk to the poor child's neck!

She shed her own cloak, letting it fall to be trampled. "Hold tight to my skirt!" she commanded. "Jane, Georgina, do the same. Horatia, help me keep everyone together. We'll stay still for a moment to let the crowd pass."

She put every scrap of calm and confidence that she could muster into her words, and the girls did press close, but staying still was easier said than done. Most of the crowd seemed hell-bent on the free ale, and the rest were struggling to get free.

Rocked and buffeted, she was seized by blank panic.

Cries and screams all around flung her back to other screams, and blood.

To the thunder of a pistol.

Shattering glass.

Blood, so much blood . . .

And a woman quoting Lady Macbeth. *"Who would have thought the old man to have had so much blood in him?"*

Darkness crept in at the edge of her vision.

No. Stay in the present. The girls need you. You will not fall apart again in a crisis!

She pinched her left hand hard to get her wits back, then clutched terrified Ricarda close. She began to ease her little group sideways to a nearby brick wall where perhaps the mob would flow past them.

"Stay close!" she yelled. "Hold on!" Her voice seemed swallowed by the cacophony around, but the girls were all with her, clinging, dragging on her arms and gown.

The press of squirming, elbowing bodies had her sweating with heat and terror, but she would not weaken. Lose their footing here and they could be trampled. The stench turned her stomach. Her foot slid on something squishy, almost making her fall. She prayed it was as innocent as a piece of dropped fruit.

One, two, three, four, five.

Horatia—good girl—had wrapped an arm around her waist so they were locked into a huddled unit.

Then her bonnet was knocked forward over her right

eye, so she couldn't see from that side at all. She didn't dare raise her hand to straighten it for fear of losing one of the children. The crush was so tight, she'd never get her arm down again.

All the younger girls were wailing now, and she wanted to wail herself. But she was the protector here. "It's all right," she said meaninglessly. "Hold tight. It will be all right."

When someone crushed into them from behind, she didn't hesitate to jab back with her elbow.

There was an *"Ooof!"*; then a strong arm came around them and a voice said, "Hold back, hold back, make way, make way there." He didn't shout—in the tumult there would be no point—but somehow his commanding tone seemed to cut through and create a moment's pause so they could slide sideways.

The crowd sealed tight behind them, but his voice opened the way until they landed entangled against the wall.

There was no indent here, however, no doorway to press back into. No barrier except a simple iron lamppost. Had they fallen out of the pot into the fire? They could be crushed. Terrified screams said that might be happening elsewhere in the maddened crowd.

But the man grasped the lamppost and made himself a barrier that the crowd must flow around, creating a tiny pocket of sanity.

Clarissa held her crying charges closer, trembling. "It's all right, dears," she said again. "Don't be afraid. This kind man is making sure we don't get hurt."

It was, of course, the wicked rake, to whom she'd been so cold. Horatia had better instincts. He was a true hero. He had rescued them and was now their protector.

Chapter Three

~

Clarissa could see only the man's back, for he was facing the throng. She could see the faces of the passing crowd, however—young, old, angry, fearful, excited, greedy, impatient. She watched them see him, see him as a barrier to the direction they wanted to take, then shift away as if he wore spikes.

She wondered what expression he was using to warn them off, but she could only be grateful. Now that she had a measure of safety her knees felt like limp lettuce. If not for the girls she might have sagged to the ground and given in to tears herself.

But she'd done it! She'd been terrified, the memories had tried to overwhelm her, but she hadn't collapsed. Instead, she'd surely helped save them all. Though still shaking and close to tears, she felt as if great weights had fallen away, leaving her light enough to fly.

She could face fear and survive.

A woman was suddenly pushed beside them. A desperate young countrywoman in coarse, disheveled clothes with a screaming baby in her arms. She did collapse, her legs giving way so that she sank down, back against the wall. Even Ricarda stopped wailing to stare at her.

Clarissa couldn't help thinking about fleas, but the mother needed help as much as she and the girls did. As the woman lowered her dirty shift and put the frantic baby to her big breast, Clarissa looked away, looked again at their savior and guardian.

She didn't generally allow herself to study men, but since his back was to her, she could indulge.

He was tall—her head barely came up to his shoulders. His olive coat lay smooth across broad shoulders and down his back, suggesting a lean, strong body. He stood with strong legs braced apart.

She ripped her gaze away. Studying a man like that was not only immodest, it was dangerous. Looks said nothing about a man's true qualities, but they could weaken a woman's mind.

Yet she couldn't resist sneaking another look. He'd lost his hat in the riot, revealing disordered honey-brown hair.

She remembered earlier assessing him as a London beau. She'd sensed that danger, but never imagined him the stuff of which effective heroes are made. Another lesson about judging by appearances.

She suddenly realized that the nature of the crowd had shifted like a change in the air, danger fading, shock lingering. Pressure eased as people began to mill around, many pale and dazed while others sharpened to bring order and assistance. Through wails, and the cries of parents trying to locate their children, she heard the beat of a drum, doubtless calling the soldiers to riot control.

She quickly counted, even though she knew they were all safe. *One, two, three, four, five.* She found a smile for Horatia, whose bonnet was down her back, revealing all her lovely curls, but who clearly was not thinking of that at all. "Thank you. You were magnificent."

The girl smiled back, proud but a bit wobbly.

Horatia, too, had probably learned in a test of fire that she was braver than she'd thought.

"Quite an adventure, girls," Clarissa said in as light a tone as she could manage. "Let go of me now and help one another to straighten bonnets and bodices."

They did so, and with Horatia's encouragement, even began to giggle a bit as they repaired one another's appearance. Clarissa made sure her own gown was straight, wondering what had happened to her cloak. She took off her crooked bonnet, using it to fan herself for a moment before putting it back on.

The man turned.

She was caught hatless and staring, because there was nothing grim and indomitable about him. Instead, he was all rake again, with a wicked glint in those blue eyes and a slight smile on his well-shaped lips.

And a wavery, warm feeling skimmed over her.

None of that! No amount of willpower, however, could halt her blush, so she turned away as she settled her bonnet back firmly on her head.

No amount of willpower could stop her from wishing she looked her inadequate best. She tried to at least tuck her hair away neatly, knowing it was a forlorn gesture. It was unruly by nature, and it had just been given an excellent opportunity to riot.

She firmly tied the ribbons, then looked at him. "I don't know how to thank you, sir. We might have been in terrible trouble without your assistance."

"I was pleased to be able to help."

She was braced to resist flirtation, but he hunkered down in front of the countrywoman. "Are you all right, ma'am?"

Well, of course.

Men didn't flirt with her.

All the same, a foolish part of her envied the mother, who was blooming under his attention. "Oh, yes, sir," she said in a country accent. "So kind, sir! I thought for sure I was to be crushed to death, or have poor Joanie here torn from my arms."

But then her eyes widened and she paled as she tried to push herself up one-handed.

He helped her, not seeming conscious of her half-exposed breast or the attached suckling infant.

"My littl'uns!" she gasped, her hand going up to push straggling brown hair off her face. "They're out there somewhere. I must go—"

"No, no," he said calmly. "Tell me what they look like and I'll find them for you. What of your man?"

"He's back tending the cows for Squire Bewsley, sir. There be three of 'em, sir. Three boys, and they do stay together if they can. Four, seven, and ten. All brown hair."

Clarissa wondered how anyone could find three urchins on that description, but the man didn't seem daunted.

"Names?" he asked, as Clarissa looked out at the street, hoping three young brown-haired lads were in sight.

"Matt, Mark, and Lukey," the woman said, and even produced a smile when she added, "Little Joanie was going to be John."

The man grinned. "Stay here, and I'll return soon to report. Hopefully with your little evangelists in tow."

His grin, Clarissa discovered, could shatter a lady's common sense. How fortunate that Horatia wasn't looking. She'd be in a swoon.

He turned to leave, but suddenly Clarissa couldn't bear for this strange encounter to end like that. "Sir, could I know the name of our rescuer?"

He turned back and bowed. "Major Hawkinville, ma'am." He raised his hand to his hat, then said, "The deuce. I wonder where it is."

"Wherever, I fear it will be sadly flattened."

Then she found herself sharing a smile that left her feeling positively light-headed.

"Better a hat than people," he said, those richly blue eyes on hers, making her heart race.

How rash she had been to come to names with a man she knew nothing about. Especially with one who seemed able to spin her out of common sense with a look.

It was done now, however, so she curtsied and gave him her name in return. Suddenly at a loss to describe her status, she added, "Of Miss Mallory's School here."

He turned to the wide-eyed girls. "As are you all, I suppose. All right?"

"Yes, sir," the girls chorused adoringly.

Oh, no. Horatia was gazing at him as if he were a god, and now the man could probably claim to have been introduced. Clarissa realized that she'd rashly created a very improper situation, and she winced at what Miss Mallory would think of this whole affair.

"Were you at Waterloo, Major Hawkinville?" Horatia asked breathlessly.

"Yes, I was."

"In the cavalry?" asked Jane.

"No."

Before anyone else could ask a question, however, he bowed farewell. "But now, ladies, I must be off to other battles."

And thus he was gone, striding away through the dazed stragglers, looking, to Clarissa's dazzled eyes, like a hero among lesser men. Finding three young strangers in the chaos seemed impossible, but if anyone could do it, Major Hawkinville could.

Definitely a hero, but judging by his swift departure, one who sought no glory in war.

Not cavalry, so infantry. He had shown great steadiness in the face of the crowd. She could imagine him leading his men to assault the walls of an impenetrable fortress, or keeping them steady in the face of a French cavalry charge.

"Wasn't he handsome, Clarissa?" Jane sighed. "And one of our noble soldiers!"

"A warrior angel," Georgina said. "I shall draw a picture of him as Saint George when we get back."

Clarissa didn't point out that Saint George was not one of the angels. This wasn't the right time for a lesson, and she wasn't a teacher, thank heavens.

"A major," sighed Horatia. "Mentioned in dispatches a dozen times. He must have met the Duke of Wellington."

"Doubtless." But Clarissa was shocked that her thoughts had been so like those of the younger girls. "Come," she said crisply. "We must return to school. If news of this crush has reached them, they'll be worried."

After their fright, the girls made no trouble on the return journey. Clarissa chose a roundabout route that should avoid any problems and determined to put any thought of handsome Major Hawkinville out of her mind.

That was hard to do when the others were determined to chatter about him. There was a great deal of romantic babble, despite their youth. Horatia was silent, probably drifting in a true hero-worshiping ecstasy.

Clarissa supposed that wouldn't hurt. She'd certainly done the same at times.

Florence Babbington's handsome brother had rendered half the school breathless when he'd come to take his sister out to tea. Clarissa remembered writing a poem in his honor, and she'd only been twelve at the time.

O noble man, tall, chaste, and bold.
So like a gallant knight of old,
Turn on me once, lest I expire,
Those obsidian orbs full of manly fire.

Her lips twitched at the memory. What nonsense people could create in the throes of romantic fervor.

Then there'd been the groom at Brownbutton's livery.

The stables were behind the school, separated by a high wall. From the attic windows, however, a person could see over the wall, and it was a wicked amusement for the senior girls. A stalwart young groom had been a special treat two years ago. He'd generally worked without his jacket, and with his sleeves rolled up, revealing wonderfully strong brown forearms.

One deliciously naughty day Maria Ffoulks had caught him working without his shirt. She'd run to gather as many of the senior girls as she could, and they'd pressed to every available window for about ten minutes until he'd gone into the stables and emerged covered again.

That hadn't been infatuation, however. It had been more like worship from afar. Worship of the male of the species, and of the mysterious, forbidden feelings he stirred in them all.

That sort of thing was probably why she'd been such a ninny as to hope when her parents had finally summoned her for a London season.

A ninny. She'd been in danger of being ninny over Major Hawkinville, too. "Come along, girls," she said briskly. "Cook was making Sally Lunns when we left." Mention of cakes removed any tendency to dawdle.

Hawk moved swiftly down the Promenade, following the flotsam of the crowd toward the Wellington Inn. The innkeeper deserved to be flogged for causing this mayhem.

He guessed the three boys would have gone along with the crowd, and as long as they kept their feet would have come out of it all right. He passed some people being attended to, but none of the injuries seemed serious. The only boy he saw among them was clearly being attended to by his mother.

A bunch of lads ran by, but they all seemed happy and purposeful, and none particularly fit the description of the evangelists. A wail caught his attention and he turned to look, but then a man scooped up the crying child and carried her away.

There were people scattered around, many of them disheveled or dazed, some on the ground. Since they were all being cared for, he followed the trail again, part of his mind scanning for the boys, part assessing the puzzle that was Clarissa Greystone.

A thief and a murderer?

Not a whore called Pepper, that was for sure, not even by deception.

The image of her face rose up, blushing, freckled, frankly thanking him for his help. No, she wasn't a beauty, but astonishingly, his heart had missed a beat there. One of these quirks that comes after battle, and she had been remarkably gallant.

Damnation, he must not let her under his guard! What was to say she hadn't played the whore, and wasn't playing a part now?

Because no one played a part in battle. In battle, the truth about a person spilled along with the blood and guts, and that riot had been a minor battle.

He paused to question two brown-haired lads hun-

kered down to play with ants in the road, but they said
they lived in a nearby house. A blond urchin wandered
by eating a plum, not seeming to be in distress other
than the juice all over her hands and dress. Hands on
hips, he looked over the untidy groups of people but
didn't see any children who seemed likely.

He spotted a young brown-haired boy standing tear-
fully alone and went over to him. "What's your name,
lad?"

The boy looked up, knuckling his eyes. "Sam, sir."

Hawk suppressed a sigh. "Who were you with, Sam?"

"Me dad, sir. I lost 'im, sir. He'll be cross."

This wasn't one of his targets, but he couldn't leave
him here. Hawk held out a hand. "Why not come along
with me? I'm going to check out the Wellington. Perhaps
your father's having a drink there."

A damp, sticky hand wrapped trustingly around his,
and they progressed down the street. Soon he gathered
two frightened sisters, and another lad who was older
but seemed slow-witted. Then stray children began to
attach themselves like burrs collected during a march
through rough country, and he eventually found the
evangelists.

"Your mother's worried about you," he told them.

"We couldn't help it, sir," the wild-eyed eldest said.
"And we stuck together."

Hawk ruffled his hair and looked around at his collection, all putting their absolute trust in him.

Clarissa Greystone would probably trust him too—if
she was as honest as she seemed to be. The encounter
had tangled all his threads, but she was still his only lead
to the heart of the conspiracy, and he had to pursue her.

Once he dealt with his present duties.

He and his burrs turned a corner and faced the Duke
of Wellington Inn. The Great Man would not be amused.

The place was jam-packed, with free-ale patrons spilling out into the street in all directions, many of them
already drunk. He spotted the town crier leaning boozily
against a horse trough, and guided his squadron there.

He pulled out a notebook and began to take down names.

When he had them all, he ripped out the page and commanded the town crier's attention. "These children are lost. You are to go around town announcing their names, and that they are to be found here."

He used his military voice, and the rotund man stood straight. "Yes, sir."

"Good. Start with the Lord Wellington."

In moments, the man's mighty bellow was breaking through the din. Hawk turned to the children. "Stay here. Your parents will find you." He put the oldest boy in charge of making sure the little ones didn't wander, then took Matt, Mark, and Lukey back to their mother.

He was not surprised to find that the heiress and her charges had left. That was no problem. He now had an excellent excuse to call on the school.

Chapter Four

Clarissa settled the girls at their tea under the eye of the cook, then carried a tea tray upstairs. She hoped Althea was recovered enough to talk.

As she put down the tray on the small spindle-legged table by the window, she thought of how much she would miss this room. She'd once itched to be out of school and in the world. Now it and the walled garden were her comfort and safety.

But then she realized that the wall was the one around Brownbutton's livery stable. From this low level, however, she couldn't see into the yard. Muscular men could be wandering around there stark naked and she wouldn't know.

Safer so.

Safe. But she was going to be forced to leave.

Someone knocked at the door, and Clarissa opened it. "Come in, Thea. I was just going to invite you for tea." But then she realized that there was something different about her friend. "You've put off your mourning."

Althea was in a pretty gown of cream sprigged with pale blue flowers, and she looked lovely. Even more lovely. Suave Major Hawkinville would probably trip over his feet if he set eyes on Althea looking like this.

Clarissa didn't like to examine why that depressed her.

It was over. They would never meet again.

"It's been a year," Althea said, smoothing the soft

fabric. "Gareth would not have wanted me to wear dull colors forever. He . . . he liked this dress." She pulled out a handkerchief and pressed it to her eyes, then blew her nose. "It will get easier."

"Yes, I'm sure," said Clarissa helplessly. "Come and have some tea."

Althea sat and Clarissa poured. "Today must be difficult for you." She offered the cake.

Althea took a piece, her eyes still glossed with tears. "For you, too."

Oh, lord.

Clarissa had let Althea think they shared a bond of mourning. It had just happened, and then she hadn't known how to set things right. It had been impressed upon her that no one must know the truth about Lord Deveril's death, and that it would be better if she didn't show her relief over it.

Now, suddenly, however, it was intolerable to be lying to Althea, and after all, who could think that she didn't loathe Lord Devil?

"An anniversary," she said, "but not a sad one."

Althea stared.

"I'm sorry for letting you think otherwise. I— I never wanted to marry Lord Deveril. He was my parents' choice. I have never grieved for him."

"Never?" Althea asked, eyes widening. "Not at all?"

"Never." Clarissa thought for a moment and then admitted a little more. "In fact, I was glad when he died. More than glad. Over the moon."

Althea just looked at her, and it was clear that her Christian soul was shocked.

"Lord Deveril was my father's age," Clarissa hurried on, beginning to wonder if she should have kept silent after all. "But age wasn't the problem. He was ugly. But that wasn't it either." She met her friend's eyes. "Put simply, Thea, he was evil. Despite his wealth and title, he was accepted hardly anywhere. Nobody spoke to me of such matters, but I couldn't help realizing that he indulged in all kinds of depravity."

She started at the touch of Althea's hand. "I'm sorry.

I wish you'd told me sooner, but I'm glad you've told me now. It explains so much. Why you're here. The way you think about men." After a moment, she added, "Not all men are like that."

Clarissa laughed, her vision blurring a little. "It would be an impossible world if they were. Truly, Thea, I doubt you've ever met anyone as foul. The mere thought of him makes me feel sick."

Althea refilled Clarissa's teacup and put it into her hand. "Drink up. It'll steady you. Why did your parents permit such a match?"

Clarissa almost choked on a mouthful of tea. "Permit? They arranged it and forced me to agree. They sold me to him," she went on, hearing the acid bitterness in her voice, but unable to stop it. "Two thousand upon my betrothal in the papers, and two upon my wedding. Then five hundred a year as long as I lived with Deveril as a dutiful wife."

"*What?* But that's atrocious! It must be illegal."

"It's illegal, I think, to force someone into marriage, but it's not illegal for parents to beat a daughter, nor for them to mistreat one in all kinds of ways."

Instead of distress, Althea's eyes lit with outrage. "Though it may not be entirely in keeping with the Gospels, Clarissa, I, too, am delighted that Lord Deveril died."

Clarissa laughed with relief. "So am I. Glad he died, and glad I told you. It's been a burden to lie to you."

Althea cocked her head. "So why did you tell me now?"

Clarissa put down her cup. "I dislike dishonesty." She sighed. "Miss Mallory says I must leave, and my guardian agrees."

"What will you do?"

"That's the puzzle."

"What do you want to do?"

Clarissa rubbed her temples. "I've never quite thought of it like that. Last year I wanted balls, parties, and handsome gallants."

"There's nothing wrong with that."

"But now I'm a walking scandal. The Devil's Heiress. And a Greystone to boot. I don't think I'm going to receive many invitations. And of course, any gallants I do attract will be after my money."

"Not all of them, I'm sure," Althea said with a smile.

"Thea, please, be honest. No man has ever shown interest in my charms." Then she winced at Althea's distress. "I'm sorry. It's all right. I truly don't want to marry, and with money I don't need to."

"But you want the balls and parties."

"Not anymore," Clarissa said, aware that it was a lie. If it could be done without scandal, she still wanted what most young ladies wanted—a brief time of social frivolity.

Althea fiddled with her sprigged muslin skirts. "I might be leaving Miss Mallory's, too."

"But you've been here less than a year."

Delicate color enhanced Althea's beauty. "A gentleman from home has approached my father. A Mr. Verrall."

Though Clarissa had just talked about leaving, this felt like abandonment. "Approached your father? Isn't that a little cold-blooded?"

"Bucklestead St. Stephens is seventy miles from here, and Mr. Verrall has four children to care for."

Worse and worse. "A widower? How old?"

"Around forty, I suppose. His oldest daughter is fifteen. His wife died three years ago. He's a pleasant gentleman. Honorable and kind."

Clarissa knew it was a reasonable arrangement. Althea would live near her beloved family, and this Mr. Verrall would doubtless be a good husband. As Althea's father was a parson with a large family, she wouldn't have many desirable suitors. All the same, Mr. Verrall sounded like dry crumbs to her.

"Don't you think perhaps you should look around more before committing yourself to this man? You attract all the men."

Althea shook her head. "I will not love again."

"You should give yourself the chance, just in case."

Althea's eyes twinkled. "By all means. With whom? Mr. Dills, the clock mender? Colonel Dunn, who always raises his hat if we pass in the street? Reverend Whipple—but then, he has a wife."

Clarissa pulled a face. "It's true, isn't it? We don't meet many eligible men. At this time of year, there aren't even any handsome brothers passing through."

"And handsome brothers are usually dependent on their fathers, who would turn up starchy at the thought of marriage to a penniless schoolteacher."

"Surely not quite penniless," Clarissa protested.

"When it comes to eligible gentlemen, I am. My portion is less than five hundred pounds."

It was virtually nothing. Clarissa took another bite out of her bun and chewed it thoughtfully. If only she could give Althea some of her money—but her trustees were sticklers for not letting her be imposed upon. And it didn't sound as if Althea would wait until Clarissa was twenty-one.

"Beth Armitage married the heir to a dukedom," she pointed out, "and though I admire her a great deal, she has not a tenth of your beauty."

Althea laughed gently. "The sort of story to make idiots of us all. Such things cannot be relied on."

"True," said Clarissa, remembering the dark side of the fairy tale.

Althea was right. She had nothing but her beauty and good nature to recommend her. The world would say she should be grateful for any suitable offer, even that of an elderly widower with a daughter not many years her junior.

"I came to thank you again for taking the girls," Althea said, clearly changing the subject. "I'm so sorry you ended up in such trouble."

"It wasn't too bad."

"The girls seem to see it as a wonderfully perilous adventure, including rescue by Saint George, complete with halo."

Clarissa laughed. "Hardly, but Major Hawkinville did help us, yes." She gave her account of the event. "I wonder if he found the woman's lost evangelists. He seemed capable of it."

Althea cocked her head. "Heaven, purgatory, or hell?"

"I'm a nonbeliever, remember? No marriage for me."

"Nonsense. I'm sure Lord Deveril was as hellish as you say, but when you meet heaven you'll change your mind."

"I won't trust heaven." Major Hawkinville somehow merged in her mind with handsome Lord Arden, afire with rage. "Any man, if angered enough, can turn into hell."

"Not Gareth," Althea said firmly.

Clarissa couldn't hurt her by arguing. "Perhaps not, but how are we to know?"

"A decent period of courtship. Gareth and I had known each other for years, and been courting for two."

Clarissa pounced. "So you shouldn't consider marrying this widower without a decent period of courtship."

"But I've known Mr. Verrall for years too, and I like him."

Balked, Clarissa still protested, "You need to meet some other men first."

"Perhaps it's a shame I didn't take the girls to the parade and fall into an adventure with the handsome major."

Clarissa chuckled, but a plan stirred. Althea needed to meet eligible men, and, as she'd said, that was unlikely here in the school. Once the last girls went home, Althea would return to Bucklestead St. Stephens and marry her doddering widower.

What was needed was what the army called a preemptive strike.

"I wonder where I should go?" she mused. " 'The world's mine oyster . . . ' "

" 'Which I with sword will open'?" Althea completed.

"With money, perhaps. It frightens me, Althea. Miss Mallory says I should not stay in the familiarity of Cheltenham, and Bath is so dreary."

"London, then."

"No." It came out rather abruptly, but then Althea

would guess that London had bad memories for her.
"Anyway, it's the end of the Season there. The place
will soon be empty."

Clarissa still hadn't worked around to her true purpose—persuading Althea to accompany her for a few
weeks and meet a suitable husband. "Where would you
go if you were me?" she asked.

But Althea shook her head. "I'm a country mouse. I
like life in a village."

"I think I might, too," Clarissa said, "though I've
never tried it. My father sold his estate when I was in
the cradle to pay debts and buy a London house."

A village, however, would be an unlikely place in
which to find Althea a prime husband.

Her frustrated thoughts were interrupted by a knock
on the door. Clarissa answered it and the school's upstairs maid said, "There's a gentleman inquiring for you,
Miss Greystone." Her expression was a combination of
disapproval and interest. "Miss Mallory isn't home
yet . . ."

"A gentleman?"

"A Major Hawkinville, he says." Mary added with disapproval, "But he's not wearing a hat."

Clarissa actually squeaked with surprise, but managed
to compose herself. The major. Here!

Then she saw Althea's smiling interest and realized
that this was a chance to introduce her to at least one
eligible man. He must be eligible, mustn't he, and Althea
clearly favored a military man.

"Major Hawkinville lost his hat saving me and the
girls, Mary. We cannot turn him away. Miss Trist and I
will be down in a moment."

As soon as the maid left, Clarissa whirled to the mirror. She could hear one of Miss Mallory's favorite ad-
monishments: *Only God can give beauty, girls, but
anyone can be neat.* It had usually been accompanied by
a pained look at Clarissa. God had neglected to give her
tidiness, too.

She began pulling the pins out of her hair.

Althea came over and pushed her hands away. After

a few moments with the brush and a few more with the pins, Clarissa's hair was pinned in an orderly, and even slightly becoming, knot.

"I don't know how you do it," she said somewhat grumpily.

Althea just laughed again. "Don't you have any ribbons?"

"No, and they'd look silly with this plain gown." Clarissa felt that she'd exposed enough folly for now. "Thank you for tidying me. Now let's go and thank the hero of the day."

"Don't you have any other clothes?" Althea asked, frowning at the beige dress.

Clarissa ignored the trunks in the attic. "No. Come along, Althea. It hardly matters what I look like."

"No?" Althea teased.

Certainly not as long as I'm with you, Clarissa thought without acrimony, leading the way downstairs. Despite that, her heart was racing on nervous little feet, and she tried to command her senses. The major was here out of courtesy. Despite his earlier behavior, there was no chance that he had been slain by her wondrous charms.

And, of course, she did not desire any man's serious interest.

He was just the sort of man, however, likely to shock Althea's heart out of the past and into thinking beyond the hoary ancient awaiting her back home.

They arrived in the neat front hall, and after a steadying breath, she led the way into the parents' parlor—so called because it was where parents were taken when they visited.

Oh, my. Speaking of wondrous charms . . .

The image in her mind had not been fanciful.

Even without a hat, he was strikingly elegant, not just in the quality of his clothes but in the way he wore them, and the way he moved. There was all the straight-shouldered authority of the military, but surprising grace as well.

He bowed—perfectly. "Miss Greystone. Excuse my intrusion, but I wished to be sure that you and the girls were not harmed in any way."

Clarissa dropped a curtsy, commanding her heart to settle so that she could think clearly. Her heart, however, was a rebel, as was her awestruck mind. "So kind, sir. We are all safe." She introduced Althea and then took a seat on the sofa, inviting him to take a chair.

They talked of the riot and the consequences—apparently two people were seriously injured, but most had merely been frightened. All the time, Clarissa was fighting her tendency to be dazzled, and observing Althea to see how she was reacting to this gem.

Althea was sparkling, which was a truly remarkable sight. Clarissa thought she was seeing the Althea that Gareth Waterstone had loved, and she was amazed that the major managed to pay herself any courteous interest at all.

Yet he did. He seemed to share his attention between them, and when he looked at her— Clarissa fought for reason, but his attentive eyes, his quick smiles seemed meant for her.

She didn't need a man.

She didn't want a man. And she must be mistaken. Such men were never interested in her.

But she wouldn't mind the company of one if, amazingly, he did find something about her to admire.

Perhaps it was her behavior during the riot. She had done well. Was it possible that he *admired* her?

Her heart scurried again. "Do you live in Cheltenham, Major?" she asked.

Those eyes. Those eyes that seemed to like looking at *her*. "No, Miss Greystone. I am passing through on my way to visit a family property. My home is in Sussex, not far from Brighton."

"Have you seen the Pavilion?" Althea asked with interest, drawing his attention.

"A number of times, Miss Trist, as a youth. I have been out of the country with the army for many years, however."

Clarissa saw thoughts of the army, and of Gareth, mute

her friend's spirits, and spoke quickly, "Brighton is the most fashionable place to be in the summer, isn't it, Major?"

"Indeed it is, Miss Greystone. I recommend it to you."

She stared at him. "To me?"

"To anyone who would like a pleasant place in which to pass some summer months," he responded smoothly, but she didn't think that was quite what he had meant.

Was he a mind reader? Here she was, in her well-worn schoolgirl clothes, and he was suggesting a move to the most fashionable, and expensive, resort in England.

Some of the glow disappeared from the room.

"Cheltenham is delightful," he went on, "but it does not have the sea, never mind the Prince of Wales and most of the *haut ton*."

"How true." She met his smiling eyes, sorting through her tumbling thoughts.

Althea broke in. "Miss Greystone is to leave here soon, Major, and enter fashionable life."

Clarissa felt herself color, and knew it did nothing to improve her looks. Althea meant well, but Clarissa wished she hadn't said that.

The major smiled as if he'd received good news. "Then perhaps you and your family will visit Brighton, Miss Greystone."

Her family. Mustn't such a man-about-town know the Greystones? And know about the Devil's Heiress.

Hiding foolish hurt, Clarissa retreated behind a formal smile and a slightly cool manner. "I doubt it is possible to move there this late in the year, Major Hawkinville. Perhaps next year—"

She rose to hint that the visit was at an end.

He rose too, with admirable smoothness. "You are thinking of the difficulty of finding good houses to rent, Miss Greystone?" He took out a card and pencil and wrote something on the back. "If you should think of visiting Brighton, apply to Mr. Scotburn and mention my name. If there is a house to be had, he will doubtless find it for you."

Clarissa took the card, though she felt it would be

safer to take nothing tangible from this encounter. How could she refuse, however, short of pure incivility?

Then he was gone, and that should have been the end of it, except that she had his card, and his even, flowing handwriting. She turned it and confirmed what she suspected.

She also had his address.

Major George Hawkinville, Hawkinville Manor, Sussex.

Major George Hawkinville, who almost certainly was a fortune hunter who knew exactly who she was and what she was worth. Whose admiration had been stirred by her money, not her charms.

But, she thought, looking at the card again, that admiration had been deliciously enjoyable. Why should a lady not play games too, and enjoy such company, especially if she was awake to all his tricks?

Hawk left the school and didn't allow himself a pause to savor success. People leaving were often watched.

His quarry had cooled for some reason, but he didn't think she was beyond reach. In fact, he'd be willing to bet that she was already thinking of a move to Brighton. If not, he could come up with some other ways to persuade her. It was the obvious resort for a wealthy young lady in search of social adventure in the summer, and he was sure that Miss Greystone was in search of social adventure.

In fact, she was ripe for trouble, and his pressing instinct was to protect her! Damnation, why couldn't she be the harpy he'd imagined?

He wasted a few moments seeking other ways to the Deveril money, but knew he'd worn that path bare. He simply didn't want to be doing what he was doing, playing on an innocent young woman's vulnerability.

Hawkinville, he reminded himself.

And no matter how innocent she was, that money was not hers by right.

He decided, however, to move on immediately to inspect Gaspard Hall. He knew how useful a strategic absence could be. Before seeing his father's new property he loathed it, but if there was something to be made of it, perhaps they could survive somehow without the Deveril money.

Twenty thousand pounds?

And, damnation, that will was a forgery. It galled him to think of anyone, even that lively young woman, benefiting from it!

For the first time in his life he was being deflected from battle by a pretty face. Not even pretty, but with power all the same.

Hawkinville, he reminded himself.

But even for Hawkinville, was he really willing to see Clarissa Greystone hang?

Clarissa retreated back to her room, card in hand. "Brighton," she announced.

"Clarissa! You can't. You hardly know the man."

Clarissa laughed. "I'm not going to *marry* him, Thea, but it is the obvious place to go. Think of it. I'm the Devil's Heiress and no matter where I go, sooner or later people will learn of it. I might as well be brazen and enjoy myself in a fashionable spot."

"But that doesn't mean the major—"

"Of course not. He merely put the idea into my mind. However," she added, twirling the card, "if we happen to meet it will not be unpleasant."

"What if he's a fortune hunter?"

Even though it put Clarissa's own thoughts into words, it stung. "Oh, he probably is," she said lightly. "As I said, I have no intention of marrying him. If he wants to play escort and charming companion, well, why not?"

"If he is a fortune hunter, I wish nothing more to do with him."

Althea had what Clarissa thought of as her Early Christian Martyr face on. Clarissa was trying to work around to the topic of Althea's accompanying her, and this was not the right direction. Unless she gave it a twist.

"I do have to leave and join the world, Thea," she said meekly, "but it will be hard. I did nothing wrong, but I am a Greystone, and I was engaged to marry Lord

Deveril, and he did meet with a very unfortunate
death—"

"He did?" Althea asked, disapproval thawing to
curiosity.

"Stabbed in a very poor area of town."

"Stabbed!" Althea gasped.

Clarissa tried to stay focused on the part she was playing, and not let memories of the truth invade to over-
set her.

"Doubtless something to do with the company he
kept," she said, "and well deserved. The point is, Thea,
that I'm a little worried about being accepted by
society."

Althea took her hand. "None of it was your fault."

"That is not how people will see it. What I am thinking," Clarissa plunged on, "is that I would feel easier
with a companion. A friend." She looked at Althea, realizing that her words were true. "With you. If I go to
Brighton, Thea, I ask most sincerely that you accompany
me for a little while."

"Me?" Althea gasped, eyes wide. "Clarissa, I couldn't!
I know nothing of fashionable circles."

Clarissa gripped her hand. "Your birth is respectable,
and you have excellent manners, and unquestioned
beauty."

Althea broke their handclasp. "I'm only twenty. I'm
not old enough to be your chaperon in a place like
Brighton."

"But I don't want you to be that. I want you to come
as a friend, to enjoy Brighton with me. Do say you will."

Althea blushed and covered her cheeks with her
hands. "It's still impossible, Clarissa. I don't have the
sort of clothes that are needed in a place like Brighton,
and I certainly can't afford to buy them."

Clarissa absorbed the truth of that. She knew her trustees would not allow her to buy Althea new clothes. She
considered sharing, for she would have to buy a new,
fashionable wardrobe herself. But she and Althea did
not suit the same colors, and her friend was a good few
inches shorter.

An idea burst upon her. She seized Althea's hand and dragged her out of the room.

"Where are we going?"

"To the attic!"

"Why?"

"To look at my London clothes!"

They clattered up the narrow stairs into the storage rooms. In the dusty gloom, Clarissa eyed the two hardly used trunks. She didn't want to open them and stir revolting memories, but she'd do it. For Althea.

At the very least Althea deserved a few weeks of pleasure in Brighton. At the best, with her beauty, virtue, and sweet nature, she might attract a wonderful husband.

A lord. A duke, even!

So she lifted one heavy lid and pushed back plain muslin to reveal a froth of pale blue trimmed with white lace.

"If you're going into society, you'll need these clothes," Althea protested.

Clarissa pulled out the blue and passed it over. "I'll never wear these again." She tossed aside that layer of muslin and unfurled the second. The pink.

She shuddered. She'd been wearing that when Deveril had kissed her. Her mother had screeched about the trouble of getting the vomit stains out of it, but it seemed someone had managed it.

"These were all chosen by Lord Deveril and paid for by him," she said, tossing the ruched and beribboned gown to Althea. "Anything connected to that man revolts me, and they don't even suit me. Imagine me in that shade of pink! If you don't take them, I'm giving them to the maids for whatever they can get for them."

Althea put down the blue and studied the pink. "The color would suit me, but it's a bit . . ."

"Overdone? In bad taste? Oh, definitely." Overcoming her distaste, Clarissa held the dress in front of her friend. "The shade is lovely on you, though."

"Won't it bother you to see me in these dresses?"

Foul memories were swirling with the attic dust, but Clarissa pushed them away. "Everything will have to be altered. You're slimmer and shorter. We can strip off the

trimming at the same time." She gave Althea the dress.
"A wardrobe is here for you, if you're brave enough to
come adventuring with me."

"Adventuring?" echoed Althea, but her eyes were
bright and her color high.

Heartbreaking that her Gareth wasn't here to enjoy
the Thea he'd known and loved, but Clarissa resolved
that she would find her friend someone almost as good.
Not just an adequate husband, but another chance at
heaven.

"Well?" Clarissa asked. "Will you do it?"

Althea stared into a distance, and perhaps for a moment she thought of Gareth, for she sobered. But then
again, perhaps he spoke to her, for she smiled in a steadier, no less glorious way. "Yes. I'll do it."

The next day Hawk rode slowly down a driveway
clumped with foot-high weeds, taking in his father's hard-
won inheritance. One chimney of Gaspard Hall had
crashed down onto the roof, partly accounting for the
broken and missing tiles. A substantial crack ran up one
wall, suggesting that the foundations had given way, and
the wood around the broken windows flaked with rot.

He directed Centaur carefully around the side of the
house, keeping to the grass rather than the drive. Less
danger of potholes or falling debris.

A couple of years ago, with farming prices high and
industry profitable, this place might have been worth
something for the land alone. The end of the war had
brought hard times, however. Trading routes were open
to competition, and prices had fallen, sometimes to disastrous levels. In various parts of the country farms were
even being abandoned.

Gaspard Hall in its present state was nothing but an
extra burden. There must be tenants here still, and others
dependent on the place, all hoping that the new Lord
Deveril would help them.

At the back of the house he found the deserted stableyard. He swung off the horse and led it to a trough and
pump. As expected, the pump was broken.

"Sorry, old boy," he said, patting Centaur's neck. "I'll find you water as soon as possible."

He looked around and called out, "Halloo!"

Some birds flew out of nearby eaves, but there was no other response.

A quick check of the stable buildings found only ancient, moldy straw and rat-chewed wood. From here, the back of the house was in as bad a state as the front.

It offended his orderly heart to see a place in such condition, but it would take a fortune to restore it. He wondered why the late Lord Deveril hadn't spent some of his money here. He assumed he simply hadn't cared.

Hawk could easily go back in his mind fifty years or so, however, and see a pleasant house in attractive gardens and set amid excellent farmland. A family had lived here and loved this place as he loved Hawkinville Manor. That raised the strange notion of there once being a pleasant, wholesome Lord Deveril. Lord Devil had likely been born here fifty years ago or so. Had he been a normal child? What had his parents been like? His grandparents?

He put aside idle speculation. The plain fact was that Gaspard Hall offered nothing. No money to pay off even part of the debt. No home for the squire without a fortune being poured into it. He was back to the duty he was trying to escape.

He led Centaur back the way they'd come. There'd be an inn in the nearby village where he could stay the night. Tomorrow . . .

Tomorrow he should return to Cheltenham and seduce the secrets out of Clarissa Greystone. But he turned and ran from that. He'd return to Hawk in the Vale and hope that she came to Brighton. It might be easier to hunt and destroy her amid that tinsel artificiality.

Chapter Five

~

July, Brighton, Sussex

Clarissa and Althea arrived in Brighton in a grand carriage with outriders. Her guardian, the Duke of Belcraven, had sent his own traveling coach and servants to ensure her comfort and safety. Her trustees, Messrs. Euston, Layton, and Keele, whom she called the ELK, had arranged every other detail in magnificent style.

This was all rather unfortunate when she still didn't have any stylish clothing, and Althea did. At every stop, innkeepers and servants had groveled before Althea and assumed that Clarissa was the maid. She'd found it funny, and at one place had even slipped off to hobnob with the servants in the kitchen. Poor Althea, however, had been mortified.

The problem should be fixed soon. A stylish Brighton mantua-maker had all her measurements and should have a complete wardrobe, chosen by Clarissa herself, ready except for the final adjustments.

Despite a number of fears, she could hardly wait for any of this adventure. Now, looking out at the lively, fashionable company strolling along the Marine Parade in the July sun, she felt like a bird taking its first terrified but exhilarating flight.

Or perhaps like a bird being pushed out of the nest and desperately flapping its wings!

From the first, impulsive decision, everything had been snatched from her control. Miss Mallory had completely approved. Althea had bubbled with excitement. The duke and the ELK had immediately put the idea into operation. All that had been left for her to do was consult fashion magazines and samples of fabric and choose her new clothes.

Major Hawkinville's recommendation had not been necessary. The ELK had assured her that there were always houses available for people willing to pay handsomely for them, and they had engaged Number 8 Broad Street, which boasted a dining room, two parlors, and three best bedrooms.

It seemed a lavish amount of space for two people— but then there was also the lady hired to be chaperon and guide to society, a Miss Hurstman. Clarissa had been somewhat surprised that the lady was a spinster rather than a widow, but she had no doubt that the ELK would have chosen the very best. The lady had been described as "thoroughly cognizant of the ways of polite society and connected to all the best families."

The ELK had also arranged for a lady's maid and a footman in addition to the staff that came with the house. Clarissa had chuckled over this entourage, but in truth it made her nervous. In her parents' penny-pinched household, one overworked upstairs maid had had to attend to the house and play lady's maid as well.

In fact, she was still rather uncomfortable with all the lavish spending, especially when she didn't really feel she deserved Deveril's money. She'd loathed the man, and it was only a quirk in the wording of his will that had led to her inheriting it. At least there was no one else entitled. When she'd expressed her doubts, she'd been told that he'd died without an heir. Without the will, the money would all have gone to the Crown.

To provide more gilded onion domes, perhaps, she thought, catching a glimpse of the Prince Regent's astonishing Pavilion. She couldn't wait to visit it, but she couldn't regret not having funded it.

She couldn't regret any of this, and in part that was

because of the secret anticipation of meeting Major Hawkinville again. She'd discouraged Althea from talking about him, pretending that he was of little interest, but now, as the carriage rolled along the Marine Parade, the sea on one side and tall stuccoed buildings on the other, she surreptitiously fingered the oblong card that she'd tucked into the pocket of her simple traveling dress.

Hawk in the Vale, Sussex. She'd looked it up in a gazetteer. It lay about six miles out of the town. Not far, but perhaps he didn't visit here very often.

Or perhaps he did.

Perhaps they wouldn't meet. Perhaps when they did she would find him less fascinating, or he would not be interested in her.

Or perhaps not.

After all, if he was a fortune hunter he would find her and pay her assiduous attentions.

She did hope so!

The gazetteer had mentioned his home, Hawkinville Manor, an ancient walled house with the remains of an earlier medieval defense. Picturesque, the author had sniffed, but of no particular architectural elegance.

Would she see it one day?

Then she noticed the attention they were attracting. A number of *ton*nish people were turning to watch the grand coach and outriders pass along the seafront, ladies and gentleman raising quizzing glasses to study it. Mischievously, Clarissa waved, and Althea pulled her back, laughing.

"Behave yourself!"

"Oh, very well. Did you see the bathing machines drawn into the water? I intend to sea-bathe."

"It looks horribly cold to me, and they say men watch, with telescopes."

"Do they? But then, men bathe too, don't they? I wonder where one buys a telescope."

Althea's eyes went wide with genuine shock. "Clarissa!"

Clarissa suppressed a grin. She loved Althea like the

sister she had never had, but like sisters, they were different. Althea would never feel the wild curiosity and impatience that itched in Clarissa. She didn't understand.

But Clarissa knew she had to control that part of her. It would be hard enough to be accepted by society. For Althea's sake, there must be no hint of scandal.

The coach began to turn, and she looked up to see the words "Broad Street" painted on the wall. "At last. We're here."

"Oh, good. It's been a long journey, though it seems ungrateful to complain of such luxury."

"And not a highwayman to be seen."

"Praise heaven!" Althea exclaimed, and Clarissa hid her smile.

Despite its name, the street was not very wide, and the massive coach took up a great deal of it. The terraced houses on either side were three stories high, and with bay windows all the way up. All that stood between the house and the road, however, was a short flight of stairs and a railed enclosure around steps down to the basement servants' area.

Clarissa had glimpsed even narrower streets nearby, however, and knew this was indeed grand by Brighton standards.

The coach rocked to a stop outside number 8, an ELK-ishly perfect house, with sparkling windows, lace curtains, and bright yellow paint on the woodwork. The door opened to reveal an ELKish housekeeper, too. Plump and cherry-cheeked.

One of the outriders opened the door and let down the steps, then assisted them from the coach. Clarissa went toward the house feeling rather like a lost princess finally finding her palace.

"Good afternoon, ladies," said the housekeeper, curtsying. "Welcome to Brighton! I'm Mrs. Taddy, and I hope you will feel perfectly at home here."

Home.

Clarissa walked into a narrow but welcoming hall with a tile floor, white-painted woodwork, and a bowl of fresh flowers on a table. Home was a singularly elusive concept, but this would do for a while; indeed it would.

"This is lovely," she said to the woman, but then found that Mrs. Taddy was looking at Althea, also assuming that she was the heiress. What a powerful impression clothes made.

"I'm Miss Greystone," she said with a smile, as if merely introducing herself, "and this is my friend, Miss Trist."

She covered the housekeeper's fluster with some idle comments about Brighton's beauty, wondering where their chaperon was.

"Ah, you've arrived," a brusque voice barked. "Come into the front parlor. We'll have tea."

Clarissa turned to the woman standing in a doorway. It couldn't be!

She was middle-aged, with a weather-beaten face and sharp, dark eyes. Her graying hair was scraped back into a bun unsoftened by a cap, and her gown was even plainer than Clarissa's simple blue cambric.

"Don't gawk! I'm Arabella Hurstman, your guide to depravity."

The ELK must have run demented. This woman could never gain them entrée to fashionable Brighton!

"I'll bring tea, ma'am," said Mrs. Taddy to no one in particular and hurried away. Clarissa felt tempted to go with her, but Miss Hurstman commanded them into the room.

It was small but pretty, with pale walls and a flowered carpet, and Miss Hurstman looked completely out of place. This was ridiculous. There must have been a mistake.

The woman turned and looked them over. "Miss Greystone and Miss Trist, I assume. Though I can't tell which is which. You"—she pointed a bony finger at Althea—"look like the heiress. But you"—she pointed at Clarissa—"look like the simmering pot."

"I beg your pardon?"

"Don't starch up. You'll get used to me. I gave up trying to act pretty and pleasing thirty years ago. Someone described Miss Greystone as a simmering pot, and I see what he meant."

"Who?"

"Does it matter? Sit. We have to plan your husband hunt."

Clarissa and Althea obeyed dazedly.

"I gather you're a protégée of the Marchioness of Arden," Miss Hurstman said.

Clarissa didn't know what to do with that statement.

"Lady Arden was a teacher at Miss Mallory's School," Althea said, filling the silence. "She was kind to Clarissa last year in London."

Clarissa supposed that summed up a very complex situation.

"That explains Belcraven, then," said Miss Hurstman. "He must be thanking heaven to see his heir married to a woman of sense."

Mrs. Taddy hurried in then with a laden tea tray and put it in front of Miss Hurstman.

"London," continued the lady, pouring. She handed Clarissa a cup. "Lasted all of two weeks there, and got yourself engaged to marry Lord Deveril. At least you ended up with his money, which shows some wit."

"He was hardly my choice," Clarissa stated, wondering what would happen if she ordered the woman out of the house. She had a burning question first. "Why would anyone describe me as a simmering pot?"

A touch of humor flashed in the dark eyes. "Because a simmering pot needs to be watched, gel, in case it bubbles over. 'Bubble, bubble, toil and trouble'? Oh, I expect trouble from you two." Miss Hurstman switched her gimlet gaze to Althea, who almost choked on a cake crumb. "You're a beauty. Here to catch a husband?"

"Oh, no—"

"Nothing wrong with that, if it's what you want. If you don't like your choices, I can find you a position. One where you won't be abused. Bear that in mind. There are worse things than being a spinster."

"Thank you," said Althea faintly.

"What about you?" Miss Hurstman demanded of Clarissa. "You want a husband too?"

"No."

"Why not?"

"Why should I? I'm rich."

"Sexual passion," said Miss Hurstman, causing Clarissa and Althea to gape. "Don't look like stuffed trout. The human race is driven by it, generally into disaster. If you wait long enough, it cools, but in youth, it simmers."

Clarissa felt her face flame. Surely whoever had said she was a simmering pot could never have meant *that*.

Who could it be? The duke? Hardly. Lord Arden? She didn't think so.

Major Hawkinville?

That thought proved her mind was spinning beyond reason.

"There's all the romantic twaddle as well," the astonishing woman continued. "That alone can turf man or woman into an unwise marriage."

She surveyed the plate and chose a piece of seedy cake. "I was young once, and reasonably pretty, though I doubt you believe it, and I remember. I decided early not to marry, but I was still tempted a time or two. And *I* wasn't fool enough to visit Brighton in the summer, where romantic folly is carried on the breeze. What's worse," she added with a look at Clarissa, "you're an heiress. You'll have to fight 'em off."

Clarissa eyed the woman coldly. "Isn't that your job?"

Miss Hurstman gave a kind of snort. "If you really want me to. You probably won't. You'll probably scramble after the most rascally ones around. Young fools always do. I'll have no scandal, though. No being caught half naked in an anteroom. No mad dashes to Gretna Green. Understand? Now, you two go off and settle yourselves in. There's nothing we can do today."

Clarissa found herself on her feet, but regrouped. "Miss Hurstman, my trustees *employed* someone"—she emphasized the word—"to gain us entrée to the highest circles. I appreciate—"

"You think I can't? Don't judge by appearances. If

there's a member of the *ton* here I'm not related to, they probably have shady antecedents. And though I don't spend much time in their silly circles, I know most of 'em, too. If you want to waltz with the Regent at the Pavilion, I can arrange it. Though why you'd want to is another matter."

"Even though I'm the Devil's Heiress?" Clarissa challenged.

"Stupid name. Concentrate on the heiress part. That'll open every door. A hundred thousand, I understand."

Clarissa heard Althea gasp. "More. It's been well invested, and I've been living simply."

"Obviously." Miss Hurstman looked her over. "With a fortune to hand, why are you dressed like that?"

"You are," Clarissa pointed out sweetly.

"I'm fifty-five. If you want to be a nun, enter a convent. If you want me to introduce you to Brighton society, dress appropriately."

Clarissa desperately wanted to state that she'd wear plain gowns forever, thank you, but she could see a pointless rebellion when it was about to cut off her nose. She admitted to the clothes waiting for her at Mrs. Howell's.

Miss Hurstman nodded. "Good. We'll go there first thing tomorrow and hope no one of importance sees you before you're properly dressed. You should have borrowed something from Miss Trist. Off you go."

Clarissa longed to sit down again and refuse to be removed, but that was pointless too. As she went upstairs with Althea she muttered, "Intolerable!"

"Perhaps she's able to do what she's supposed to do," Althea suggested.

"If so, she can stay. Otherwise, out she goes."

"You can't!"

Clarissa wasn't sure she could either. Moving Miss Arabella Hurstman might require the entire British army and the Duke of Wellington to lead it. But could she endure much more of Miss Hurstman? The woman was going to turn this delightful adventure into misery.

She went into the front bedroom that Mrs. Taddy indicated, finding their luggage already there and a sober-faced maid beginning to unpack.

"Who are you?" Clarissa demanded.

The woman dropped an alarmed curtsy. "Elsie John, ma'am. Hired to be maid to Miss Greystone and Miss Trist." She, too, was clearly having trouble deciding who was who.

"I'm Miss Greystone," said Clarissa, beginning to lose patience with this farce. "That is Miss Trist."

The maid rolled her eyes and turned back to her work. Clarissa sucked in a deep, steadying breath. She had failed to stand up to Miss Hurstman, so she was taking out her anger on the innocents.

Then Althea said, "Would you mind if I lie down, Clarissa? I have a headache."

"No, of course not. It's probably because of that dreadful woman."

Clarissa knew, however, that it was as much her fault as Miss Hurstman's. She reined in her temper, and even found a smile for the maid. "Elsie, you may go for now."

She helped Althea out of her gown and settled her in the bed with the curtains drawn, but then didn't know where to go. She couldn't stay here and be quiet. She didn't feel at all quiet. She needed to pace and rant.

She left the room, closing the door quietly. There were supposed to be three bedrooms, and there were three doors. What if the third was the housekeeper's? She crept downstairs, but she suspected the only rooms below were the front parlor and the dining room. She headed for the dining room.

"Ah, good!"

Clarissa jumped.

Miss Hurstman had emerged from the parlor like a spider from a hole. "Come back in here."

"Why?"

"We have things to discuss. Believe it or not, I'm your ally, not your enemy."

Clarissa found herself too fascinated to resist.

"You're strong," Miss Hurstman said, as Clarissa reentered the room. "A bit of brimstone, too. That's good. You'll need it."

"Why?"

"You're the Devil's Heiress. And you're a Greystone. Even under my aegis, you'll receive some snubs."

"I don't care, except if it hurts Althea."

"It'll hurt her if people are cruel to you. She can't take any fire at all, can she?"

"She doesn't like discord, but she can be strong in fighting for right and justice."

"Pity we don't have lions to throw her to. She might enjoy that."

Enough was enough. "Miss Hurstman, I'm not at all sure you will suit, but if you are to be caustic about Miss Trist, you certainly won't."

The woman's lips twitched. "Think of me as your personal lion. Now sit down. Let's talk without a delicate audience.

"I like you," Miss Hurstman said as she returned to her straight-backed posture in her chair. "Don't know what fires you've been through, but it's forged some steel. Unusual in a gel your age. Your Althea is doubtless a lovely young woman, but tender lambs like that give me a headache. They can always be depended on to say the right thing and to suffer for the stupidity of others."

"It wasn't stupidity that killed her fiancé."

"How do you know? War is stupid, anyway. Do you know we lost ten times as many men to disease as wounds? Ten times, and a regiment of women with sense could have saved most of 'em. Enough of that. I want to have things clear. We're to find her a good husband, are we?"

Clarissa imagined that Wellington's troops must have felt like this before battle, and yet there was a starchy comfort in it. Miss Hurstman, despite her unlikely appearance, radiated competence and confidence.

"Yes."

"Any dowry at all?"

"A very small amount."

Miss Hurstman *humphed*. "The right man will find that romantic. What's her family?"

"Her father is the vicar of Saint Stephen's in Bucklestead St. Stephens. He's brother to Sir Clarence Trist there. Her mother is from a good family, too. But there's no money and seven other children."

"Where did the fine clothes come from, then?"

"I gave them to her."

"Why?"

Clarissa considered her answer. "Do you know Messrs. Euston, Layton, and Keele, ma'am?"

"Only by repute and a letter."

"Thorough," said Clarissa. "Conscientious. Determined to pass over my fortune when I'm twenty-one with scarcely a nibble out of it."

"Very right and proper."

"Carried to ridiculous lengths. I can buy what I want and they will pay the bills, but they allow me virtually no money to spend on my own. They would never have let me hire Althea to be my companion—and you have to admit that having her here will be much more pleasant than being here alone."

"You have me," said Miss Hurstman with a wicked smirk.

Clarissa swallowed a laugh, and suspected it showed.

The truth was that she was beginning to like Miss Hurstman. There was no need to pretend with her. With Althea, dear though she was, Clarissa always felt she had to watch herself so as not to bruise her friend's tender feelings. With Miss Hurstman, she could probably damn the king, pick a fight, or use scandalous language and stir no more than a blink.

"Clothes," Miss Hurstman prompted.

"Oh, yes. The ELK didn't object to my bringing Althea as a friend, but she needed fashionable clothing. They'd not pay for that, but they'd pay for new clothes for me."

"Shady dealings, gel." Miss Hurstman waggled her finger, but the twinkle might be admiration.

Clarissa was surprised to feel that Miss Hurstman's

admiration might be worth something. "It wasn't a noble sacrifice. I would never have worn those gowns again. They were bought for me to parade before Lord Deveril."

"Ah. And that shade of blue wouldn't have suited you any better than the one you're wearing now. Hope you chose better this time."

Clarissa looked down at the tiny sprigged pattern that had been the best material Miss Mallory's seamstress had to hand. "So do I. I chose rather bold colors."

"Bold seems suitable," said Miss Hurstman dryly. "If they don't suit, we'll choose again. Won't make a dent in your fortune. So, Miss Trist needs to marry money. And generous money, at that."

"What she needs is a man who loves her."

Miss Hurstman's brows rose. "When she can't love him back? She'd go into a decline under the guilt of it. And if she doesn't marry money, she'll feel she's let down her family."

Clarissa wanted to object, but the blasted woman had clearly taken Althea's measure to the inch. She needed to be of service to all.

"I want her to be happy."

Miss Hurstman nodded. "She'll be content with a good man and children, and plenty of worthwhile work to do. You, on the other hand, need a man who loves you."

Major Hawkinville, Clarissa thought, and reacted by stating, "I don't need a man at all. I'm rich."

"You're obsessed by your money. Guineas are uncomfortable bedfellows."

"They can buy comfort."

Miss Hurstman's brows shot up. "Planning to buy yourself a lover?"

"Of course not!" Clarissa knew she was red. "You, ma'am, are obsessed with . . . with bed! My trustees cannot have known your true colors."

Despite that, she could see the wicked twinkle in Miss Hurstman's eyes, and felt its reflection in herself. She'd never known anyone so willing to say outrageous things.

"Why are you my chaperon?" she demanded. "You

are clearly a most unusual choice, even if you are well connected."

"Nepotism," said Miss Hurstman, but that twinkle told Clarissa that there was more to the word than there seemed to be. "And you come into your money at twenty-one," Miss Hurstman carried on. "Unusual situation all around. Unusual that Deveril leave you anything. Even more unusual that he arrange for you to be free of control at such a tender age."

"I know, and sometimes I wish he hadn't." After a moment, Clarissa admitted something she'd never told anyone before. "It frightens me. I've tried to learn something about management, but I don't feel able to deal with such wealth."

Miss Hurstman nodded. "You can hire Euston, Layton, and Keele to manage your affairs, but it will still be a tricky road. It's not just a matter of management. A woman is not supposed to live without male supervision, especially a young unmarried lady of fortune. The world will watch every move you make, and scoundrels will hover with a thousand clever ways to filch your money from you."

Major Hawkinville, she thought, though she couldn't see him as a scoundrel. "Fortune hunters. I know."

"At the end of a few weeks with me," Miss Hurstman stated, "you'll be more ready, and in ways other than administrative. But don't put the thought of a husband out of your mind entirely. There are good men in the world, and one of them would make your life a great deal easier. I don't see you as content with celibate living."

Put like that, Clarissa wasn't sure she would be content, either, and she knew part of that feeling was because of the heroic major, even though he hadn't touched her in any meaningful way. She wasn't ready to expose such sensitive uncertainties to Miss Hurstman's astringent eye, however.

Her companion rose in a sharp, smooth motion. "There's a lot about you that I don't understand. I won't pry. As long as it doesn't affect what we're doing here, it's no business of mine. But I'll listen if you want to talk, and I can keep secrets. You probably won't believe it, but I can be trusted, too."

Clarissa did believe it. She was tempted to lay all her burdens on the older woman's shoulders—Lord Deveril and his death; Lord Arden's cruelty to Beth; even the Company of Rogues, Lord Arden's friends, who had helped her, whose burden of secrets she carried, who frightened her in vague, elusive ways.

That the idea tempted her was alarming in itself.

Chapter Six

～

Hawk rode into Brighton at half past eight, before the fashionable part of town was stirring. He turned into the Red Lion Inn and arranged to stable Centaur there. He had a standing invitation to stay with Van and his wife, who'd taken a house on the Marine Parade, but he wouldn't disturb them at this hour.

He wasn't sure why he was here so uselessly early except that he'd wanted to get on with his pursuit of Miss Greystone. Time was shortening before Slade's deadline, but more than that, like a novice before battle, he feared losing his nerve.

Miss Greystone might seem innocent, but he couldn't imagine how she could not have been involved in Deveril's death and that forged will. She was, as far as he could see, the sole beneficiary. Anything he discovered was likely to lead to her destruction, and quite simply, he balked at that. He'd spent the past weeks seeking some other way of claiming the Deveril money.

He'd failed.

If he'd failed, he doubted it was possible. He'd used every angle and connection to try to find the forger, or a hint of the killer. Nothing, which meant he was up against a clever mind and that line of inquiry was dead, especially given his shortage of time. One day, however, he hoped to know who had constructed the deceit, and how.

And why. That in particular puzzled him. The heiress had the money. Why had a clever mind gone to such illegal lengths for no obvious profit?

A lover? He didn't want to think he'd been as deeply fooled by her as that.

From servants and gossips, he'd compiled a list of people Clarissa had been seen with during her time in London, but it was short and unhelpful. The Greystones and Deveril had only been tolerated, so her social circle had not been wide. The highest-born connection was Lady Gorgros, a vastly stupid woman who couldn't be the genius behind anything.

Viscount Starke had hung around Deveril, but he'd shake hands with anyone for another bottle of brandy, and his hands perpetually shook on their own, anyway. There'd been others of his sort, and a couple of upstart families who had wined and dined the Greystones under the illusion that it was a step toward the *haut ton*.

After Deveril's death, however, she'd been taken up by the Marchioness of Arden. That had struck him as strange enough to be interesting until he'd discovered that Lady Arden had been a teacher at Miss Mallory's School. Obviously, in time of need Clarissa had turned to her. Hawk would have spoken to the marchioness to see if she had anything to tell, but the lady was living in the country, expecting to be confined with her first child at any moment.

It was perhaps as well. Poking in such high-flowing waters was likely to be dangerous. That explained, however, why the heiress's guardian was the Duke of Belcraven, Arden's father. Her own father had been persuaded to sign away all his rights for five thousand pounds. With the Greystones, it would appear, everything was for sale.

So, after weeks of work, he had facts but no clue about Clarissa Greystone's mysterious partner in crime. Thus his only key was Clarissa herself. Perhaps her honesty and innocence were a deep disguise, and she was a thorough villain. Perhaps she was the puppet of some undiscovered manipulator.

Whatever the truth, Hawk was going to uncover it, and he would do whatever it took.

As soon as the post office opened he went to speak to his obliging informant there. Since Hawk was from a well-known local family, Mr. Crawford had made no difficulty over accepting a crown to send word when Miss Clarissa Greystone arrived in town.

"Came to register with me yesterday, Major Hawkinville," the rotund man said with a wink. "Miss Greystone, a pretty friend, and their chaperon."

"Any other notable arrivals?" Hawk asked, attempting to mask his interest a little.

Crawford consulted his book. "The Earl and Countess of Gresham, sir. Mrs. and Miss Nutworth-Hulme . . ."

When the man had run down the list, Hawk thanked him again and left, pausing to allow a couple to enter the room. An arresting couple.

The woman was a silver-haired beauty in pure white, from the plumes on her bonnet to her kid slippers. Somehow she tweaked at his memory, though he didn't know her. Certainly no man would forget her. Her companion was a tall, darkly handsome man with an empty sleeve tucked between the buttons of his jacket. Military, Hawk guessed, but again, no one he knew.

"Mrs. Hardcastle!" Mr. Crawford exclaimed, coming around his counter to bow to the lady.

Ah, he remembered her now. She was the actress they called the White Dove of Drury Lane. She'd been playing Titania when he'd tracked Van down in the theater a while ago. His mind had been entirely on Van's danger, but even so, her grace and charm had made an impression.

She was irrelevant to his current concerns, however.

As he continued on his way he heard Crawford greet the man as Major Beaumont, confirming that he was military and a stranger. All the same, that irrelevant name would now have slotted into his mind.

He found it tiresome to have nearly every detail stick, even something like a chance-met actress and her escort, but he'd learned to live with it, and it was the basis of his skill. He still had time to kill, so he walked over to the seafront, hoping the brisk breeze would clear his mind.

He wasn't used to having a tangled mind, but Clarissa Greystone had achieved it. Looked at from the angle of the evidence, she could not be an innocent. Hell, she was a *Greystone,* and even if she had spent most of the recent years at Miss Mallory's School, that had to carry a taint.

As well, he knew better than most that appearances could be completely deceptive. He remembered a wide-eyed child in Lisbon who had mutilated the soldiers he had murdered and robbed.

The ethereal White Dove was probably a foulmouthed wanton, and wholesome Clarissa Greystone was neck-deep in slime. He need have no qualms about pleasing her and wooing her until she let something slip that would open the puzzle-box of Deveril's affairs.

If only he felt that way.

He watched the dippers lead their horses down to the beach and harness them to the bathing machines, getting ready for the first bathers of the day. Business might be light, given the clouds graying the sky. Even so, perhaps he should sea-bathe despite the weather, and try to be washed clean of the stink he felt creeping over him.

Maudlin thought, but he'd never used lovemaking as a weapon before.

He suddenly remembered recruiting someone to do just that, however—if coupling with a notorious whore could be called lovemaking. It had been two years ago, just after the taking of Paris. Napoleon had abdicated, and Richard Anstable, an inoffensive British diplomat, had been found stabbed to death.

The man who'd found him had been Nicholas Delaney, and Hawk had recognized the name. Delaney had been the creator and leader of the Company of Rogues, Con's group of friends at Harrow School.

Hawk, curious about a person he'd heard so much about, had immediately wondered what Delaney was doing at the liberation of Paris. He'd sought Delaney out, and there'd been an instant liking, though Hawk had instinctively blocked the man's charisma.

That charisma, however, had landed Delaney with the very devil of a job, and because of their acquaintance, Hawk had been given the task of putting it to him.

The Foreign Office, the Horse Guards, and the military command all had files on a woman called Thérèse Bellaire. A daughter of the minor nobility, she had risen in wealth and power as mistress and procuress to Napoleon's most important men. In 1814, with Napoleon abdicating, she had turned to Colonel Coldstrop of the Guards, and begged his help in fleeing to England. No one thought her purpose innocent.

It had been decided to support her plan so as to find out what she was up to and whom she contacted. The files showed that a few years before, Delaney had been her resident lover for months. The files also said that he'd left her, not the other way around, and that she still cared.

Hawk's orders had been blunt. "She's up to something," General Featheringham had said, "and we need to know what. Only idiots think Boney's going to sit on Elba growing violets, and there are Bonapartist sympathizers everywhere, including Britain. Tell Delaney to get back into the woman's good graces and rut the truth out of her."

Hawk had put it more politely, but Nicholas Delaney's eyes had turned steady and cool. All he'd said, however, was, "And to think I felt guilty about not fighting in the Peninsula."

Hawk had tried to sugar the pill. "I hear she's a very beautiful woman, and skilled at the erotic arts."

Delaney had stood up at that. "Then you do it," he'd said, and left.

It hadn't been a rejection. Hawk had known that, and within days he'd heard that Delaney was part of a wild circle including Thérèse Bellaire. Soon after that, he'd left for England with the woman, presumably doing his noble service.

Hawk had heard no more of it, and hadn't cared to, but when Napoleon, as predicted, had returned to France and power, the Bellaire woman had reappeared in the inner circle. She'd disappeared around the time of Waterloo, and now, surely, her goose must be cooked.

It had all come back to him because he'd met Delaney again recently—in Devon, at Con's place there. Delaney's country estate lay not far away, and he'd come to look over the strange collection left by Con's predecessor and to help Con with a dilemma to do with Susan.

Delaney and Hawk had both pretended not to have met before, and it hadn't seemed that Delaney held a grudge. All the same, Hawk wondered how many thorns from his past would turn up to jab him.

Thorns from his present, as well.

He returned to the Red Lion and ate a mediocre breakfast, waiting for fashionable Brighton to emerge. Waiting for Clarissa Greystone to become vulnerable to his Hawk's eye and talons.

The fashionable throng kept earlier hours at Brighton, so by eleven he could go out to stroll among them. He circled the open grassy area called the Steyne, chatting to the occasional acquaintance, many of them military, casually keeping an eye out for his quarry.

He recognized Miss Trist first. Or rather, he was alerted by a swirl of attention around a lovely lady in a white dress trimmed with periwinkle blue, and then saw who it was. It took him a moment to recognize the lively creature beside her as Clarissa Greystone.

No sign of the unsophisticated schoolgirl now. What an excellent actress she was.

She wasn't wearing a bonnet. Instead, a daringly elegant hat with a small curved brim revealed all of her face and quite a lot of her stylishly dressed curls. It didn't make her a beauty, but it gave a vibrancy to her features. To protect her complexion, she carried the latest thing, a pagoda-style parasol. Or, to be precise, she twirled it. Even at a distance she looked confident, full of the zest of life—and dangerous.

Her gown was an off-white color strongly trimmed with rust-colored braid and edged around the hem with a deep fringe. As she walked, that fringe swung, giving tantalizing glimpses of shapely ankles emphasized by cream-and-rust-striped stockings.

Every man on the Steyne was doubtless looking at those ankles.

He jerked his own eyes up, steadied himself, and planned his intercept. He saw others making a direct line, including a number of military men. The last thing he wanted was the heiress in the protection of another man. Disguising his urgency, he moved in swiftly for the kill.

"I say, Aunt Arabella, fancy seeing you here! And in such charming company!"

Clarissa started. She'd been so intent on looking carefree and confident despite feeling sick with nerves that she hadn't noticed the dark-haired, dark-eyed young officer until he was upon them.

Miss Hurstman stopped and looked him up and down. "Afraid the mold'll rub off on them, Trevor? You were a big-eared gawk when I saw you last. Heard you did well at Waterloo, though. Good boy. You don't want to chatter to me, I'm sure. I know what you want. Miss Trist and Miss Greystone. Consider yourself introduced. Lieutenant Lord Trevor Ffyfe. He'll be a safe flirt for you because he knows I'll cut his nose off if he ain't."

The young man laughed. "Remarkable woman, my aunt. Are you new to Brighton, ladies? You must be. I couldn't possibly have missed two such beauties . . ."

After a few moments of his flattering, chattering company, Clarissa's nerves began to settle, and tentative joy crept in. Was it really going to work? Was Miss Hurstman going to perform the miracle and gain her entrance to society? This was what she'd dreamed of—becoming clothes, a fashionable throng, and a gallant, even titled, flirt.

She and Althea had lived in seclusion for two days while Mrs. Howell and her assistants rushed backward and forward doing final fittings on the gowns. They hadn't been bored, because there had been the hairdresser, the dancing master, and Miss Hurstman's own drill in perfect, confident behavior.

"Never fluster!" she commanded Clarissa. "Althea can be as demure and uncertain as she pleases, but if you are, they'll eat you alive. Look them in the eye, remember your fortune, and dare them to turn their backs."

Now she was being hatched, and in very fine feathers. She loved the bold colors of this one, and the deep, daring fringe. Perhaps in fine feathers she became a little bit of a fine bird?

She kept her chin up, her smile in place, and prepared to look anyone and everyone in the eye.

"Do say that you'll give me a dance at the assembly on Friday, Miss Greystone."

Clarissa focused on handsome Lord Trevor, and her smile became genuine. "I'd be delighted to, my lord."

"I consider myself the most fortunate of men, Miss Greystone!" He was attempting to sound sincere, but she could tell that his dazed attention was more on Althea than herself. She didn't mind. That was the true purpose of this adventure.

More or less.

She couldn't resist glancing around in search of Major Hawkinville. There was no reason under the sun for him to be here today, but she couldn't help but look.

Imagine being able to talk with him at leisure.

Imagine him asking her to reserve a dance.

But then, perhaps the dazzling appeal had been a figment of the moment and here, among so many fine military men, he would be ordinary.

There was only one way to find out.

Another survey showed no sign of him. Patience, she told herself, and concentrated on the increasing number of fine military men. It was as if Lord Trevor had breached the walls—they were surrounded by uniforms, all seeking introductions.

Only one said to Clarissa, "Oh, I say, aren't you—?" and then shut up, turning red.

"Dunce," said Lord Trevor with a reassuring smile at Clarissa.

But her nerves started to churn again. She was still the

Devil's Heiress. It was all very well to be swarmed by young officers. Would other parts of society accept her?

The officers all had excellent manners, at least, and shared their attention between Althea and herself. Since all she wanted from them was the lightest flirtation, it was heavenly.

But what about the major? She glanced around again, searching the clusters of people dotting the fashionable gathering place. She was sure that if he was here he would stand out for her . . .

And he did!

After just one glimpse, her heart started a nervous patter.

She instantly turned back to the group, smiling brightly at a lieutenant whose name had flown right out of her head, chattering to him in what was probably a stream of nonsense.

Remember, he is a fortune hunter. This is only for amusement, not for life.

"Miss Greystone. Miss Trist. How delightful to see you here."

Clarissa turned, putting on what she hoped was a merely warm smile. "Major Hawkinville. What a lovely surprise."

His smiling eyes held a distinct hint of wickedness. "Not entirely a surprise, Miss Greystone. We did speak of it."

A little shocked by that betrayal, Clarissa was still seeking the right response when a poke in her side alerted her to Miss Hurstman, expecting to be introduced. She grasped the escape, and her chaperon asked a few pointed questions before giving him the nod. Clarissa was surprised to detect something negative in her dragon. Wariness? Concern? Was there something wrong with his family? His reputation?

But then she had it. Probably Miss Hurstman knew him to be a man in need of marrying a fortune. Sad to have that confirmed, but not a shock. She could still enjoy him. In fact, it could be seen as educational. Once word escaped, she was bound to be swarmed by fortune hunters. She would learn from the major what to expect, and how to handle it.

"Major Hawkinville!" Lord Trevor said. "I say, sir, how good to see you again. And now you meet my redoubtable Aunt Arabella."

Miss Hurstman's eyes narrowed. "Been gossiping about me in the mess, Trevor?"

Lord Trevor went red and stammered a denial.

"He was singing your praises," said the major, "about some work you did helping young workhouse girls."

Miss Hurstman looked between them. "Strange topic for officers."

"We try to be eclectic. Educate the subalterns, you know." Hawk turned to Clarissa. "Are you enjoying Brighton, Miss Greystone?"

"Perfectly," she said, adding a silent *now*.

She'd wondered whether he would seem as special away from riot and adventure, but if anything, he was more so, even when surrounded by other eligible men. He was remarkably elegant, without being foppish. She wasn't sure how that came about, but she would be happy to study the question.

What was her fortune hunter going to do next?

He chatted to the other men for a moment or two, then he held out his arm to her. Concealing a smile, she put her hand on it, and let him cut her out of the group to stroll about the Steyne.

A simple and direct first step. She approved.

How would he open his wooing?

"You've acquired a formidable dragon, Miss Greystone."

She looked at him in surprise. "Miss Hurstman? She was hired by my trustees, Major."

"Ffyfe's aunt?"

"Is that so extraordinary?"

"Ffyfe's aunt, I believe, is actually cousin to his father, the Marquess of Mayne, rather than sister. However, she's sister to one viscount, aunt to another, and granddaughter of a duke. Hardly the type to hire herself out for the season."

"You're surprisingly well informed, Major." She supposed a fortune hunter needed to gather information about his quarry, but such blatant evidence of it dismayed her. And where was the amusing flattery and charm she had anticipated?

But then he smiled rather wryly. "I'm blessed—or cursed—with a retentive memory, Miss Greystone. Facts stick. You may wish to be a little on your guard."

"Against your retentive memory?"

It came out rather snappishly, and he looked startled. "Against Ffyfe's aunt." But then he added, "Ignore me, please. Someone who's been in battle often jumps at loud noises. My active service had more to do with puzzles than cannon fire, but I'm left with a sharp reaction to things and people that seem amiss."

"You see Miss Hurstman as amiss?" Clarissa asked, beginning to be intrigued by the puzzle. "I'd think her eminent background would put her beyond reproach."

"High rank doesn't always go hand in hand with virtue, Miss Greystone. I would think you would know that."

"I?" she asked, a nervous tremor starting. Was he referring to her family?

"I could not help but be curious about you, Miss Greystone, and I learned that you were betrothed to Lord Deveril."

Despite the sun, Clarissa felt as if a chill wind blew around her. Something must have shown on her face, for he said, "Have I offended you by mentioning it?"

She looked at him. He did not seem repentant. Only watchful. Was this really how fortune hunters behaved? And, she suddenly thought, if he was honest about his curiosity, had he not known in Cheltenham that she was rich?

"It is common knowledge, Major."

"As was Lord Deveril's vice. I confess to being curious as to how you came to be committed to him. It cannot have been by choice."

She silently thanked him for that, but could not, would not, talk about it. It made her almost physically sick.

"My parents compelled me, Major. But it is a matter I prefer not to discuss. I must thank you for the name you gave me, though it was not required. My trustees have found me a pleasant house in Broad Street."

"A good address. Close enough to the Steyne for convenience, but not so close as to be affected by rowdiness. What with bands, parades, and donkey races, this is often not a restful place."

She glanced at him. "But do I want to rest?"

He returned her look, and it was suddenly like the time when they had been watching the parade, when he'd silently challenged her. Had he not known then who she was? It seemed crucial, but she had no way to be sure.

"I see," he said. "You enjoy riot and mayhem?"

She twirled her parasol, sending the fringe dancing at the edge of her vision. "Not precisely that, but some little adventures . . ."

"You could creep out of your house tonight to explore Brighton with me in the dark."

"Major!"

But he was teasing, and she loved it.

His smile crinkled his eyes and dug deep brackets beside his mouth. "Too extreme? Or simply too early?" Before she could find a reply, he added, "We must establish boundaries, Miss Greystone. Could I tempt you to stroll beyond this treeless space and find more privacy?"

"To do what?" she asked, glancing away, but as if she might consider something so outrageous.

"Part of the adventure, Miss Greystone, is the mystery involved."

She looked back. "But a mystery, Major, might prove to be pleasant, or very unpleasant."

"There would be no excitement otherwise, would there?"

She met his eyes. "No danger, you mean."

His only response was a slight deepening of his tantalizing smile.

Suddenly she wanted to say yes. To go off with him and discover just how dangerous he could be. If this was a fortune hunter's trick, then she could begin to understand why some ladies fell victim to them!

Time to be wise. She looked back toward Miss Hurstman, Althea, and the group of red coats around them. "I think we had best return, Major. I cannot afford to endanger my reputation, for Althea's sake. I hope she will make a good connection here."

He turned back without complaint. "You do not seek a husband yourself?"

It pleased her to be able to say, "No." How would he deal with that?

"That is unusual in a young woman, Miss Greystone."

"I am an unusual woman, Major Hawkinville."

She meant merely that she was—or soon would be—independently wealthy, but when he said, "Yes, you are," it seemed to mean a great deal more.

Despite reason, warmth stirred within her, and it was caused by the admiration in his eyes. She tried to dismiss it as a fortune hunter's trick, but she could not.

"Your good sense and courage during the riot made a strong impression upon me, Miss Greystone. It also cannot have been easy to be put into such a situation with Lord Deveril, and yet you have survived unscathed."

She wished he would stop referring to that, but said, "Thank you."

"You are free of your parents' cruelty now, I hope?"

"I am under the guardianship of the Duke of Belcraven." Then she remembered his curiosity, and her wits sharpened. "You did not find that out, Major?"

A quirk of his lips seemed to be acknowledgment of a hit. "Yes, but not why. Or how."

"Then that puzzle can lend excitement to your life, Major."

His brows rose. "I am newly back from war, Miss Greystone. I am in no need of excitement."

She stopped to face him. "That was an unfair blow, sir!"

"Are we duelists, then? I thought us conspirators against your dull world."

"My world is not at all dull." *Especially not with you in it!*

"Ah, of course. You are new to Brighton. Perhaps I should return in a week or two when the novelty has worn off."

A second too late she knew she had let her dismay at that show. She had forgotten that he didn't live here. When would she see him again, enjoy his sparring again?

From inside a posy of scarlet coats, Althea flashed Clarissa a speculative look. Clarissa realized that she and the major were standing face-to-face in a way that must look particular. What now? She didn't know how to do this any more than she knew how to swim. Was she being wooed, or simply toyed with? How should she react? How far could she go without endangering her liberty?

She fell back on frankness. "When you do return, Major, I hope you'll call. Broad Street. Number eight."

He bowed, and by accord they moved on to join her party. "When in Brighton, I am based at number twenty-two, Marine Parade. It has been taken by my friend Lord Vandeimen and his bride." He glanced past her. "Ah, and here they are, lured by curiosity. Or," he added softly, "your delectable fringe-veiled ankles."

Stupidly, she looked down at her fringe as if she wasn't aware that it effectively made her skirt three inches shorter. By the time she looked up again to greet his friends, she was thoroughly off-balance.

Delectable? He thought her ankles delectable?

Chapter Seven

Major Hawkinville's friends were an elegant couple, though Lord Vandeimen's skin was darker than Hawk's, and a jagged scar marred his right cheek. Another officer, she was sure. Lady Vandeimen's complexion was perfect, her eyes heavy-lidded and fine, and her smile warm.

Clarissa thought that the lady must be older than her husband, but little smiles seemed to speak of the warmest feelings.

"Maria!" Miss Hurstman marched over. "Good to see you. This must be the scamp you just married." She gave Lord Vandeimen a swift perusal. "Good for you."

"Jealous?" murmured Lady Vandeimen, breaking a laugh from her husband, who captured Miss Hurstman's hand and kissed it.

"The redoubtable Miss Hurstman. Honored, ma'am."

Astonishingly, Miss Hurstman might be blushing. "Scamp," she repeated. "But twenty years ago you might have deprived me of my wits, too. At least you're safely chained and one less rascal I have to guard these flighty creatures from."

She seemed to emphasize that with a sharp glance at Major Hawkinville. After a little more chat, Miss Hurstman turned to Clarissa. "We'd best be off. We have things to do."

We do? wondered Clarissa, but Miss Hurstman was in

command of this expedition, so she said farewells attended by promises of meeting at the assembly. It was frustratingly unclear whether they included the major or not.

As she, Althea, and Miss Hurstman headed out of the Steyne, the younger officers trailed along. "Not good enough," complained Lord Trevor to Clarissa. "Letting yourself get stolen by a staff officer, Miss Greystone. What are we poor fellows to do about that?"

"Fight?" Clarissa teased.

"Hawk Hawkinville? I think not."

Hawk Hawkinville. Yes, it suits him.

"He has a formidable reputation?" She knew she was showing her interest, but was unable to resist. Folly blowing on the wind in Brighton, Miss Hurstman had said. It was more as if it shone down with the emerging sun, melting will and wits to a soggy mess.

"Right-hand man to Colonel De Lancey, Wellington's quartermaster general. Crucial work. But he enjoyed some action too. Saved one battalion at St. Pierre single-handed, they say, when all the officers were killed."

"Really?" prompted Clarissa. Of course, a military hero could still be a scoundrel in other areas. A fortune hunter. Insidiously, it was ceasing to be so appalling a notion.

"I heard his main work was in investigations, Miss Greystone."

"Of crimes?"

"Yes, but also problems. When we were sent cartloads of shoes when we needed meat, or meat when the horses needed hay. When boots turned out to have paper soles, and rifles were off. No shifty supplier wanted to come under the Hawk's scrutiny, I assure you. It's said that he rarely misses or forgets a detail."

So finding out about her engagement to Lord Deveril and her guardian would have been child's play. With sudden unease, Clarissa wondered what Hawk Hawkinville might find out if he began to look more closely. He had no reason to look into the details of Lord Deveril's death, but it seemed as if danger brushed against her.

"He did immediately know all Miss Hurstman's connections," she said.

"Did he?" Miss Hurstman's question was rather sharp. "Was he right, though?"

"I confess, I've forgotten exactly what he said, ma'am. I think that Lord Trevor is the son of your cousin rather than being a nephew, and that you are the granddaughter of a duke."

Was she silly to think that Miss Hurstman also looked worried? Did she have something to hide, too? Why *was* she employed as a chaperon?

But Miss Hurstman only said, "Ha! Not infallible, then. I'm the great-granddaughter of a duke. Trevor, take yourself and your friends off. You'll have another chance tomorrow."

Miss Hurstman swept Althea and Clarissa away with suspicious urgency. "You want to watch a man with a name like Hawk Hawkinville."

"Why?" Dirty laundry in Miss Hurstman's cupboard? Out of sheer, mischievous curiosity, Clarissa wanted to know what it was.

"A hawk's eye for detail and a close-to-infallible memory? A woman would never be able to wear the same gown twice."

"As if I cared. And you certainly don't."

Miss Hurstman didn't respond directly. "You'd be wiser to avoid him. Come along."

They were already out of the Steyne and heading back to Broad Street. Miss Hurstman was upset, and Clarissa found herself feeling more protective than curious. She understood what it was not to want a hawkish eye on one's past.

But Miss Hurstman? Her overactive imagination began to play. A scandalous affair when young? Cheating at whist? Time in the Fleet for debt? All seemed highly unlikely.

But then her own involvement in violence probably seemed that way too—a thought that wiped all whimsy and humor from her mind. Major Hawkinville was, in effect, a professional hunter of criminals. He was the last person she should encourage to take an interest in her affairs.

The immediate resistance she felt to the idea of giving him up was warning that her feelings were stronger than she thought. For the first time she let herself seriously contemplate being caught by her fortune hunter. Merely needing to marry money did not make a person a villain. Althea needed to marry a man with at least a comfortable income.

But Clarissa knew she shouldn't indulge in this particular predator.

She arrived home queasy with worry. Mr. Delaney, leader of the Company of Rogues, had stressed that she mustn't let out a hint about Deveril's death, or those who had helped her could hang. She might hang for her involvement.

Beth Arden, who had been so kind, would be involved too, just when she was expecting her child. And Blanche Hardcastle.

She needed a quiet place to think, but Miss Hurstman ordered her and Althea into the parlor. Once there, she fixed Clarissa with her gimlet gaze. "How do you know Hawkinville?"

Clarissa had not expected this attack. She knew her color was flaring, though she had nothing really to be ashamed of.

"We met in Cheltenham. He rescued me and some of the schoolgirls from a riot."

"Cheltenham?" The woman's eyes narrowed. "What was he doing in Cheltenham?"

"Why shouldn't he be in Cheltenham?"

"His home lies near here, unless I'm mistaken. So why Cheltenham?"

"He was en route to some property his father had recently acquired."

"Ah." Miss Hurstman suddenly seemed thoughtful.

"Ah?" Clarissa echoed. "What does that mean? Miss Hurstman, if you know something to the major's detriment, I wish to know it too."

Of course Miss Hurstman knew he was a fortune

hunter. Clarissa wanted that minor problem out in the open and dealt with.

But Miss Hurstman said, "To his detriment? No. According to Trevor, a fine officer. One of the oldest families, too. They go back to the Conquest." She waved a bony hand. "Off you go and do something."

Clarissa stayed put. "Why were you sounding so suspicious?"

"Why? I was told that you'd lived in almost nunlike seclusion, and then a buck of the first stare with no connection to Cheltenham claims acquaintance. Of course I wonder. And from the way the two of you were looking into one another's eyes, you were up to more than you're telling me!"

Clarissa knew she'd turned red, but she said, "It was exactly as I have told you." She couldn't help but add, "So you don't know anything shameful about him?"

"No."

But Clarissa heard a frustrating shadow of doubt. She changed tack. "Do you know anything about Lord and Lady Vandeimen?"

"Another gallant rescue in Cheltenham?" Miss Hurstman asked caustically. "If so, he's escaped your net. Married a few weeks back. She was Mrs. Celestin, wealthy widow of a foreigner. She's older than he, of course, but there's nothing wrong with that, and she's of the best blood. A Dunpott-Ffyfe. We're cousins of the more distant sort. His family's quite new here. Dutch originally, but his mother was a Grenville. Why are you so curious?"

Clarissa felt as if she'd turned on a tap and been drenched in information, all of it irrelevant. "Major Hawkinville gave me their direction as a place to contact him."

"And why, pray, would you be contacting him?"

An excellent question. Clarissa had felt that she'd dealt with the major's risqué behavior well, but he had still pushed her into impropriety. "I don't know why. I did say he would be welcome to call here."

"Nothing wrong with that. But neither of you will receive a gentleman here alone, do you understand?"

"Of course," said Clarissa for both of them. Althea looked as if another headache was coming on.

"No clandestine meetings, and no clandestine marriages. And if either of you ends up expecting a bastard child, I'll be disgusted at your folly."

Althea squeaked and stuttered something about *never* and *shock*.

Clarissa, however, dropped a meek, schoolgirl curtsy. "Yes, Miss Hurstman."

The woman's snort of amusement said she'd deflected suspicion, but inside she was a churning mass of confusion and anxiety. Hawk Hawkinville was a danger to both her virtue and her secrets, but the only safety lay in cutting herself off from him entirely.

She wasn't sure she was strong enough to do that.

When the young women had left, Arabella Hurstman stood frowning in thought. Then she walked to the small desk, sat, and pulled out a sheet of writing paper. In dark, neat script, she told the man who'd sent her here what was happening.

> *You warned of possible danger from the new Lord Deveril, and here is John Gaspard's son, as wickedly handsome as his father, dancing attendance and clearly having already made inroads. What's more, Major Hawkinville is not a man to be taken lightly. I sense a great deal more going on than I was led to expect. I require full and complete details immediately. Preferably in person.*
>
> *And bring my goddaughter with you. It's too long since I saw her.*

She folded it, sealed it, and addressed it to The Honorable Nicholas Delaney, Red Oaks, Near Yeovil, Somerset.

In the sanctuary of their room, Althea pressed her hands to her cheeks. "That woman says the most outrageous things!"

"She does, doesn't she? I rather like it."

"You would." Althea blew out a breath and began to remove her elaborate bonnet. "So, are you still pleased with the major?"

Clarissa suppressed a sigh. Still no peace. She was going to have to discuss beaux.

"He will serve to pass the time," she said lightly, dropping her hat on a chair.

"Is that fair?"

"I doubt that his heart is engaged, Thea. So, are you smitten by Lord Trevor?"

Althea gave her a look. "He's far too young. Stop trying to change the subject." She put her bonnet carefully into its box. "You must not become a flirt, Clarissa."

"But I want to flirt! And as I don't intend to marry, that is all it can be. I have warned the major of that."

Althea's eyes widened. "What did he say?"

Clarissa grinned. "I think he took it as a challenge." Her humor faded. It would be perfectly delightful if he hadn't turned out to be a Hawk.

"What is it, Clarissa?"

She couldn't explain, because that would involve explaining about Deveril's death. "This is all very new to me. I want to enjoy it, but without creating a scandal."

"Simply behave properly."

"But that would be so boring!" Irresistibly, Clarissa thought of slipping out at night to explore Brighton.

Impossible, of course, but oh, so tempting.

At school she had often slipped out into the garden at night. A minor wickedness, but she'd loved it. If she had not discovered that Major Hawkinville was so dangerous, she might perhaps have been tempted eventually into that adventure.

Althea was shaking her head. "I heard that you were not the best-behaved girl at Miss Mallory's, and now I'm coming to believe it."

Clarissa had to chuckle. "Guilty, I'm afraid. But I never created a scandal, and I won't now, Thea. So don't worry."

Then, to Clarissa's relief, Althea sat down to write her

daily letter to her family. She pretended to read a book so as to have time to think.

The only sensible course was to rebuff Major Hawkinville and get him out of her life. But would it do any good? If he wanted her fortune, he would pursue, and besides that, his interest in Lord Deveril's death might already have been stirred.

Perhaps it would be better to continue the acquaintance and watch what he was doing. That was pure sophistry, of course, for if he was investigating her past, what could she do about it?

Kill him?

She'd intended the thought to be humorous, but it sparked a new fear.

The Rogues had been kind to her, but she didn't underestimate their ruthlessness. What might they do when it came to defending those they loved?

She suddenly felt as if she were a Jonah, bringing ruin to whoever she touched—Beth, the Rogues, even Lord Deveril. And now innocent Major Hawkinville. Perhaps she should lock herself away in a convent to keep the world safe!

Hawk returned with the Vandeimens to their house, though he'd decided not to stay the night. His encounter with Clarissa Greystone had left him damnably unbalanced. Was she innocent or wicked, honest or false? He needed time and distance to regroup.

Every instinct reported that she was the same gallant, unsophisticated young woman he had met in Cheltenham. Every fact pointed to the opposite.

What was she? He had no idea except that she was surprisingly dangerous to him on a personal level. He enjoyed bandying words with her. He was feeling peculiarly protective. He was even beginning to find her pretty in the way the French referred to as *une jolie laide*, a woman who is not beautiful but almost becomes so through vitality.

"Do you like this design of porte cochere, Hawk?"

Maria's voice snapped him out of his thoughts, and he

looked at the drawing spread on the parlor table. Maria and Van—mostly Maria—were engaged in refurbishing Van's neglected home. That was why they were in Brighton for the summer. To be away from dust and noise but close enough to supervise.

"It would serve the purpose." He glanced at Van. "You're adding a porte cochere?"

Van shrugged. "Maria wants one."

"Of course I do! What if we return home one night in the pouring rain?"

"Umbrellas?" Van suggested.

Maria simply gave him a look, but it sizzled.

Hawk sighed. Newlyweds. Another reason not to stay. He felt intrusive, and also a touch envious. And where had that come from? He stood, putting down his half-drunk cup of tea. "I should set off back to Hawkinville."

Maria rose, too. "Wait just a moment, Hawk. I have something for you to take, if you would be so kind. Special nails." She hurried out of the room.

"Rushing away?" Van said. "You would be welcome to stay. I saw you gazing soulfully into Miss Greystone's eyes."

Hawk threw him a scathing look, though he'd created that moment of contact for precisely that effect. To alert others, especially other men. To put his mark on her.

"Perhaps I'm fleeing soulfulness," he said.

"She seems charming."

"She's a minx."

"A charming minx, then. There's nothing wrong with marriage, Hawk. I recommend it. And Miss Greystone would be an excellent choice. I hear she's quite an heiress."

"You think I need to marry for money, too?"

The "too" made it a jab at his friend, who had married a very rich woman. It was deliberate. Hawk didn't want Van digging into these matters.

Van leaned against the table, completely unruffled. "Running scared?"

"Running cautiously. I hardly know the chit, so why the talk of marriage?"

"I'm like a convert. Ardent to recruit new disciples."

Hawk laughed. "I'm delighted to see you happy, Van, but it isn't my path at the moment. Can you imagine me bringing a bride home to Hawkinville Manor, to live among the incessant skirmishing between me and my father?"

"Tricky, I grant you."

"And I must stay there until the squire recovers strength enough to run the estate."

He hadn't told anyone about the squire's title, or about the threat to Hawk in the Vale. The title was an absurdity, and he hoped to block the threat. At the back of his mind was the thought that if desperate he could apply to Van and Maria for a loan to pay off Slade.

Twenty thousand pounds?

When on earth could he repay a sum like that? And he doubted Maria now had much money to spare.

Hawk knew that she'd been returning money to people her first husband had cheated, and giving generously to charities for veterans because Maurice Celestin had made profits from shoddy military supplies. With the extensive renovations to Steynings, cash was probably in short supply.

More than that, however, he didn't want to admit what he was doing to try to get the Deveril money. Though he could justify it, he didn't want anyone to know what he was up to with the heiress.

"I hope you can take time for frequent visits here, at least," Van said equably. "Con and Susan are speaking of joining us for a few days."

"Of course."

Hawk was spared more conversation when Maria came in with a satchel over one shoulder and a leather bag in her arms. "The nails are rather heavy, I'm afraid."

He took the bag, pretending that his knees buckled under the weight. "Centaur will never make it home."

She chuckled. "If I can importune, the carpenter is waiting for them. The decorative heads are part of the design."

"I'll get them there this evening."

"And you'll be back soon, I hope," she said with a wide, friendly smile. Remarkable, when he'd done his best at one point to turn Van away from her.

"In pursuit of Miss Greystone, perhaps?" she teased.

"After a fashion," said Hawk, and escaped.

Chapter Eight

~

Miss Hurstman was everything she claimed. Despite her unfashionable appearance and brusque manner, she led Clarissa and Althea neatly into the very heart of Brighton's fashionable world. Clarissa went with delight, savoring her dreamed-for season like a fine wine. She would have been in heaven if not for her secrets and the worry about Major Hawkinville. He had returned to his home, but he had promised to ask for a dance at the next assembly at the Old Ship.

She knew she should hope never to see him again, but the thought of another encounter was like the last cream cake on the plate.

She couldn't resist.

He couldn't really be a danger, she rationalized. He wanted her fortune. Why would he spend time poking around in stale matters of a year ago?

And, she realized, if he wanted her fortune, he would do nothing to upset the situation. Nicholas Delaney had also said that the truth about Deveril's death could make her ineligible to inherit.

Relieved, she flung herself into every day, her circle of acquaintance constantly growing. Word was out that she was the Devil's Heiress, but this did not seem to have reduced her appeal. Instead she found herself something of a curiosity, and a lodestone for nearly every unmarried man, along with his mother and sisters.

As common wisdom said, *Money will always buy friends.*

There were also true friends, however. Althea, of course, but also Miriam Mosely, and Florence Babbington of the famous brother. Unfortunately he was now married and fixed in Hertfordshire, so she couldn't find out whether his manly orbs still stirred her to poetry.

Even Lord and Lady Vandeimen were friends of a sort, for they always came over to speak to her, and Clarissa and her party had been invited to take tea with Lady Vandeimen one day.

Clarissa understood that this was probably because their friend would like to marry her money, but she didn't mind.

Now, however, with the night of the assembly here at last, she teetered on the brink of something thrilling. As Elsie assisted her with her lovely *eau de nil* silk evening dress, Clarissa tried to disguise the shivers of excitement and nerves that seemed to be skittering over her skin.

It was very strange. Perhaps she was addicted to Major Hawkinville as people were said to become addicted to opium. Miss Mallory had arranged lectures for the girls from Doctor Carlisle on the dangers of the overuse of laudanum. He had described in awful detail the progression of the dependency, so that in the end the addict could not resist the drug, even knowing that it held destruction, in part because of the terrible physical suffering of withdrawal.

But after two—no, three—meetings?

The addict also, according to Doctor Carlisle, lost interest in all other aspects of life. A mother would neglect her child. A father would neglect his work. Even nourishing food and drink were unimportant to the person ruled by opium.

Clarissa bit her lip on a laugh. She wasn't so far gone as that. She had taken a second helping of Mrs. Taddy's jam pudding this evening, and she was enjoying all aspects of this stay in Brighton. Her unsteadiness now was simply that this would be her first grand affair here, her first trial before society en masse.

London didn't count. In London, Lord Deveril had not wanted her to go to any event unless he was with her.

Her dress, at least, was perfect. The subtly colored silk skimmed her curves and exposed just enough of her bosom to be interesting. The delicate gold-thread embroidery shimmered in the evening light. It would be magical under candles. Her hair looked as pretty as possible, and the bandeau of gold and pearls set it off very well.

Thank heavens for Miss Hurstman.

There had been no jewelry in Lord Deveril's possession, and Clarissa owned only a few valueless pieces. It was not a matter she had thought of. Miss Hurstman had, however, and had sent an urgent message to the Duke of Belcraven. A messenger had soon arrived with a selection of items.

None of them were precious, which was a great relief. Clarissa would have hated to risk losing an heirloom. They were all lovely, however. The gold filigree set with seed pearls went perfectly with her gown. She'd offered Althea her pick, but Althea had insisted on wearing only her own very simple pearl pendant and earrings.

Clarissa looked at her friend and sighed with satisfaction. In a pure white dress, stripped down to simple lines, and adorned only by her beauty, Althea would outshine every other woman present tonight and have every available man on his knees by tomorrow. She was sure of it.

She held out her gloved hand to her friend. "Onward to our adventure!"

Their hackney coach rolled up to the Old Ship Inn, which stretched along the seafront, every window illuminated to welcome the guests. The stream of people was continuous, the men in dark evening wear or uniforms, the ladies a rainbow of silk, lace, and jewels. All of fashionable Brighton would be here, and excitement danced in the air on a drifting mélange of perfume.

Clarissa pulled up the hood of her cloak to protect her coiffure from the brisk wind and stepped down from the coach. She worked hard to keep her smile at a suitably subdued level, but excitement was bubbling up in her like water in a hot pot. Her first true ball, and already she had promised dances to five men! Althea would never sit one out unless from exhaustion. It would be a splendid evening.

She caught Miss Hurstman's eye on her and tried to rein in her smile even more, but her dragon said, "Enjoy yourself. Though everyone puts on an air of boredom, it's a pleasure to be with people prepared to admit to a little excitement."

Clarissa set her smile free, this time at Miss Hurstman. Her liking and admiration for the woman grew day by day. It was so typical that her dress for this grand event was only slightly more festive than her daywear—a maroon gown and a very plain matching turban. Clarissa was reveling in fine clothes, but she relished the fact that Miss Hurstman did not care, and did not care what anyone else thought about that.

Quite possibly, she thought, as she entered the brilliantly lit hotel, she would be like Miss Hurstman one day. A crusty spinster who did and said exactly as she wished. But not yet, not yet. Tonight was for youth, and excitement, and even, perhaps, a little judicious folly.

Major Hawkinville had asked her to go apart with him on the Steyne. What would she do if he made the same invitation tonight, at the assembly?

If he was here.

He'd said he would be, but until she saw him . . .

She tried not to show it, but as she looked around, enjoying the company and acknowledging acquaintances, she was looking, looking, looking for Major Hawkinville.

Then she saw him enter, smiling at something said by one of his companions—the Vandeimens and another couple. He wore perfect dark evening clothes, but a blue cravat the color of his eyes was a playful touch that made her want to run over to him to tease. Then he laughed and raised the second woman's hand to his lips for a hotly flirtatious kiss.

A surge of pure fury hit Clarissa, but then the woman laughed too, rapping his arm hard with her fan, and it was clear that she was with the other man and no threat.

Clarissa realized that she'd been staring and looked hastily away, praying that no one had noticed. But, oh, she hoped he would kiss her hand that way.

She couldn't help it. She had to glance back. He and his party were approaching!

They were all still in the spacious entry area, for Miss Hurstman had paused to speak to someone, but all around, guests were flowing toward the ballroom. The major and his friends had to navigate the stream.

It was only when they arrived that Clarissa realized that she had watched him all the way. Immediately she decided she didn't care. She didn't know how to play sophisticated games, and she didn't enjoy them, so she wouldn't.

Hawk approached Clarissa Greystone with increasing concern. It was no good. Time away had not altered anything. He could not see her as a disguised villainess.

Look at her now! Beneath the Ship's chandeliers, she sparkled and shone, but it wasn't light on gold and embroidery, it was unabashed excitement. She was innocently, honestly delighted to be here and anticipated a magical evening.

That, surely, couldn't be faked.

As he crossed the lobby smiling, he was rapidly rearranging the pieces in his mind.

She was someone's innocent dupe, and that someone would plan to get the money back somehow.

How?

By marriage, or by inheritance.

Theft was a possibility, but as dangerous as the original crimes. Gaming was another, but not until she left her minority and was in independent control of her money.

He almost paused in his step. That would explain that strange provision of the will that put a fortune in her hands at twenty-one. An unpredictable device, however. Who was to say she would become a rash gambler? And who could say that she wouldn't marry before she reached twenty-one and have a husband to control her? In fact, it was highly likely.

Marriage? Illogical to put the money in her hands, then plan to marry it, especially as no one seemed to have made any attempt to secure her affections during the past year.

Inheritance, then. But Deveril's will stated that if Clarissa died before her majority her family should have no right to the money and it should go to the Middlesex Yule Club.

That was an absurdity, out of keeping with what he'd learned of Deveril, unless it was a cover for some depraved enterprise. In his week in London, he'd failed to find any trace of such an organization.

His main emotion, however, was a chill fear.

Inheritance necessitated death.

It was only as he introduced Con and his wife to Clarissa's party that he remembered there was another way to get the money from her—by proving the will false and being Deveril's default heir.

The course he was pursuing.

It didn't threaten her life, but seeing her here, shining with the pleasure of this wealthy, privileged life, he suspected that it was close.

Hawk in the Vale, he reminded himself. All the people of Hawk in the Vale, not to mention his own dreams, hinged upon this. He would take care of her, though. She would not be abandoned to the cruelty of the world, or of her family.

As they moved to follow the crowd toward the ballroom, he offered an arm to Clarissa and Miss Hurstman.

The latter immediately said, "You spend much time in Brighton, Major?"

He recognized an attack, though he had no idea why she was hostile. "When the company pleases me, Miss Hurstman."

At her narrow look, he went on. "My friends the Vandeimens are fixed here at the moment, and the Amleighs have joined them for a week or so."

"Thought he'd inherited the earldom of Wyvern," Miss Hurstman said, as if Con's title was suspicious too.

"It's under dispute, so he has reverted to the viscount-cy. He'll be happy to have it stay that way."

"The old earl was certainly a dirty dish. Bad blood." But it was said with an eye on him. He came to the alert. What did she know? It would be disastrous if Clarissa discovered his connection to Deveril.

"There's bad blood in every family, Miss Hurstman," Hawk replied, meeting that look. "Wasn't it your paternal grandfather who tried to stake his daughter in a game of hazard?"

Clarissa was astonished and alarmed to see Miss Hurstman silenced, and she leaped into the conversation. "So are you fixed here for a few days, Major?"

He turned to her, his expression warming. "I am, Miss Greystone. I anticipate a great deal of pleasure from it."

Clarissa didn't think she mistook his meaning, and she turned away to hide a smile. He was here to hunt her. She still wasn't sure if she should let herself be caught, but the pursuit promised extraordinary pleasure.

She had promised the first dance to dashing Captain Ralstone, and forbade herself to regret it. She couldn't dance every dance with the major. She had to confess to being relieved, however, when he led out Lord Amleigh's wife rather than some other unmarried woman.

Jealousy? That was ridiculous.

She made herself pay full attention to Captain Ralstone during their dance, but this had the unfortunate effect of increasing his confidence. By the end of the set, his comments were becoming a little warm, and his manner almost proprietary. She was delighted in more ways than one to move off with Major Hawkinville in preparation for the next set.

"Ralstone is a gazetted fortune hunter, you know," he said, as they strolled around the room.

"And you are not?" It popped out, and she immediately wished it back.

His brows rose, but he didn't immediately answer. Eventually he said, "My father owns a modest property, and I am his only son."

She knew she was red. "I do beg your pardon, Major.

I had decided to put off affectation and behave naturally, but I see now why it is unwise."

She was rewarded with his smile. "Not at all. I would be delighted if you would be natural with me, Miss Greystone. After all, as we see, it dispels misunderstandings before they can root."

"Yes," she said, but she didn't think his talk of natural behavior related entirely to dispelling misunderstandings.

He covered her gloved hand on his arm. "Perhaps we can begin by using first names with each other, just between ourselves."

She glanced down at their hands for a moment. He wore a signet ring with a carved black stone, and his fingers were long, with neatly oblong nails.

She smiled up at him. "I would like that. My name is Clarissa."

"I know. And mine is George, but no one uses it. You may if you wish, or you may call me Hawk, as most do."

"Hawk? A somewhat frightening name."

"Is it? You are no pigeon to be afraid of a hawk."

"But I am told that you investigate everything, and forget nothing."

He laughed. "That sounds tiresome rather than frightening."

"Then what about the fortune hunting? Are you hunting me, Hawk?" She longed to have everything honest between them.

He touched her necklace where it lay against her throat, sliding a finger slowly beneath it. "What do you think?"

Clarissa wasn't sure whether to swoon or be outraged.

"And be assured," he murmured, lowering his hand, "if I capture you, my little pigeon, you will enjoy it."

She escaped by looking around at the company and fanning herself. "It is not pleasant, you know, to be prey, no matter how benign the hunter."

"Bravo," he said softly. "Well, then, you will have to be a predator, too. I think I will call you Falcon."

She looked back at him. "Ah, I like that."

"I thought you might."

But then she realized that he had brought them to a halt and was gazing into her eyes. Fortune hunting, she realized, could take many subtle forms. He was trying to mark her as his. She probably should not allow it, but it was too exciting to decline.

"Electricity," she said.

"Definitely. You have experienced that mysterious force?"

"At school. We had a demonstration."

"Education is wonderful, is it not?"

It was perhaps as well that the warning chords sounded then for the next dance, for Clarissa wasn't sure what she might have done. The simplest fortune-hunting technique, she realized, would be to compromise her.

She must certainly guard against that, but she could certainly enjoy this.

It was only a dance.

Clarissa tried to remind herself of that, but she had danced with a man so rarely. The dancing master at the school hardly counted. Last year in London, she had attended two balls, but on both occasions she had been on Lord Deveril's arm and had danced only with him. She wasn't sure if her lack of partners had been because of her own lack of charms or because of Deveril.

And here she was, dancing with a man who seemed able to generate electricity without any machine at all!

It was a lively country dance that gave little opportunity for talk, but that didn't matter. It would be an effort to be coherent. The movements allowed her to look at him, to smile at him, and to receive looks and smiles in return. They held hands, linked arms, and even came closer in some of the moves. She began to feel that she was losing contact with the wooden floor entirely . . .

When it came to an end, she fanned herself, trying to think of something lightly coherent to say. Suddenly she found herself in a cooler spot, and realized that he had moved them into the corridor outside the ballroom.

She half opened her mouth to object, to say that she would be looked for by other partners, or by Miss Hurstman, for that matter, but then she closed it again.

What next?

She couldn't wait to find out.

The corridor—alas?—was not completely deserted, but as they strolled along it he captured her fan, sliding the ribbon off her wrist, and began to ply it for her. The cool breeze was not adequate competition for the additional heat swirling inside her.

"What are you doing, Hawk?"

His lips twitched. "Hunting?"

"Pray, for politeness' sake, call it courting, sir."

"Courting? I have much practice at the hunt, but little at courtship. How should we go on?"

She put on a mock flirtatious air. "Poetry would be welcome, sir. To my eyes. To my lips . . ."

"Ah." He ceased fanning, but only to capture her gloved hand and raise it to his lips. *"Sweet maid, your lips I long to kiss / To seal to mine in endless bliss / Let but your eyes send welcome here / And I, your swain, will soon be near."*

His lips pressed, and she resented her silk gloves, which muted the effect. "A sweet rhyme, but it comes rather easily to you, sir."

His eyes lit with laughter. "Alas, it is commonly used. Written on a scrap of paper and slipped to a lady."

"Not always with proper intentions? Tut, tut! Let me think what I can contribute."

Her hand still in his, she recited, *"O noble man, tall, chaste, and bold / So like a gallant knight of old / Turn on me once, lest I expire / Those sapphire orbs filled with manly fire."*

He laughed, covering his face for a moment with his free hand. "Manly fire?"

"And sapphire orbs," she agreed. "Though I feel obliged to confess that the original was obsidian."

"Ah. That probably explains the 'chaste' too."

Clarissa blushed, though heaven knows she'd not expected him to be inexperienced. "He was one of my friend's brothers, and I was twelve. It's a very romantic age, twelve."

"And you're so old and shriveled now."

She looked into his teasing eyes and quickly, before she lost courage, drew his hand to her lips for a kiss. Warm skin, firm flesh and bone. A hint of cologne and . . . him.

Remembering that they were not alone, she hastily dropped his hand, grabbed her fan, and fanned herself frantically.

"It is hot, isn't it?" He put a hand at her elbow and moved her sideways.

Into a room.

She stopped fanning, though she was certainly no cooler. It was a small withdrawing room set with armchairs, and with copies of magazines and newspapers available. At the moment it was deserted.

He made no attempt to shut the door. If he had, she thought she would have objected despite her riveted fascination.

To be compromised would be disastrous, she tried to remind herself, but a part of her simply didn't care.

That part seemed to be the one in control. And the door, after all, was wide open.

"Major?" she said as a light query.

"Hawk," he reminded her.

"Hawk." But she blushed. The word seemed wicked, here, alone.

He touched her lips. "You only have to fly away, my dear."

She met his eyes, her heart thundering. "I know."

He took her hand and drew her across the room. When he stopped, she realized that they were no longer visible to anyone in the corridor.

But the door was still open . . .

Then he raised her chin with his knuckles, and kissed her.

It was a light kiss—a mere pressure of his lips against hers—and yet it sent a shiver of delight through her.

Her first kiss!

But then she stiffened. Not her first. Deveril had been her first. A memory of vomit made her pull back.

He stood absolutely still. "You do not like to be kissed?" Then, perceptively, he added, "Deveril?"

Her silence was all the answer he needed. "What a shame he is already dead."

"You would have killed him for me?"

"With pleasure."

He was serious. And he was a soldier. The idea of having a champion, a man ready to defend her with his life, was even more seductive than kisses. It was too soon, ridiculously too soon, but she wanted this man.

"Lord Deveril was murdered, I understand," he said. "I don't suppose it was you, was it?"

The seductive mist froze into horror. "No!"

He caught her arm before she could run away. "It was a joke, Falcon, but I see it's no matter for humor." The touch turned into a caress. "You must forgive a soldier still rough from the war."

She was struck dumb by fear of saying the wrong thing, and by the tender pleasure of his hand against her arm, her shoulder, her neck . . .

"If I were persuaded into marriage with a person I disliked," he said, "and had unpleasant kisses forced upon me, I would do away with the offender."

"But you're a man."

"Women are capable of violence too, you know."

Lulled, relaxed, she said, "Yes. Yes, they are."

As soon as the words escaped, she knew she had finally said too much. It shouldn't matter. It was of no significance to him. But she had said too much.

Making herself be calm, she moved away from his touch, wondering whether to spill more words to cover what she'd said. No. "We must return to the dance. As I said, Major, I do not plan to create a scandal."

Even to her own ears it sounded brittle.

He merely said, "Of course." But as they moved toward the door, he put his hand on the small of her back. She felt it there through silk—possession and promise.

She had overreacted. He'd been joking, teasing.

And, as she'd decided before, her future husband

would not want the truth about Deveril's death to come out. Perhaps it was her sacred duty to marry him!

As they moved into the corridor, he linked their arms again. "You mustn't let one man have such a victory over you, Falcon. You are entitled to enjoy kisses, and kisses are not so very wicked." He waited until she looked at him, then added, "I hope you will soon let me show you how pleasant they can be."

She was tempted to move back out of sight for an immediate demonstration, but she made herself be sensible and return to the ballroom. For one thing, she had another partner waiting. For another, she needed time and peace to think this all through.

A hollowness ached in her, however. Harmless as it had been, she should not have said that about a woman and violence. Nor should she have panicked at a joke about her killing Deveril.

Could she not engage in simple conversation without perilous shards of truth slipping out?

She danced one later set with the major, and it was the supper dance, but she made sure that afterward they stayed with a group. He didn't seem to mind. He was, she was sure, a very patient hunter, and if he felt confident, it was hardly surprising.

As they returned home, Miss Hurstman said, "I warned you, Clarissa, about slipping off into anterooms."

Foolish to hope that the dragon had not noticed. "It was hot in the ballroom."

"That is the usual excuse. If you'd been gone any longer I would have found you."

Clarissa sighed. "I'm sorry, Miss Hurstman, but Major Hawkinville was a perfect gentleman."

It wasn't really a lie.

"So I would hope, but have a care. I have no doubt he has an eye on your fortune."

"Nor do I." The coach drew up in Broad Street and they climbed down. "But tell me, Miss Hurstman, which of my partners tonight did not?"

Althea exclaimed, "Clarissa!" but Miss Hurstman, consistently honest, made no rebuttal.

Althea would have liked to chatter about the evening, but for once Clarissa claimed a headache and even accepted a little laudanum in the hope that it would still the whirling doubts and questions in her head.

It worked, but in the morning all the doubts and questions were still there, along with the acceptance of a simple fact. Hawk Hawkinville was winning. She was beginning to fall in love with him.

Chapter Nine

As they sat at a late breakfast the next morning, a note came from Lady Vandeimen inviting Clarissa and Althea to walk with her. Miss Hurstman made no objection and remarked that Maria Vandeimen would be a strict chaperon. "She was spun off her feet by a handsome opportunist once."

"A fortune hunter?" Clarissa asked.

"There are different types of fortunes."

"What was hers?"

"Her blood. Celestin had money and wanted the entrée. But it wasn't her, you see. It could have been anyone of high enough birth."

Clarissa nodded, understanding the warning. "Yes, I see."

As expected, when Lady Vandeimen arrived, she was accompanied by her husband, the Amleighs, and Major Hawkinville.

Hawk.

And the question was, Did he simply want money, or was there something of her about it?

Clarissa was not at all surprised when Althea ended up walking with the Amleighs, leaving her to Hawk's escort. Nor could she regret it. One thing was certain—she could not make any kind of decision without learning more about Hawk Hawkinville, and the lessons were perfectly delightful.

It was not a delightful day, being overcast and somewhat chilly. But as Lady Vandeimen had remarked when she'd arrived, in this unsettled summer, overcast was a pleasant alternative to rain. The weather had given Clarissa the opportunity to wear a very stylish Prussian blue spencer with bronze braid and frogs, so that was a silver lining.

As they paused to look at the unused bathing machines, however, she said, "I wish the weather would turn warmer. I might brave the water."

"Do you swim?"

She looked at him. "Not at all. But the dippers take care of the bathers, don't they?"

"And keep to the shallows."

He turned to lean back against the wooden railing. A deliberate ploy, surely, to make her breathless at the long, lean length of him, and the strength that was clear, even when he was at rest.

A ploy did not mean that any of it was false. She'd met any number of men in the past days, many of them handsome, but none had the power over her that this man seemed to have.

"We have a river back home," he said. "The Eden. Perhaps I will take you there to swim one day."

"Perhaps." She tried for the same light manner but feared her feelings must show. "But can I trust you not to lead me into deep water?"

His slight smile acknowledged the double entendre. "You can't really swim in the shallows."

"I can't really swim at all."

"I could teach you."

"Or drown me."

His brows rose. "O ye of little faith."

"O me of great caution, Major." Lord above, but this verbal play alone could seduce her into folly, never mind all his other charms.

"Hawk," he reminded her.

"Very well, Hawk. I wonder where the others are," she asked, looking back.

"Nervous?" he murmured.

"Of course not." Yet the mere suggestion had stirred nerves within her. The others were only a few yards away, speaking to another party. There were people all around. There was nothing to fear, except the reactions inside herself, which seemed to be rapidly spinning out of control.

"Perhaps you should be nervous."

She swiveled back to face him. "Why?"

"Because we are already in deep water. Can't you tell?"

Oh, yes. "We are in public on the Marine Parade in Brighton."

"Even so . . ."

The others joined them then, and Clarissa could only be glad. She wasn't sure she had a coherent response to make.

"The Pytchleys were just speaking of the fair," Maria Vandeimen said. "They say it is very amusing. Lord Vandeimen and I are thinking of driving out there this afternoon. Perhaps you would care to come if you are free, Miss Greystone, Miss Trist."

"The fair?" Clarissa asked, trying to surface from deep waters.

"Out on the Downs," Lord Vandeimen said. "A little wild, but perfectly safe with good escorts."

She couldn't help but look at Hawk.

What if the escorts were a little wild?

"I will have to ask Miss Hurstman," she said.

When asked, Miss Hurstman again made no objection, though to Clarissa she did not seem entirely happy.

"Be sure to stay with your party," she said to both of them, though it seemed to be directed particularly at Clarissa.

The sun broke through the clouds as the two open carriages rolled up to the sprawling fairground set up on the Downs. Clarissa looked back toward the town spread out before them, with the silvery sea beyond, then turned to the gaudy, hurly-burly jumble of the fair.

"Your eyes are sparkling, Miss Greystone," said Hawk from his seat opposite her.

"I've never been to a fair before."

He smiled. "Then I'm particularly glad Maria had this fancy."

They were sharing the vehicle with Lord and Lady Vandeimen, while Althea came behind with the Amleighs and Lord Amleigh's secretary, Mr. de Vere. Clarissa hoped he wouldn't catch Althea's fancy. He could hardly have a fortune, and seemed mischievous.

They descended from the carriages and headed for the first tents, but they had to pick their way, for the ground was soft after the wet weather and much trampled. This meant that Clarissa must keep a firm hold on Hawk's arm, which did not displease her at all.

"What fairground pleasure most appeals?" he asked her.

"I don't know. Everything!"

He laughed, and they paused at a miniature model of Paris, complete with a glassy River Seine.

"Is it true to life?" Clarissa asked.

"Yes, it seems to be," he said, dropping a coin in the box there, "except that Versailles is not so close."

She looked at him. "You must have seen many countries."

"Not so many. My service was confined to Europe."

She looked at another model, which claimed to be Rome. "I would like to travel. I would like to see Spain, and Italy, and the ruins of Greece."

"When you have your fortune and your independence, there will be nothing to stop you."

"True." But she knew she was not brave enough to wander the world alone. A weakness, but it must be faced. Coming to Brighton was enough of an adventure for her so far.

There was a more popular display, but their party wandered past it without a close look. Clarissa peered and saw that it was a representation of the Battle of Waterloo.

No wonder. But it amazed her to think that their ur-

bane escorts had, not long ago, been part of that dire
and desperate affair.

Had killed.

She glanced at Lord Vandeimen of the smooth and
silky blond hair—though there was that scar.

Lord Amleigh was more saturnine, but when he
smiled, dimples showed.

No one would think that smiling de Vere had been to
war. As for Hawk, he looked as if he would hate to have
his clothes disarranged, and yet he had been a hero at
least once, according to Lord Trevor. And even if he
hadn't raised a sword at Waterloo, he'd been there,
among the carnage.

She realized how little she really knew of him. She
must be careful.

For the moment, however, she was reveling in innocent
fun. They all progressed merrily from sideshows to trials
of skill to prizewinning animals. The men teasingly en-
couraged the ladies to try their hands at everything, applauding successes and commiserating with failures. Lady
Amleigh proved to have a very good throwing arm at the
coconut shy, and Lady Vandeimen was skilled at archery.
Clarissa had no such skills, but she managed a lucky roll
at dice, which doubled her sixpence to a shilling, and
Althea hooked a cork fish with a little fishing pole to
win a carved fan.

They paused outside a black tent spangled with golden
stars. "Madame Mystique," said Lord Vandeimen.
"She's the latest sensation here in Brighton. Would any
of you ladies like to have your fortune told?"

Althea said an emphatic no, and the other ladies both
made a laughing comment about already having their
excellent fortune. Clarissa was tempted, but she didn't
want to be the only one, so she said no as well, and they
moved on to the next stall, where sticky buns were for
sale. The men hailed this as if they were starving, and
soon they all had a bun in their hands, though the ladies
had to remove their gloves first.

"This feels wonderfully wicked," Clarissa declared,
licking sweetness from around her lips.

"Wicked?" Hawk asked.

"Standing in a public place eating, and eating so messily! Miss Mallory would definitely not approve."

He smiled. "We can be a great deal more wicked than this, I assure you, Falcon. But perhaps just as sweetly."

The others were laughing together and trying to clean sticky fingers. Clarissa savored her last mouthful, looking at him, thinking about the tantalizingly light kiss they'd enjoyed.

"Perhaps you are a devil that tempts rather than a hawk that hunts."

"Any good hunter knows to lure his prey. And the devil hunts souls, that's for sure."

"To their destruction."

"True."

Then he grasped her wrist and inspected her hand. For a heart-stopping moment, she thought he would start to lick her fingers clean, but instead he drew her toward some enterprising children who were offering a handwashing service next to the bun stall.

She staggered. His warm, firm fingers were light against her skin, but they were there, sending her nerves jumping.

He let her go, and Clarissa found herself clasping the wrist his fingers had circled, aware of her own frantically pounding pulse.

One smiling girl took his penny, and a second poured cool water over Clarissa's hands into a bowl. A third offered soap, and Clarissa rubbed away the stickiness, but was careful not to wash her wrist. She wanted the memory of his touch.

A fourth child, a pretty red-haired urchin, offered a towel, and Clarissa dried her hands while watching the other members of the party follow. This was all innocent fun, but something stronger beat beneath it. She knew it, and knew it to be dangerous, but she couldn't resist.

Then she was snapped out of her dreamy thoughts by a spot of rain.

She realized that the sun had disappeared again, and a heavier layer of dark clouds was sliding in. The rain was only a hint on the air at the moment, but Lord Vandeimen said, "Back to the carriages, I think."

No one protested, though Clarissa wanted to. What would have happened next?

Lady Amleigh said, "I do wish that volcano had kept its head!"

To which her husband responded, "Perhaps it was in love."

The look in his eye and the lady's blush said it had special meaning for them. Clarissa wondered what it would be like to have that sort of private connection, that sort of love.

It was beginning to seem a prize worth more than a mere fortune.

A number of people had the same idea of leaving the fair, but then, as the rain held off, some turned back. Suddenly there was a swirling crowd that reminded her of the riot in Cheltenham.

Hawk put his arm around her and held her close. "Don't worry. There's limitless space here, so it can't become a deadly crush."

All the same, they were jostled a little, and he eased them between two stalls and into more open space. Clarissa couldn't help noticing that the other couples had gone in another direction.

Accident, or design?

She glanced at him, not at all nervous. He'd mentioned her going apart with him. She was ready to find out what it involved. She glanced at the darkening sky, praying that the storm would hold off for a while.

Then the wind squalled, almost flinging her skirts up. She fought to hold them down. "I think the storm's about to hit!" she called, in case his wicked purposes had blinded him to nature.

"I know." He glanced around, then said, "Come on!" His arm around her, he ran toward a large tent. The rain hit like a gray sheet just as they made it to safety.

It was a rough stable with lines of tethered horses, many of them moving restively with the storm. They became even more agitated as people rushed and staggered in in various states of wetness.

A couple of grooms tried to stop the invasion, but it was no good. The rain was coming down in torrents, driven hard by the wind, and the ground outside was already a swamp.

They ended up with only about twenty people in the tent, but with everyone squeezing away from the nervous horses, it was a crush. The stink of dung, horse, wet clothing, and unwashed bodies made Clarissa almost wish that she was out in the torrent.

Hawk eased them into a corner, but said, "I apologize."

"It's not your fault, but I do wish there was some fresh air."

Suddenly he had a knife in his hand, a slender knife that, all the same, cut a slit in the canvas wall as if it were muslin. When it was clear that the rain was coming from the other direction, he made the cut into a rectangular flap.

"Do you have a pin?" he asked.

"What lady would be without one?" Clarissa said, shocked by that efficient blade. She had never imagined a gentleman carrying such a thing and had no idea what to do with the information.

She gave him a pin. "You are very resourceful, Hawk. And very well equipped."

He was pinning up the flap. The knife had somehow disappeared. He looked at her for a moment, then held out his hand. Pushing back his cuff, he slid the dagger out again.

"An interesting fashion accessory," she said.

"More of a bad habit."

"I thought soldiers went more normally armed."

"Wise soldiers go armed in any way that will keep them alive. I've been in places where a secret weapon was almost expected, however." His lips quirked. "Don't think me a hero. It was generally a matter of dealing with shady merchants, thieves, and even pirates. And there being little difference between the three."

She smiled, content now that she had fresh air to breathe. They were hardly alone, but the people all around seemed to be country folk or fair workers. No one to care what she and Hawk did or said.

"You have to know that I find that exciting," she remarked.

Hawk almost had her where he wanted her, where he had to want her, but as usual her disarming frankness was like a shield, turning away all weapons.

He made himself smile teasingly. "Is it? Most ladies find killing knives frightening."

She tried. She tried very hard. But he saw the flicker of muscles that registered a hit.

"Killing?" she said, in the way of a person who knows they have to say it.

He handled his stiletto, carefully out of the way of nearby people. "A knife like this is not for mending pens, Falcon. Though it does that job very well." He turned the handle toward her. "Here."

She stared at it, all guard shattered. "What? I don't want it!"

"You said it excited you."

"No, I didn't!" She was fixed on the knife like a rabbit on the snake that will kill it. He saw her swallow. It was like a knife in his own gut. A knife he had to push in deeper rather than draw out.

"What did you mean, then?"

She looked up. Tried to step back, but a tent support blocked her from behind. She was pale, her eyes stark, but she managed a kind of lightness. "I meant pirates and such. Romantic things."

"If you think pirates romantic, I should definitely equip you with a knife, and teach you how to use it."

"No, thank you."

"No?" He moved the knife again. *Did you kill Deveril? If not, who used a knife on him?* "I call this my talon. A Falcon should have a talon, too." When she didn't respond, he pushed. "Why does it bother you? Something else to do with Lord Deveril?"

For a moment she looked shockingly like a man who realizes that his guts are hanging out, that he's dying. "No!"

People nearby turned to look. Damn. He slipped the knife back in its sheath and took her gloved hands. "Have I upset you? I'm sorry."

She stayed silent, though her chest was rising and falling.

"It's Deveril's death, isn't it?" he said softly, sympathetically. "These things heal when they're spoken of."

It was usually a surprisingly successful ploy. He'd had men talking their way to the gallows this way. No words spilled, so he asked a simple, factual question. Often once people started to talk, they couldn't stop.

"When did he die?"

She blinked at him. "June the eighteenth. When so many others were dying . . ."

Against reason, he pulled her into his arms. "Hush, I don't mean to upset you. Don't talk about it if you don't want to."

But the words he'd wanted were like lead in his heart.

June 18. The day of Waterloo, when, indeed, so many others had been dying. But Deveril's body hadn't been found until the twentieth, and the date of his death had never been certain.

To be so sure, Clarissa had to know all about the murder, and he knew now that he'd been stupidly hoping that she didn't, that she was the innocent she seemed.

How had it been? Had she killed Deveril to stop him from raping her? And was he going to send her to the gallows for it?

That or Hawkinville, he reminded himself.

He knew, abruptly and with astonishing relief, that he could not do it. Not even Hawkinville was worth that.

Perhaps his father had had the right idea after all. Persuade her to marry him. He would not be like his father, after all, courting callously for gain. He truly admired his gallant Falcon. He would protect her, cherish her. A picture began to unfold of them together at Hawkinville. Children . . .

But then a dark curtain fell. He wasn't simply Hawk Hawkinville, fortune hunter. He was heir to Lord Deveril!

It was hard not to burst out laughing at the farce of it. When did he tell her she was going to have to live her life with the name she loathed? Not before the wedding, for sure. She would run away. Right after the ceremony? No, he'd better make sure of her and wait until it was consummated.

Damnable.

And how did he expect to marry her? If she'd killed Deveril, she hadn't done it alone. And there was that forged will, and someone after her money. Announce their betrothal and the other parties would have to act.

Elope, then. But the other objection still stood. Could he really persuade a woman into a clandestine marriage knowing she would loathe him once she knew the truth?

For once, he was totally adrift.

He gently eased her away. "It's stopped raining. It's a sea of mud out there, but we should try to find the others."

She looked up, a little pale but much restored, perhaps even with a hint of stars in her eyes. Stars he'd been working so hard to put there. Pointed stars, that could do nothing but hurt her, one way or another.

People were moving out of the tent, but slowly. Suddenly needing to be free of the place, he pulled out his knife and extended the hole, stepped through, then helped her out. They emerged into a field, so they escaped the trodden mud, but she still had to teeter over a deep puddle. That seemed to drive the clouds away entirely. She laughed, looking up at him, clinging to his hand.

He put his hands at her waist and swept her over the puddle, wishing he could sweep her away entirely. Wishing he were someone other than the Hawk, and heir to John Gaspard, Viscount Deveril.

They picked their way down the back of the tents toward the carriages as the fair slowly came back to life around them.

"How optimistic people are," she said, looking at the sky.

"Another torrent on the way," he agreed. "But optimism is good. *Carpe diem.*"

She glanced at him, seeming almost completely restored now. "Is that optimism? Surely optimism should say that tomorrow will be as pleasant as today?"

"Whereas Horace advised us to put no trust in tomorrow."

They were apart from the crowds, but he wasn't sure he cared about proprieties anyway. He felt as if this might be his last moment. He drew her into his arms, and she came willingly, a trusting pigeon.

"This is most improper," he murmured against her lips.

"Improper, yes. But most?"

It broke a full smile from him, which he gave her in the kiss, then lost as he tasted her fully for the first time. Soft, sweet. With wondrous amusement he found he could actually taste her delighted curiosity as he teased her mouth open to him.

Her hands clutched, holding him tighter. He could feel all the promising, firm curves of her body and a faint tremor that might even be partly his own.

When had he last kissed for the kiss alone? When had he last lost himself in a kiss so that when their mouths slid free he felt dazed, as if from too much hot sun—which there certainly wasn't today on the rainy downs.

Her eyes were wide, but not with horror. After a moment she said, "I don't think I need to worry about the memory of Deveril's kiss anymore."

He pulled her close and held her. "Then I'm glad of that." Did it mean Deveril was no longer such a power in her mind? If he told her the truth now, would she shrug it off?

If she didn't, he would have burned every conceivable bridge.

She pushed slightly free. "You are not glad of other things?"

What could he say? Hardly surprising that she expected more after a kiss like that. Hardly surprising if she expected a proposal.

"I am glad that the rain has stopped, and for the tip of your nose." He kissed it.

She chuckled, blushing.

"I'm glad to be out of the tent, and for your elegant ankles."

Her eyes shone.

"I'm glad that I might, one day, discover other elegant parts . . ."

He was saved from pursuing that insane course when something hurtled through the air and hit her.

Clarissa screamed, but he grabbed the thing and discovered that it was a muddy, raggedy cat, hissing, squirming, and doing its damn best to sink in its claws.

"Don't!" Clarissa screamed.

"I'm not going to break its neck." He usually had a way with animals. He held it close to his body and started murmuring to it. In moments it calmed.

She staggered closer. "Is it all right? Where did it come from?"

"Hush." He worked at shrugging out of his coat one sleeve at a time without letting the cat free, murmuring to keep it calm as he gradually swathed it. Then a purr started and quickly grew in volume.

Chapter Ten

Clarissa watched him with astonishment. She never would have thought that her hawk of elegant plumage would go to such trouble for a scrawny cat.

Now that the cat seemed calm, she looked around. A man came out of the back of a nearby tent and chucked a handful of dead rats into a sack, then ducked inside again. She heard squeals, yowls, and shouting from inside.

She marched over to yank back the canvas curtain. As she thought, it was a ratter's tent, where cats and dogs were set to kill rats. People were packed onto ranks of rough benches cheering on the hunters and calling out bets. Assaulted by noise, stink, and pure violence, she staggered back.

Then a burly man blocked her view. "If yer want to come in, go round the front and pay."

Clarissa remembered her purpose. "Who threw that cat?"

"What frigging business is it of yours?"

"It hit me! What's more, it's wounded and needs care."

"I didn't wring its neck. What more does it need? Useless piece of scrag."

"You may not have heard," said a calm voice behind her. "The cat hit the lady."

The ratter whipped off his hat. "Hit the lady, sir? Well, I never! Are you all right, miss?"

How infuriating not to be taken seriously without a man at her back! This was an active lesson on the points Mary Wollstonecraft had been making in her writings.

"What about the cat?" she demanded, though she was beginning to realize that the last thing the poor creature needed was to be returned to the ratters. People nearby were turning to look, too, their avid faces suggesting that they expected another juicy battle.

The ratter put on an apologetic expression. "Didn't turn out to be much of a ratter, you see, miss. If you'd like the dear creature, please, take her."

The purring vibrated the air by her side. Clarissa glanced once at Hawk, almost distracted by the fact that he was in shirtsleeves, but hoping he would take over. He had his arms full of purring cat, however, and his look seemed to say, This is your game. You play it.

"Very well. I will take her. Does she have a name?"

"Fanny Laycock," said the man with a very false smile. Someone nearby sniggered.

"Take her," Hawk said.

Clarissa found herself with her arms full of coat and cat. The purring stopped, and a slight shivering began. She tried murmuring to it, and it calmed a little. Her attention was all on Hawk, however, as he walked toward the ratter. The man's eyes suddenly widened. Whatever it was Hawk did to impress people, he was doing it again.

"You can't go around throwing cats," he said, almost lazily. "I'm sure that when my companion gets into clear light, she will find that her gown is snagged and stained with blood. I doubt you can afford the cost of a replacement, but a guinea will serve as penance."

"A guinea—!"

He stopped and swallowed. Slowly, he dug into a pocket, but Clarissa caught a movement and saw the two other men moving closer. They were all so big!

"Hawk!" she said sharply in warning, just as the first man ran for him.

"You really shouldn't," Hawk said. But his fist had

already shot out, hurtling the first man back into the stands, causing a yelling commotion among the people sitting there. He'd somehow avoided the other two.

But then men leaped out of the stands and fists flew. Rats escaped and were darting underfoot, pursued by ferocious dogs and cats. Women screamed and wood shattered.

It was the riot all over again!

Trying to protect the frantic cat, Clarissa was forced back, right out of the riotous tent into a gathering crowd.

What was happening?

Hawk!

What if he was dead?

She tried to soothe the poor cat, tried to soothe herself, but tears trickled down her face. Another disaster, and entirely her fault. She truly was a Jonah . . .

But then she heard chattering and realized the tumult had calmed. The flap opened, and Hawk appeared in the midst of a group of cheerful, admiring men.

Hard to imagine him so disordered and muddy, but he seemed unharmed. A giggle escaped. He'd lost his hat again! Then someone hurried after and gave it to him.

He thanked all the men, who presumably had been on his side, then looked around for her. "Are you all right?"

"Yes, but what of you?"

"Nothing serious." He brushed a tear off her cheek. "I'm sorry if you were frightened."

"It wasn't your fault."

"It's an escort's duty to protect against all affront. I clearly need practice." He took the cat, and the ungrateful beast immediately started purring again. "Let's find the others before they call out the army."

As they walked away, navigating to avoid puddles, she glanced back. "What of the ratters?"

"They decided not to be any more trouble. Oh, that reminds me," he said, stopping. "One of them relieved his master of a guinea for you. It's in my right pocket."

She glanced at his tight-fitting breeches. "I'm sure you can give it to me later."

"Are you encouraging me to be in debt?"

She met his eyes and hid a smile. "I am rich enough to ignore a guinea. Please, consider it yours."

"Falcon, I'm disappointed in you. Think of it as storming a spiked wall under enemy fire."

Fresh from violence, it made her shiver. "Have you done that?"

"Yes."

Despite what he said about his military life, he must have risked death so many times. "Then I can hardly retreat, can I?"

"I didn't think so." It was almost a purr of his own.

She wanted to laugh, but found a frown instead. "I'm perfectly aware of what you're doing. You think I can't resist a challenge."

"I seem to be right. Perhaps you need lessons. Sometimes it is wise to retreat."

"In this case?"

"Probably."

"It's only a pocket," she said.

She glanced around. They were still off to one side of the fair, with no one else nearby. They were in sight of the dozens of waiting carriages, but she couldn't make out the rest of their party, so she doubted they could see her.

Truth to tell, she didn't care. She wanted this excuse to touch him. Perhaps it was something to do with the violence, the danger, the thought of his perilous past . . .

She moved behind him and slid her hand into his pocket.

Of course it meant standing close. It meant sliding her hand against his hip as if there was scarcely anything between her and his naked body. Well, there *was* scarcely anything between her and his naked body, his warm naked body, but she would do it anyway.

In fact, since it was a challenge, she would raise the stakes. She pulled her hand out and stripped off her glove, then slid her hand in again.

She heard a choked laugh, and grinned. "Feeling for a small coin with gloves on would be so awkward," she said, spreading her fingers and exploring with them, hoping it tickled. What she discovered through two layers of cotton was strong, hard bone and warm muscle.

And pleasure in the firmness of it beneath her hand.

He was still, but she could feel tension. He'd invited this, however, challenged her to it. If it embarrassed him, it was his fault. She supposed she should be embarrassed, but she wasn't. Truly, she felt as if she was blossoming into someone very unlike Clarissa Greystone!

She moved slightly closer, curling her left arm around his torso, and pressing her cheek against his hot back. How firm he was. Muscle everywhere. Used to being close only with female bodies, she found this to be a magic all its own.

An image flashed into her mind—the groom's naked chest, rippling with well-defined muscles. The major wasn't as big a man, but would his naked chest look like that?

Would she ever find out?

Suddenly, so closely and hotly entwined, it seemed a moment for bald truth. "You're a fortune hunter, aren't you, Hawk?"

She felt his instant tension.

"Why else were you in Cheltenham? You knew about me and came to steal a march on the others. You tempted me into coming to Brighton, and you've been stalking me ever since. I'd rather there were truth between us."

She felt him breathe, three steady breaths. "And if I am?"

"I don't mind." Then she felt that went too far too soon. "But I make no promises, either."

"I see. But you won't blame a man for trying?"

"No," she said, smiling against his back. "I won't blame a man for trying."

And truth is, I can't wait until he wins.

Smiling at her golden future, she angled her hand down and forward, following the deep pocket of the man who would one day be her husband. Whose body would be intimate with hers. She sucked in a deep, steadying breath and wriggled her fingers in search of the coin. She felt him suddenly stiffen.

"Am I tickling you?" she said unrepentantly.

"After a fashion."

Her fingers touched a bone, but then she realized there couldn't be a bone in the middle of his belly. Her little finger caught the edge of the coin as her mind grasped what she had to be touching.

A girls' school is not a haven of innocence. There had been many discussions, much sharing of knowledge, and not a few books stolen from fathers and brothers and smuggled into school.

According to a slim, alliterative volume called *The Annals of Aphrodite,* she was brushing against the Rod of Rapture. But didn't men only Mount to Magnificence just prior to Carnal Conquest?

She seized her coin, pulled her hand out, and retreated a few steps, pulling on the armor of her sensible glove.

He turned, not changed in any drastic way. A quick glance, however, showed that he was still Mounted to Magnificence. She knew her face had to be bright red.

"So," he said, "the raw recruit has scaled the walls but is defeated by the sight of fire within."

"Not defeated. Just not willing to be burned."

"Even if duty calls?"

"Duty, I think, calls in another direction entirely." She set off briskly for the carriages.

He soon caught up. "I'm not planning a rape."

"Good. I don't want to talk about it."

"How disappointing."

She fired a mock glare at him. "No, you are not going to challenge me into it." But she was loving, loving, loving this. To be able to talk this way with a man!

He laughed. "Another time, then."

But then Hawk sickeningly remembered that there were not going to be other times. Now that he was certain his Falcon had been involved with Deveril's death, he had hard choices to make—and he could see none that would lead to a happy ending.

For him or for her.

When they arrived back at the carriages, Van gave him a rather steely look. Since Maria was the chaperon for this excursion, Van would feel responsible, and he wasn't liking what he saw. Hawk wondered exactly what he saw.

The short version of their story satisfied Maria, but Hawk thought Van was still watchful. Not surprising. Despite long periods of separation, they knew each other very well.

"But what are we to do with the cat?" Maria asked, clearly not taken with the creature.

Hawk looked at the sleepy animal, which was filthy, scrawny, and missing part of an ear. "I'll keep it."

"Your father's dogs will eat it," Van predicted.

"I shall have to stand protector." Hawk climbed into the carriage, cat still bundled in his coat, feeling a maudlin need to protect something.

Clarissa needed advice, and Althea did not seem likely to help with this. Instead, once she'd changed from her soiled dress, she sought out her chaperon. Miss Hurstman, as usual, was in the front parlor reading what looked like a very scholarly book.

"Miss Hurstman, may I talk to you? About Major Hawkinville."

The woman's brows rose, but she put her book aside. "What has he done?"

"Nothing!" Clarissa roamed the small room. "Well, he's wooing me. He's a fortune hunter, I'm sure, even though he says he will inherit his father's estate. He admitted that it isn't very large, and he's as good as admitted that he does want to marry me. For my money—" She stopped for a breath.

Miss Hurstman studied her. "I assume there is no need for this panic?"

Clarissa, suddenly bereft of words, shook her head.

"Then what has caused it?"

The woman's calm was infectious. Clarissa sat down. "I didn't plan to marry. I saw no need to. But now, it is beginning to be appealing. You did warn me. I don't know if this all shows a flexible mind, or a weak one."

Miss Hurstman's lips twitched. "Clever girl. The difference between the two can be hard to judge. The main question—the only question, really—is, Will he make you a good husband for the next twenty, forty, sixty years?"

Clarissa could feel her eyes widen at the idea. "I don't know."

"Precisely. He is a handsome man, and I assume he knows how to please and interest a woman. His father certainly did."

"His father?"

"I knew him when I was young. A dashing military man with an eye to bettering himself."

A fortune hunter. Like father, like son? And yet the father had clearly settled for his modest estate.

Miss Hurstman was looking at her as if she could read every thought. "You cannot know enough about Major Hawkinville yet to make a rational decision, Clarissa. Time will solve that. Take your time."

"I know, but . . ." Clarissa looked at the older woman. "You speak of when you were young. Don't you remember? Just now, reason has nothing to do with it!"

Miss Hurstman's eyes twinkled. "That, my dear, is why young women have chaperons. Did Lady Vandeimen not play her part?"

Clarissa bit her lip, then said, "We were separated for a little while by a squall of bad weather."

"For a sufficiently little while, I hope?"

"Oh, yes. Nothing . . . nothing *truly* happened."

Miss Hurstman gave one of her snorts, whether of disapproval or amusement was hard to tell. "I do enjoy an enterprising scoundrel." Amusement, then. "Panic over?" she asked.

Surprisingly, it was. Perhaps it was simply being away from Hawk, or perhaps it was Miss Hurstman's dry practicality, but Clarissa didn't feel so caught in swirling madness anymore.

Time. That was the answer to her dilemma over Hawk Hawkinville, and she had no shortage of it other than that created by impatience. She would make herself wait a week or two without commitment. And without being compromised.

She did not fool herself that it would be easy.

She wished she could discuss her other problem with Miss Hurstman—the matter of Deveril's death, the way she kept speaking of it, the disastrous effects she seemed to have on other people's lives—but her trust did not go so deep as that.

Chapter Eleven

⁓

Hawk entered the Marine Parade house with his friends, but he went straight up to his room with the cat. He hoped to avoid Van, but wasn't surprised when he walked in not long after.

Hawk had taken the cat out of his jacket and was gently checking it for serious injuries.

"What are you going to do with it?" Van asked.

They might as well get to the topic at once. "I suspect Miss Greystone will wish me to care for it."

"And what Miss Greystone wishes is of importance to you?"

"Yes." The damnable thing was that he didn't want to lie to his friend, not even by implication, but he couldn't tell the truth. Above all, he needed time to think.

Surely there had to be some way to save Hawkinville from Slade, and Clarissa from the gallows.

The cat squawked as he touched a sore spot, but it was a polite complaint without claws attached.

"Quite the lady, aren't you?" he murmured.

Van came over. "Is it? Female, I mean."

"Yes, and not in bad shape, considering."

He finished his examination and put the cat down on the carpet. After a body-shaking shudder, it picked its way around the room like a tattered lady bountiful inspecting a lowly cottage.

"No problem with movement at all," Hawk said. "In

fact, quite a dainty piece. Tolerable quarters for you, your ladyship?"

The cat gave him an inscrutable look.

Hawk picked up his jacket and contemplated its sorry state. He hadn't bothered to hire a valet since returning home, but he needed one now.

Van took it and went to the door. "Noons!" he shouted, and in moments his valet appeared, complained about the jacket, and went off to put it right.

The cat had sat to clean itself with dogged persistence.

"Tidiness above all. That's the spirit," Hawk said, scooping it up and carrying it to his washstand. There was a slight chance that if he was busy enough Van would put off the talk to another time.

"What you are about to get," he told the cat as he gingerly sat it in the wide china bowl, "is some assistance in the cleaning department. Do not be so rude as to scratch me."

He heard Van laugh and wondered if he was going to get away with it.

The cat had stiffened, but it wasn't frightened.

"Bear up like a good soldier," he said soothingly, and poured a little warm water over the side where blood was thick and sticky. The animal gave a yowl of complaint, but turned its head to lick. "No, no," he said blocking its head. "Let me. You can clean up the remains later."

He gently rubbed the blood till it softened, then washed it away under a new dribble of water. He was careful of the gash above it, and to soothe the cat, he kept talking.

"Not all of this blood is yours, is it? You must have done a fair bit of damage. It's my guess you could take on any rat you wanted. Beneath your dignity, was it, duchess? Risked having your neck broken over it, though, didn't you?"

As he started on a patch on one shoulder, Van interrupted his monologue. "What exactly are your plans in regard to Miss Greystone?"

Hawk hadn't really expected to get away with it.

"*In loco parentis* are you?"

"After a fashion, yes."

Hawk tried a mild deflection. "Marriage is making you damn dull."

Watching, Hawk could see Van control his temper. Damn. When they were boys a comment like that would have led either to a fight or to Van slamming out to work his temper off elsewhere. Either would have cut short the discussion.

They weren't boys anymore.

The cat licked his hand. It was probably a command for more water, so he supplied it, working on another spot.

"Maria thinks she is assisting a courtship," Van said. "A courtship very much to your advantage. Generous of her, wouldn't you say?"

Hawk winced at that one. "I do not necessarily need assistance."

"You are likely to get it anyway, women being women. The question is, Do you deserve it?"

Hawk lifted the cat from the muddy, bloody water and wrapped it in a towel for a quick dry. Though not scratching, it wasn't purring either.

He had to say something. "I'm not sure what you mean by that, Van."

Van rubbed a hand over his face. "I'm not either. Damn it all, Hawk, Maria likes Miss Greystone. She's playing at matchmaking. I don't want her hurt."

Ah, that Hawk could understand.

He put the cat down, and it stalked to a corner and began furiously cleaning itself.

"I don't want anyone hurt, Van. Not even a damn cat. A fine state of affairs for a veteran, isn't it?"

"A pretty natural state, I'd say. What's going on?"

Hawk realized that it was no good. Van wouldn't be deflected, or satisfied with a denial, and a good part of it was probably concern for him. The past was a strange beast. It lay dormant, appearing to be harmless, but it had claws and fangs and leaped up to take another bite at unexpected moments.

A poor analogy. He would embrace the past and the future it promised, if he could.

He would have to tell Van part of it, at least.

He emptied the dirty water into the slop bucket and washed his hands in fresh. "My father has mortgaged Hawkinville to Josiah Slade."

"That damned ironmonger? Why?" After a moment, Van asked, "How much?"

Hawk turned to him, drying his hands. "More than you can afford."

Van smiled. "Come on. I'm not ashamed to use my wife's money in a good cause."

"How much of it is left? Maria returned the money that her husband cheated your family out of. She's been doing that elsewhere, too, hasn't she? She has her dependents to take care of and Steynings to restore."

"You think patching the plaster at Steynings is more important than keeping Slade out of Hawkinville? Perdition, he'd be squire too, wouldn't he? Intolerable! How much?"

"Twenty thousand."

Van stared, struck silent.

"Even if you could lend me that much, when could I pay it back? Even squeezing the tenants for every penny, it would take decades."

"But what option do you have?" Van asked. "You can't let Slade . . ." But then he answered himself. "Ah. Miss Greystone."

Lying by implication, Hawk said, "Ah, indeed. Miss Greystone."

Van was frowning over it. "Do you love her?"

"How does one know love?"

"Believe me, Hawk, you know. Do you at least care for her?"

"Yes, of course. But will she marry me without protestations of love?"

Will she elope with you, you mean.

Van grimaced. "Probably not."

"With my father's example before me, I am naturally reluctant to woo an heiress under false pretenses."

But wasn't that exactly what he was doing?

The cat came to rub against his leg, miaowing. He scooped it up.

"The ratter told Clarissa the cat was called Fanny Laycock."

"I see why you had to thrash him."

It was cant for a low whore.

"But I'd better find another name before she remembers it." He looked into the cat's slitted green eyes. "Care to give me a hint? No, I don't think 'Your Highness' acceptable. I will call you Jetta. You are jet black, and you were *jeter'd*, as the French would say. *Getare* in Italian, but I'm afraid in Spanish it would merely mean 'snout.'"

He looked at Van, who was grinning at this byplay. At least he'd managed to change the subject. "I'd better go down to the kitchen and beg some scraps for her. I never thought to ask if you minded a cat in the house."

"No, of course not. But your father's dogs are going to eat her when you take her home."

Hawk looked at the cat again. "Somehow I doubt it."

He didn't escape scot-free. Van left the room with him and said quietly, "I need your word, Hawk, that you won't go beyond the line with Miss Greystone."

Hawk bit back anger. He had no right to it anyway.

"You have it, of course," he said and left, wondering if his friendships, too, were going to die in this bloody mess.

He got milk and bits of chicken for Jetta, then since the cook didn't seem to mind the intruder, he escaped out through the kitchen door. There was no thinking room there, however, so he went round to the street, to the seafront.

He was coatless and hatless, but he didn't care. The rough weather had driven nearly everyone off the seafront anyway, even though it wasn't raining at this moment. The wind still whipped, carrying damp air and even spray off the churning waves. He saw the packet from France bucking its way in and could imagine the state of the poor passengers.

It was good weather for hard thinking, though. Rough and clean.

Did he love Clarissa? He had no experience of love, so how could he know? But Van said he'd know, so it couldn't be love. Or not that kind of love. His feelings were close to those that he had for Van and Con, and that he'd had for some other friends in the army.

Friends, then. He and Clarissa were, in a fragile way, friends. He groaned into the wind. That made it worse. Betrayal in love was a theoretical evil. Betrayal of friendship . . .

And damn it, now Maria and thus Van—a deep and necessary friend—were tangled up in the affair.

He reined in his panicked mind. When had his mind last been panicked?

Fact one. Clarissa had at the least been present at Deveril's murder. It was the only rational explanation for her reaction to the knife and her knowing the exact date.

Hypothesis. She might have killed him herself, but it would have been in self-defense, not to get his money.

Was he besotted to think that? No. He hadn't known her long, but he knew her well enough to know she couldn't be a coldhearted, greedy villain. A crime of passion was much more in keeping.

Fact two. If it came out that she had killed a peer of the realm under any provocation, she might hang for it. Or at least be transported. At best, she would have to await trial in prison among the scum of the world.

Therefore, her crime could never be made public.

It settled Hawk to realize that as an absolute certainty.

He would tear down Hawk in the Vale himself before it came to that.

Having reached that bleak point, he found he could think properly again.

What if she had only been witness to the killing? Perhaps someone else had killed Deveril to save her. Did that really fit better, or did he just want it to be so? It was no great improvement. She would still be an accessory to the murder and liable to the same punishment, and he could hardly send a man to trial for defending her.

However, if he could not prosecute anyone for murder, he was unlikely to break the will.

He leaned against a wooden railing, cursing softly into the snarling sea.

Always, always, always was the fact that the will had been forged and planted in Deveril's house. It shattered any illusion of noble deeds. A cunning rogue was behind that, and Hawk couldn't believe that he intended to leave Clarissa in peaceful possession of a fortune.

So, even walking away from Clarissa and leaving her in peace was not an option.

He circled and circled it, and came down to the heart of the matter. He could persuade her to elope.

No question of marrying her in the normal way. As soon as he applied to the Duke of Belcraven his family would be investigated. The most casual search would uncover that his father was a Gaspard, and probably that he was within days of being pronounced Viscount Deveril. Even if Belcraven was willing to permit the marriage, he would tell Clarissa, and that would be that. He wasn't sure she would be able to bear the thought of being Lady Deveril one day, but he knew she wouldn't forgive the deception.

Elope, then. He would have to pretend love, but he was at least very fond of her. He would not be like his father. She would not have cause to complain of neglect. With luck she wouldn't have to be Lady Deveril for a long time, so perhaps it wouldn't be a terrible blow.

But what if it was? What if the blow, in particular the deception behind it, was enough to kill all affection? Would he end up in a marriage as bitter as that of his parents', with one lost wedding-night child to show for it?

He could do that to himself for Hawkinville, but not to her. Not to his Falcon, who was in such fledgling flight in search of life.

And anyway, he thought with a wry laugh, he'd promised Van. He was sure Van would see an elopement as going far beyond the line.

Which brought him, via a sharp sense of loss, back to the killer. Was there, perhaps, another way . . . ?

Clarissa and Althea were promised to a birthday party being given that evening by Lady Babbington for Florence. Clarissa didn't really want to go, but Florence was an old school friend, and it would do no good to stay home drowning in longing, doubts, and questions. It was to be an event for young ladies only, so at least she wouldn't have to deal with Hawk again.

She found that the Babbingtons' small drawing room felt almost like the senior girls' parlor at Miss Mallory's and slid with relief into the uncomplicated past. Soon she was chattering and giggling, and the high spirits continued over dinner since, unlike at school, wine was served with the meal.

Perhaps that was why the after-dinner chatter turned naughty, especially when it was revealed that Florence had made a transcription of *The Annals of Aphrodite*. As those new to the book huddled to read it, whispering aloud the more exciting phrases, Clarissa wondered how many of them had acquired a little practical experience of the Risen Rod of Rapture.

Then Florence placed letter cards in a bag and invited everyone to pick two to find the initials of their future husband. Clarissa was interested to note how many of the ten young women clearly hoped for a particular set of initials.

Clarissa's heart pounded when her first letter was a *G*, but then she lost all faith when the second turned out to be a *B*.

Suggestions were called out.

"Gregory Beeston."

"Lord Godfrey Breem."

"Florence," said one, "isn't your brother called Giles?"

"But he's married," Florence pointed out.

"Is he still as handsome?" Clarissa asked, and recited her poem. It received great applause, and they all began to put together admiring doggerel.

"George Brummel," Lady Violet Stavering suggested.

She had been at Miss Mallory's too, but had considered Clarissa beneath her notice. She still liked to cloak herself in an air of bored sophistication and was not taking part in the versification.

"He could certainly use your fortune, Clarissa," she added.

Clarissa might sometimes feel at sea in society, but she could swim like a fish in schoolgirl malice. "So could nearly everyone," she said, dropping her letters back into the bag. "Including your brother, Violet. But I am hardly likely to bestow my riches on an elderly and broken dandy like Brummel. If I enter into trade, I will buy the highest quality."

"Such as Major George Hawkinville?" purred Lady Violet.

So their meetings had been observed. Clarissa willed herself not to blush. "Perhaps." But she added, "Or some other young, honorable man."

Florence leaped in with suggestions, and Clarissa regretted the spark of unpleasantness at her friend's party. Soon every eligible man of Brighton was being assessed with startling frankness.

Mr. Haig-Porter's legs were too thin, Lord Simon Rutherford's fingers too short and fat. Sir Rupert Grange laughed like a donkey, and Viscount Laverley had a chest so narrow it was surprising he could breathe.

"But a viscount," said Cecilia Porteous tentatively. "It is a consideration."

Nearly everyone agreed that a peer of the realm might be excused some flaws.

"Even Lord Deveril," murmured Lady Violet.

"Don't be a cat, Vi," snapped Florence. "We all know poor Clarissa didn't want to marry him."

"And we thanked heavens for his timely death," agreed Lady Violet sweetly.

Clarissa stiffened, wondering if Lady Violet suspected. But that was ridiculous. She was simply scratching for the fun of it.

She was saved by an interruption from Miriam Mosely. "I don't know how it is that men like Lord Vandeimen and Lord Amleigh, who have both title and physique, are snapped up before they properly appear on the market. I think it vastly unfair!"

"But remember," said Lady Violet, "Lord Vandeimen was thought to be as rolled up as Brummel, and drowning in gaming and drink as well, before he married the Golden Lily."

This was news to Clarissa, and she recognized that Lady Violet had raised it because the Vandeimens were friends of Clarissa's. She would very much like to put snails in Violet's bed. Again.

She hoped the comment would be ignored, but some others demanded details. Lady Violet chose a sugarplum and bit into it. "Oh, Vandeimen came home from the war to find his father dead and the estates quite ruined."

"Hardly like Brummel, then," said Clarissa.

Lady Violet was not silenced. "He consoled himself with drink and the tables, but then had the good fortune to snare the rich Mrs. Celestin. Trade, you know."

"That's not true!" objected Dottie Ffyfe. "She married a merchant, but she was born into a good family. She's a connection of mine!"

Lady Violet's lips tightened, but she shrugged. "A woman moves to her husband's level upon marriage. First trade. And a foreigner. Then a demon." She allowed a pause for effect before continuing, "According to my brother, in the army he was known as Demon Vandeimen."

Everyone was now leaning forward avidly, and Clarissa felt wretched for having started this. Lord and Lady Vandeimen were both properly behaved and kind, and obviously in love. Someone else who was being tarnished by association with her.

"My brother says that they've been close friends forever," Violet continued, lapping up being the center of attention. "Vandeimen and Amleigh. And," she added with a sly look at Clarissa, "Major Hawkinville."

Clarissa smiled back in a way that she hoped said she was politely bored to death.

"All born and raised near here," Violet continued.

"Reggie said that they each have a tattoo on their chest."
Someone gasped. "Said he'd seen Lord Amleigh's in the
army, and been told about the others."

She looked around, licking sugar off her fingers. "A
hawk for Major Hawkinville, a dragon for Lord Amleigh." Then she added, pink tongue circling her lips,
"And a demon for Lord Vandeimen."

The synchronous inhalation made a kind of *oooh*
around the room.

"What a pity," said Miriam, "that we are unlikely to
ever see that."

But Clarissa was thinking how wonderful it would be
to see that, because it would mean she was seeing
Hawk's naked chest. Impossible, of course, short of
marriage.

Marriage.

It was all very well for Miss Hurstman to talk about
reason, and waiting, and thinking of the years of marriage, but could she bear *not* to do it? Wouldn't she
regret it all her life, wondering what it might have been?
Whether it might have been true heaven . . .

". . . Hawkinville."

With a start, she realized that they were talking about
Hawk—as if he were a piece of meat on a butcher's slab.

"Handsome."

"Perhaps a little lightly built."

"But wide shoulders."

"And excellent thighs!"

*Thighs! Sally Highcroft had been looking at Hawk's
thighs?*

"Delicious blue eyes."

"I prefer brown myself," said Violet.

Clarissa was astonished to find that her fingers were
trying to make claws.

It was Althea, however, who spoke up. "I don't think
it at all seemly to talk about a gentleman in this way."

Violet laughed. Her practiced laugh that said that others were silly, unsophisticated ninnies. "They do it about
us all the time, according to my brother."

"Ladies," said Althea, "should set a higher standard.

And we should be more respectful of those who fought
for us in the war."

This did subdue everyone, and Clarissa flashed Althea
a grateful smile.

"But did he fight?" asked Violet, who never stayed
subdued for long. "Quartermastering, I believe."

Again Althea was there first. "Such administrative
matters are extremely important, Lady Violet. My late
fiancé was in the army, and he often said so."

"You cannot deny that an officer who was often in
battle is more dashing."

"No. But I can deny that dash is the most important
thing about any gentleman!"

Althea was in her Early Christian Martyr mood, and
clearly ready to throw herself to the lions. Or turn into
one. Poor Florence was looking close to tears, so Clarissa
rushed in. "There are any number of eligible names
being discussed here who never went to war at all. We
can surely assess each gentleman as to his qualities." Remembering Miss Hurstman's words, she added, "Their
qualities as husbands over the next twenty, forty, sixty
years."

"Lud!" exclaimed Florence, but with a grateful look,
"what a dismal thought. They'll all be boring, bulging,
and bald by then."

"So will most of us," said Althea, still looking militant.

"Not bald," Clarissa pointed out.

"Gray, then," said Althea, but she relaxed.

"Thank heavens for the dye pot—"

Violet was interrupted by a maid, and Florence leaped
up with obvious relief. "Speaking of futures, I have a
special treat for us. The fortune-teller Madame Mystique
has been engaged to give us each a reading. I'm sure
one of the things she will be able to predict will be our
marital fate. Now, who would like to go first?"

Everyone politely urged Florence to be first, and when
she left, Clarissa led a determined foray into talk about
fashion. Violet would still be a cat, but it was unlikely
to become quite so personal.

Florence returned blushing, and Violet leaped up to go next.

"Well," Sally asked, "what did she say? Are you allowed to tell?"

"It's not like a wish, Sally." Florence sat down among them. "She spoke of a man of honor and good family. And she mentioned his high brow." She looked around, blushing. "That does sound rather like Lord Arthur Carlyon, doesn't it?"

So, that was where Florence's interest lay. A pleasant man who was showing signs of losing his hair. A high brow. Madame Mystique was clearly tactful, and clever as well.

They had played at fortune-telling at school, so she understood how it was done. If possible, the fortune-teller learned about her clients beforehand, and, of course, certain things could please almost everyone. Promises of happiness in love and of good fortune. Flattering comments about strength and wisdom. In addition, and most important, a fortune-teller watched to see what random comments triggered a response.

Having been engaged for this event, Madame Mystique would have learned about Florence, at the very least. She might even have been given the guest list. Clarissa assumed she would be told about Hawk. Handsome, honorable, and a war hero, and perhaps something cryptic about a bird.

Violet returned not so pleased, having been told that the ideal husband for her was not highborn, but wealthy. "The woman is a charlatan!"

But Miriam returned with high hopes of Sir Ralph Willoughby. "But Queen Cleopatra said I must be bolder with him!"

"Queen Cleopatra?" Florence asked.

"Apparently sometimes Queen Cleopatra speaks through Madame to give a special message. She said that if I want Sir Ralph to show the depth of his feelings, I . . . must not be so nervous of being alone with him." She looked around for advice.

Clarissa, thinking of her time at the fair with Hawk,

knew that Queen Cleopatra had the right idea, but she wouldn't say so with Violet listening.

Althea said, "She is right, after a fashion, Miriam. I have, after all, been engaged to marry. Some men find it hard to show their feeling when constantly under the eye of others. This does not mean that you should go far apart with him, or put yourself in danger."

"Oh," said Miriam, her thoughts obviously churning. Her eyes flickered around the group. "She also said . . ."

"Yes?"

"That touch could encourage a gentleman."

Touch! Clarissa couldn't imagine Miriam sliding her hand into Sir Ralph's pocket.

"She said that when most touches are improper, they can have great power. That since ladies are generally gloved, our naked hands have"—she looked at her own pale hand—"sensual power."

"Naked!" exclaimed Florence, looking at her own hand. "I suppose we are gloved when out of the house. So we make an excuse to take off our gloves—"

"And then touch his skin," said Miriam, who looked as if she didn't quite believe what she was saying.

Clarissa thought about the fair, about sticky buns, and Hawk's hand on her wrist. A naked wrist . . .

"Lud!" said Lady Violet. "You're all talking like Haymarket whores. The woman is depraved."

Miriam flushed. "We're only talking about touching hands, Violet!"

"Or faces, I suppose," said Florence, eyes bright with mischief. "Hands and faces are the only naked spots available, aren't they? No wonder men go around so wrapped up. It's probably like armor."

They fell into a laughing view of a world where men were terrified of attacking female hands, but then it was Clarissa's turn to visit Madame Mystique.

Chapter Twelve

~

She was smiling as she followed the maid to the room set aside and hoping that she, too, would be advised by the naughty Queen Cleopatra. The dispensing of such titillating advice doubtless explained the woman's popularity.

The maid opened the door to reveal a curtain. Clarissa pushed it aside and entered the room.

Gloom halted her. If this room had windows, the curtains were drawn, for there seemed to be no natural light.

There was some light, however. Hanging oil lamps with dark, jewel-colored glass turned the room into a mysterious cave of swaying shadows. The oil must be perfumed, for a sweet, exotic tang wafted through the air, making this place like an otherworld, nothing to do with fashionable Brighton at all. Clarissa shivered, then reminded herself that this was all theatrics.

Madame Mystique sat behind a table covered with a pale, shimmering cloth. She wore some kind of dark silken robe and a veil over the lower half of her face. Her hair was covered by a helmet of silver coins that hung down to her shoulders in back and to her eyebrows in front. Her large eyes were heavily outlined in black.

"Sit," she said in a soft foreign voice, "and I will reveal the secrets of your heart."

Clarissa knew that running away now would make her look the fool, so despite a flash of irrational panic, she took the few steps and sat down across the table from the woman.

There was nothing to fear here, and yet wariness was tightening her shoulders and causing her heart to pound. Perhaps it was simply the intent look in the woman's eyes, but, of course, she would only be studying her for things to use in her "predictions."

There was no crystal ball. Instead, the table was scattered with an assortment of items—well-used cards with strange designs, carved sticks, disks with markings, unpolished stones in many shapes and colors, and ornate ribbons, some of them knotted.

"Surely I know the secrets of my own heart," she said as lightly as she could. "I would rather you tell me something I do not know."

"Indeed? Then consider the items on the table," the fortune-teller said with an elegant sweep of a beringed hand, "and pick the three that interest you most."

Clarissa stared at the objects, wondering what each meant. She didn't believe in fortune-telling, but even so she was suddenly nervous of letting this woman probe. She picked ordinary, unrevealing things—one stick, a plain length of ribbon, and a clear chunk of crystal.

Madame Mystique took them, holding them. "You have secrets. Many secrets. And they trouble you greatly."

Clarissa stiffened with annoyance. Of course someone who picked the plainest items was trying to hide things. "Everyone has secrets."

"Not at all." The large eyes smiled. "Have you not noticed how many people long to tell their secrets if they can only find an excuse? You, however, have true secrets. You would be afraid to whisper them into the ground for fear that the growing grass would speak of them."

Clarissa almost rose to leave, but she remembered in time that any sharp reaction would tell Madame Mystique that her guess was correct. She produced a shrug. "Then I am managing to keep them secret from myself as well."

But why was the woman touching on such matters?

Was it possible she truly did have powers? That could be disastrous!

Cradling the items, the woman asked, "What did you come here to learn?"

"I didn't. You are simply a party favor." She intended it to be a slight.

The woman was as impassive as the Sphinx, however, and Clarissa realized that her eye decoration was in the Egyptian style. "But you came. What brought you here? What do you wish to learn?"

After a moment, Clarissa said the obvious. "Something about my future husband." That should not lead to dangerous matters.

"Very well." The fortune-teller let the objects fall on the table and picked up the three cards they landed on. She laid them in front of Clarissa, each with a sharp snap. "He will be handsome. He will be brave . . ."

Snap. "He will be poorer than you."

Clarissa stared, her heart thundering now. Few young ladies married poorer men. But then she almost sagged with relief. Madame Mystique had done her preparatory work and knew Clarissa was the Devil's Heiress.

"How tedious," she drawled. "Can you tell me nothing more?"

"What do you truly wish to know?"

Will Hawk offer marriage? Should I accept? Will he stir the issue of Deveril's death to our destruction? Whom can I trust?

Unable to ask the questions that mattered, Clarissa stared at Madame Mystique.

The woman exclaimed with exasperation. "Ah! You are so guarded. Knotted. You will strangle yourself!"

She seized Clarissa's right hand to peer at the lines. Clarissa thought of fighting free, but part of her had to know what the woman would say next.

"Ah," said Madame Mystique again, but softly this time. "Now I see. I see blood. I see a knife."

Clarissa began to drag her hand away, but then she remembered. The woman was fishing for a reaction. That was how fortune-tellers worked. That and prior knowledge.

But a chill swept over her, as if the cold wind outside was whistling through the curtains. What strange waters to fish in.

She calmly pulled her hand free. On the slight chance that Madame Mystique might have the true sight, she must get away from her.

"You have nothing to fear from me," said the woman, "but you are right to be afraid. Your secrets are dangerous." In a very soft voice she added, "A murder, yes?"

Clarissa was nailed in place, not knowing whether to stay or flee.

"A murder linked to money. Much money. But it is poisoned, my dear. It comes from evil and will always carry evil. You must escape its toils."

"I don't know what you're talking about." Clarissa instantly knew she shouldn't have spoken, because all the willpower in the world couldn't make her voice sound convincing. But her silence must have been eloquent, too.

Sweat was sending chills down her spine, and she didn't know what to do. It was as if the woman were forcing open a door into the past, into secrets and places that must stay in the dark forever.

"Listen to me." The fortune-teller leaned forward, capturing Clarissa with her large, dark eyes. "The money will bring you nothing but pain. You must tell the truth about it or it will cause you agony and death. Guard yourself, guard yourself! There are rogues around you who will cause your ruin."

Rogues? Clarissa felt her heart rise up to choke her.

The Company of Rogues?

But then she shivered with relief. "Rogues" was just a word. A word for scoundrels. Of course a person should avoid scoundrels. This woman couldn't possibly know about the Company of Rogues.

And all she had said could come from common knowledge. She was the Devil's Heiress. Lord Deveril had been stabbed to death, and she'd ended up with his undoubtedly dirty money. She couldn't imagine why Madame Mystique was making such high drama out of it except for effect.

Perhaps having at least one guest totter out of the room white and shaking was good for business.

"I inherited a great deal of money from a man who was murdered," she said flatly. "The whole world knows that. I thought you were going to tell me something new."

The flash of annoyance in the woman's eyes was satisfying, but Clarissa wanted to leave. Would it hint at guilt?

"You refuse to recognize your danger," the woman said. "I will ask Queen Cleopatra to advise you."

Ah, the sensual advice. That she could deal with. But then the clear chime of a bell almost shocked her out of her chair.

"I am Cleopatra, Queen of the Nile," said Madame Mystique in a high-pitched, ethereal voice. "My handmaiden speaks for me."

Despite herself, Clarissa couldn't help a shiver.

"Beware," the voice sang out. "Beware all rogues!"

It's just a word.

"Beware a man with the initials *N.D.*"

Clarissa stopped breathing.

Nicholas Delaney?

Could Madame Mystique have found out the name of the leader of the Rogues? Impossible!

Could she have the true gift?

If so, how much had the woman had seen in her hand? Had she seen whose blood, whose knife? And what was this danger that surrounded her, connected to the money?

"N.D. does not want you to tell the truth," the eerie voice continued, "but you must. Only then will you be free. Heed my words. Heed them, or you will die within the year."

Die? Clarissa felt as if she were fighting for breath. Tell the truth? She couldn't! She couldn't possibly.

The dark-lined eyes opened. "Queen Cleopatra does

not speak to everyone," Madame Mystique said in her ordinary voice. "I hope what she said was useful."

"You don't know?"

"I am merely the vessel for her words." The dark eyes studied her. "You are upset. I am sorry. She usually brings good advice."

Clarissa somehow dragged herself out of her trance. The woman must never know how close her words had come to dangerous matters. "Everything I've heard here was nonsense," she said. "In fact, you didn't really predict my future at all."

Madame Mystique did not seem upset. She picked up the plain crystal and placed it in Clarissa's hand, closing her fingers over it. "You do not believe, but keep this stone. It will help you when your troubles begin."

Clarissa could only think how Hawk's touch had made her shiver, and this one made her shudder. She wanted to leave the woman convinced that her predictions and warnings had been meaningless, but hunt as she might she could not find the right words. In the end she simply turned and walked out of the room.

She took a moment to steady herself, slapping her cheeks a little since she was sure she was pale. Then she returned to the drawing room, trying for a light smile.

Someone else left to see Madame Mystique, and the others began questioning Clarissa.

"What did she say?"

"Whom are you to marry?"

"Was it frightening?" Althea asked. "You look a little pale."

Clarissa found a shrug. "Terrifying! She said I would marry a man poorer than myself."

"But a truth," said Violet.

"Yes, of course. Clearly she has the gift. Althea, do you have one of your headaches?"

Althea, bless her, took her cue. "I'm afraid so, Clarissa. I don't wish to spoil your enjoyment . . ."

"Not at all. It is late." She thanked Florence for the party, and soon they were out in the fresh air with their footman for escort on the short walk home.

"You seem upset," Althea said as they walked.

"Not really, but it was a silly event."

Althea glanced at her. "Because they were discussing Major Hawkinville?"

That was a much safer speculation than any other, so Clarissa smiled and admitted it.

In bed, however, anxiety defeated sleep.

Madame Mystique had clearly seen more than could be guessed or discovered. What if she talked? She might even go to the magistrates to tell them about a young woman involved with blood and murder. When people realized the young woman was the murdered Lord Deveril's betrothed and heir, might that not start speculation?

The Rogues had clearly covered up the events of that night very skillfully, but was it skillful enough to resist an intense investigation?

She tried to tell herself that Madame Mystique would see no profit in going to the authorities. Magistrates tended to look sourly on such fairground tricks, and the woman had no proof.

Clarissa couldn't be sure, though. She couldn't be sure!

And the woman had predicted her *death* if she didn't somehow get rid of the money.

No, if she didn't tell the truth about the money.

What truth? The will, at least, was honest.

"Truth" must refer to the fact that a person involved in a death could not benefit from it. That had been explained to her. Mr. Delaney had not been crude about it, but she'd understood. If she let slip the truth about Lord Deveril's death, many people would suffer, including her. She was ashamed to think that at the time she'd appeared to be the sort of ninny who would gabble, but she hadn't been at her best.

And perhaps she was that sort of ninny. She knew she'd said a few things to Hawk that she shouldn't have.

She couldn't tell the truth, though. That was completely impossible.

What should she do?

She chewed on her knuckle. The Rogues should be

warned about this danger. She didn't want to contact Mr. Delaney. She would have to confess to being less than reliable, but on top of that, they all made her uneasy. They seemed to be good men, honorable men. Except perhaps the brutish Marquess of Arden. But they were also ruthless. Only think how coolly they'd reacted to bloody murder! Mr. Delaney had seemed almost amused.

Perhaps, behind their superficial gloss, they were too like Arden, given to violence when crossed.

But she had to tell them. They had risked much for her, so she must guard them. She slipped out of bed and lit a candle from her night-light. When Althea did not stir, she wrote a very carefully phrased warning to Nicholas Delaney. She folded it, sealed it, and returned to bed to plot how to get it into the post without anyone knowing. She might be going to extremes, but Miss Hurstman was bound to question her about the connection, and she didn't want to tangle in any more deceit.

Madame Mystique collected the items from the table and left her assistant, Samuel, to clear away the lamps and curtains. She left the room, hearing the last of the guests taking an excited farewell, and dispatched a maid to tell Lady Babbington that she was ready to leave.

The plump and amiable lady bustled into view, beaming. "Thank you so much, Madame Mystique! The girls are thrilled with your prognostications."

Thérèse smiled. Young women were always excited by ways to entice and entrance men.

Lady Babbington extended the guineas, then tittered. "They talk of crossing a gypsy's palm with gold, don't they?"

Older women, too.

"But I am not a gypsy, madame. My art is an older one than theirs." She held out her hand, and when the flustered woman put the money into it, she added, "But sometimes visions come to me. You are a very fortunate woman, madame, blessed by the fates with a healthy family and a loving husband."

"Oh, yes. Yes indeed!"

"But the fires perhaps only smolder?" She reached into her bag of items and pulled out a ribbon at random. A blue one. "Blue," she said, "is your color of power. Take this ribbon, Lady Babbington, and wear it on your person at all times. It reminds you of your younger days, yes? When you and your husband first fell in love?"

Lady Babbington looked a little blank, but then said, "I'm sure I had ribbons of all kinds then."

"You will recall. You will recall much about those times. Then you will look at your husband and see that man who thrilled you so, and it will be so again."

The woman was pink but fascinated. She even looked younger.

Madame Mystique patted her on the hand. "You and your husband are really no different, are you, now? Good night, my lady, and thank you for engaging me."

"Oh. Good night, I'm sure."

Madame Mystique made her way out of the back of the house. Or rather, Thérèse Bellaire did, not totally disappointed by her night's work. A number of women might lead more interesting lives because of it—and she had met Deveril's heiress.

Not what she had expected. More brain and steel. But she'd confirmed by her reactions that the Rogues were involved.

That Nicholas was involved.

She waited in the basement for Samuel, telling fortunes for free for the servants, promising them windfalls, handsome admirers, and appreciation for their talent.

For so many people, that was all they wanted, to be appreciated, though often for talents they did not possess. The cook was not the finest, but a simple compliment about her cake and she preened. When she was told she was appreciated, she doubtless saw herself the talk of Brighton for her culinary skills.

The lanky footman in the overlarge livery, Adam's apple bobbing, probably saw himself as the object of every housemaid's lust. The shy, dough-faced maid envisioned being snatched up by a solid tradesman because of her unpretentious goodness.

This fortune-telling was such an easy business that she could no doubt make her living at it forever. But she would have her fortune.

If Deveril had not already been dead, she would have killed him for stealing it from her two years ago. Now her sole purpose was to get it back. It was hers, earned in the sweetest ploy ever imagined, and Deveril would not have been able to steal it if not for Nicholas Delaney and his Company of Rogues.

Samuel arrived, the curtains in a bundle and the empty lamps dangling from his big right hand.

A strapping lad for seventeen, and of course he was devoted to her.

She adored him, as she adored all handsome young men . . .

As a tiger adores goats.

She rose and took her leave of the dazzled servants, who would spread the word. No, Madame Mystique would never lack work here in Brighton. But her main concern was her plan.

Would the heiress heed her warning? Would she confide in someone that the Rogues had killed Deveril and forged that will? Alas, it was unlikely, and she hadn't spilled any information.

Too much brain and spine.

As she walked to her Ship Street establishment, she mourned her pretty, elegant plan. Prove the will false—and entangle the Rogues in a murder charge at the same time—and the new Lord Deveril would have the money.

Mrs. Rowland's invalid husband would die, and after a short interval, the widow would become Lady Deveril. A little while longer and she would be a widow again, possessed of all that money. The son could have the paltry estate.

So delightfully devious. Whatever suspicions people might have, she would leave for the Americas legally possessed of the wealth. But she had failed to find evidence. Her only hope now was the Hawk.

If he did the job for her, the plan could still work. She had Squire Hawkinville in the palm of her hand. It had

added spice to this rather tedious work to dance beneath
the Hawk's nose and be overlooked. Perhaps it would
be even more delicious if he squeezed the heiress dry
for her.

She climbed the steps to her house and unlocked the
door, sending Samuel off to put the things away, but with
a look he recognized, that made him blush.

Ah, seventeen.

She went to her room and stripped off Madame Mystique, slipping into a silk robe that had been appreciated
by Napoleon himself. Tomorrow, alas, she would have
to return to Hawk in the Vale for a while, to be that
dreary Mrs. Rowland. Her excuse for absence was that
she was pursuing an elusive inheritance. But it would not
do to be away too long.

All the more reason to enjoy tonight.

She rang her bell and summoned her dinner—and
her goat.

Hawk slept that night. If he'd not learned to sleep
through external and internal turmoil, he wouldn't have
survived a month in his army work. He'd formed his plan
anyway. He'd found the way out, but it would be
stronger if he could squeeze a bit more information out
of Clarissa.

It was a way out that would mean that she would never
speak to him again. He preferred to think of it as freeing
her from him.

Over breakfast he felt Van observing him, but the talk
was all gossip and chatter. Maria had received a letter
with a new view on Caroline Lamb's novel, *Glenarvon*.
It kept her interested, as she'd witnessed several of the
scandalous incidents between the lady and Byron.

Con, Susan, and de Vere were to leave today, claiming
that a little Brighton was enough for them. Everyone
rose to see them on their way.

Then Maria said, "The sun's shining! We must go out
immediately before it rains again."

Van laughed. "It's not quite that dire, my dear."

"Is it not?"

"I'll send a note to see if Miss Greystone and Miss Trist wish to join us."

Hawk met Van's look blandly and received a distinctly warning look in return.

"Don't worry," he said as they left the room. "I have absolutely no intention of seducing Miss Greystone today."

It was, alas, damnably true.

Chapter Thirteen

~

By the time breakfast was over, Clarissa had come up with and discarded any number of cunning plans for posting her letter. In the end, she chose the simplest. While Miss Hurstman was reading the newspaper, and Althea was writing her daily letter home, she slipped out of the house and hurried through the few streets to the post office.

If Mr. Crawford thought it strange to see a young lady alone, he made no comment.

Clarissa gave him the letter. "Can you tell me how soon it will be there, please?"

He studied the address. "Near Yeovil? Tomorrow, dear lady. I will make sure it leaves on the earliest and best mail."

His benign smile said he thought it was a love missive. But then he looked at the letter again. "Mr. Delaney of Red Oaks? Why, I am almost certain that your companion, Miss Hurstman, sent a letter to exactly that address not many days ago."

It hadn't occurred to her that a man like Mr. Crawford would keep track of letters passing through his hands. Lord help her, had she just done something else stupid?

But then the full meaning struck her.

Miss Hurstman!

Miss Hurstman in league with the Rogues?

She hadn't time to analyze it now, with Mr. Crawford

smiling at her. She took the letter out of his fingers. "If Miss Hurstman has already written to Mr. Delaney, then this is old news, I'm afraid." She pasted on a carefree smile. "Thank you, Mr. Crawford."

She hurried away, going two streets before she let herself pause to think. It was absurd, but she felt as if someone was watching her, looking for signs of guilt.

It was still early, so only the most hardy were out for brisk walks, but she couldn't stand here like a statue. And if she didn't get home, she would be missed. She felt like tearing up the letter and throwing the scraps into the sea, but she immediately thought of someone chasing after them and piecing them together.

Ridiculous. She was going mad.

At the very least, she was thoroughly rattled and needed someone to talk to. Someone to trust. First Madame Mystique, now Miss Hurstman.

She pushed the letter to the bottom of her pocket and hurried back to Broad Street, trying to make sense of things.

Crawford could be wrong, but that was outlandish.

So, Miss Hurstman knew Mr. Delaney.

There was no getting around it. It was likely that Mr. Delaney had arranged for Miss Hurstman to be Clarissa's chaperon here in Brighton. And she could see why. It must have worried him that she was moving out into the world, so he had installed what amounted to a warder. Miss Hurstman hadn't been a very good one or she'd have stuck with Clarissa at all times, but perhaps the lady didn't understand all that was at stake.

The huge question was, What was Miss Hurstman supposed to do if Clarissa posed a threat?

What could the Rogues do—except kill her?

She couldn't believe it, but she forced herself to be logical about it. They would have no other way of keeping themselves and their loved ones safe. It wasn't just the Rogues and herself. Beth Arden was at risk. Blanche Hardcastle was at greatest risk of all.

Madame Mystique had warned of death . . .

She came to a sudden stop, then stepped hastily into

Manchester Street. After a moment, she carefully peered around the corner. On the opposite side of the Marine Parade, the distinctively straight and drab figure of Miss Hurstman was talking to a blond man.

To Nicholas Delaney!

He was already here, because Miss Hurstman had summoned him. And it must have been at least two days ago, perhaps because Hawk was courting her. The Hawk. Miss Hurstman had been alarmed to hear that he was a skilled investigator.

Clarissa headed up Manchester Street to come down Broad Street from the other end.

Mr. Delaney was here, so she could go to him and tell him about Madame Mystique. If she trusted him. She could also assure him that she was no danger to him. Would he believe her?

He'd been kind to her once. He'd been the only one to realize that night that she had been ignored. Beth was being comforted by the marquess, Blanche by Major Beaumont, but she had been left shivering alone. He'd taken her in his arms and somehow given her the feeling that it wasn't so bad and that everything would be all right.

But still, what was she to expect of a man who entered a bloody scene of murder and complained that he'd "missed the action"?

She paused outside the door to her house, vaguely understanding people who threw themselves into the ocean to escape a dilemma. She would not be so weak, though. She had to do the right thing—the right thing for Beth and Blanche, and also for herself. She did not want to die over this.

She slipped in but did not make it upstairs undetected. Althea came out of the front parlor. "Have you been out? I thought it must be Miss Hurstman. She received a note and went out. There's a message here from Lady Vandeimen."

At least Althea didn't ask where Clarissa had been. Clarissa took the note and opened it. "We're invited to walk with them again."

"And Major Hawkinville?" teased Althea.

Everything stopped for Clarissa, then moved again in new patterns. "And Major Hawkinville. I will send an acceptance and then change into a prettier dress."

As she went to the desk she asked, "Where did Miss Hurstman go?"

"She didn't say. Where did you go?"

"I wanted a bit of fresh air before the crowds."

Clarissa dashed off the note and summoned the footman to take it. Then she called for Elsie and went to change. She chose the rust-and-cream dress she'd worn on the first day, and took her parasol as well. It had so little chance to be useful.

Hawk. The one person she could trust was Hawk. Well, she trusted Althea, but Althea was of no use in this predicament. In fact, she was another burden for Clarissa. Althea must not become embroiled in this.

With Hawk, Clarissa knew exactly where she was. He was a fortune hunter. Other than that, he was as honorable as could be. And he was the Hawk. He would protect her.

Especially, she thought suddenly, if they were married. Once they were married his interests would entirely match hers. She would have to tell him the truth, of course—but not until they were married. For Beth, and Blanche, and the Rogues, she could not tell him the truth before.

She grieved for that, for she would like to marry him with full honesty between them, but it was the only way. And she couldn't believe that it would be a terrible blow to him. After all, he'd said he wished he could kill Deveril for her. No one could look on Deveril's death as a wrongful act. Except perhaps a court of law.

So. Enough of playful games. She must bring Hawk to the point of offering for her hand, which surely could not be so very hard. Then she would have to insist on a rapid marriage. The thought of marrying Hawk, of capturing him for her own, was enough to put a golden glow around all the darkness. If she could persuade everyone, it could happen within the week!

Miss Hurstman returned and made no objection to the outing, though she declined to go herself. "Mindless gallivanting," she said, but she looked a little grim.

"Was there something in your message to distress you, Miss Hurstman?" Clarissa asked.

"No." But that was all she said, and since the Vandeimens and Hawk arrived at that point, Clarissa could not probe. She doubted it would do any good anyway, though she'd love to know exactly what Miss Hurstman and King Rogue—as Nicholas Delaney was called—had discussed.

Soon Clarissa was alone with the man she needed to marry, but found herself alarmingly tongue-tied. Hawk could fluster her with a look, but she was generally able to keep her wits. Now, knowing she was hunting him, she couldn't think what to say.

She found a safe subject. "How is the cat, Major Hawkinville?"

He offered his arm as they went down the shallow steps. "Thriving on a diet of liver and cream. It caught three mice last night, and has become the cook's pet."

"Then why didn't it please the ratters?" They turned to stroll down toward the seafront.

"Pure pride. Would you have worked for them?"

She returned his smile. "Oh, I approve!"

"I have called it Jetta from its color, and because it was thrown."

"Jettisoned. I hope it has a better future."

"Do you want the cat?"

"I? I have no place to keep a cat just now."

"You have more of a place than I do."

Clarissa realized that they'd slipped into their usual easy exchange, which was not likely to take them to marriage. A conversation about homes might, however.

"But you have a home in Hawk in the Vale, do you not?" she asked.

"That is my father's."

A strange thing to say. "A father's home is generally thought of as his son's home. Especially his heir's."

"Perhaps my years away have made it less homelike to me."

"Then where will you live, when you settle down?" There. That was a hint.

He didn't seem to notice it. "I have to live there for a while. My father is not well and needs help in managing his affairs. Jetta can return with me to Hawkinville when I go."

They crossed the road to the seafront, where the bathing machines were still doing poor business. Clarissa, however, was fixed on other matters. "Do you plan to return soon?"

If her concern showed, all the better.

He glanced at her. "I cannot stay away for long periods. What of your home, Falcon? When the season ends here, will you go to live with your guardian?"

When the season ended—she hoped to be married to him. "I don't think so. I don't know what I'll do."

How exactly did a woman edge a man into proposing?

"Will Miss Hurstman stay with you?"

Not if I have anything to do with it. "I don't know that, either. I haven't been looking very far ahead. After all," she said with a twirl of her parasol, "something might occur . . ." *Like marriage,* she thought at him.

As usual, Althea was being swarmed by suitors, and the Vandeimens had stayed with her. Clarissa wondered if she should go back, but she couldn't do much to help decide which gentleman should have the honor.

"Perhaps you will stay with Lady Arden," Hawk said.

Clarissa stared at him. Surely she'd never spoken of Beth to him.

"Why do you suggest that?"

But of course. He was the Hawk. And that was part of the reason she must marry him. If only he'd get around to asking her! He was doubtless acting the proper fortune hunter, but here she was, like a deer in his sights with a label on saying, Shoot me, and nothing was happening!

"She was a teacher at Miss Mallory's," he said. "It

was a simple assumption that she asked her father-in-law to oversee your affairs."

"I suppose I could stay with her for a little while," she said. "By then her baby should be born and past its first weeks."

"But you do not want to? She is still the harsh schoolmistress?"

Clarissa laughed at that. "She never was."

"But . . . ?"

She looked at him. "You're very persistent, Hawk. What is this to you?"

He smiled. "It pleases me to see you challenging."

"Does it please you to answer?" Something about his manner unsettled her.

"But of course. I would not want you moving to, for example, County Durham."

His manner was flirtatious, which was promising at least.

Clarissa turned away, as if fascinated by the sea. "I have no relatives in County Durham, as best I know."

"It's surprising what you can find on the family tree," he said in a tone that made her wonder what it meant. Before she could ask, he added, "But you ease my heart."

Aha! She turned back. "*Heart,* Hawk?"

But the moment was shattered by a sharp yapping and a tug at her skirt. A ball of white fur had its teeth in her dangling fringe.

"*Stop!*" She tried to drag her skirt free, and Hawk swooped to capture the dog. But when he picked it up, the skirt came with it.

"*Hawk!*" Clarissa shrieked, trying to hold her hem down.

He laughed and went to his knees, grabbing the growling dog's jaws to force them open. Clarissa was laughing at the absurd scene, but burningly aware of being the focus of all eyes and still showing too much leg.

"Button, no!" a woman cried, running over and leaning to slap the dog's muzzle. "Let go! Let go!"

And the dog obeyed, wriggling frantically in Hawk's hands toward its mistress.

It was Blanche Hardcastle, dressed as always in white, but stunningly flushed pink with annoyance and exertion.

She held the small dog close, and she and Clarissa stared at each other. Major Beaumont and another couple were nearby, but everything was, for a moment, frozen and silent.

For a panicked moment Clarissa felt that Hawk would immediately know all the truth about Deveril's death. But then sanity returned, and her only concern was scandal. Blanche was an actress, and though she was highly regarded in her profession, the world knew that her past was not unblemished. She'd been Lord Arden's acknowledged mistress, for a start.

However, it revolted Clarissa to think of snubbing the woman who had been so kind—more than kind. "Blanche," she said with a smile. "Is that monster yours?"

Blanche looked a little worried too, but she smiled back. "Alas, I found him abandoned, and he is white, but I cannot teach him manners."

"That's because you're not firm enough with him," said Major Beaumont.

Blanche retorted, "You'd doubtless like to thrash the poor mite."

But the smile they shared took any sting out of it. Clarissa was genuinely delighted to see the two of them so relaxed and happy. She certainly couldn't let anything destroy that.

Major Beaumont turned to her. "Miss Greystone, you have to take some blame. That fringe of yours is designed to provoke madness in males."

It made her laugh, even though she was frantically thinking, *He was involved too! Would there be anything in that for Hawk to weave the truth from?*

"I confess it," she said as lightly as she could. "Do you know Major Hawkinville?" She performed the introductions, noting that the other couple had wandered off. Probably other actors being discreet.

Hawk and Major Beaumont exchanged some comments about the military, which seemed to establish each other in a few words. There was time for Blanche to say, "You're looking splendid, Clarissa, and your 'Hawk' is very handsome."

Clarissa blushed to think that she'd shrieked that in front of half the world, but she agreed. And here was someone she could go to for advice. Blanche knew all the secrets, and she had worldly wisdom for ten.

"Could I come to see you?" Clarissa asked.

Blanche's eyebrows rose, but she said, "If it won't get you into trouble. I'm in Prospect Row. Number two. I'm performing here at the New Theater." With a watchful look, she added, "In *Macbeth*."

Clarissa knew she gaped for a moment, but covered it. She smiled at something Major Beaumont said, but inside she was wondering whether she could even depend on Blanche.

Madness to play Lady Macbeth!

She was sinking into the past, to Blanche saying, "I have always wanted to do *Macbeth*." Even Lord Arden had been shocked by that after hearing her quote from the play earlier. *Who would have thought the old man to have had so much blood in him?*

A squeeze on the hand pulled her back. It was Blanche. "I hope my little pet didn't frighten you, Clarissa."

She laughed. "No, of course not!" And she told the story of the ratters the day before.

"So that was you," said Major Beaumont. "There's an account in today's *Herald,* but the names of the lady and gentleman are not given."

"Not known, we hope," said Hawk, and after a little more chat, Blanche and her major walked on.

"May I be curious?" Hawk asked. "A famous London actress is an unusual friend for a Cheltenham schoolgirl."

Clarissa had expected it, and had prepared a response. "It is a strange connection, and slightly scandalous. Can I trust you with it?"

To her concern, he seemed to think about it, but then said, "Of course. I'm no gossip."

They strolled back toward the Vandeimens and the well-attended Althea. "Blanche was the mistress of the Marquess of Arden until just before his marriage. You might think that this would create a rift between her and the marquess's wife—"

"I'd think it would make any meeting impossible."

"Ah, but you don't know Lady Arden."

"And how do you know of these things?"

How did she explain that? She hadn't thought this through.

"It slipped out." It wasn't entirely a lie. She looked at him. "I'm not an innocent, Hawk, and I won't pretend to be with you."

His lips twitched. "I hope not. So, how did these two unlikely ladies meet?"

"Beth heard about Blanche and contrived a meeting."

"Strange. Mrs. Hardcastle seemed unscratched."

Clarissa frowned at him. "You would of course think that two ladies would fight over a man. In fact, they discovered they shared an interest in the rights of women and the works of Mary Wollstonecraft, and became firm friends. The marquess," she added, "was somewhat disconcerted."

Hawk laughed. "An understatement, I'd think."

"Definitely." Clarissa's smile widened and she lost herself in thinking how very handsome he was when he laughed . . .

"And Lady Arden introduced you?"

She collected her wits. "Yes. Though I went to Blanche's house only once."

She prayed not to show how that once had changed her life.

He was studying her. Why? "Are you a follower of Mary Wollstonecraft?"

She almost laughed with relief at such a prosaic concern. "Would you mind?"

"I would have to study the lady's writings to be sure. But the proof is in the product, I think."

He was looking at her, surely, with warm approval. She stopped, waiting, hoping . . .

"And Major Beaumont?" he asked. "How does he come into the picture?"

Clarissa was hard-pressed not to scowl. "He's a close friend of the marquess's from their school days. And as you see, he now has a special relationship with Blanche. According to Beth, he wants to marry her, but Blanche thinks it unsuitable. She clearly thought speaking to me unsuitable, too. Sometimes our world does not please me."

Especially having to play these silly games!

His brows rose at her sharp tone, but he said, "I see you as too much of a free spirit, Falcon, to be severely constrained by society."

That could almost be an opening for *her* to propose to *him*, but Clarissa's nerve failed her. What if he said no? What then? Perhaps he would say no on principle if she broke the rules so thoroughly.

She took a cowardly escape. "I'm trying to be good for Althea's sake. We should rescue her."

"From admirers? Will she thank you?"

"Definitely. She becomes flustered by too much flattery, and men will insist on saying the most absurd things."

Unlike you. She'd felt so certain that he was at least pursuing her fortune, but now sickening doubt invaded. Was he slow to capture her because he didn't find her appealing after all? Was she completely fooling herself?

"Perhaps men say absurd things because women like it?" he commented. "Would you be offended to be told you are like a golden rose?"

She stared at him. "Skeptical, perhaps," she said with a dry mouth and a racing heart.

"You would accuse me of lying?"

"Of flattering."

"In fact," he said almost prosaically, "you do remind me of a golden rose. Not red, which is too deep and dark, nor white, which is too calm. Nor even pink, which is too coy and blushing, but golden, like warm sunshine, brightening what you touch."

She had to lick her lips, and she knew she was blushing. She should protest again that it was not true, but she wanted it to be. She wanted him for any number of reasons, but she wanted to be loved by him more than anything in the world.

Because she loved him.

Breath-stealing, panic-building, but true. She loved him. She could not bear to lose him.

In the end, she simply said, "Thank you," and prayed for more.

Hawk wondered what demented demon had taken control of his tongue. He'd come out today to learn more about Clarissa and the Ardens, and had succeeded beyond his hopes because of that chance encounter.

He had not come out to break her heart even more. He feared he could read the glowing expression in her eyes.

"Miss Trist," he reminded her, turning toward her friend.

He sensed her disappointment, but after a moment she spoke calmly enough. "With such eligible men around her, you'd think Althea would be developing a preference."

Strong Clarissa. If only . . . "Do you think that perhaps she dislikes the fuss of it?" he asked.

She looked at him in surprise, in control. "Dislikes being the toast of Brighton?"

"It is possible."

"How else is she to find a grand husband?"

"Perhaps she doesn't want one."

"She does, Hawk. If she doesn't find something better, she'll have to go home and marry a stuffy widower with children nearly as old as she is."

He couldn't help but smile. "You are charmingly ardent in her cause. And kind."

"It's not kindness. It's friendship. You understand that, surely. I hear that you and Lord Vandeimen are old friends."

Yes, he understood that. "From the cradle."

"Althea and I have been friends for less than a year, but true friendships can happen quickly."

It was said with meaning, as a challenge to him. She was right. Over and above any emotions, they had discovered friendship. Friendship in marriage. It had been his ideal once.

Ah, well. Ideals often drowned in war.

She turned to study her friend. "You think she is not finding what she wants?"

"I don't think she seems happy," he said honestly, "but as you say, somewhere in Brighton the perfect man must exist."

They moved in, and Miss Trist clearly was relieved to be rescued.

"Are you not happy here, Thea?" Clarissa asked quietly, studying Althea.

"Of course I am." But she added, "I do miss the country a little, though."

It was said quietly, but Lady Vandeimen heard. "We could drive out to visit Hawk in the Vale."

"Why?" Hawk asked.

To Clarissa, that sounded rather sharp, and Lady Vandeimen was looking at him with surprise. "Why not? Trips to the nearby country are all the rage, and I would enjoy a chance to check on the work at Steynings. If we set off early tomorrow, we can enjoy a whole day."

"It will probably rain."

"Hawk, if we stayed at home for fear of rain, none of us would do anything this summer!"

Clarissa watched this exchange, wondering why the project displeased him. She longed to see his home. The home she hoped would be hers. Did he think it wouldn't appeal?

She wished she could reassure him. It could be a hovel and she wouldn't care. After all, with her money they could build a better place, and it was Hawk she wanted.

Hawk.

Perhaps on a trip to the country, to his home, there'd be more opportunity to progress. Queen Cleopatra had given her very strange messages, but her advice to Miriam had been promising. Get the man apart, take off her gloves, and touch.

Perhaps, in the country, she could do that.

And now, with Hawk's attention drawn to Blanche, she must succeed. She must bind him to their cause.

Chapter Fourteen

~

As they strolled back, Van said to Hawk, "Wasn't that the White Dove you were talking to? Not done to introduce her to a proper young lady, you know."

"What proper young lady? Clarissa introduced her to me."

Van laughed, but didn't look as if he entirely believed it.

"The White Dove?" Maria said. "Oh, the actress. We saw her play Titania, Van. Do you remember? She's very good. In fact, she's playing Lady Macbeth here."

"A violent change of roles," Hawk said. "And it's hard to see her as the bloodstained power behind the rotten throne."

Maria gave him a look. "Are you saying that a beautiful woman cannot also be dangerous?"

He blew her a kiss. "No man of sense would."

"Especially armed with a pistol," Van said, which seemed to be a private joke.

Hawk, on the other hand, was thinking that classical beauty had little to do with it either.

It would be so damn easy to take the beckoning path. Marry. No, elope. He suspected he could get her to do it.

Roses. Hades.

Think of the three-day journey to the border, surrounded by her glowing enthusiasm, knowing he was leading her to the slaughter. Imagine a wedding night. Her innocent, trusting surrender.

God, no, don't. Don't even think of that.

Better by far that she simply hate him and be free.

Carpe diem, whispered the devil in his mind.

He could probably steal one more day before the morrow.

And he might as well be Hawkishly practical. He still didn't know quite enough about her and the Ardens. If he played his cards right, he might learn the details he needed.

Tomorrow.

In Hawk in the Vale.

The next day, Clarissa looked excitedly out of the Vandeimen coach windows as it rolled over the humpbacked bridge into the village of Hawk in the Vale. She was full of curiosity, but also primed to take any opportunity to pursue her cause. If Hawk didn't propose, she vowed she would do it before they left.

The ladies were in the coach, and the gentlemen—Hawk, Lord Vandeimen, and Lord Trevor—rode alongside. Althea had muttered that she did not need a partner, but Clarissa thought she was relieved it was Lord Trevor, who was excellent company without showing any sign of wanting to be a suitor.

Miss Hurstman was not with them, since today was her weekly meeting of the Ladies' Scholarly Society, which she declared to be "an oasis of sanity in Bedlam." She did not seem particularly different in her manner, and there had been no sign of Mr. Delaney. Clarissa was relieved, however, to be out of Brighton and safe.

The gentlemen were all superb riders, but Clarissa couldn't help but smile at the cat riding proudly erect in front of Hawk. Jetta had refused to ride in the carriage, clearly thinking the company of other females inferior.

Hawk stroked her occasionally, and her eyes slitted with pleasure. Clarissa could rather imagine reveling in his touch in just the same way. She wondered if men ever stroked women the way they stroked cats.

During the journey, Lady Vandeimen had insisted that they all be on first-name terms. Clarissa had happily agreed, thinking that soon they would be true friends. The lady shared what she knew of Hawk in the Vale, and Clarissa savored every morsel, especially as it felt as if she was being welcomed into the community.

She now knew that Hawk's family was the most ancient, and in many ways the most important, in the area, though there was no title except squire, which went with the manor house. If someone else were to buy the manor, he would become squire.

The other principal families were the Vandeimens and the Somerfords, headed by Lord Amleigh. Both families had estates outside of the village, but Hawkinville Manor was in Hawk in the Vale in the old style.

Maria had shared some interesting gossip along the way. "Lord Amleigh recently inherited the title of Earl of Wyvern. The seat is in Devonshire. However, it appears that the late earl might have had a legitimate son who has a prior claim. Quite a strange story. The earl and the woman—a member of a good local family—married in secret. They were both so displeased with each other, however, that they kept the matter secret, and she took up with a local tavern keeper, who is reputed to also be a smuggler!"

"And now the secret heir emerges?" Clarissa inquired. "It's like a play. Or a Gothic novel."

"Except that in this case the 'wicked earl' is Lord Amleigh, and he doesn't want the inheritance at all."

"That's an interesting idea, however," Clarissa said. "A trial marriage. I imagine any number of disasters could be averted."

"Clarissa!" Althea objected, but she was laughing.

"Well, it's true."

"Indeed," said Maria, and seemed to mean it.

It made Clarissa wonder about her first marriage, for there could surely be no disillusion with her second. "However, there is the matter of offspring," Maria continued. "What if the trial has consequences?"

What, wondered Clarissa, if the trial was discovered?

Could *she* compromise *Hawk*?

"I have sent a message inviting the Amleighs to take lunch with us at Steynings," Maria said. "If, that is, the dining room plasterwork is finally finished."

Clarissa then learned more than she really cared to know about the trials of repairing a decade's neglect of a house that had not been well built in the first place.

Hawk's home was older. Was it in even worse repair? She, like Maria, had the money to repair it.

He'd ridden ahead to make sure all was ready for them. Already she was longing to see him.

The coach was lurching along a rough road around the central village green, past a row of ancient stone cottages that looked in need of as much care as the road.

Perhaps this was why Hawk was hunting a fortune.

A swarm of piglets suddenly dashed out between two cottages, chased by three barefoot children. It was fortunate that it was after the coach had passed, not before. Clarissa watched with amusement as the urchins tried to herd the piglets back home.

Maria directed her attention to the church. "Anglo-Saxon, of course."

Yes, it looked it, complete to the square stone tower. Age made the village picturesque, but it was something more subtle that made it feel . . . right. Clarissa had never visited a place where the varied bits and pieces fit together so well, like the assorted flowers in a country garden.

Her eye was caught—hooked, more like—by a discordant piece, a monstrous stuccoed house with Corinthian pillars flanking its glossy doorway. There were other new buildings, buildings from every period over hundreds of years, but only that one seemed so appallingly out of place.

"What is that white house?" Clarissa asked.

"Ah. That belongs to a newcomer. A wealthy industrialist called Slade." Maria pulled a face. "It doesn't fit, does it? But he's very proud of it."

"Couldn't he be stopped?"

"Apparently not. He seems to have ingratiated himself with the squire. Hawk's father."

The carriage halted, and the footman leaped down to assist the ladies out. Lord Trevor and Lord Vandeimen dismounted, and a groom trotted out through open gates to take the horses. Through those gates Clarissa could see an ancient building.

Hawkinville Manor. It must be.

She was astonished that she hadn't spotted it more easily, but it did blend in with the row of cottages and other nearby buildings, and was surrounded by a high wall covered by a rampant miscellany of plants. Ivy cloaked the tower, too.

Wall and tower had doubtless been necessary for defense in the past, but now the double gates stood open, and Clarissa could glimpse a garden courtyard and part of the house—thatched roof and old diamond-pane windows. Roses and other climbing plants ran up the wall, making it seem more a work of landscape than architecture.

She vaguely heard the carriage crunch on its way to the inn, but she was moving forward, through the gates.

"How charming," Althea said in a polite way.

"Yes," Clarissa agreed, though the word seemed completely inadequate. Only a poet could do justice to the sheer magic of Hawkinville Manor.

The courtyard was sensibly graveled, but that was the only modern touch. In the center, an island full of heavy roses held in its very heart an ancient sundial. It was tilted in a way that surely meant that it couldn't tell the time, but then she doubted that sundials had ever been accurate.

This place had formed before the counting of minutes or even precise hours had any meaning.

Both courtyard and house were bathed in sunlight. Warm sunlight, for a miracle, and it gave the illusion that the sun always shone here. Many windows stood open, as did the iron-mounted oak door. The view through the doorway gave a tantalizing glimpse of a tiled hall that seemed to run, uneven as the river surface and worn in the middle by many feet, to another open door and a beckoning garden beyond.

She took a step forward.

A dog growled. She blinked, seeing four large hounds sprawled near the threshold in the sun. One was looking at her lazily, but with a warning eye.

"Daffy."

At the word, the dog subsided. Hawk walked past, out of the house, Jetta still in his arms.

He stroked the purring cat, but his eyes were on Clarissa. "Welcome to Hawkinville."

Now why, thought Hawk, did he feel almost shocked to see Clarissa here when she was fully expected? It was as if the air had thinned, or as if he'd been riding and working to the point of wavering exhaustion.

He pulled himself together and answered questions. Yes, the sundial was very old and had come from the monastery at Hawks Monkton when it had been destroyed in the sixteenth century. Yes, the tower did date back to before the Conquest but had been fixed and improved a number of times.

Clarissa's dress was a simple one for this day in the country. It had not seemed special before. Now the color reminded him of the richest cream in the cool dairy and made him want to lick something.

Yes, he said to Lord Trevor, there was a home farm, and this was it. The manor house also served as a modest farmhouse. There were more buildings beyond the wall to the right.

That dress was doubtless the simplicity of a very expensive modiste, but the effect was charming and comfortable and fit here like the roses. Her wide straw hat was caught down at either side with golden ribbons.

Why hadn't he noticed before that it would prevent kisses?

She turned to look more closely at the sundial, leaning in but laughingly trying to protect her flimsy skirts from the rose thorns. He stepped forward to help, and she smiled up at him.

The buzz of insects among the flowers turned into a buzz in his head. Her hat shaded her face from the sun, but cast a golden glow and a hint of mystery. Her smiling lips were pink and parted, and he could almost taste their warmth.

What was beauty if not this?

With frightening clarity he could imagine her here as his wife. He would sweep her laughing into his arms and carry her upstairs to a bed covered with smooth sheets fresh from hanging in the sun. And there he would slowly, perfectly, ravish her.

He remembered to breathe, and when his hand was steady, he pulled out his penknife. "Let me cut you each a rose, ladies."

He cut a pink one for Miss Trist, and carefully stripped the thorns before giving it to her. He cut a white one for Maria. But then he looked for a golden one, a perfect golden rose, just beginning to unfurl from bud, and gave it to Clarissa.

She remembered. He could tell by the way she blushed within the golden mysteries of her hat and raised the rose to inhale its perfume. He remembered his foolish, thoughtless words about roses . . .

And that she wasn't for him.

Carpe diem.

The morrow was not for them.

He ached to reach out and touch her, simply touch her cheek. He wanted to tell her that this moment, at least, was true. He wanted to lock her in a safe and private place where she would never be in danger again.

The church clock began to chime, pulling him back to reality.

By the time it had struck the full ten, he could speak normally and invite his guests into the house. He steered them to the right, into the front parlor, then escaped, his excuse being having to tell his father they were here.

Clarissa looked around the modest but lovely room. The ceilings were low, and she'd noticed that Hawk had to duck slightly to get through the door, but it all created a coziness that wrapped itself around her. She could imagine sitting here on a stormy winter night, a huge fire burning in the hearth, curtains tightly drawn. A person would always feel safe here.

Even the Devil's Heiress.

She knew without doubt that she would be safe in Hawk's arms, and in his home.

She raised the golden rose to her nose. The scent was light, almost elusive, but it was sweet and seemed to carry the charm of sunlight. A golden rose. That had to mean that his fondness was real, and her plan was good. Whatever the reason for his hesitation, it was not from reluctance.

Perhaps he simply felt it wrong to hurry her. Though it seemed like a lifetime, she had been in Brighton for only a week. Perhaps he'd set himself a restraint—that he not propose inside a fortnight, for example.

She inhaled the rose again, smiling. She was sure that restraint could be broken.

Maria sat in one of the old wooden chairs with crewel-work cushions. "Do you like the manor, Clarissa?"

Clarissa pulled her wits together. "It's lovely."

"Perhaps it's as well you think so. But at the least it needs new carpets."

"Maria," said her husband, "don't start doing over someone else's home."

They shared a teasing smile, and Maria said, "That will be for Hawk's wife to do."

"Not until his father's dead," said Lord Vandeimen, and Clarissa saw a slight reserve touch his face. At thought of wife, or thought of father? Maria Vandeimen was discreet, but there might have been coolness in her mention of Squire Hawkinville during the journey here.

That was a small cloud on the horizon, she had to admit. She adored this house, but what would it be like sharing it with Hawk's father, especially if he was an unpleasant man?

A small price for heaven.

"So," said Maria, "what do you think on the subject of carpets, Clarissa?"

Clarissa looked at the faded and worn Turkish carpet that covered the rippling dark oak floor and felt that any change would disturb something as natural and perfect as the roses in the garden. When she looked carefully, she could see that the cushions on the old chairs sagged and the embroidery was faded and worn with time.

"I think they suit the house," she replied with a smile, and Maria laughed.

"It's as well we have different tastes, isn't it?"

Clarissa glanced at Lord Vandeimen, a fine-looking man and pleasant, who stirred her not at all. "Yes, indeed."

Maria chuckled.

A huge fireplace took up most of one wall, and an old oak settle sat to one side of it. The front wall was a bank of small-paned windows that stood open to the sunny courtyard. Clarissa wandered over. Soft perfume drifted in—rose, lavender, and many other plants she could not even name. Sparrows chirped in the eaves, doves cooed nearby, and all around, birds sang.

Oh, but she wanted Hawkinville Manor!

It seemed almost wrong to feel that way. It was Hawk she should want, and she did, desperately, but she was tumbling into mad love with his home as well.

More than love. It was as if the place was her setting, where she fit perfectly. She felt as if she were putting down roots now, tendrils winding through faded carpet and old oak floor into the earth beneath, determined to stay.

A gig rattled by outside the gates, startling her out of her impatient thoughts. Two women hurried past, chattering, laughing. Clarissa stepped back as if they might look and see her there, might see her yearning, but all the same she loved the way the house was part of the village, not stuck far away in a huge park.

Then Hawk returned, making her heart do a dizzying dance. The cat was still in his arms. "Let me show you around this floor. I'm afraid the manor isn't a showplace, just a simple home."

Clarissa went forward into the flagstoned hall.

The walls were wainscoted in blackened oak and painted white above, hung with the occasional painting. A small table against one wall held a bowl of mixed garden flowers. It wasn't a formal arrangement, any more than this was a formal house, but it was pretty and entirely right for the setting.

A faint purr hummed from Jetta. Clarissa knew she would purr too if Hawk was stroking her in that absent-minded but continuous way.

"It's lovely," she said.

"I think so. It is doubtless impractical of me, but I don't want to see it change."

"Who would?"

He flashed her a smile. "Most people, especially if they had to actually live here. And are tall." He ducked slightly to lead her into a dark-paneled dining room with another huge fireplace, ancient oak sideboards, and a thick table. That table had been polished so long and lovingly that the glossy top seemed to have the depth of a dark pool.

A mobcapped, aproned woman came in bearing plates. She bobbed a curtsy and went on with her business.

"Aren't you tempted to have the doorways made higher?" she asked.

"It would be a serious structural challenge. I'm learning by painful experience."

He led the way through an adjoining door into another parlor.

Another bank of windows almost filled the wall, and a window seat ran the width of it. Beyond lay a simple garden with lawn, rockery, and beds of flowers. And beyond that flowed the river. Two swans glided past as if completing the picture for her particular delight.

How wonderful to spend long summer evenings on this seat, by this river.

With Hawk.

It was not just wishful thinking.

Clarissa was determined that it would be so.

Chapter Fifteen

~

They walked over, as if in perfect accord, to look out at the view. Beyond the river lay peaceful fields, some with crops and some with cows. The land rose in the distance to the downs that lay between here and Brighton.

"What is the big white house up there?" she asked. "Steynings?"

"Yes."

"Why is the village only on this side of the river?"

"The Eden's deep here and tricky to cross, and the bridge is quite recent. Before that a person needed a boat or to go downstream a mile to Tretford to cross."

She saw an old boathouse off to one side, unused now, wrapped around and split by wisteria.

"So Lord Vandeimen's house wouldn't have been built over there before the bridge."

"Not unless he wanted to keep his inferior neighbors at bay."

She sat on the seat and smiled up at him, simply happy. Happy with everything. "And did he?"

His hand continued to stroke the blissful cat. "When the first Baron Vandeimen settled here, he was inclined to look down on our simple ways, they say. Foreign, you see. Over the generations, they are beginning to fit in."

Clarissa heard a laughing comment from Lord Vandeimen, but her attention was all on Hawk. His eyes were warm and full of humor. And something else?

He was very hard to read.

He looked out at the view again. "My bedroom is directly above here. We experimented with flashing candlelight messages in the night. Van and I could see each other's lights, then Van and Con could send messages clear across the vale."

"I'm surprised that isn't done more often."

"It is used—especially by smugglers—but, of course, it's subject to bad weather. Come on, I'll show you something else."

He guided her back across the hall and up a short flight of stairs into another room as if she were the only one on this tour.

"But this is too big," Clarissa said, looking around at a space that seemed as big again as the house.

"We call it the great hall, which is a little grandiose, but it serves the function. My mother held the occasional small ball here." He led her further in. "Now you're in the old tower."

Then she understood where the extra space had come from. Most of the room was inside the hexagonal tower. To her right were the arrow slits she'd seen from the courtyard. Now she could see that they were glazed. There were more at regular intervals, but in the side of the tower opposite the door, another bank of windows had been cut. Since the tower walls were deep, the window seat was in an alcove of its own.

She went to kneel on the cushions to look out. This view was on a diagonal, looking out at a kitchen garden and an orchard, the trees already laden with small fruit. To the right she glimpsed the farm buildings he'd mentioned, and beyond, the river wound on through yet more fertile countryside.

"The kitchens and such are below, which is why this is raised." He had come over to stand close behind her, so Jetta's purr almost vibrated through her. If she turned, how close? "And that, I'm afraid, is all I can show you today. My father does not want to be disturbed."

She swiveled and found that her knees almost touched his. "He is very unwell?"

"He's partly paralyzed. He's improving, but it's slow and he prefers not to show himself to strangers. He's also often out of temper." He took her hand and gently tugged her off the cushioned seat. "Let me take you out into the garden."

It was a surprise to find the others in the large alcove with them, and frankly she wished they weren't. According to Queen Cleopatra, she needed to be apart with him.

Then she realized that Hawk held on to her hand. She still wore her gloves, but they were cotton lace and it was almost skin to skin. Queen Cleopatra had been right about the potency of that.

His other arm still cradled the cat, who was eyeing Clarissa suspiciously through slit eyes, but at least wasn't hissing as yet. She liked the thought that the cat was jealous. Animals were supposed to have good instincts.

As they followed a stone-paved path down to the riverbank, she felt as if she and Hawk blended at palms and fingers to become one, but when they reached the riverbank he abruptly disentangled them. Almost as if he'd only just noticed the joining.

She was lost without a map in a wilderness of emotions and touches.

A family of ducks paddled busily around, bobbing for food, ducklings quacking and dashing. Jetta leaped down from Hawk's arms to lie in the sun watching the ducklings, as if she hoped one would come close.

"Don't you dare," Clarissa warned.

The cat only blinked.

Clarissa decided to stay close, just in case, but she turned back to look at the house. It seemed contentedly slumberous in the sun, wrapped in its blanket of climbing plants and thatch. The sun was warm on her skin and gave a glow to everything.

This was one of life's perfect moments. She hadn't had many, but she recognized it. It was a moment she would never forget, but she hoped there would be many more like it.

"Penny for your thoughts?" he said.

Now that was an invitation, but she wouldn't rush in until he had been given his chance. She could wait.

"My thoughts are that this is a lovely home, and you are very fortunate to have grown up here."

"Ah."

At the tone she glanced at him.

"True fortune is to grow up surrounded by love, wouldn't you say, despite the circumstances? If this had been your family home, would it have made your youth happy?"

"If this had been my family home, it would not be in nearly such good repair. And anything of value would have been stripped from it years ago."

"I see. You think I should count my blessings?"

She met his eyes. "I think we all should. And the main blessing is a future. Whatever the past has been, the future is always ours to make."

He was clearly listening and thinking.

"A future without the tendrils of the past?" He looked at the manor. "A house like this says otherwise. The future is not a road stretching cleanly in front of us. It is a layer built on the foundation of the past."

She thought of her family, her childhood, Deveril, Deveril's death. "Does no one ever get to start building anew?"

His smile was wry. "Perhaps. But not someone who belongs to a place like Hawkinville Manor."

"Belongs to," she said. "I like that."

But a movement on the ground caught her eye. Jetta had risen to a hunting crouch, and one little duckling was paddling close to the bank.

Clarissa stepped forward and shooed it away.

"She wouldn't, would she?" she asked Hawk.

"She's an excellent mouser."

"That's different."

"Not to the mouse. The cat is a predator, Clarissa. It is its nature to hunt."

She turned back to watch the ducklings. "It is a hawk's nature too."

"And a falcon's."

She glanced at him. Was that a hint? Did he want her to ask him? Why? "I assure you, I won't bring you gifts of small victims."

He reached out and lightly touched her cheek. "Whereas I would like to bring you your enemies, headless."

"Enemies?" His touch and the word had her dazed.

"People who wish you ill. People you fear."

She laughed, though to her own ears it sounded shaky. "Alas, I have no enemies worthy of a hawk."

"Alas, indeed. But lacking a true enemy, I will make do with a petty one. No one has spoken to you unkindly? No carriage has splashed mud on your gown? No servant has served your soup cold?"

He was teasing, but he hadn't been teasing before. Why should he suspect enemies? How much of the picture had he put together?

"I wouldn't demand anyone's head for that," she said. "In fact, I want no more violence in my life."

"More?"

She was stuck, but then Lord Trevor said, "Someone's waving, sir."

They both looked around to see an aproned figure waving from the manor door.

"Ah," Hawk said. "The carriage must have returned to take us up to Steynings."

As the others went ahead, he scooped up the cat, then put his free hand on Clarissa's back to direct her toward the house. As he had in that room in the Old Ship . . .

Her dress was fine, and she was wearing the lightest of corsets. She felt the heat, and a thread of excited pleasure up and down her spine as she retraced her steps to the house.

Hawk and Hawkinville.

She would have both. She must have both!

*   *   *

Steynings was certainly a complete contrast to the manor—all clean, modern lines and symmetry. Inside, however, the place was a hive of mending, hammering, painting, and cleaning. The smell of wet plaster, sawdust, and linseed oil stole any sense of comfort for Clarissa. She followed Maria's guided tour, wondering if her husband minded his family home being taken over in this way by his new wife.

She didn't think Lord Vandeimen minded much that his wife did, just as she would find it hard to mind much that Hawk did. He wasn't by her side now—the men had disappeared, probably to find a quiet corner and drink ale—and every moment of this tour seemed a waste of time.

Since there was no escaping, however, she tried to pay attention and make intelligent comments. One day soon, she hoped, the Vandeimens would be neighbors.

When she studied things, it did seem to her that most of the work was an improvement. Some doors had been moved, and two rooms had been opened up into one. The pale paintwork was fresh and airy and suited this building. It was easy to comment approvingly.

As they all returned to the marble-floored entrance hall, the men emerged.

Hawk came over to her. "More to your taste, I gather?"

Clarissa checked that her hostess was out of earshot before answering, "Not at all, I'm afraid. It's too cool and big."

He looked skeptical. Did he really think everyone preferred the modern style?

"Truly, Hawk. I think the manor house is lovely."

Frustratingly, he seemed to take her comment as mere good manners. What else could she say? That she loved his house so much that she would marry Lord Deveril for it? Well, not quite that, for sure.

Then Lord Amleigh and his wife strode in in riding dress and high spirits. Clarissa did not think she imagined their sharp looks, as if she was being assessed. That was a very hopeful sign, if both of Hawk's friends thought her of interest.

They all sat down in the dining room for a cold luncheon. Though the room was in a state for guests, Clarissa could see that work had been left half done in various spots. The food was excellent, however, and a general peace suggested that the workmen were also taking their meal.

She began to take in a sense of the house as it would be, and amid the relaxed conversation, indulged herself in imagining dinners here with these couples as her good friends. Her mind sped ahead to children growing up together as the three men had, but all in completely happy homes.

Not in a home like hers, or like Hawk's.

In some things, at least, a new beginning was possible.

She heard about the Vandeimens' wedding feast. It would be wonderful to be married like that, to be introduced to the village like that.

"You'll have to choose a bride soon, Hawk," teased Lady Amleigh, "so we can have another party before the summer is out."

"Greedy, aren't you, Susan? Wouldn't it be better to wait a summer or two? There aren't likely to be any more of that sort for a generation."

"Speaking of generations," Lady Amleigh responded, "we can celebrate christenings!" She blushed and grinned. "And yes, that does mean that I think there's going to be a christening in February."

Everyone congratulated the Amleighs, but Hawk said, "Hardly the time for a village fête, I'm afraid."

Clarissa detected a touch of wistfulness in Maria Vandeimen's expression, and wondered. The lady had been married and had no children. Could that happen to her? She supposed it could happen to any woman.

With talk of fêtes and babies, everyone was lazy about rising from the table, but eventually Maria said that the workmen needed to get back to their tasks and they'd been told to be quiet while the guests were here.

They all walked out into the hall, and the Amleighs took their departure. The Vandeimens, however, were

approached by an aproned man holding rolls of plans,
and soon they were embroiled in an intent discussion.

Lord Trevor and Althea wandered to study some
painted panels, leaving Clarissa and Hawk alone. It was
not a good enough separation, however. The day here
was almost done. Soon they would be in the carriage
home, all chances gone. And she'd vowed to propose
before they left.

Here?

The acoustics of the hall were such that she could almost catch what everyone else was saying. She needed
to be outside with him. For quite a long time.

"After a lunch like that," she said, "I would love a
walk. Could we walk back to the village, perhaps?"

Hawk looked at her, but then said, "Maria will probably be some time, and would be relieved not to have us
hovering. There's a pleasant footpath that should take
only a half hour or so."

Anticipation and pure nerves tied Clarissa's insides in
a knot, but she said, "That sounds perfect!"

But then he said, "I'll ask Lord Trevor and Miss
Trist."

Clarissa fiercely projected a message to Althea to refuse, but the other couple came over while Hawk went
to speak to the Vandeimens. Clarissa looked for an opportunity to whisper to Althea, but none presented itself
and in moments they were leaving the house by the back
terrace, any hopes and plans in ruins.

She tried to imagine Althea lingering behind with Lord
Trevor, but couldn't. Althea, after all, was a stickler for
the proprieties.

Halfway across the lawn toward the woodland, however, Althea stopped. "Oh, dear. I'm terribly sorry. My
ankle has begun to ache. I twisted it slightly in the mud
at the fair."

They all stood there for a moment, then Hawk said,
"We will go back."

"Oh, no! Please don't," Althea protested. "I'm sure
you were looking forward to the walk." She turned to

Lord Trevor. "But if you could give me your arm back to the house, my lord . . ."

Of course he agreed. Clarissa glanced at Hawk, wondering if he would insist on returning as well, but he said nothing.

"Well, then," she said to Althea, "if you will be all right . . ."

"Perfectly." And Althea winked.

Clarissa had to fight not to laugh as she turned again, alone with Hawk at last.

Instinct told her that this could be the most important half hour of her life.

Chapter Sixteen

~

Hawk linked arms with Clarissa and led her toward the woods and wilderness. He looked down at her, but her golden straw hat shielded her face and made her a woman of mystery—as if she wasn't enough of a mystery already.

He'd not planned this unchaperoned walk, but now that it sat in his hands he could not reject the gift. He could use it to seek details about Deveril's death, but he knew he simply wanted to enjoy this time with the woman he could not have.

It was perilous. He recognized that. Strange magic was weaving through this day, and he felt as if he were walking into a fairy circle, being slowly deprived of logic and purpose.

He would do no wrong, however. He had promised Van, and a promise like that was sacred. All the same, a stern chaperon would have been safer.

A yowl made him look back to see Jetta running after them like a thoroughbred. "Ah. A chaperon after all."

"Do we need one?"

He glanced at Clarissa, catching a wickedly demure look that made him want to groan. What was he going to do if *she* had wicked designs upon *him*?

The cat arrived with a final yowl of protest. He picked it up, saying to Clarissa, "If you don't think we do, Falcon, you are being naive."

She blushed, but it only created a more devastating glow. "I am capable of saying no to anything I do not want, Hawk. Are you saying you would force me?"

"You have a mistaken idea of the role of the chaperon, my girl." They strolled on, the cat now limply content. "Her role is not to prevent wolves from attacking, but to prevent maidens from throwing themselves into the jaws of the wolves."

She turned her head so he could see her whole face, and her expression was decidedly wicked. "I have always disliked having a chaperon."

He stroked the cat. "Jetta, I think you are truly needed here."

Clarissa laughed, a charming gurgle of laughter that was new. A few weeks ago in Cheltenham she hadn't laughed like that—relaxed and happy. Seductive.

He could vividly imagine her laughing like that in bed. Naked in a well-used bed . . .

He'd seen men bewitched by wicked women, often to the extent of besmirching their honor, once or twice to their complete destruction. Had they, too, felt careless as they fell, as if a few magical moments were worth any fate?

If he had any sense, he would return to the house now.

Instead, he went on with her, out of the sunshine and into the cool mystery of the woodland. Jetta leaped down to explore, and Hawk searched for something innocuous to say. "We played here a great deal as boys."

"Knights and dragons?" she asked.

"And crusaders and infidels. Pirates and the navy— but we were always the pirates."

The hat tilted, showing a glimpse of nose. "A criminal inclination, I see."

An opening. He could not fail to take it. "Of course. Have you never played the criminal?"

He watched carefully, but since he could still see only her nose, it was hard to judge her reaction.

"Have you?" she said.

Yes, now.

How peaceful it seemed in this other world under the

green shade, busy birdsong all around them. Jetta pounced into some ferns, then out again, thankfully without a trophy.

Hawk looked at the siren walking so demurely by his side and wished this was the innocent, unshadowed stroll it seemed.

"Not here. None of us wanted to play the true villains. We didn't consider pirates villains, of course. The dragons, infidels, and navy had to be imaginary."

She turned so he could see her complete smile. "But villains often have the best lines. I always asked to play the villain in school plays."

"A villainous inclination, I see."

"Perhaps." There was laughter in it, however, not dark meaning. "I certainly preferred it to being the heroine. There are so few good roles for a heroine."

"Shakespeare has some."

"True. Portia. Beatrice. I played Lady Macbeth once—"

He could imagine that a hand tightened on her throat, sealing off any more words. Why? What was it about Lady Macbeth that could not be spoken? Like the distant rumble of cannons, speaking of death, he remembered the bloody dagger in the play.

"But is she a heroine?" he asked, watching. "She incites a murder . . ."

He was almost certain that Lord Arden had killed Deveril, but had Clarissa incited him to it? Pressed the dagger into his hands? It was not a picture he wanted to envision.

"She suffers for it," Clarissa said.

"But some murderers benefit from their crimes."

"Only if they're not caught."

She was getting better and better at tossing words around without showing her feeling. He admired it, but he wished for a little more transparency.

Exactly how had it gone? Planned assassination, or crime of the moment? It mattered. It mattered to him because he did not want her to be guilty in the tiniest degree, and it would matter if it ever, God forbid, came to the courts.

He knew he was dicing with that. By stirring this pot, he risked everything pouring out to destroy.

"It's a difficult role for a schoolgirl," he remarked, "but playing Macbeth would be harder still."

"Oh, not really." Her voice seemed normal again. "He's caught up in circumstances, isn't he? And anyway, schoolgirls love dark drama and tragedy. Every fifteen-year-old girl longs to die a martyr. We used to enact the story of Joan of Arc for amusement."

She'd slid deftly away from the edge.

"You played Joan of Arc, while we played Robin Hood. Saint and thief. That probably reflects the difference between girls and boys."

"Militant saint and honorable thief. We girls weren't attracted to the kind of saint who spent her life in prayer and peace, just as none of you wanted to play the true villains."

"We conscripted some." He lifted a trailing branch out of her way. "The head groundsman here was unknowingly our sheriff of Nottingham. Avoiding him was a challenge, especially as he didn't always approve of what we were doing and carried a sturdy stick."

"And what about Maid Marian?" she asked with a look.

"Not until we were *much* older."

She laughed again, that charming chuckle.

He suddenly stopped, and without question or apology loosened her bonnet ribbons so the hat flattened and hung down her back.

She looked up at him, unresisting.

Tempting. Demanding, even.

With difficulty he remembered his promise to Van. A kiss, perhaps?

No, even a kiss was too dangerous now.

"We did a play about Robin Hood once," she said.

"Who were you? Robin? Maid Marian? The wicked sheriff?"

"Alan-a-dale."

"The minstrel? Do you sing, then?"

It shocked him that there might be something significant about her that he didn't know.

She smiled, a lovely picture of freckled innocence under the green-and-gold filtered light of the summer woods. Then she began to sing.

Under the greenwood tree
Who loves to lie with me,
And turn a merry note
Unto the sweet bird's throat.

She began to back away, still singing:

Come hither, come hither, come hither.
Here shall you see
No enemy but winter and rough weather.
Come hither, come hither, come hither.

Hawk stood, almost breathless, caught by her sweet, strong voice and the invitation in her eyes.

No enemy but winter and rough weather . . .

If only that were true.

He walked slowly forward. "Shakespeare? I didn't know he wrote about Robin Hood."

"As You Like It. It's mostly set in the forest, so we stole bits."

"You have a lovely voice. And," he added, "you issue a lovely invitation."

" 'All the world's a stage,' " she quoted lightly, " 'and all the men and women merely players . . .' "

He wanted to shoo her away, as she'd shooed away the duckling. *You are in the company of predators. Flee, flee back to safety.* Instead, his will crushed, he held out a hand.

A kiss. Just a kiss.

Her eyes still and thoughtful, she loosened the fingers of one lacy white glove and slowly pulled it off. Then she began on the other. He watched her unveil creamy, silken skin, a shiver passing through him.

Hands touched, hers cool and soft, and he drew her

close, drew her hands to curl behind him. Dappled light turned her hair to a deep, burnished gold, and he loved the rioting wildfire of it. In every way, it suited her. The curve of her full lips and the look in her steady eyes were pure perfection.

She moved a little closer and raised her face expectantly for the kiss. The very boldness was a warning, but he couldn't heed it now. He took the offered kiss that he needed.

Clarissa took the kiss that she needed.

As their lips blended and sweet satisfaction rippled through her, she didn't regret anything, past or future. She sank into the spicy pleasure of his mouth and gladly drowned. She held back nothing, holding him tight to her so every possible inch joined with him, absorbed him.

When the kiss ended, she shivered. It was partly pleasure, but more the ache of drawing apart and the hunger for more. For eternity.

She waited for the words that would speak the message in his darkened eyes, in his hands that played gently against her cheeks, but then he stepped carefully away. "I wonder where Jetta is."

She caught his hand. "Do we care?"

His fingers tightened on hers, but he said, "Yes, I think we must."

He was right. If they wanted to be honorable, they could not keep kissing like that. But why would he not speak? She felt she might die of this restraint, but she would give him till they were almost back in the village. She would give him that much.

She was the one who turned to follow the path, he the one to be drawn along by their interwoven fingers. "Tell me more about yourself, Hawk. Tell me about your work in the army." She hungered for everything about him, and there was so much she did not know.

She thought he might resist, but after a moment he led her onward and answered. "I started out in the cavalry, but I was seconded to the Quartermaster General's

Department. It's a separate administrative unit. There is also the Commissariat, and the duties often overlap.

"The main purpose is the management of the army. It's no easy matter to move tens of thousands of men and all the hangers-on around efficiently and bring them to battle in good order. In addition, an army is like a city. Everything that happens in a city happens there. Brawls, theft, crimes of passion. Most matters are sorted out by the officers—think of them as magistrates." He helped her over a spot where a crumbling hole spanned the path. "Sometimes there are more complex problems. Organized thievery, forgery, murder."

"Murder?" She hoped she sounded merely curious. She'd reacted to the word like a spooked horse.

He gave her one of his sharp glances. She told herself it didn't matter. Soon they would be bound, and then she would tell him everything.

"Murder," he agreed, "but rarely of any cleverness. It was usually a case of following the bloody footprints."

She hoped she didn't shiver at that.

"We mostly looked into crimes involving officers or civilians, and of course there were always spies, some of them traitors."

"Men in the army who turned traitor?" she asked, genuinely shocked.

"Sometimes."

"Why would anyone do that?"

"For money. There's no limit to what some people will do for money."

There seemed a dark tone to that. Was it because he was thinking of himself as a fortune hunter? Was it simple guilt over that which made him hesitate?

They were talking of crimes, however. It was an excellent opportunity to see just how strictly he kept to the letter of the law.

"Did you always enforce the law?" she asked. "Sometimes there must be excuses. Should a starving person hang for stealing a loaf of bread?"

"No one should hang for stealing a loaf of bread. Our

punishment system is barbaric and irrational. But those with wealth live in fear of those who are poor."

She made herself ask the next question. "What of those who steal life? Should a person always hang for murder?"

He glanced at her, and she could glean nothing from his expression. "You think there should be clemency?"

"Why not? The Bible says an eye for an eye. What if it's a crime of revenge?"

"The Bible also says, 'He that smiteth a man so that he die, shall surely be put to death.' "

That wasn't what she wanted to hear. "What of a duel? Should the victor who kills his opponent be executed?"

"That is the law. It's generally ignored if the affair is handled according to the rules."

She took a risk and referred to the heart of the matter. "Yet you said you would have liked to kill Lord Deveril for me."

He was looking at her intently. She met his eyes, waiting for his answer.

"Some people deserve death," he agreed.

"So in such a case, you wouldn't want the law to run its course?" She was being too direct, too bold, but she must know.

He didn't instantly agree. "Who are we to play the angel of death or the angel of mercy? Who are we to subvert justice?"

"Subvert justice?"

"Isn't that what you're suggesting? Shielding a criminal from the wrath of the law?"

It was precisely what she was suggesting, and she didn't like his answers.

"I was thinking more of a jury," she said quickly. "Often they let people go rather than expose them to harsh penalties."

"Ah, true, and why our system does not work." They had stopped, and he rubbed a knuckle softly in the dip beneath her lips. "We are being very serious for a summer afternoon. You think often and deeply about justice and the law?"

"We had to discuss such matters at Miss Mallory's," she said, beginning to melt again—and at such a slight touch. "Do you mind a thoughtful, educated w . . . woman?"

She'd almost said *wife*!

His eyes crinkled with laughter. "Not at all. So," he added, soberly, "what is it you want to know about my views on the law?"

She thought for a moment, then asked a direct question. "Did you ever let a guilty person go because you thought it just, even though the law would have punished them?"

His hand stilled. After a thoughtful moment, he said, "Yes."

She took what felt like the first deep breath in minutes. "I'm glad."

"I thought you might be. In at least one case, I was wrong and thus responsible for another death."

"But—"

Jetta leaped out of the undergrowth just then, and Clarissa started with shock. She put a hand to her chest and Hawk laughed. "That cat will be the death of me. Come on. We are commanded onward by our chaperon."

Jetta was walking haughtily ahead.

Chaperon or not, Hawk put his arm around her as he had that day at the fair. Here, however, there was no need to protect her from a crowd.

She relaxed into the gentle protectiveness of it, but dared another question. "Did you ever have to investigate a friend?"

"Once. I had no choice. He was guilty of repeated cowardice, and a danger to all around him."

"What happened to him?"

"Nothing dramatic. He was allowed to resign his commission on the grounds of ill health. Last I heard, he goes around recounting his brave deeds and regretting that his weak body forced him to leave the scene of battle." After a moment, he looked at her and added, "Sometimes we do not know our friends."

Was that a warning?

"Can we know people at all?" she asked. "Can we ever know another person too well to be surprised?"

"Can we ever know ourselves too well to be surprised?"

She frowned over that. "I feel I know myself fairly well, faults and all."

"But—forgive me, Falcon—you have flown in circumscribed territory. If you were plunged into the extraordinary, you would doubtless surprise yourself. One way or another."

She looked up at him. "If we are uncertain of everything, even ourselves, how do we go on?"

"Ultimately, blind faith and trust."

Trust. That was the key. "I trust you, Hawk."

His eyes shifted away. "Ah," he said. "Perhaps you shouldn't."

Chapter Seventeen

~

She looked ahead, to find that the path wound around a large boulder. Jetta, following it, glanced back, then disappeared.

"What's the matter?" she asked.

He took her hand and pulled her along. "Come."

Beyond the boulder the path tumbled down long, rough steps. It didn't go very far before it divided, seeming to wander through shrubs and rocky outcroppings. She could hear splashing water somewhere.

"I have led you," he said, "like the children of Israel, into the wilderness."

Then she realized what this was. A wilderness garden. "So you have. But surely that isn't such a terrible thing."

"It has not, I fear, received Maria's efficient care as yet, and thus is rather more realistically wild than it should be. Yet it stands between us and our goal." He looked at her. "Do we go on, or back?"

A wilderness was designed to look wild but to also provide safe, smooth paths for civilized enjoyment. She could see that some paths here were almost overgrown, and there might be other hazards.

She smiled at him. "We go on, of course."

His smile suddenly matched hers. "So be it."

He helped her down the rough, rocky steps. "This is all completely artificial, of course. Dig here and you'll hit chalk, not granite. Careful."

The final rock was covered in tangling ivy. He stepped on it in his riding boots, grasped her at the waist and swung her completely over to the path beyond.

She landed feeling as if she'd left her stomach and her wits behind her entirely. When he stepped down beside her, she curled a hand around his neck. "A hero deserves a kiss," she said, and rewarded him, rejoicing in the first kiss she had taken for herself.

When they drew apart, she dared to caress his lean cheek with her fingers, her delighted fingers. "Knight errant and princess."

"Or," he said, "dragon and princess . . . ?"

"With sharp teeth?"

He turned and nipped at her fingers, and she snatched them away. "But you are Saint George! Georgina West said so that first day."

He captured her hand and drew it to his mouth, to his teeth. "I'm no saint, Clarissa." He pressed teeth softly into her knuckle. "Remember that."

Astonishingly, she wanted him to bite harder.

But then he lowered her hand and tugged her along a path. "Come on."

She laughed and went, their bare hands clasped as if it were the most natural thing in the world. And it was. They were friends. They were joined. He was hers, and she was his, and before they returned to the civilized world she would be sure of it.

He often had to hold back invading branches. At one point, Clarissa raised her skirts to work past a brambly spot. It was necessary, but she didn't mind showing an extra bit of leg.

"Daisies," he said, admiring her stockings with a grin. "Are all your stockings fancied in some way?"

She deliberately fluttered her lashes at him. "Why, sir, that is for you to find out!"

When he reached for her, she ducked under a drooping branch and evaded him. Something snagged at her, and she realized that her hat was still down her back. She didn't mind, but waited for him to unhook her. Then froze at the tender touch at her nape . . .

They seemed magically transported out of the real world and real cares, to a place where wild rules reigned. She turned slowly to look at him, but he shook his head and drew her onward.

Then they came to the water, a little stream trickling out of a rock to splash into a moss-covered dip and flow away into a weedy pond. Clarissa put her hand under the cool stream.

"Piped, of course," he said.

She flicked a handful of spray at him. "Just because you have a house that looks as if it's grown where it stands! That's no reason to sneer because others have to construct their little bit of heaven."

"Minx." Laughing, he brushed away the sparkling trail from his hair. "Nature is beautiful enough. Why try to turn it into something it isn't? But we did have fun here as boys."

He looked around. "I remember we knotted a rope onto a branch up there," he said, pointing at a tall elm that overhung them. "We were planning to swing from one side to the other, like pirates boarding a Spanish treasure ship. Van broke his collarbone."

"Your parents must have been terrified."

"We hid the rope and said Van had fallen on the path. We were going to try another time, but never did. Perhaps we did have some sense."

He put his hand under the water, letting it stream out between his fingers like diamonds in a shaft of bright sun. She watched him carefully, expecting retaliation.

He turned to her, and with his wet hand he gently traced a cool line across her brows, down her cheek, and to her lips. Then he kissed her, hot against the cool, so she hummed with pleasure.

He drew back, frowning. "This is no good. Maria will send out a search party."

She grasped his jacket and pulled him back. "Can't we hide here and never be found?"

"Hide in the wilderness?" He freed himself, gripping her hands to prevent further attack. "No, fair nymph, I'm afraid we cannot. The world is a demanding mistress and will recapture us." He looked around. "The paths wind all over, but we can cut through by going that way."

She looked where he pointed. "That's the pond."

"It's about six inches deep." He suddenly swept her into his arms.

She shrieked, but then wrapped one arm around his neck and kissed his jaw. "My hero!"

"You may want to wait and see if I can do this without dropping you. I suspect the bottom is pure slime."

As soon as he put his boots into the water she felt them slip. "Hawk . . ."

"What is life without risk?"

"This is a brand-new gown!"

"O little mind, tied down in mundane cares."

The pond was only about ten feet wide, but he was having to take each step with exquisite care. Clarissa began to laugh.

"Stop that, woman. You'll have us drowning in duckweed!"

She stopped it by sucking lightly at his jaw.

"Is that supposed to help?"

"Promise of reward?" she whispered.

He halted. "Stop that, or I drop you."

She looked into his smiling eyes. "Do I believe you?"

"Do you think I wouldn't?"

"Yes," she said, and nibbled him.

He groaned and stepped quickly, rashly, the rest of the way across, then set her on her feet. He kept one arm around her, however, and swung her hard against him for a kiss that made their others seem lukewarm.

Clarissa sagged, her knees weakening under that assault. The next she knew she was sprawled back against a rock, a sun-warmed rock, grit and heat clear even through cloth. It was only slightly inclined. Perhaps if his legs weren't so pressed to hers she would slide down.

All she could think of, however, was his passionate eyes, on her. On her. Everything she wanted in life was here.

"Your gown is probably becoming stained with moss,"

he whispered, leaning closer, supported by one arm. The other hand rose to play on her cheek, her neck . . .

"Is it?" Her own voice astonished her with its husky mystery.

"Your new gown," he reminded her.

"Am I supposed to care?"

"Yes," he said. "I rather think you are."

"But I'm rich, Major Hawkinville. Very rich. What is one dress here or there?"

His lips twitched. "Then what about the evidence of moss on a lady's back?"

"Ah. But isn't the damage done? And I can always claim that you were a poor escort and let me tumble in the wilderness."

" 'Tumble,' " he said, brushing his lips over hers. "That has two meanings, you know."

"Like 'rod'?" she dared.

Those creases dug deep beside his mouth. "Very like 'rod,' yes. You frighten me, Clarissa."

"Do I? How?"

"Don't look so pleased. You frighten me because you have no true sense of caution. Aren't you at all afraid?"

"I'm not afraid of you, Hawk."

"You should be afraid of all men here, alone in the wilderness."

"Should I? Show me why."

With a laugh that sounded partly like a groan, he looked down, down at her bodice. Her gown's waist was very high and the bodice very skimpy, though made demure by a fine cotton fichu that tucked into it.

He pulled that out.

Clarissa lay there, heart pounding, as he softly kissed the upper curves of her breasts, a feather-stroke of lips across skin that had never known a man's touch before. A wise and cautious woman would stop him at this point. She raised a hand and let her fingers play with his hair as his lips teased at her.

Then his hand slid up to cup her breast. A new, strange feeling, but she liked it. His thumb began to rub and she caught her breath. Ah, she liked that even more!

She realized her hand had stilled and was clutching at the back of his neck. Her eyes half-focused on sunlight on his hair . . .

A sudden coolness made her start and look down. His thumb had worked both gown and corset off her nipple! She watched numbly as his mouth moved over and settled . . .

She let her head fall back and closed her eyes, the sun a warm haze behind her lids as he stirred magic in first one breast, then the other.

No, not just in her breasts.

Everywhere. Perhaps because his hand was beneath her skirt, up on her naked thigh. At some time her legs had parted and he pressed between them. She moved her body against his, holding him closer.

So, this was lovemaking.

Ruin.

How very, very sweet.

A deep beat started between her thighs, teaching her what wanting truly was. Wanting a specific man, in a specific way, at a specific moment.

Now.

She wriggled to press closer.

"Good God!"

He pushed away, jerking her up straight. Clarissa opened dazzled eyes to see him in a shimmering halo of light. He pulled up her bodice and searched around for her discarded fichu.

She put a hand on the rock to stay upright, but she was laughing. "That was astonishing! Can we do it again?"

He straightened, fichu in hand. "You're an unrepentant wanton!" But he was flushed and half laughing too. "You've bewitched me completely out of my senses. Heaven knows how long we've been here." He flung the soft cotton around her neck and began to tuck it in with unsteady fingers.

Then he stood back. "You do that. Maria will want my head. And Van will want—"

He stopped what he was saying, and she fixed the fichu over her breasts, fighting back her laughter. She was incapable of anything except total delight. That kiss, that encounter, had wiped away the last trace of doubt about his feelings. He'd gone further than he'd intended. He'd lost track of time.

He, the Hawk, had been lost in his senses with her.

She knew he was appalled, and that spoke of the power of their love.

Their love . . .

"We need only say we were lost in the wilderness, Hawk."

"We need to get out of here. Where's our damned inadequate chaperon?"

He took her hand and virtually dragged her up some more steps and around another boulder out into an open grassy space. There sat Jetta in front of a gate in the estate wall, waiting.

"Don't ask how she knew where we were going," he said. "She's never been here before." He strode forward and grasped the iron bolt, then swore. "It's stuck. My apologies."

"For language or gate?" But Clarissa knew laughter was in her tone. She couldn't help it. She'd laugh at rain at the moment, at thunder, or at hurricane. He was anxious to get through the gate for fear of her! Of what more they might do here.

She rather hoped the latch was fused shut.

He struggled with it for a moment more, then suddenly stood back and kicked at the rusty bolt. The gate sprang open, the bolt flying off the shattered rotten wood.

She caught her breath.

Crude, effective violence.

A side of Hawk Hawkinville that she had not seen before, suddenly reminding her of handsome, civilized Lord Arden lost in rage, hitting his wife . . .

He shook himself and turned, the elegant man again. "Come."

Chapter Eighteen

Clarissa went through the splintered gate. All the beautiful certainty she'd floated in had gone, and she was jolted to dubious earth. Would his next violent outburst be against her? When she told him the truth?

Beyond the gate lay civilization. The English countryside. A well-trodden pathway ran along the edge of a field of barley, winding up the hill behind them, and down toward the village in front.

The path to where? She had vowed to ask him to marry her if he didn't propose first. Now she faltered before uncertain flames.

"The path rises up to Hawks Monkton," he said in a very normal voice. "It's about three miles."

Jetta rubbed past their legs and headed down. What was there to do but follow?

"Perhaps you would care to visit it one day," he said as if giving a guided tour. "We have the remains of a monastery there. Very remaining remains. The stones were too useful to be left untouched."

"We?" she asked. "Does the manor hold this land?"

"No, this is Van's. The only manor land on this side of the river is around Hawks Monkton. On the other side, we own the village, and land nearly all the way to Somerford Court up there."

From this height Clarissa could see more of Lord Amleigh's home—a solid stone block with a lot of chimneys. "Jacobean?" she guessed.

"Early Charles I, but close enough. It doesn't have the elegance of Van's house, or the age of mine, and the Somerfords haven't been wealthy since the Civil War, so it's shabby in places. But it was always my favorite place to be." He'd come to a halt considering it. "It was always a place of love and kindness and tranquil days."

"What happened to them?"

More violence?

He looked at her as if coming out of memories. "Was I speaking in the past tense? That comes out of my mind rather than reality. But Con's father and brother died while we were in the army. It was his father's heart. His brother drowned. Fred was boating mad. His mother and younger sister still live there, however, and he has two older sisters who are married with families of their own."

Clarissa gave thanks for what sounded like a normal family. She was beginning to think such things a matter only for fable!

"And Lord Vandeimen? He doesn't mention any family."

He gestured for them to walk on, and she obeyed. She noted, however, that he didn't touch her this time as he had so many times before. Had that burst of violence indicated a change of mind in him, as well as for her?

What was she to do about that?

"Sadly, Van has none left. It's hard to believe. Steynings was always so full of life. His mother and one sister died in the influenza that swept through here. His other sister died in childbirth a year ago, on the exact day of Waterloo. God alone knows, death was not short of business that day." He collected himself. "It's not surprising that his father went downhill. He shot himself."

"And Lord Vandeimen came home from battle to all that? How terrible."

"But his marriage has begun to heal the wounds."

Marriage. Capable of healing, capable of wounding. She suddenly saw it not as a device, as a comfortable matter of orange blossoms and beds, but as an elemental force.

"My parents were not like that," she said, half to herself. "I'm sure their marriage was always . . . arid."

"Perhaps not. Many marriages begin with dreams and ideals."

She looked at him, realizing that they were talking about marriage—now, when she had become dreadfully uncertain.

"What of your parents, Hawk?"

"Mine?" His laugh was short and bitter. "My father tricked my mother into marriage to gain her estate. Once he had it, he gave her no further thought other than to push her out of his way."

She stared at him, thinking perhaps she at last understood his lack of action. "You fear to be like your father?" she asked softly.

They had stopped again. "Perhaps," he said.

She grasped her courage. "If we were to marry, would you give me no further thought other than to push me out of your way?"

Humor, true humor, sparked in his eyes. "If I found you in my way, I'd likely ravish you on the spot."

She laughed, feeling her face burn with hot pleasure. "Then marry me, Hawk!"

And thus Hawk found himself frozen, pinned to an impossible spot by the words that had escaped him. If he said no, she would shrivel. If he said yes, it would be the direst betrayal.

He could not trap her without telling her the truth. If he told the truth, she would flee.

He'd been silent too long. Mortification rushed into her cheeks, and she turned to stumble away down the path.

He caught her round the waist, stopping her, pulling her against him. "Clarissa, I'm sorry! You are being very generous, and I . . . Dazzled by sunshine and wilderness adventures with you, I'm in no state to make a logical decision."

She fought him. He felt tears splash on his hands. In fear of hurting her, he let her go.

She whirled on him, brushing angrily at her eyes with both hands. "Logical! Do you deny that you went to Cheltenham in search of the Devil's Heiress?"

"No."

"Then why, for heaven's sake, when the rabbit wants to leap into the wolf's jaws, are you stepping back?"

"Perhaps, dammit, because rabbits are not supposed to leap into jaws!"

She planted her fists on her hips. "So! You will hold my boldness against me and cling to conventional ways!" Her look up and down was magnificently annihilating. "I thought better of you, sir."

With that salvo, she turned and marched away, and this time he did not try to stop her. He watched for a moment, transfixed with admiration and pure, raging lust.

My God, but he wanted this treasure of a woman in every possible way. He forced his feet into action to follow, plunging madly back into thought to find an answer, a solution. And it was as much for her as for him. He could not bear to see her suffer like this.

He could accept her offer of marriage. He recognized it for the worm it was, but he could make a clear case in favor.

She loved him. Perhaps she would forgive. Perhaps she would accept a future as Lady Deveril. If not, she would be the offended party, and could march off, banners flying. He'd keep not a penny more of her money than he absolutely needed, and would never try to restrict her freedom. He'd give her a divorce if she wanted it.

But divorce always shamed the woman. She would never be restored to the promise of life that she had now. He would be stealing that from her.

And it would have to be an elopement, with all the problems he'd already considered. All the problems that had made him reject that course. He had always prided himself on courage and an iron will, but now he'd found his weakness. He seemed able to stick to nothing where Clarissa was concerned.

Van.

He had made his friend a promise. He'd already gone further than he ought. Elopement, though—that would be an outright violation. Van might even feel obliged to call him out.

God Almighty! That would be the hellish nadir, to risk killing or being killed by one of his closest friends.

The path separated from the high stone wall, and Clarissa took the branch heading toward the river and the humpbacked bridge. He watched her straight back and high-held head.

Such courage, though he was sure she was still fighting tears. She hurt. He knew that. She wouldn't agree now, but it was a minor hurt that time would heal.

He must stick to his other plan and let her fly free.

Clarissa watched a crow flap up from the field in front of her and wished she could simply fly away from this excruciating situation. All she could do, however, was hurry to rejoin her party and return to Brighton.

Empty, purposeless Brighton.

No more Hawk.

Why had he pursued her if he did not want her? Why had he kissed her like that in the wilderness if he did not want her? Was it true what they said, that a man would kiss and ravish any woman, given the chance?

It hadn't felt like that, but what did she know of the reality between men and women?

But, oh, it hurt to think that all her money was not sweetening enough to make her palatable.

She was sure that he was still coming along behind her, and she longed to turn and scream stupid, pride-salving things at him. That she didn't want him. Didn't need him. That she thought his kisses horrid.

She bit her lip. As if anyone would believe that.

All she could do was escape with the shreds of her dignity intact.

And then what?

No more Hawk.

No Hawk in the Vale.

No heaven for her. Ever.

She came to a stile, and for a stupid moment the wooden structure seemed like an insurmountable obstacle, especially with tears blurring her vision. She gathered her skirts in order to climb it.

Hawk suddenly stepped past her to climb over and offer her a hand. She had to face him again. Was she fooling herself that his eyes seemed to mirror her pain?

She put her hand in his, realizing by sight that it was gloveless. Somewhere in the wilderness she had mislaid that symbol of the well-bred lady.

As she stepped up on her side, he said, "I'm sorry. You know how to turn a man topsy-turvy, Clarissa."

"It's entirely an accident, I assure you. I know nothing."

"I shouldn't have criticized you for making that proposal." He was blocking her way, but at a point where she was nearly a foot taller. Deliberately giving her that superiority?

"I meant what I said," he went on. "I'm dazzled. This has been an unexpected and remarkable day, and our adventures in the wilderness were enough to turn any man crazed. You must see that."

The splinters of ice in her heart started to melt, but he wasn't really explaining. Or accepting her offer.

"I can't answer you now," he said. "I told you about my parents. My mother flung herself into marriage with my father in a state of blind adoration, then clung to her disappointment for the rest of her life. Marriage is not a matter to be decided in emotion."

She stared down at him. "You're likening me to your father? You, sir, are the fortune hunter here!"

"Then why did you ask me to marry you?"

She knew she was turning red again. "Very well. I, like your father, lust after Hawk in the Vale. At least I'm honest about it. And I won't push you aside if you get in my way."

There was something to be said for anger, she realized, and for an additional foot of height!

"And," she added, "*you* went to Cheltenham looking for *me*."

"Yes."

"Checking me out before making a commitment?"

A smile twitched his lips. "I liked what I found."

"And you suggested that I come to Brighton."

"Yes."

"And kissed me at the fair."

"Yes."

"And took me into the wilderness."

He looked rather as if she were raining blows on him. That didn't stop her. She would not play coy games anymore.

She stepped over the middle of the stile to loom over him even more. "So, Major Hawkinville, what happens next?"

"You fly like the falcon you are." He put his hands at her waist and lifted her, spinning her in a circle twice, then down to the grass beyond.

She landed, laughing despite herself. "No one but you has ever done that to me, Hawk. Made me fly." She meant it in many more ways than a spin through the air, and she knew he'd know that.

What now? Should she risk devastation by asking him again . . . ?

A scream severed the moment.

A young child's shriek.

After a dazed moment, Clarissa realized that a splash had gone with the scream. Hawk was already running, already halfway across a field to the river—the river so deep it had kept the village on one side until the bridge was built. She picked up her skirts and raced after him, dodging around slightly startled cows.

The child was still screaming, but she couldn't see the riverbank for bullrushes. Screaming was good, but then she realized that there might be more than one child. One screaming, one drowning.

Hawk could swim. She remembered that and thanked God.

The screaming stopped, and she saw that Hawk was

there, and a small child was pointing. Then he waded through the rushes.

She ran the last little way, gasping, and took the girl's hand. She could see a boy flailing, but in quite shallow water near the edge. Hawk grabbed the boy's arm and hauled him close.

Safe.

Safe.

Clarissa sucked in some needed air, collapsing onto the grass with the little girl in her lap. "There, there, sweetheart. It's all right. Major Hawkinville has your friend."

The dark-haired child was very young to be out without an adult, and the lad didn't look much older. No wonder they'd fallen into such trouble.

Wondering at the silence, she turned the girl's face toward her and found tears pouring from huge blue eyes, but eerily without a sound. "Oh, poppet, cry if you want." She raised her cream skirt to wipe the tears.

A hiccup escaped, but that was all. But then suddenly the child buried her face in Clarissa's shoulder and clung, shivering like Jetta that first day. Clarissa held her tight and crooned to her.

She thought to look around for the forgotten cat and found it there, lying in the grass, eyes on the child in Clarissa's lap. Clarissa made a little room, and Jetta leaped up.

The child flinched, but Jetta pushed closer, purring, and the little girl put out a grubby hand to touch her. Then shivering little arms encircled, and tears fell onto the silky fur.

Hawk had the other child out of the water and was hugging him too. He and she were both going to be muddy, but Hawk didn't seem to mind, and she certainly didn't. She was glad that he wasn't wasting breath yelling at the frightened boy.

Clarissa hid her face in the girl's curls. She was besotted by everything about Major Hawk Hawkinville. She could even, in a way, admire him for not snatching the prize she'd dangled in front of him.

He would be a wonderful father, though. She'd never thought that way before, but she wanted him as father to her children.

He carried the boy over. "He seems to mostly speak French, and be of a taciturn disposition, but he's one of Mrs. Rowland's children, so this must be the other."

"Who's Mrs. Rowland?"

"A Belgian woman married to an invalid English officer. She has rooms in the village."

"Her children shouldn't be out alone."

"No, but there's little money. She has to go away sometimes, seeking an inheritance. People have offered to help, but she's proud. We'll take them home as we go."

Clarissa separated reluctant child and cat, then held out a hand. He helped her up with the little girl still clutching.

"At least," he said, looking her over, "no one is going to be commenting about stains on your dress now."

Clarissa chuckled. "I'm definitely not still tied down by mundane cares."

She didn't want to think back to all that had happened, however, and she had no idea how to go forward. She focused instead on the fact that the little girl was barefoot, and the boy too.

"Where are your shoes, little one?" she asked the girl in French.

The dark curls shook, no.

The boy said, "We were not wearing any."

"That's not uncommon in the country," Hawk said, "and even less so on the continent. But I suspect that these two slipped out of the cottage without permission. Their mother is probably frantic."

They crossed the bridge into the village, passing a sinewy woman with a basket who clucked her tongue. "Those little imps. Do you want me to take them, sir?"

Hawk thanked her but refused, and led the way behind the clanging smithy to a door in the back of another building.

"Bert Fagg lets out these rooms," he said.

"A rough place for an officer and his wife," Clarissa said.

"I know, but she's living on my father's charity. She claims to be a connection of his. He certainly enjoys her company. He said he invited her to live in the manor house, but she refused. She's a strange, difficult woman."

He knocked on the door of the very silent building. Rough cloths covered the windows, so Clarissa couldn't see inside.

"Perhaps she's out looking for the children," she said.

But then the door swung open and a dark-clothed woman stepped out. The only brightness about her was a stark white cap that covered her graying hair and tied under her chin with narrow laces. She did not look well. Her skin was sallow, and dark rings circled her eyes.

"Oh, mon dieu!" she exclaimed, snatching the little girl from Clarissa's arms. "Delphie!" Then she went off into a rapid tirade of French that Clarissa could not follow.

She heard a noise and looked down to see Jetta, back arched, hissing at the woman. She hastily picked up the cat. "Hush."

Jetta relaxed, but still looked at Mrs. Rowland with a fixed stare. Clarissa could almost hear a silent hiss, and knew just how the cat felt. Yes, any mother might berate a child who had fallen into danger, but there was something coldly furious rather than panicked about Mrs. Rowland.

Clarissa glanced at the boy, whom Hawk had put down. He looked suitably afraid. Any child could be afraid after being caught in such naughtiness, and he had taken his baby sister into danger with him. All the same, there was something *old* about his fear. She desperately wanted to stand between the woman and her children, as she'd stood between Jetta and the duckling.

Mrs. Rowland suddenly put the girl down and said in clear French, "Come, Pierre. Take Delphie inside."

Pierre walked over to his sister, head held high, and led her into the cottage.

"Thank you, Major Hawkinville," said Mrs. Rowland

in heavily accented English. She sounded as if she'd rather be eating glass.

"Anyone would have helped. May I ask that you not be too harsh on them, Mrs. Rowland? I think they have learned their lesson through their fright."

The woman did not thaw. "They must learn not to slip away." She went back into her house and shut the door.

Clarissa blinked, startled by such lack of gratitude, and also by a flash of recognition. Who? Where? She was certain she'd never met Mrs. Rowland before.

Hawk drew her away. "There's nothing we can do. Any family in the village would spank the pair of them for that."

"I know. But I don't like that woman." She stroked the cat in her arms. "Jetta hissed at her."

"Understandable. That's only the second time we've spoken, and she makes the hair on the back of my neck stand on end. I'd think she was avoiding me except that she avoids everyone except my father."

They walked back around the smithy onto the green.

"She visits your father?"

"Yes, and surprisingly he frets if she stays away too long."

"You don't like it?"

He glanced at her. "I told you once, I'm inclined to be suspicious of every little thing."

"I suspect your instincts are finely tuned."

His look turned intent. "At the time, as I remember, I was speaking of Miss Hurstman. You have reason to worry about her?"

Clarissa almost told him. But no. At this point she wasn't at all sure that he could be trusted with her secrets.

"Surely Hawk Hawkinville can find out about a Belgian woman married to a British officer called Rowland."

"Hawk Hawkinville has been somewhat busy. But certainly the next time I'm in London I'll check on them both at the Horse Guards. She rubs me the wrong way, but she's probably simply a poor woman in a very difficult situation and with a prickly nature."

Then he said, "Gads, Maria is probably already at the Peregrine, steaming! Come on!"

He took her hand and they hurried across the green. This was the moment when Clarissa had promised herself that she would propose.

But she had, and she'd been rejected. It was so painful that she couldn't imagine how men plucked up the courage to do it, especially the second time.

She'd spiraled up to heaven in his arms, then plunged into fear at his violence, and then to hurt and furious shame at his rejection. But she still loved him. Silly, besotted fool that she was, she still loved, still hoped.

They were almost at the inn. She said, "That is a horrid house," meaning the stuccoed one next door.

"Thoroughly."

"If your father owns the village, didn't the builder need permission?"

He stopped and turned her toward him. "Clarissa, I need to tell you something."

"Yes?" Her heart speeded. She sensed this was something crucial.

"My father is deep in debt to Slade, the man who owns that house. That's why he couldn't stop it. My father has mortgaged Hawkinville Manor and all its estates to Slade. If we don't get a lot of money soon, Slade will be squire here. And the first thing he plans to do is to rip down the manor and the cottages to build an even more monstrous house on the river."

She stared at him, struck by an almost physical sense of loss. "You can't permit that! My money. It's my money that you need, isn't it? Then why . . . ?"

He winced. "I can't explain everything now, Clarissa. But I wanted you to know the truth. So you'd understand."

"But I *don't* understand."

"Major Hawkinville! Good day to you, sir."

They both turned to the man who had come out of the white monster. He was middle-aged, fit, and well dressed. If Clarissa had been a cat, she would have hissed.

Hawk put an arm around her as if in protection and moved to avoid the man.

"A lovely day, is it not?" Slade persisted.

"It is becoming less so." Clarissa could feel tension in Hawk—the leashed desire for violence. The wretched Slade must know it and was deliberately tormenting him.

"You and your lovely lady have had an accident, Major?" the man asked, narrow eyes flicking over them.

Clarissa realized that in addition to being a mess she still had her hat hanging down her back, and her hair was doubtless rioting. A glance showed her that Hawk for once was almost as disordered.

"Only in meeting you, sir," said Hawk.

"So I suspect," said Slade in a voice full of innuendo.

Clarissa felt Hawk inhale, and hastily stepped between the men. "You must be Mr. Slade. Major Hawkinville has told me how kind you have been to his poor father."

Slade froze, and his narrowed gaze flicked between her and Hawk.

"Clarissa . . ." Hawk put his hand on her again to move her away.

"How happy you will be," she said, evading him again, "to know that soon your generosity will be repaid. I am a very wealthy woman."

It was delicious to see the odious Slade turn pale with shock and fury, but Clarissa didn't dare look at Hawk. He was probably pale with shock and fury too, but she hadn't been able to stand seeing him baited.

"My congratulations, Major," Slade spat out.

"Thank you, Slade." Hawk's voice sounded flat. "It must be a great relief to know that your generous loans will be repaid in full, with interest, before the due date."

"A hasty marriage, eh? Doubtless wise."

Clarissa blocked Hawk again, facing the iron founder. "Not at all, sir." She wanted to knock the man down herself! "It will take time to arrange a suitably grand affair. On the village green, no doubt, since Major Hawkinville's family is so important here."

Oh, lord. She could feel Hawk's anger blistering her back.

"The loans come due on the first of August, young lady."

She assumed what she hoped was a look of astonished distaste. "If you insist on payment on the dot, sir, it will be arranged by my trustees. Under no circumstances will I permit Hawkinville Manor to change hands."

Hawk's arm came around her then, pulling her to his rigid, angry side. "As you see, Slade, there is no point in your further residence here."

The man's face was still pale, but now splotches of angry color marked his cheeks. "I believe I will wait to dance at your grand wedding, Major."

"If you insist."

Hawk turned Clarissa toward the inn, but Slade said, "Is the name of the bride a dreadful secret?"

Clarissa twisted back to say, "Not at all, Mr. Slade. I am Miss Greystone. You might have heard of me. Some call me the Devil's Heiress."

She was then swept away by an arm as strong as iron. Lord, that had been thoroughly wicked, but also thoroughly satisfying. Slade was probably drooling with fury.

So was someone else. Not drooling, but furious.

Chapter Nineteen

Hawk dragged her not to the main door of the inn, but through the arch into the inn yard. Ignoring, or perhaps oblivious to, the various servants there, he thrust her against the rough wall. "What exactly do you think you are doing?"

"Trouncing the odious Slade!" she declared, grinning even though her knees were turning to jelly with fear. Glory in the battle warred with memories of Beth's bruised face. "Don't tell me you didn't enjoy that."

"Enjoy being taken by the scruff and dragged through a bramble patch?"

"Enjoy watching him drink bile."

Suddenly his furious eyes closed, and then he laughed, leaning his forehead against hers. "Zeus, yes. It was worth a thousand torments."

Clarissa knew she should feel hurt by that, but she didn't. She was suddenly certain that all was right in her world. She didn't understand his reluctance, but she was sure it could be blasted into dust. Above all, she was sure that she wanted him, and that he would be all she wanted and more.

She poked him hard in the belly. "If you're rude again about the prospect of marrying me, I'll go right back and tell Slade he can have Hawkinville, every last post and stone."

He straightened to look at her, eyes still wild with

laughter. "Clarissa, there is nothing I want more than to marry you."

"Well, then—"

His kiss silenced her, a hot, enthralling kiss that sent fire into every part of her, though she couldn't help thinking of the watching servants.

With glee.

He'd certainly have to marry her after this.

"Hawk! Clarissa! Stop that!"

Clarissa emerged from a daze to find Maria hitting Hawk's back with a piece of wood. Fortunately it was rotted, and was flying into pieces with each blow.

Hawk turned to her laughing, hands raised, and she threw the remaining fragments away in disgust. "What do you think you're doing?" she demanded. Then she stared at Clarissa. "Or more to the point, what *have* you done?"

"I ravished her in the wilderness, of course."

"What?"

"Don't be a goose, Maria. That wilderness of yours, by the way, is too damn wild. But most of the damage to our appearance was done by our gallant rescue of two children from the river."

"Rescue?" Maria collected herself. "That doesn't explain such a shocking kiss in front of the servants."

"A certain madness comes upon us all after battle."

"Battle?"

Clarissa was threatened by incapacitating giggles, for a hundred reasons. She simply leaned against the wall and enjoyed the show.

"Clarissa just routed Slade by telling him we are engaged to be married. I thought I had better compromise her thoroughly before she changed her mind."

She'd won! She didn't know how, but she'd won. She lovingly brushed some fragments of rotted wood off her future husband's shoulders.

He turned, and the look in his eyes turned her delight to cold stone. The laughter had gone, and was replaced by something dark and almost lost. A movement beyond him caught her eye, and she saw Lord Vandeimen emerge from one of the stable buildings, suddenly deadly.

Why on earth would she think that?

As if alerted, Hawk swung around. "Nothing happened."

"Nothing!" exclaimed Lady Vandeimen, but then she seemed silenced by the crackling tension.

"Nothing of any great significance," Hawk said with precision.

Clarissa wanted to protest that, but she too was frozen by something ready to burst out of this ordinary place into the world of claw and fang.

Lord Vandeimen said, "A word with you, Hawk." His head indicated the stable behind him.

Clarissa put her hand on Hawk's arm as if to hold him back, but Maria pulled her away. "Come into the inn and tidy up, Clarissa."

"But—"

"You can't possibly return to Brighton looking like that." She ruthlessly steered Clarissa into the building, chattering.

"Lord Vandeimen is not my guardian!" Clarissa broke in, forcing a halt. "What's going on out there?"

Maria looked at her. "More to the point, what went on during your walk?"

"Nothing," said Clarissa, "of any great significance." Then the whole tumultuous half hour burst out of her in tears, and Maria gathered her into her arms, hurrying her along to a private room.

"Hush, dear. Hush. Whatever went on, we'll arrange matters. I know Hawk loves you."

Clarissa looked at her and blew into her handkerchief. "You do?"

"Yes, of course."

"Then why doesn't he want to marry me?"

Maria's smile was close to a laugh. "Of course he does!"

Clarissa shook her head. "Men are very hard to understand, aren't they?"

Maria hugged her again. "There you have a universal truth, my dear."

Hawk followed Van into the pleasantly pungent stable thinking that the day couldn't get much worse, but knowing that in fact it could.

Van turned and merely waited.

"That kiss probably did go beyond the line," Hawk said. "But nothing worse happened." Then he remembered the wilderness. "More or less. That bloody wilderness of yours is a disgrace."

He saw Van fight it, then laugh. "It's almost worth it to see you in this state, Hawk. What the devil are you up to?"

"I'm trying to save Hawkinville."

"I assume you have decided to woo Miss Greystone. Is it necessary to be so crude about it?"

"She told Slade we were engaged to marry."

Van visibly relaxed. "Why the devil didn't you say so? Congratulations!"

"I'm not going to marry her, Van."

Van leaned back against a wooden post, frowning in perplexity. "Would you care to start at the beginning? Or at some point that makes sense?"

Hawk said, "My father is the new Viscount Deveril."

Van frowned even more. "You're the son of Lord Devil? The one Miss Greystone inherited from? And I've never heard of it?"

"The new Lord Deveril. You know my father changed his name as a price of marrying my mother. He was born a Gaspard, and that's the Deveril name. When Lord Devil died last year, he chased back up and down the family tree and discovered that he's the heir. It's taken him the best part of a year to settle it, but it's just about done."

"Congratulations. You'll outrank me one day."

"Bugger that. The name's fit to be spat upon."

"A name's a name. The first Lord Vandeimen was a spineless lickspittle. Is this where the debt comes from?"

"More or less. The squire's been obsessed by the Deveril money. He thinks he should get it along with the title, that the will was a forgery." Hawk looked around and spotted a room with a door. "Come in here."

Van followed, and Hawk shut the door. The room was small and seemed mostly to hold nostrums for treating horses.

"Unfortunately," Hawk said, "my father is probably right." He didn't want to say it, but he had no choice. "I've been dangling after Miss Greystone not to woo her but to entice her to spill something about the will."

"You're a damn fine actor, then."

"I've learned to be. Van, for God's sake, there's no question of marriage! Once Clarissa discovers what I've been up to, and that I'm a future Lord Deveril, it'll all be over."

"Hawk, this doesn't sound like you."

"What, underhanded trickery and sneaky investigation? It's my stock-in-trade. I've softened up plenty of villains for the gutting."

"But not an innocent young woman."

"If she was innocent, there wouldn't be any gutting to be done."

Van frowned. "All right, let's talk about this. What exactly do you think her guilty of?"

"Murder, or conspiracy to murder."

"*Murder?*" Van managed to keep it soft. "If I'm any judge, Miss Greystone would run from killing a mouse."

"The mouse wouldn't be forcing vile kisses on her, and threatening worse."

"You think she killed Deveril when he tried to rape her? You'd send her to the gallows for that?"

"No, dammit. But remember, she ended up with the dead man's money."

It was a detail he tended to willfully ignore.

"All right," said Van, "do you have any reason other than wishful thinking to believe that Lord Deveril's will was forged?"

"When have you ever known me to indulge in wishful thinking?"

But his thinking about Clarissa came perilously close.

"It was handwritten," he said crisply, "witnessed by servants who have conveniently disappeared, and it left everything not entailed to a young woman, to come to her completely and without control at age twenty-one."

Van's expression lost its indulgence. "Hell."

"Hell, indeed. I can add, from Clarissa's own lips, that she was sold to Deveril and hated him, which he must have known. She threw up over him when he tried to kiss her."

"It does look damned bad. How did Deveril die?"

"Knifed. Viciously."

But then Van shook his head. "It still doesn't fit. I know I don't have your acute sense for truth and lies, but Clarissa Greystone makes an unlikely thief and an impossible murderer."

"Appearances can be deceptive. Did I ever tell you about an innocent-looking, big-eyed child in Lisbon? Never mind. You don't want to know."

Van's brows rose. "Are you protecting Demon Vandeimen from sordid details, Hawk?"

Hawk sighed. "I would if I could. We none of us need more darkness in our lives. But I have to save Hawkinville. You must see that, Van."

"Yes, of course. Perhaps I'll simply cut Slade's scrawny throat."

It was a joke. Hawk hoped, but he shook his head. "No more blood if I can help it."

"So, let's sort it out."

Hawk put up a hand. "Maria will be waiting. We can talk later if you want."

"No, let's deal with this now. If necessary we can stay the night and get Con in on it. You really think Clarissa Greystone committed a vicious murder and planted a forged will?"

"No, dammit, but that could be willful delusion."

Van smiled slightly at the implied admission. "I'm not willfully deluded. Let's consider this. If someone else was the murderer and thief last year, who could it have been? From what I've heard, she left school and went to London. She can't have known many people who would kill and forge for her—" He broke off. "Talk about teaching a grandmother to suck eggs. You must have been through this."

Hawk resisted for a moment, but he knew Van wouldn't let it go. "Arden," he said.

"Arden?"

"The Marquess of Arden was the killer. Last year he married a teacher at Clarissa's Cheltenham school."

Van's jaw dropped. "The heir to Belcraven? Are you mad?"

"High rank means honor? You know better than that, Van."

"It means hell's fires if you meddle there and can't prove it beyond doubt. And what motive could he have?"

"Maria has that pretty niece, Natalie. What if she were in the power of a man like Deveril? Couldn't Maria persuade you into doing something illegal to rescue her?"

"I'd knife him in public if necessary."

Hawk knew Van was speaking the literal truth. He himself would do it too. And so would a man like Arden, he was sure.

"If that was the way it was," Van said, "give the man a medal."

"Then how do I get the money?"

"How do you get the money this way?"

Hawk put it into plain words. "I blackmail him for it."

Van braced himself against a worktable. "You'd destroy essentially honorable people?"

"Don't get too misty-eyed. Disposing of Deveril was a virtuous act, but misappropriating his money was straight-out, deliberate theft."

"How in God's name do you think to go about this? Men like Arden and his father can destroy with a word."

"Ah, yes, the Duke of Belcraven. He's Clarissa's guardian, by the way."

"Zeus! They're all in it? But why?"

"Simply protecting her, I assume. Which has my sympathy. But I must save Hawkinville, and I see no reason not to have enough of that money to also rebuild

Gaspard Hall and get my father off my back. And do something for the poor Deveril tenants."

Van was looking slightly alarmed. It took a lot to alarm Demon Vandeimen. "You'll have to convince the duke that you would make it public. And," he added, "watch your back."

"I'm good at that. Van, I'm depending upon the fact that these are essentially honorable people. Deveril was thought to be without an heir. Surely they'll see that it's wrong to divert all that money."

"And Clarissa?"

"She'll hardly be left penniless."

"She's an innocent party."

"Innocent! She shows no guilty conscience over enjoying the ill-gotten gains." Then another piece clicked into place. "Devil take it, the fortune is *payment*. She was present at the murder, so Arden arranged the forgery to pay her off. No wonder she's as closemouthed as a tomb about it."

"Hawk, this is wrong."

"No, dammit, forgery is wrong. My father, damn his eyes, is right. The money belongs to Hawkinville, and I won't see Slade destroy it because I was too squeamish to hurt Clarissa's feelings!"

"You can't do it."

Hawk was about to wring Van's neck when he saw the expression on his friend's face. As if he'd suddenly seen an unpleasant vision.

Van straightened. "Arden will call your bluff."

"He daren't risk it."

"Why not? If you prove anything, you will destroy Clarissa as well as him."

"With any luck, he won't know that's a factor."

"More to the point," said Van slowly. "Arden is a Rogue."

"What?"

"One of Con's Company of Rogues. I can't believe that slipped by your brain. Roger, Nick, Francis, Hal, Luce . . ." Van recited. "We heard enough about them. And Luce is Lucien de Vaux, Marquess of Arden."

It had slipped by him. Devil in flames. Something about Arden had been niggling him, but Con had always talked about the Rogues by first names—unusual enough. Luce.

"And Hal Beaumont," he said. "The man with Mrs. Hardcastle. Clarissa said he was an old friend of Arden's. But being a Rogue doesn't give Arden immunity."

"No, but he has to know who you are. I'm sure Con spoke of us to them as much as he spoke of them to us. And there's only two of us. Unless he has the brain of a sheep and the spine of a rabbit, he'll have to know that you could not possibly attempt to destroy one of Con's Rogues. However, perhaps Con can act as go-between."

"No!" Hawk's rejection was instinctive, but reason followed. "That's an intolerable position to put him in. 'Admit to murder and forgery of your free will and quietly move half of Clarissa's fortune to my friend Hawk.' No," he repeated, standing among ruins. "I'll come up with something else."

"You don't have much time. Why not simply tell Clarissa the truth? Perhaps she will be able to forgive your deception and overlook a future as Lady Deveril."

"But how will Arden and his father feel about it? She still needs her guardian's permission."

"Damn."

"Strange, isn't it? I have all the cards in my hand, and yet it still seems possible that I might lose."

"We have to tell Con. He can't be left out of this."

"Haven't you thought that he might know? The Rogues don't keep secrets from each other."

"You think he knows that they set up a will that defrauded you?"

Hawk shook his head. "I haven't told him anything about the debt or the Deveril title. Someone in the Rogues has to know, though, with my father chasing it through the courts."

"I can't believe Con would do nothing about a situation like that."

"He'd be caught in the middle."

"No," Van said. "It's more likely that they're protecting him from it. He's only recently started to recover from Waterloo and Dare."

Hawk considered it and knew it might be true. "All the more reason not to tell him yet." He went toward the door. "I need a little more time, Van. Perhaps if I shuffle the cards again. At the least I need to go down to the manor to get clean clothes."

They emerged from the room and separated, but as Hawk walked to the manor, he couldn't seem to shuffle the cards into anything but disastrous patterns.

Who should suffer? Himself, for certain, but he was choosing the pain.

What of Con, or Clarissa?

What of the Dadswells, the Manktelows, and the Ashbees? Was Granny Muggridge to have the roof torn down around her head?

But at what point did the price of Hawkinville become too high?

Cut the loss.

It was a process he'd done often in the war, even when it meant choosing between one set of soldiers or another. Perhaps if he thought of everyone as troops of soldiers.

The option with the least loss was to elope with Clarissa. He would have the money, or at least the expectation of it. He knew the will, and the money came to her at her majority, regardless of what she did or whom she married. As her husband, he could easily borrow against it.

Hawkinville would be safe.

There would be a fighting chance of happiness for them. There was something deep and true between them, and he would work to gain her forgiveness for the deception.

Van might never forgive him for breaking his word, but he could hope that time would heal that, especially if he could make Clarissa happy.

Con. At the moment, Con was an unknown. If he saw this as a betrayal of the Rogues, it could lead to a rift. The Rogues certainly weren't going to like it. They were going to have to damn well trust him not to expose their criminal acts.

But it was the only way.

Gathering the detached purposefulness that had carried him through scenes of carnage, he went swiftly to his room to change, then gathered the money available in the house. He thought about leaving a note for the squire, but then knocked and entered his father's room.

The squire was lying on his daybed fondling—there was no other word—some papers. "They have come," he said, with shining eyes. "The documents. You may now officially call me Lord Deveril!"

Hawk had to stop himself from seizing the papers and ripping them to shreds. Pointless. Pointless.

This settled things, however. In moments his father could begin spreading the word. Since Clarissa was in the village, she would hear about it, and that would be the end of that.

"Congratulations, my lord. You may congratulate me, also. I am about to marry Miss Greystone."

His father beamed. "There, you see. All's well that ends well. And her money will pay to refurbish Gaspard Hall."

"Not a penny of her money will go on Gaspard Hall, my lord. We will pay off Slade, but the rest will remain under her control."

If he had to do this, it had to be that way.

"What? Are you mad? Leave a fortune in the grasp of a chit like that? I will not allow it."

"You will have no say in it." He turned toward the door. "I merely came to say that I will be gone a few days."

"Gone? Gone where? We must arrange a grand fête to announce my elevation to the village! I outrank Vandeimen now, and I'll see him recognize it."

The fury boiling inside Hawk threatened to burst out of control, but he'd not struck his father yet. Now was definitely not the time to start.

"It will have to wait, my lord. I am off to Gretna Green."

He closed the door on his father's protests—not about the elopement but about delay in his fête—and ran down the stairs. Somehow he had to get Clarissa out of the Peregrine and on the road north before his father set the news spreading.

He fretted even over the time it took a groom to saddle up Centaur, imagining his father leaning out of his window above to shout the news. He wouldn't do that, but he would tell his valet—might already have told his valet. His valet would tell the other servants and . . .

Perhaps a servant had already hurried home to spread the word.

He led Centaur up to the inn, considering how to steal Clarissa. Perhaps he'd have to snatch her on the way to the coach, like Lochinvar snatching his beloved from her wedding.

So light to the croup the fair lady he swung.
So light to the saddle before her he sprung!
"She is won! We are gone, over bank, bush, and scaur;
They'll have fleet steeds that follow," quoth young Lochinvar.

And that, of course, was the problem. He was dubious about young Lochinvar riding so rashly with a lady at his back, and he'd no intention of attempting it with Van and Con—especially Van, an incredible horseman now equipped by his rich bride with the finest horses—in hot pursuit.

He would have to go in and try to lure her out.

Then he saw Clarissa—beloved, unconventional, impetuous Clarissa—in the arch to the inn yard. Alone. Her hat shaded her face again, and some order had been brought to her curls, but her dress was irredeemably stained.

When he reached her, she stepped forward. "I've told them all what I did with Slade and that I kissed you, not the other way around."

If he hadn't adored her already, he'd have crumpled then. He held out his gloved hand. "Elope with me."

Her eyes widened, but she only said, "Why?"

"So that this can't be snatched from us."

She looked down and away, obviously flustered, but then back at him. "Do you love me, Hawk? Don't lie. Please don't lie."

"I adore you, Clarissa. And that is no lie."

Then she smiled and put her hand in his. "Then, of course. It's a mad, impetuous notion, but that probably suits us both."

He laughed as he swung his fair lady to the crupper and settled in front of her. "I used to be a very sane, thoughtful man," he said. "Hold tight. We're going over bank, bush, and scaur."

And he set off, past a few startled villagers, along the road that would eventually take them north to Scotland, where minors could still legally marry without the permission of parents, guardians, or Rogues.

But he soon turned off, going west instead of north. He couldn't outride Van. But, by heaven, he could probably still outthink him.

Chapter Twenty

〜

The rest of the party was in the entrance hall of the Peregrine, waiting with some impatience for Clarissa to return from the privy. Eventually, Maria asked Althea to find her, but Althea returned frowning. "She's not there. I don't know where she can have gone to. Perhaps she's returned to the room upstairs."

But then one of the Misses Weatherby trotted in, cheeks flushed. "My dear Lady Vandeimen!" she gasped. "Oh, my lords." She curtsied around, clearly breathless with excitement. "Are you by any chance looking for your companion? We saw you earlier. My sister and I. Saw you on the green, and returning. And the handsome major returning with the lady."

"Miss Weatherby," Maria interrupted ruthlessly. "Do you know where Miss Greystone is?"

"Why, yes," said the lady, not well concealing her glee. "She's just ridden off behind Major Hawkinville."

Maria looked at her husband. "Van?"

He'd turned pale with anger in a way she'd never seen before.

He was actually moving when she grasped his sleeve. "Wait! Talk." She smiled back at Miss Weatherby. "Thank you so much. I know I can trust you not to spread this around."

Unlikely hope, but it might stop the news for a minute or two. She didn't think there'd been any inn servants nearby to hear. She dragged her husband into the adjoining parlor, the rest following, and shut the door. She couldn't have done it if he'd resisted, so she knew she was right.

"I think he truly loves her," she said. "And I know she loves him."

But Miss Trist wrung her hands. "Why run off together? She's refused him, and he's abducted her!"

"Nonsense," Maria snapped. "Abduction is completely illegal these days. He can hardly drag her against her will to Scotland."

Van said, "I have to stop this, Maria. For everyone's sake. I'm sending a note up to Con."

He left before she could stop him again, and indeed, she wasn't sure she should. But he'd looked for a moment as if he would kill his friend.

Demon Vandeimen. Did she know what he was really capable of?

Van returned with a letter in his hand. "I've sent for Con. When he arrives, give him this."

Maria took it, but she knew he was setting off in pursuit. "Don't kill him, Van. For your own sake, don't."

He relaxed slightly. "I won't. I might beat him to a pulp, but I won't kill him." He kissed her quickly, tenderly, then rubbed at what must be lines in her brow. "Don't worry. This is a mess, but I'll find a way to bring it all out right."

"He hasn't abducted her," she said. "Clarissa's besotted with him, and I'd say he feels the same way about her. What's going on?"

"It's complicated." He kissed her again quickly, then left.

Maria could have screamed with frustration. Complicated! She'd give him complicated. She considered snapping the seal on the letter in hopes that it explained, but long training in proper behavior would not permit it.

Instead she called for tea and settled to soothing Althea. Poor Lord Trevor was looking as if he wished himself elsewhere, but he was bearing up like the well-trained officer he was.

It took remarkably little time for Con to turn up, though it had felt like an hour. He strode in, another man behind him.

"Mr. Nicholas Delaney," he said. "My guest at the moment, but he's probably involved." He took the letter, opened it, and read.

Then he passed it to his friend.

"Con," said Maria, "if you don't tell me what is going on, I am going to do someone serious injury."

He laughed, but sobered, looking around the room. "Ffyfe, I'm sure you're as curious as any human would have to be, but it would simplify things if you weren't here. And Miss Trist, you could help Miss Greystone as well by strolling on the green."

Lord Trevor accepted his orders remarkably well, but Althea looked around. "What's going on? Is Clarissa in danger?"

Lord Trevor took her arm. "Truly, Miss Trist, it would be simplest if we left. I trust Lord Amleigh to take care of everything."

Maria watched him coax Althea out of the room, and said, "He'll go far."

"Doubtless. Listen, Maria. The squire has mortgaged Hawkinville to Slade. More than mortgaged. He's deep in debt to the man, and Slade plans to tear down most of the village to build a preposterous villa on the river. Of course Hawk has to stop him."

"Of, course, but— Ah, I see. Clarissa's fortune. But why elope?"

"Because, according to Van's letter, the squire is about to become Lord Deveril. Sorry," he said, passing over the letter. "Read it yourself."

Maria took it and read quickly. "He really thought she would reject him for the name?"

"And for the deceit of it all. It was more a case, I assume, of him not being willing to risk everything on the chance that she might. It's the way Hawk's mind has learned to work. Pinpoint the one thing that must or must not happen and work toward it, damn the incidentals."

"Incidentals," Maria muttered, scanning through the letter again. "Some of this is so cryptic!"

"Judiciously so," said Mr. Delaney, whom she'd forgotten entirely, which was surprising, since he was a good-looking man with presence. "Con," he said, "you should follow to assist Vandeimen. I'll hold the fort here. Talking of things that must not happen, Clarissa must not marry Hawkinville without knowing the truth."

Con nodded and strode out, and he must have narrowly missed colliding with Althea rushing in. "That Miss Weatherby says that Major Hawkinville's father is now Lord Deveril! *Lord Deveril!*"

"We know," said Maria with a sigh. "Sit down, Althea, and have some more tea."

Thérèse Bellaire stood by the smithy, observing confusion on the village green and seething.

She'd been uneasy about that encounter with the heiress, though the girl had shown no sign of recognition. Her main concern, however, had been the relationship between the two. To her experienced eye it hadn't looked like a man bewitching a silly young woman, but like a man bewitched.

By love. The greatest traitor of all the emotions.

The Hawk was supposed to remove the heiress and leave the old man in possession of the money! If he married the heiress there would be three lives between her and victory. Two accidental deaths could be arranged. Three, however, would be perilously suspicious, especially if she survived as Squire Hawkinville's wealthy widow.

And now what was going on? One of the silly, nosy Weatherby sisters was flitting around in an ugly, over-ornamented bonnet. People were appearing from buildings like worms from bad apples.

Surely she'd seen Lord Vandeimen ride north out of the village. Not at a dangerous gallop, but with some urgency, and yet his wife's carriage had not left.

Then two men rode to the inn at speed.

Lord Amleigh, she thought, and . . .

Nicholas?

Danger skittered down her spine, but excitement too. Ah, if he was here it would become a great game. And perhaps she would have the chance of true revenge. There was his dull wife. And a child now, as well. She'd checked on him, and he rarely left their sides. What if they were here too?

She licked her lips. This was almost as good as a tender goat in her bed.

It would be so deliciously dangerous to go over to the other side of the green, to be close to the inn, where Nicholas might see her.

Would even Nicholas know her in this disguise?

She began to walk across the green, wondering whether she dared to go into the inn and seek a meeting to see if he would know her like this. If anyone would, he would. They had been so spicily intimate six years ago, when he had been so young, so tender. None other of her young conquests had been like him.

They had been so wickedly intimate two years ago, as well. Compelling him had added a delightful twist. If she held his child captive, would he surrender again?

Fatally tempting, but too much so. It was time to be sensible if she was to have the life she wanted. She would have her fortune back, or as much as she could get, and escape.

As she neared the groups of people, she heard the name Deveril.

"Why, Miss Rowland," said one of the Misses Weatherby. "Have you heard? Our dear squire has become Viscount Deveril! He has just received the news!"

"Amazing!" she said. "I must go and congratulate my cousin."

Miss Weatherby's scrawny face pinched. She and her sister had never quite believed the supposed connection. But then, both sisters were enamored of Squire Hawkinville in their pathetic, spinsterish way. What would they think to know that Thérèse could have him at a snap of her fingers because she provided flattery, a clever mouth, and opium?

One of the inn's grooms was out here, and he smiled his crooked-tooth grin. He was proof that she could still enslave men in this ugly guise. It was never entirely a matter of looks. So few women realized that.

Probably the poor man was bemused and guilty about the lustful urges he felt toward the drab foreign woman with the sick husband.

He sidled over. "Grand news, ain't it, ma'am?"

"Wonderful."

"And such a coming and going." He was almost bursting with news.

"Yes?" she asked, as if he were clever and important.

"Here's Lord and Lady Vandeimen at the inn with a party, visiting the village. And one of the young ladies has disappeared! Miss Weatherby,"—he tipped his head in the lady's direction—"she says she saw the lass off with Major Hawkinville on a horse! And," he added in a whisper, "now Lord Vandeimen's hurried off in a fine old mood. Known him since he was a lad, I have, and there'll be blows before the night's out, even if it is another George."

Sometimes the English idioms escaped her. She ignored the last comment, but inside she was cursing.

Eloped. She'd feared as much.

"And here's the other one arrived with a friend."

Since the groom clearly had no more to say, she thanked him and hurried down to the manor. The new Lord Deveril was of no use to her anymore, but it was best not to drop a part. And he would be good for a few guineas.

When she left, it was with guineas, and confirmation that the Hawk was off to Scotland with the heiress.

She paused to look at the bucolic setting and the robust English peasantry still gossiping. Thank God she could escape this place. If only she could set fire to its smug prettiness before she went.

She might try if not for the wet weather. It had doubtless left the thatch too sodden to catch.

She had survived a perilous life by recognizing when

to drop one plan and pick up another. She headed briskly for her home here.

She still had Lieutenant Rowland, and there was a chance of Nicholas's child. All was not lost. Possibly, just possibly, she could have her money and Nicky on his knees begging before it ended.

Once Althea was calmed, Maria looked at Mr. Delaney. "You're the leader of the Company of Rogues, aren't you? I heard of you from Sarah Yeovil, and of course some more from Van."

"Leader?" he said, looking strangely both relaxed and poised for action. "That was at Harrow. Now we're simply a group of friends."

Maria glanced at Althea, wishing she could send her away again. Sensible Lord Trevor had not reappeared.

"But what connection is there between a group of school friends and Clarissa that leads to you giving Con a command? Ah, no, I'm sure you'd call it some friendly advice."

His eyes sparkled with amusement. "The connection is Lord Arden," he said, and it was fencing for the hell of it. "He's a Rogue. His wife was one of Clarissa's schoolteachers and is by way of being a friend and mentor now."

"You Rogues are very willing to put yourselves out for each other, aren't you?"

"Of course. Is that not the root of friendship?"

They were interrupted by Lord Trevor, carrying Hawk's cat. "Lady Vandeimen? This cat's hanging around and making a nuisance of itself. Someone said it was the major's."

"It belongs at the manor, I suppose . . ." But Maria remembered Van saying the squire's dogs would eat it.

The cat leaped out of Lord Trevor's arms and up onto the table to look around with what could only be described as severe annoyance. Maria sketched the rescue story for Delaney, and he laughed. "I'll take her up to the Court and try to keep her there until Hawkinville returns. One certainty in all this is that he will return."

He picked up the cat, and though still radiating grievance, she stayed in his arms. "What do you wish to do now, Lady Vandeimen? There is nothing you can accomplish here, I think."

Maria sympathized with the cat's feelings. "I am not one of your Rogues, Mr. Delaney." Even so, she rose. "I see that I get the task of explaining to Clarissa's chaperon that I have allowed her to be carried off to a clandestine marriage."

He put on a look of mild alarm. "Definitely. I'm not going to take that news to Arabella Hurstman."

"You know the lady, I see," she said, pulling on her gloves.

"Oh, yes. I asked her to take care of Clarissa."

"Nepotism!" gasped Althea, who was looking dazed.

He glanced at her. "Did she say that? She would. As it happens, she's godmother to my daughter. Tell her that Arabel is nearby and will come to visit when this is straightened out—if she doesn't eat anyone in the meantime."

"Your child has cannibalistic tendencies, Mr. Delaney?"

He grinned. "More than likely. But I was referring to Miss Hurtsman. Don't worry. This all seems high drama at the moment, but it will sort out readily enough with a little attention."

"Indeed! What a shame you weren't involved in the war."

Though he scarcely twitched, it hit home, and she shepherded Althea out of the room regretting her sharp words. She was irritated at being excluded from the inside circle, however, and deeply worried about Van.

All had been delightful since their marriage, but it wasn't that long since he'd tried to blow his brains out. His estates were in no danger, and he had many reasons to live, but some of those reasons were rooted in Hawk in the Vale and the Georges.

What would happen if this caused a deep breach with Hawk?

They climbed into the waiting carriage, and Lord Trevor appeared, leading his horse, ready to escort them.

Such an excellent young man, and thank heavens he'd been spared both physically and mentally by the war.

Unlike Con. Con had left to follow Van, but she suddenly realized that Con could be put in a position of having to choose between two groups of friends.

She almost left the carriage, driven to stay here. But why? There was nothing she could do. Whatever happened would happen far from here, presumably on the road north. Could Hawk really outrace Van? What would happen when Van caught them?

Van said that Con was the steady one, the one who had anchored them to prevent extremes. But the Con Somerford she had known in the past weeks did not strike her as rock solid, even with Susan and his new happiness.

Van said it was Waterloo, and the loss of his fellow Rogue, Dare Debenham, there.

Maria had known Dare. His mother, the Duchess of Yeovil, was a distant cousin. Dare had been a young man put on earth to make others smile, and Sarah Yeovil had not even begun to recover from his loss, especially as there had been no body to bury. It had taken months for her to accept that he was gone.

Con Somerford hadn't deceived himself that way, but apparently, despite all reason, he blamed himself, as if he could have nursemaided Dare through the battle and kept him safe.

He couldn't afford to lose another friend.

Chapter Twenty-one

Tollgates, thought Van, were a very useful institution. Not only did they provide the funding for decent roads, they marked the passage of travelers, especially unusual ones such as a man with a lady up behind him.

When he joined the London road, the keeper of the first tollbooth north told him that no such couple had gone that way, on horse, by carriage, or on foot. Of course. Hawk would hardly try to outrace him on the direct route, double-laden.

He had to turn back toward Brighton to check the side roads, but there were dozens of them weaving off into a complex network linking village to village. Damn Hawk. He was going to have to waste hours, and he didn't have the patient nature for this kind of work.

Con might follow, so he left a quick note with the tollkeeper explaining his actions, and saying that he would leave a clue on the signposts of the roads he went down. It would be one of their old boyhood signs. A twist of wheat. The fields were full of it.

Then he turned back, stopping to ask anyone he passed if they'd seen the couple, and also to cut a handful of wheat from the edge of a field. He turned off onto the first side road after sticking a crude wheat dolly in a crack on the top of the signpost.

Damn Hawk! He'd throttle him when he caught him. And yet a part of him hoped his friend would get away, marry Clarissa, and that it would all somehow work out for the best.

Hawk followed side roads and did some cross-country work, though he couldn't jump hedges with Clarissa at his back. They didn't talk and he was glad of it. He didn't know what to say.

Speed wasn't important at this point; concealment was. At an out-of-the-way village he stopped at a small inn and asked if anyone in the area would have a gig to hire out. Luck was with him, and Mr. Idler, the squint-eyed innkeeper, admitted to having one available himself. "Mostly used to go to market day, sir."

Despite the squint, Hawk assessed the man as honest, and the type to hold his own counsel. "May I hire your gig, sir, for a week or more?"

The man pursed his lips. "A week or more, sir? That'd be a bit of an inconvenience."

"I'd pay very well. And I'd leave my horse as security."

The man's eyes sharpened, and he went over to give Centaur an expert scrutiny. "Nice beast," he said, but he still looked suspicious. "Where you and the lady be going, then, sir?"

Hawk gave him the true answer. "Gretna Green. But I'll only take the gig as far as London. Perhaps not even so far as that. I won't be able to return it until we come back, though."

The man looked between them, then fixed his eyes— more or less—on Clarissa. "You going willingly, miss?"

Hawk watched her response. She smiled brilliantly. "Oh, yes. And I'm not being duped by a worthless rascal, either. My companion is an army officer who served well with the Duke of Wellington."

Mr. Idler was not impressed. "There's many a gallant soldier no sane woman would want to husband, miss, but that's your affair." He turned to Hawk. "Right, then, sir."

They settled terms quickly, then Idler added, "Your lady might want a cloak, sir. I could sell you one my daughter left behind for a shilling."

The deal was struck, and Clarissa climbed into the gig wearing a typical hooded country cloak of bright-red wool over the shambles of her fashionable gown. She smiled down at the innkeeper and said, "Thank you. You've been very kind."

"Aye, well, I hope so."

Hawk extended his hand to the man, and after a surprised moment, Idler shook it. "I'll take good care of your horse, sir. But if you're not back here in a few weeks with my gig, I'll sell it."

"Of course. I make no demands on you, but if my lady's brothers should happen by, we would appreciate it if you didn't tell them of our business."

But Idler didn't make any promises. "Depends on what they say, sir, and what I make of them."

Hawk laughed. "As is your right. My thanks for your help."

He climbed up, accepted Clarissa's bright smile wishing he were worthy of it, and set a rough course east to pick up the Worthing road north of Horsham and work his way to London by that roundabout route.

They went four hours on the Worthing-to-London road, able to make only a steady pace because of the one horse. He wanted to push closer to London, but the sun set and then darkness crept in, with rain threatening. Hawk turned off into a narrow road to a village called Mayfield, which he hoped would have some sort of inn.

He halted the gig partway, however. "We'll have to stop here for the night. Any regrets?"

She looked at him with a calm, direct gaze. "None, except that you can't tell me why."

He was tempted, but he said, "No, I can't. But we'll stay here as brother and sister."

She smiled as if she was hiding laughter. "No one will believe it. We look completely unalike. We might as well stay as husband and wife. It is what we will be, isn't it?"

His heart began to thump, but she was right. "Yes, it is." He dug in his pocket and took out the rings he'd brought—a plain gold band, and the one with the smooth ruby between two hearts.

"It's been the betrothal ring in my family since Elizabethan times," he said, taking her left hand and sliding the ring onto her finger. "A perfect fit. We do seem to be fated."

"I think so." She blinked away tears. "I didn't know I could be so happy as this. And the other?"

He held it in his fingers. "My mother's wedding ring. I'm not sure we want to use it. She wore it all her life, but apparently refused to be buried with it."

She closed his hand around the ring. "You are not your father, Hawk, and neither am I. We are marrying because we love each other. Nothing else matters." She opened his hand again to look at the ring. "I wish I could wait until we say our vows, but I suppose I should wear it."

Her complete trust was undermining him, but he'd known how it would be. Rather as a man facing amputation knows how it will be. Knows it has to be.

He slid the ruby ring back off her finger and put the gold band on. "With this ring," he said to her, "I promise that I will always cherish you, Clarissa, and will do everything in my power to make your life happy."

He meant every word, but even so they were tainted by what was really going on.

She shone without reservation. He put the ruby ring above the other and clicked the tired horse into motion again. "We'll wait until the real vows are said before we go any further with this, of course."

She didn't say anything, but when he glanced at her she was smiling in a damned mysterious manner.

The Dog and Partridge was small, but the buxom landlady admitted to a room for the night. He didn't think she believed for a moment that they were married, even with the rings, but she was willing to mind her own business.

He saw Clarissa blush as they were led upstairs and into a clean, surprisingly spacious bedroom, but she showed no sign of doubt or hesitation. What would he do if she did begin to get cold feet? Compel her to go through with it?

Impossible.

The woman lit a lamp and went to arrange their washing water and their dinner. Then they were alone.

As well as the bed, the room contained a table and chairs, and two good-sized armchairs with cushions on the seats. A washstand occupied one corner and a chamber pot another, both with screens, thank heavens, though he would use the outside convenience.

Clarissa hung up her cloak, then sat in a chair. "I'm astonishingly happy. But, then, you know I have an impatient nature. Waiting weeks for a church wedding would have been torture. I only wish it were possible to fly to Gretna Green."

Hawk laughed, wondering if it sounded like a groan. "I wish that too."

He meant that he'd not have to worry about pursuit anymore, and would be sooner done with deception, but he saw her take it as a longing for her delightful body naked in a bed with him.

Another groan threatened. He did long, and from her slight, totally wicked smile, he feared his bride longed too.

How the devil had it come to this? And yet this was the only option that would save the village and give at least a fragile chance of winning Clarissa too. But if he didn't win her . . .

He could shoot himself. Hawk in the Vale would be saved.

But then it would end up sold when the squire died with no heir. Damnation. He had to get her with child to see this through?

After a knock, the door opened to admit two maids with their meal and jugs of washing water. He gave them their vails and they curtsied out.

Hawk pulled himself together. He'd never been one to do things halfheartedly. These moody silences didn't serve at all. He smiled at Clarissa. "Do you want to wash first, or eat?"

"Eat," she said with a grin. "But I'll wash my face and hands at least. I am starving, though. I was in too much of a tizzy to eat much at lunch." She looked at him, rosy with some kind of humorous guilt. "I'd vowed to propose to you, you see, if you didn't get around to it. I wasn't leaving Hawkinville without trying to capture you."

He could not resist. He went over and kissed her. "I am certainly thoroughly snared."

"No regrets?" she said to him, direct and sober.

He couldn't flat-out lie. "Given a different world, Falcon, I would rather have married you in a church before your friends. But I do not regret the marriage."

It was enough to make her smile. Soon they sat to their meal, divided by large amounts of very welcome food.

It seemed almost inappropriate to be so hungry at such a time, but life marched on in the midst of even the most extraordinary events.

Clarissa considered it unfortunate that the chairs had been placed at either end of the table. It put five feet between them. All the same, they were alone, and in a more steadily intimate situation than they'd ever been.

And, by some miracle, on their way to their wedding.

With only one bed for the night.

Her heartbeat was already fast, but she was willing to wait for the first seductive moves.

Hawk poured wine into her glass and indicated the plates. "It's probably best if we help ourselves."

Though she'd honestly claimed hunger, now she wasn't sure she could eat, but she took a chicken breast and some vegetables, then sipped her wine, watching him in the pool of lamplight.

It touched gold in his hair and picked out the handsome lines of his face and the elegance of his hands. Was it kind to her? A flutter of uncertainty at her appearance started inside. The small mirror had told her that neatness, as usual, had totally escaped her. Perhaps she should have asked to borrow his comb. He'd used it to restore his usual elegance.

Then he looked up, and something heated danced in his eyes that smoothed the flutter away. He raised his glass to her. "To our future. May it be all you deserve."

She raised her own. "And all you deserve, too."

As she sipped, she saw a twitch of expression.

"Hawk! Don't you think you deserve happiness?"

"You forget. Any future is built on the past."

It was as if Deveril were trying to bully his way into the room. She should tell him before he committed himself . . .

But she thrust it away. "Tonight, can't we forget about the past?"

"The past is always beneath our feet. Without it, we walk on nothing."

"Perhaps without it, we fly."

And he smiled as if the shadows fled. "Perhaps we do, wise Falcon. Perhaps we do. Eat. You'll regret it later if you don't."

"Advice from experience?" she asked, but she cut into the tender chicken and made herself eat a mouthful. Then she discovered that she was hungry, and she ate a few more forkfuls of food in silence.

"See?" he said, his lips twitching.

Lamentably, she flicked a piece of bean at him.

He caught it in his mouth. "Army tricks. Never waste food."

They laughed together and she thought, *friend.*

She'd had friends at school, some of whom she'd felt close to, but she'd never felt as she did about Hawk. She didn't know how to say it—it seemed almost childish—but it was a warm glow near her heart. Something steady and dependable. Unlike the rather frantic burning of her love.

She talked a bit about Miss Mallory's and he shared some of his time at his school, Abingdon.

"Van, Con, and I went to different schools," he said. "Different family traditions. And I think our families thought a little variety would be good for us. Part of the purpose of schooling is to make useful connections, after all."

"Did you enjoy it?"

"Time away from the manor was always pleasant."

She sensed a hard truth being delivered. "We won't let your father destroy our happiness, Hawk."

"I pray not." But he didn't seem to believe it.

She chattered for a while about Brighton matters, but something was disturbing that warm glow of friendship like a chill draft playing on a candle flame.

They might as well talk of serious matters. "How long will it take us to get to Scotland?"

"Three days, with good speed."

"Can we elude pursuit?"

He pushed away his plate still half full. He hadn't touched it for some time. "I hope so. Van doubtless has murder on his mind." He picked up the decanter of claret. "More wine?"

She wasn't used to a lot of wine and had already drunk two glasses, but she accepted more. "He'll never catch us on this route."

"It will be luck if he does. He does, however, have amazing luck." He shrugged and filled his own glass. "We'll be in London tomorrow and can arrange some disguise and then speed north."

She looked down at her stained and muddy dress. "I'll treasure this dress, though. It has very special memories." That flicked her mind to something else. "Do you know, during the journey I've been thinking about the horrible Mrs. Rowland. I know her from somewhere."

"Where?" he asked, eyes suddenly alert. "Is there anything else to the feeling? Any connection?"

She laughed. "Always the Hawk! It wasn't anything dire or suspicious. Just curious. I wish I could pin it down."

He'd relaxed again, but she thought his eyes still seemed intent. He'd told her he couldn't resist a mystery, and it seemed to be true. She was definitely right to be binding him.

"Well, then," he said, "where might you have met her?"

"That's it. I have no idea. You have to understand, Hawk, I haven't led a very adventurous life."

He laughed, and she protested, "I haven't! Things have

happened to me recently, but most of my life has been positively boring. The only place I might have met her was last year in London."

"More or less at the time of Waterloo, when Lieutenant Rowland was in Belgium fighting and being wounded. It would be strange if his wife and children were in London then."

"And I'm sure I never encountered a Belgianwoman. I was restricted to fashionable circles, and rarely escaped my mother's eye." She shook her head. "It's probably a mistake. Some people look like others."

"But you aren't confusing her with someone else, are you?"

She could only shrug. That faint sense of recognition was becoming less substantial by the minute. The talk had passed some time, but she was no longer interested.

"Never mind," he said, one finger stroking the long stem of his glass. It reminded her of his stroking of Jetta, and of how very much she wanted him to be stroking her.

She couldn't bear it. She stood and carried her wineglass around to his side of the table.

Their eyes locked for a moment, and then he pushed back his chair, inviting her to sit on his lap. An invitation she took, heart racing, heat surging through her.

It must be the wine, but it was magical.

"Another adventure," she said, adjusting herself and looping her free hand around his neck. "I've never sat on a man's lap before."

"As usual, you get the idea very quickly." He accepted her daring kiss, then one hand rose to cradle the back of her head. His lips opened and she settled, melted, into a deep joining.

After a languorous time, their mouths parted and he whispered, "Do I want to know what other adventures you have planned?"

"Plan?" she said, exploring his jaw, his ear with her lips. "I'm a creature of impulse."

"Heaven protect me. What impulse drives you?"

"I think you know."

He moved her apart a little. "Clarissa, I promised Van that I wouldn't seduce you."

"I didn't promise anything."

She swooped in for another kiss, but he held her away. His face was flushed, his breathing unsteady. "I think perhaps you're unaccustomed to wine . . ."

"Not that unaccustomed." She cradled his face, feeling the roughness of a day's beard on his cheeks. "Why wait? What if they do manage to stop us?"

"Then it would be better."

"Or our marriage would be essential."

He captured her hands and held them away. "Clarissa—"

"There's only one bed. Where are you going to sleep?"

"On the floor. I've done it before."

"You've *eloped* before?" she teased.

The look in his eyes filled her with a sense of extraordinary power. She could hardly believe that she was doing this—trying to seduce a man. She, Clarissa, the plain one that no man ever looked twice at.

But she was, and she was winning, and it didn't seem so extraordinary, so ridiculous. She could feel it in his hands, still controlling her wrists, and see it in his eyes. She could sense it in the very air around them.

His scarce-checked desire.

For her.

For her.

"What would you do if I started to undress here, in front of you?"

His eyes closed with what looked like pain.

"You'd like it?" she asked, astonished to hear it come out in an almost Jetta-like purr.

"Would I like to be burned to a cinder?"

"Well, would you?"

His lids lifted, heavily. "It's every man's deepest longing."

That might be teasing, but she knew it went deeper than that. It was hunger.

She leaned forward, letting him keep control of her

hands, to brush her lips across his. "Make love to me tonight, Hawk. It is my deepest longing."

His lips moved beneath hers for a moment, then slid away. "What if you change your mind, if you decide you don't want to marry me?"

"You think I will be so disappointed?" she teased.

He avoided her lips again. "Clarissa, I'm trying to be noble, dammit. If anything prevents our marriage, you'd be ruined."

"Are you saying you won't marry me?"

"No. But you may change your mind."

"You forget. I'm in love with your house."

He laughed, and rolled his head back, eyes closed. "Think. You might get with child."

She nibbled down his neck. "So, I'll be the even more scandalous Devil's Heiress. I don't care."

"The child might."

"Then I'll buy it a father. But, Hawk, I want you. Nothing is going to change my mind. I love you."

His lids lifted, heavily. "You said you loved my home."

"And you. If Slade tears down Hawkinville Manor, I will still love you. But he won't do that. We are on our way to our wedding to prevent it."

He swallowed. She felt it.

"Do you feel your feet sliding, Falcon?" he said softly. "Love only greases the path. It doesn't promise a safe landing."

"Some paths lead to heaven."

"Downward?"

She chuckled and moved her lips downward, nuzzling at the edge of his collar. "It would seem so . . ."

Dimly, somewhere far away in the house, a clock began to chime. She decided to kiss his neck and jaw for each chime, and ended at ten. "Ten fathoms deep," she breathed against his skin.

He released her hand to hold her off at the shoulders. "I surrender to the depths."

Triumphant, sizzling, she relaxed away from him, and he raised her left hand to his mouth. "I give you my love and allegiance, Falcon. I swear that if this falls apart, it will be at your desire, not mine."

"Then it will never fall apart."

He slid her from his knee to lead her to the bed.

"Electricity," she said.

"Lightning."

"Yes." She knew she was blushing, but she didn't mind. Despite *The Annals of Aphrodite,* she was unclear about what was going to happen here, but she didn't mind that either.

She simply waited, for Hawk.

He raised his hands to her hair, which she knew was a mess. "I suppose your maid arranged this carefully this morning. Does that seem a very long time ago?"

"A mere century or two."

"And the destruction is considerable." Pins fell to the floor, and his fingers threaded into her curls. "But it is rioting, tempestuous hair, like its owner." His eyes met hers. "And as lovely."

"You like storm and riot?"

"Very much." He raised her hair and let it fall. "It catches the lamplight in a net of fire."

He lowered his hands and turned her to the bed. It was set high, and steps stood ready for them to climb into it. Should she take off her clothes yet, or would he do that for her?

He dropped her hand to pull off the buttercup-yellow coverlet. Meticulously, he folded it and put it on the chest that sat at the base of the bed. Then he folded down the other covers, exposing a large expanse of pure white sheet.

The precise preparations stirred a pang of panic. "Won't I bleed?"

"The people here must suspect what is going on. If it bothers you, we can stop now."

"Oh, no." Then she plunged into honesty. "It's just that this suddenly frightens me, but in the spiciest way. Does that make sense?"

He put his hands on her waist and lifted her to sit on the high bed. "Of course. It frightens me, too. Because I want it too much."

He was looking into her eyes as if searching for doubts, for retreat. She smiled and leaned forward to kiss him.

He laughed, broke free. "Stay there."

He went to pile the remains of their meal on the tray, then put it outside the door.

"You think of everything," she said, and heard a touch of a pout in it.

He came back toward her. "That is my reputation." He went to his knees and began to unlace her right half boot.

Clarissa sat there, feeling slightly like a child, but at his touch, intensely woman. Keen anticipation suddenly swirled inside her.

And impatience.

"I feel," she said, looking down at his bent head, "that at a moment like this I should be wearing satin slippers, not muddy shoes."

"At least they're leather." He put the right one on the floor and began on the left. "The mud and water don't seem to have soaked through to your stockings."

She flexed the toes of her liberated right foot. Her daisy-embroidered stockings were pretty, but sturdy. "I should be wearing silk stockings, too."

He glanced up, smiling. "For a day in the country? I'd think you a flighty piece."

"You don't think me a flighty piece?"

He discarded her left boot. "Hmmmm. Now that you come to speak of it . . ."

He began to slide his hands up her leg beneath her skirts, making her stir and catch her breath.

"Is this . . . is this the way it's usually done?"

"What?" He met her eyes, but his hands continued to move up.

"Is the gentleman supposed to remove a lady's shoes and stockings? Is that part of it?"

His lips twitched. "Are you going to analyze every step?"

"This is a very important experience for me, you know."

"Yes, I think I know that."

His hands found her garter, and undid the knot by feel,

sending the most extraordinary feelings up the inside of her thigh.

"There are a thousand ways to make love, Clarissa. Doubtless more. If this was our wedding night, I might have left you with your maid to undress and get into bed, then joined you later." He looked down again, and pushing her skirts up to her knee, rolled down her stocking.

"I bought those yesterday," she said softly. "With you in mind."

"And they are much appreciated." His voice seemed suddenly husky, and she couldn't contain a smile, even though her heart was beating so deeply she wondered if she might faint.

Dazedly, she watched her pale leg reveal itself. Doubts stirred. It was a very ordinary leg.

He stroked his fingers up and down her shin, then raised her foot to kiss her instep. "This is definitely an argument for anticipating marriage."

"What? Oh, no maid et cetera . . ."

"Precisely."

"So many places to kiss."

"And I intend to kiss every one."

So many places on him to kiss, she thought. Would she be brave enough to kiss every one?

Then he explored for the garter of the left stocking. Clarissa leaned back on her elbows, closing her eyes in order to concentrate on the feel of his hands. She felt unsteady. Quivery. She wasn't sure she wasn't actually quivering.

When he kissed her left instep, his hand cradled her foot warmly to raise it, fingers brushing against the side of her heel. Then his hands slid slowly back up her legs, opening the way for cool air. He was pushing her skirts up now.

She truly did quiver, for he must be close to her naked privacy.

Lips hot on the top of each knee in turn, hands stroking the length of her thighs.

Then he pulled her up and lifted her off the bed to stand.

Chapter Twenty-two

~

She opened dazzled eyes to see him framed in a halo from the lamp. "This is remarkable."

He laughed, and it seemed to be with unshadowed pleasure. "I hope it becomes even more so." He pulled her suddenly close for a kiss. "You're not at all afraid, are you?"

"Is there anything to be afraid of?"

"A little pain?"

She shrugged. "I'm sure it hurt to swing on ropes across the wilderness."

"That was Van, not me."

"But you'd have been next, wouldn't you?"

He grinned. "We'd already argued over it. And you're right. I wouldn't have counted the scrapes and bruises." He raised a hand and brushed some hair off her cheek, back behind her ear.

"But lovemaking is dangerous, Falcon. Be warned. At its best or its worst it takes us to places beyond the ordinary. Beyond swinging ropes, beyond battle, even. The French call it the little death. They believe that for a moment the heart stops and all bodily sensations cease, so that return to life is both exquisite delight and exquisite agony."

She quivered again, deep inside, with hunger. "Can it be like that the first time?"

He laughed, or it might have been a groan. "If I can

possibly make it so. Which at the moment," he added, turning her to unfasten her dress, "might come down to a question of how long I can stand this torture."

"Torture?" she asked, shrugging out of the dress.

"Only moderate so far. Corsets, however, are the very devil."

She giggled, but could only wait as he unknotted and loosened her laces. She turned then. "I can get out of this and my shift while you undress. Or do you need me to help you?"

"That would probably be my undoing." He began to rip off his clothes, as she struggled out of the corset. He was watching her in a way that brought back every scrap of that sense of female power, and she was clumsy with humming excitement.

He pulled off his shirt, and she froze, corset dangling from her failing fingers. Not so massive as the groom in Brownbutton's stableyard, but the stuff of maidens' dreams all the same, with ridged muscles down his belly and curved ones in his arms.

There was a dark mark above his right breast. She let the corset fall and walked over to him.

"The tattoo," she said. "I see it at last."

"Didn't you always know you would?"

She smiled up at him. "Yes. This was inevitable from the first day, wasn't it?" She raised her left hand to trace the purple lines. "A *G* and a hawk?"

"Van was a demon. Con a dragon."

"Why?"

"Why do sixteen-year-old boys do most of the things they do? Because one of them suggests it, and it seems like a good idea at the time. We wanted to be able to recognize one another's mangled bodies."

She shuddered and with her left hand on the tattoo, she ran her right down a jagged scar in his side. "You could have died before we met."

"True, though I didn't have a very dangerous war."

"What was this, then?" she asked, still touching the scar.

"A chance to swing over the wilderness. If staff duties

were light, we were sometimes given permission to join the fighting forces."

She looked up. "And I suppose you leaped at it."

He seemed surprised by her tone. "Of course. Can't you imagine how frustrating it is to be surrounded by the fever of battle—the electricity—and not be caught up in it?" He ran a hand up her side to stroke the curve of her breast. "Rather as if we were to be suspended like this for the rest of our lives, never to fall fully into the madness of desire."

At the look in his eyes, and the tantalizing touch, a shudder passed through her, a shudder of pleasure and pain such as she had never even imagined. She felt as if she contained seething power between her two hands. His heat, his breathing, his controlled patience . . .

She leaned closer to press her cheek against his hot, smooth skin. He sucked in a deep breath, moving against her like a wave, and she let her hands slide around him, encircle him, pressing to him so only the fine cotton of her shift lay between their bodies.

"What would I have done if you had died?" she murmured.

His arms came around her. "Found some other man to love."

"It doesn't seem possible."

"It doesn't, does it?" His head rested against hers. "When I watched you at the manor house today, standing near the sundial, surrounded by roses, it was as if a missing piece had fallen into my life. I give you fair warning, Falcon. You will have to fight to be free of my hood and jesses."

She smiled into his skin. "As will you. And a falcon, remember, is a superior bird to a hawk."

She heard a hum, presumably of pleasure. "The thought of you hunting me down," he said, "almost tempts me to fly."

"I have claws to catch you with." She lightly pressed her nails into his back.

His inhaled breath swayed her again. "Have you any idea," he said, "how perfectly happy I am at this moment? Or, come to think of it, it's more a state of perfectly happy anticipation."

Understanding, she moved back, though she would willingly have stood like that, so intimately close, for hours longer.

He sat on the bed and urgently pulled off his boots. She went to help, tossing first one, then the other aside. She put hands to his right stocking, but he seized her, swinging her onto the bed, and falling on her with a ravishing kiss.

At last!

She wrapped her arms and legs around him, kissing him back, pressing a burning, aching need against him. Then he broke contact, freed himself to pull off her shift.

Thus, finally, she was naked, and fear hit her. Not fear of joining, but fear of disappointing.

He put a hand to her breast, slid it down over her ribs, her hip, her thigh, then back up again. "You are so beautiful," he murmured.

"You don't have to lie to me."

He looked up at her. "I'm not lying, love. Don't you know? Your legs, your hips, your breasts . . . You're cream and gold and honey. A perfect, delicious sweetmeat."

He suddenly swooped down and licked, licked up her belly, around her breast.

She had a beautiful *body*? She'd never thought beyond her plain face, but the way he was cherishing her with touch and gaze, the hunger she sensed in every touch, tempted her to believe. The perfect jewel in a perfect day. He was taking pleasure, true pleasure, in her body.

He tongued her nipple, making her catch her breath, mostly in anticipation. This she already knew, and she remembered the way he'd been swept beyond sense in the wilderness.

She wanted to do that to him again.

Again and again.

Forever . . .

He suckled her, first gently, then more deeply, and she arched. "Hurry," she said. "Hurry."

"Patience," he murmured. "Patience."

"I don't want to be patient!"

"Trust me."

He slipped away from her breast and began to lick slowly toward the other one.

She punched at his shoulders with both fists.

He laughed.

Loving the feel of his broad shoulders, she began to knead them. She loved the feel of his tongue, too, though not as much as the suckling.

He hummed again, approvingly, so she kneaded him some more, more deeply as he suckled, kneading her need into his deep muscles again and again.

Her leg was rubbing against his and his breeches bothered her. "Undress," she commanded.

He pushed away from her, and she grabbed for him. "No, don't stop."

"Patience," he said, laughing and escaping. "A little waiting will definitely do you good."

She sat up, hands on hips, pretending annoyance, not having to pretend frustration at their separation. But it was almost worth it to watch as he stripped off his remaining clothes.

He stepped out of his drawers and looked at her, and suddenly his jutting manly part grew larger, rising.

"Oh, my," she said. "I thought the pictures exaggerated."

"Pictures?" He climbed back on the bed and gently pushed her down.

"Men have books, and women steal them." She was still looking at his Rod of Rapture, wondering if the book was right, and he would like her Felicitous Fingers. "Some of the girls brought interesting treasures back to school."

"But you didn't quite believe them? From what I've seen of such books, you were very wise." He captured her face and looked into her eyes. "Are you frightened, love?"

She thought about it. Something was beating in her, but she didn't think it was fear. She certainly didn't want to stop. "What I'm feeling is nothing I've ever experienced before."

He kissed her, laughing. "Still analyzing."

Despite the fluttering inside and outside of her skin, she chuckled. "Of course. I don't want to miss or forget any of this. Perhaps I should keep a diary."

"Now that would shock our grandchildren." His hand had found her breast again.

Grandchildren. An astonishingly beautiful thought.

Grandchildren at Hawkinville.

"I'd write it in code," she murmured, dazed by his touch. "The first sight of you. The first feel of your skin. The special smell of your body. My own strange state. Your every touch . . ."

His hand stilled. "It is somewhat disconcerting, you know, to think of you taking notes."

She looked at him. "Hawk, are you nervous?"

"You think I'm not?" When she just looked at him, he said, "I want this to be perfect for you, my heart. But perfection really isn't possible."

She smiled and ran her hand through his hair. "Whatever it is, it will be perfect."

He kissed her quickly. "Continue to take notes, then," he said, and turned his attention to her breasts.

"I like that," she said. "Oh! I feel as if I'm coming down with a fever. But not at all ill. Uncomfortable, though. Inside."

His hand slid down. "Perhaps I can heal that." He paused to circle her navel; then his fingers pushed into the hair between her thighs, close to the tingling ache.

She followed every touch and sensation in her mind, marveling.

"Open for me, sweetheart."

When had she pushed her thighs so tightly together? She hastily spread them, breath held, and his fingers slid deeper.

Slid. She could feel moisture there. "The Delectable Dew of Deliquescent Desire . . ."

"What?"

She hadn't realized that she'd spoken aloud. "A book called it that."

"A bedazzling book of bridal bemusement?"

Laughing, she said, *"The Annals of Aphrodite.* It was rather alliterative."

"So I hear. You are Definitely Delectable."

"Impossibly Impatient?"

"Dauntingly Demanding."

They collapsed into laughter, but he looked at her. "Don't you think perhaps we could take this seriously?"

"Why?"

"Because I'm becoming Desperately Desirous."

He was ruffled and rosy. She laughed again at all the *r*'s, but said, "Then I am Wonderfully Willing."

He pressed his hand back between her thighs. "But not Rapturously Ready, my Pulchritudinous Pleasure."

Beautiful pleasure. She didn't know if she was truly beautiful, but he was, and this was, made more so by the blessing of laughter. She would never have imagined being in a bed with a naked man entwined in laughter.

Her hips rose of their own accord to greet his fingers, and an ache intensified. Passion's Penultimate Pang. They were near the end?

It was deep, deep inside her. Where he would go.

Soon, she prayed. Soon.

"Does that feel good?" he asked.

"Oh, yes. But . . ."

He began to circle his hand. "Better?"

All the feelings seemed to rush to the place he pressed on, and her hips pushed up again. "Oh! The Precious Pearl of Eden's Ecstasy."

"Probably." He laughed into her dazed eyes. "By all means, tell me what else you recognize as we go."

"The Wanton Wave of Womanly Welcome," she gasped as her body rose up and fell of its own accord. "I tried it. Stroking the Precious Pearl . . . It was pleasant, but not like this!"

Her body seemed to clench itself painfully, but she wanted more.

"Books for men tend to emphasize the delicacy of the

pearl," he murmured into her ear. "Those for women should doubtless emphasize firmness. Tell me if I hurt you."

His hand pressed harder, and his mouth settled hot against her breast. Something shot between his mouth and his hand, and Clarissa let out a little shriek. "The Searing Spear of Sensual Sublimation!"

Her senses were firing off into sparks and sparkles, but she tried to comment as he'd asked, "And . . . the Final Fragrant Fragmentation. Oh, my! Don't stop!"

"I won't."

She wanted to push back, so she did, again and again, desperately seeking something that wasn't alliterative at all.

And then she died.

She felt it. That sudden, perfect stop, then the torrent of sensation that left her shaking and breathless.

Then he moved over her, and as her mind came together she realized that it wasn't his hand anymore.

It was him against her.

She was still quivering and aching, and she caught back a cry, not sure if it was of need or protest. Her body seethed with sensitivity, but he was forcing her hips wide, forcing her open in a way his fingers had not. She felt impaled—

She stifled the shriek, but then said, "That hurt!" and was shocked back to the real and awkward world.

He stilled. "Are you all right?"

She wanted to say no, that she needed time to get used to this, that perhaps they should try again another day. But she could sense his tense desperation, and could imagine what he might be feeling.

"Of course," she said, trying for laughter again. "The . . . Perfumed Portal has been Pierced." Oh, but she was invaded. "So it's time for the . . . Masculine Mastery of Maidenly Mysteries."

"Not maidenly anymore," he said, but she was rewarded by his abrupt surrender to his needs.

The Fearful Phallic Ferocity. She knew just what the *Annals* had meant.

Again, and again, and again.

She could bear it, she could bear it, she could bear it.

But then pain faded and other feelings flowed back. Fierce, thunderous feelings, shared with him. She found she was meeting his movements, harder and harder, thrust for thrust.

The Joyous Joust!

Then he froze. She could feel the rigid tension in every inch of his muscular body. She opened her eyes to revel in the sight of him, beautiful in the light and shadow of this perfect room, lost in the little death.

Oh, yes, making love was a very dangerous thing. They were more than naked here. They were naked to the soul.

He relaxed as if the Wave of Womanly Welcome had rolled over him, and collapsed to kiss her in the way she needed to be kissed. In the way that expressed the shattering experienced.

Then he rolled to the side, still tangled with her, to hold her close. They were plastered together at every possible point, sealed by sweat, and she found it impossible to imagine ever being separated again, even by clothes.

They were one. Forever. Indivisible.

She kissed his chest, then wriggled up to kiss his mouth, then looked into his sated eyes. "That was perfect."

"Perfectly Perfect? That's as close to alliteration as I can come at the moment."

His eyes were amused, but above all they were deeply content and centered on her. "Perfection will come, and we'll enjoy the practice." He closed his eyes and laughed. "Is it possible to say a sentence without two words starting with the same sound? After this, I'm going to embarrass myself every time I open my mouth."

She sprawled on his chest, looking at him. "Persistent Practice?"

His eyes opened. "You want to fly higher and higher?"

"Why not? Why stay close to ground?"

"For safety?"

"Do we care about safety?"

"Yes," he said, smile fading, "I rather think we do. I intend to keep you safe, love, even if it does mean staying in the nest."

She snuggled even closer. "That won't be too bad if the nest has a bed. When can we do it again?"

He looked at her. "I had the impression it hurt you quite a bit."

When she thought about it, she could feel soreness. "The design of the female body is very inconvenient."

"Most parts of it are thoroughly delightful," he said, cradling a breast and kissing it. "Especially yours."

She dared to ask. "Do you like my breasts?"

"I adore your breasts."

"More than other women's breasts?"

He looked up. "Don't. That's a game that no one wins. You are you. I love you. I have never loved a woman as I love you. As it happens, you have very beautiful breasts, full and pale, with generous, rosy nipples. But it wouldn't matter if they were otherwise. They would still be the breasts of the woman I love."

She put wondering hands to her body, to her breasts. "It's hard for me to think of myself that way."

"As beautiful?"

"And loved." She felt tears threaten, and she didn't want to spoil this with tears. She smiled and put one hand on his chest. "You have a beautiful body, too."

"Is that all I am to you? A beautiful body?"

He spoke teasingly, but she sensed that the same need pulsed through him as her.

"No, you're the man I love. If you went back to war and came home scarred and maimed, you would still be the man I love."

"Why?" But then he put up a hand to stop her answer. "God, no. That's another game that no one wins."

She wanted to laugh. "Why wouldn't any woman fall in love with you? You're handsome, honorable, brave, strong . . ." But she moved down to kiss the hawk on his chest. "For me, though, the most wonderful thing is the way I've been able to talk to you from the first. You are my deepest, lifelong friend. I know you have other friends—"

He sealed her lips with his fingers. "None closer. Now."

"Truly?"

His eyes were steady and deep. "Truly. For as long as you wish."

She began to cry. She couldn't help it. This was the most perfect moment of her life, but she was sobbing as if she'd lost everything that mattered. He gathered her close, rocking her and murmuring for her to stop. She tried, but she couldn't.

"It's all right," she managed. "I'm happy, not sad!"

"Lord save me from you sad, then, love. Do stop, please."

She laughed and wiped her face on the sheet. "I look a mess when I cry, too."

He helped her dry her eyes and didn't deny her statement. For some reason, that put the perfect finish on perfection.

This was all completely honest.

She ran a hand across Hawk's wide shoulders, then down the center of his chest, just wanting to touch. She traced the scar again, chilled by how close it must have been to fatal.

"It was a mere glancing blow."

"I'm surprised it didn't break your ribs."

"Cracked them. Hurt like the devil."

She stroked along the scar. "I'm glad you're not at war anymore."

"I was rarely in much danger. Unlike others."

She looked up. "Why do you blame yourself? Your work was important."

"I know."

"But you still felt as if you were shirking," she risked, sliding down and holding him, his head on her shoulder.

She thought he wouldn't speak of it, and she didn't dare to press him further. But then he began to talk, about his army life, but especially about others, including Lord Vandeimen and Lord Amleigh.

She listened, stroking his hair, blending deeper with him at every word. She kept feeling she'd found perfect happiness, only to rise up to more, and more. She truly felt she might fly away, but it would be to heaven.

Heaven. Ah, yes. No purgatory for her. Certainly no hell. Instead, miraculously, she had heaven.

Except for the small worm of her involvement in Deveril's death.

It was time to tell her story. But not quite yet. This time was for him. He was talking about Hawkinville now.

"I went into the army to escape it. When I returned a few weeks ago, I planned to deal with whatever problems my father had and ride away. I didn't intend to cut myself off from Van and Con, but I didn't think I could live there.

"But when I rode in, people recognized me. God knows how, since most of them hadn't seen me since I was sixteen. And I recognized them. Not always immediately, but within minutes it was as if the passing years had disappeared. Even my old nurse . . ."

He moved his head restlessly against her. "Nanny Briggs saved my life. She was my mother in all true senses of the word. Even after she left my father's service, I spent more time in her house than at the manor. I sent her letters and gifts. But I hadn't thought she really mattered to me anymore until I saw her.

"In ten years she'd gone from a robust woman to a frail one, shrunken, crooked, and in pain. And in ten years, I'd hardly given her a thought apart from casually sent packages. Of course, she'd treasured every one."

He suddenly shifted, moving up to look at her. "Why am I boring you with all this? Come and be kissed for being such a good listener."

The kiss was Hawk's kiss, as skillful and delightful as ever, and yet afterward, cuddled against him, Clarissa pined for the links that might have been forged with the words he had left unsaid.

"I wasn't bored," she said. "I don't think you should blame yourself for not thinking of them. When a person grows, he will often leave his home and start anew. And

I'm sure war demands a man's attention. You would not have wanted to be distracted."

His hand was stroking her back again, and she remembered him stroking Jetta, remembered wanting to be stroked that way. And now she had it. For as long as they both should live . . .

He nuzzled her hair. "I've never embarrassed myself with so much chatter before."

She smiled against his skin. "You've never been married before."

"We're not now."

"As good as. In the eyes of heaven. I've never felt like this, either, Hawk. I've never truly had someone to be with like this. It's like catching sunlight and finding it can be held in the hands forever."

"Or having heaven here on earth."

"Perfect Perpetual Paradise," she murmured on a laugh. This would be the moment to tell him. So at peace, so relaxed, so inextricably bound.

And yet, it would change things. They'd have to talk, to make sense, to leave the soft clouds. Better surely to sleep now, and do the telling in the morning.

Chapter Twenty-three

~

Clarissa awoke to sunshine and warm, musky smells, to strangeness inside and around. And then to memory.

She turned her head slowly, but he was there, beside her, still trustingly asleep, turned away. He'd thrown the covers off down to his waist, so she could indulge in luxuriant study of the lines of his back, of his muscular arm bent close to her. She longed to ease forward and kiss it, taste his warmth and skin, but she wouldn't wake him yet.

When he awoke she would have to tell him, and it pricked at her. It wasn't precisely wrong not to have told him. It couldn't make any particular difference to him. It wasn't as if she was in danger of being arrested.

But she wished this moment was enshrined in perfect honesty.

On that thought, she reached out to touch his arm.

He stirred, rolled, then his eyes opened sharply. She saw that second of disorientation before he relaxed and smiled. But guardedly. Such shadows behind his smile. Why?

Ah.

She smiled for him. "I have no regrets. I love you, and this was the first night of our life together."

He took her hand, the one wearing the rings, and

pressed it to his lips. "I love you, too, Clarissa. This will be as perfect as I can possibly make it."

She almost let go of why she'd awakened him, but she would not weaken now. "Almost no regrets," she amended. As he became suddenly watchful, she added, "I have something to tell you, Hawk, and I think it requires clothing and cool heads."

He kept hold of her hand. "You're already married?"

"Of course not!"

"You're not Clarissa Greystone, but her maid in disguise."

"You've been reading too many novels, sir."

He pulled her closer. "You eloped only because you were consumed with carnal lust for my luscious body."

She resisted. "You're beginning to sound like *The Annals of Aphrodite,*" she said severely, "and of course I lust. But I also love."

"Then nothing troubles us."

"I could have lost all my money on wild investments in fur cloaks for Africa."

His smile deepened. "You're a minor."

"I gammoned my trustees."

"I'm not at all surprised." He gently tugged her closer. "Would you care to gammon me?"

She went, let herself be drawn to his lips, but in a moment she tugged free and clambered out of the bed. "Later," she said, but then froze, suddenly aware of her total nakedness.

Then she laughed and faced him brazenly.

He sat up equally brazenly, completely splendid, tousled, smiling.

"Carnal lust," she murmured, and made herself turn away to search for her shift, her corset, and her lamentably muddy stockings.

When she looked back he was already into his drawers. "I wish I had a clean dress to wear."

"We'll find you one in London. Much though I'd like to linger here, beloved, we'd best have breakfast and be on our way."

Awareness of the world, of pursuit, drained delight.

She hurried into her shift and corset, then went to him to have the strings tied. A sweet and simple task, and yet to have a man tie her laces seemed a mark of the complete change in her life.

As he tied the bow, she turned in his hands and started what must be done. "I was present when Lord Deveril died," she said, intent on his expression.

It hardly seemed to change at all. "I guessed."

"How? Why?"

"Perhaps because I'm the Hawk." But his lashes lowered as if that might not be the whole truth.

She put that aside. "I need to tell you about it. I should have before, but I couldn't until now. You'll see why."

His eyes were steady on her again. "Very well. But you wanted clothing and cool?"

She hurried to put on her dress and stockings, though she had to hunt for her second garter. He was dressed by then, and she went to him to have her buttons fastened. As he did the last one, he brushed her hair aside and she felt heat, wet heat, up the back of her neck.

"When I saw you in this dress, Falcon, you made me think of dairy cream, and I wanted to lick you."

She laughed and turned, pushing him playfully away. Something she could do when she knew there would be tomorrow and tomorrow and tomorrow.

Even, perhaps, later. They'd clearly eluded any pursuit. There was no real need to rush on to London.

Once her conscience was clear.

She sat on the rather hard chair at one end of the table and indicated that he should sit on the other, at a safe distance. His brows rose, but he obeyed.

"You were present at Deveril's death," he said obligingly. "I assume he was doing something vile and his death was deserved. I also assume that you did not kill him, but if you did it would only make me admire you more."

She bit her lip on tears at his understanding.

"You don't have to tell me any more, Falcon. It really doesn't matter."

She smiled. "But I want to. I have many failings, and one is an incurable urge toward honesty."

"I don't see that as a failing, beloved." And yet something somber touched him.

Beloved. She plunged into it. "I don't need to tell you that Deveril was an evil man. After he kissed me, I ran away from him."

"When you threw up over him."

"Yes. Perhaps I should have been able to control myself better . . ."

"Not at all. We use what weapons we have to hand."

She laughed. "I see what you mean. It certainly stopped him! Well, then, I escaped through the window in my brother's clothes, but Deveril hunted me down and caught me at . . . at a friend's house." Even now she faltered about telling him everything. "He had two men with him, so we couldn't do anything, and he threatened . . . He was going to do horrible things to us both, but he was going to kill my friend. So . . . he was killed."

She paused for breath and pulled a face. "That wasn't much of a tale, was it?"

"It does rather skip the who, the where, and especially the how—which I admit fascinates me. But I understand, and you bear no guilt."

"You won't feel obliged to pursue justice about it?"

He reached a hand across the table. "What is justice here? I award your noble defender the medal."

She put her hand in his, knots untangling that she'd hardly been aware of. "I knew you would think like that. I'm sorry, Hawk, deeply sorry, that I didn't tell you everything before."

"Before?"

"Before we committed ourselves."

He tugged, and she understood and went to sit in his lap, to be in his arms. "There is no shame in this, Falcon. But I confess to Hawkish curiosity. About the how, and how it was concealed."

"The how comes mostly from Deveril's being taken by surprise. And from reinforcements." She reached out to touch a silver button on his jacket. "I'm not sure how much else I can tell, even to you." She looked up. "There are secrets we are bound not to share. Does that apply to husband and wife?"

"Not if it affects both husband and wife. But take time, love. Our only urgency now is to eat and be on our way."

"I long for complete honesty between us," she said. "On all things. But would you tell me something truly secret that Lord Vandeimen shared with you?"

He thought for a moment. "I might not." He touched her cheek. "Do what you think is best, love. I trust you."

Trust. It was like a perfect golden rose. She sat up slightly and faced him. "Then I have to tell you one thing, Hawk. I did not behave at all like a Falcon last year. I was frozen with fear. Paralyzed. I did nothing. And afterward . . . Afterward, afterward I was heartless to the one who saved me. Shocked because others weren't shocked—"

He put his fingers over her lips. "Hush. It was your first battle. Few of us are heroes the first time out. I threw up after mine."

His understanding was so perfect. She took his face between her hands and kissed him, without words to express the wholeness that she felt.

She drew back at a tumultuous pealing of church bells. "Is it Sunday and I didn't notice?" she asked.

"Not unless we've spent days in heaven instead of just one night. And it's very early for a wedding."

Hawk eased Clarissa off his lap and went to open the door. There were many innocent explanations for the bells, but his instinct for danger was at the alert.

It could be nothing to do with Van, surely.

A sparkle-eyed maidservant was just running up the stairs and paused to gasp, "Not to worry, sir! It's the duke's heir born at last and all safe! And free ale to be served in the tap in celebration!"

"Duke?" Hawk asked, alarm subsiding, but trying to think what ducal estate was in the vicinity.

"Belcraven, sir! Not the duke's heir, of course, but his

heir's heir. His estate is here. A fine, handsome boy born to be duke one day, God willing, just as his father was born here twenty-six years ago!"

"A true cause for celebration," Hawk said, amazed that his voice sounded normal.

Arden here? What strange star had brought this about?

He'd discovered that the marquess had a Surrey estate called Hartwell, his principal country residence. He'd not troubled to find out precisely where. Details, details. It was always in the details.

"The marquess's estate is very close?" he asked in faint hope.

"Not a mile out of the village, sir! And he and his lovely wife as easy as can be with everyone here." She gave him a sly look. "Not like in the old days, when the company was very different, let me tell you."

"Marriage reforms many a man."

"And many a man it don't!" she flashed back with a grin, and hurried off on her errand. An increasing babble could be heard below.

Hawk turned slowly back into the room, rapidly absorbing the situation and the implications. Could they get away undetected? From what he knew about the Marquess of Arden, his displeasure was likely to be expressed physically and effectively.

Clarissa, however, did not seem to realize their danger. Her eyes were shining. "Beth's had the baby and all is well! She'll be somewhat put out at it being a boy, of course."

"Put out that it is a boy?" he asked, swiftly gathering their few possessions.

"She doesn't approve of the aristocracy's obsession with male heirs."

It was sufficiently startling to make Hawk pause.

"She's a firm believer in the equal rights of women, you see, and of a rather republican turn of mind."

"The Marchioness of Arden?"

"She wrote that it would be bad enough having a son born to be duke without him being the eldest, too. She hoped for a few older females to keep him in line. Apparently Lord Arden was the youngest and has two older sisters, and she said that might have been the saving of him."

Hawk laughed. "Very likely. I'm sorry about breakfast, but we should be away from here. I doubt there'll be much service here soon, anyway."

"Oh, I suppose so." She unhooked her cloak, but said wistfully, "It does seem a shame not to be able to visit Beth, being so close."

"No," he said firmly and guided her out of the room.

"I know. I know. And she's doubtless resting. But it does seem . . . A note? No," she said for him.

"No," he said again as they went downstairs, wishing he could give her this small indulgence.

In the plain hall, he grabbed an excited potboy and asked him to find the landlady. People were streaming toward the inn from all directions.

"It's a bit like the Duke of Wellington, isn't it?" she said.

"I hope not." *Come on. Come on.*

She turned suddenly, the scarlet cloak clasped to her. "You said Deveril's death was justified," she said quietly. "So I want to tell you who killed Deveril."

Trust and honesty. Hawk wished that he could tell her now. But she could still back away. "Arden," he said, looking around for the landlady. "It doesn't matter except that we don't want to be caught by him here."

"Why . . . ? But no, it wasn't the marquess."

He turned to look at her. He had given up the plan of blackmailing the marquess and duke, but even so, it was as if solid ground disappeared from beneath his feet. Had he been wrong about everything?

"It was Blanche Hardcastle," she whispered.

"The actress?" It was probably the stupidest response he'd ever been guilty of.

"Yes. I know why you're so shocked. A woman, and one who seems so delicate. But she was a butcher's daughter, apparently. And now, of course, she's playing Lady Macbeth."

"Zeus!" He wasn't actually shocked that a woman had ripped Deveril open. A man has to be dense indeed to preserve illusions about the gentler sex during wartime. For some reason, however, the image of the killer going on to play the part of the woman with the bloody knife did outrage him.

Clarissa was looking at him slightly anxiously, and he was relieved to be able to say with honesty, "Mrs. Hardcastle is in no danger from me, Falcon. I salute her."

Wryly he acknowledged, however, that he'd held a sharper weapon than he'd known. Belcraven and Arden might well have called his bluff, secure that if he did seek a Pyrrhic victory, they stood behind high walls of power and privilege. An actress, however, was another matter entirely. An actress with a somewhat dubious past would hang for the bloody murder of a peer.

"You see, don't you," she said slightly anxiously, "that Blanche must never suffer for her gallantry. She took him . . . she took him up to her bed to get him away from his guards. . . . She was so brave."

"I see. Don't worry about this."

She smiled, a hint of tears in it again. "I'm so glad I told you. I feel truly free now. Free to be happy."

" 'And ye shall know the truth,' " said Hawk, " 'and the truth shall set you free.' "

He teetered on the edge of taking the great gamble, of trusting to her love, to the magic they'd shared.

She did love Hawkinville.

She did love him. If that survived the strain.

But years of caution tied his tongue. What if he was wrong?

He'd heard of men sentenced to death spinning out the moments with one slim excuse or another, against all reason delaying the inevitable. Now, at last, he understood.

Another moment of her untarnished admiration and trust . . .

Then a tall, athletic blond man strode into the inn smiling, gloves and crop in hand. Hawk knew instantly, fatally, who it must be. Pre-ducal arrogance radiated from every pore.

People rushed forward to bow, to congratulate. Then the smiling gaze hit Clarissa, moved to Hawk, and changed.

No chance of escape. Hawk put Clarissa behind him as the marquess smiled again, escaped his well-wishers, and came over to them, cold murder in his eyes.

Clarissa, however, slipped around him. "Congratulations on the baby, Lord Arden."

Damnation, she was trying to protect him, and he could hear the fear in her voice. Arden would never hit a woman, but Hawk pulled her back to his side.

Arden, however, softened to concern when he looked at her. "Thank you. Clarissa—"

"I do hope Beth is well," she interrupted, a tone too high.

"Beth is a great deal weller than is seemly." The marquess's voice took on an exasperated edge. "The baby was born at four in the morning, but the mother is already out of her bed and well enough to fight the midwife about the need to lie down, and me about the appropriate establishment for a future Duke of Belcraven. Having lost a night's sleep and years of my life, I wouldn't mind even a few hours in bed, never mind a week of rest and loving attention, but how can I even sit down and try to recover when Beth is bustling about? And now I find this!"

At the return of fury, Hawk expected Clarissa to falter, but her chin went up. "Are you planning to hit someone again?"

Color flared in Arden's cheeks. "Probably."

"Typical!"

Hawk forced Clarissa behind him. "Did he hit you before?"

By Hades, he'd take Arden apart!

"No!" Her hands clamped around his right arm, and he realized his hands were fists. And so were Arden's, though he looked more startled than enraged.

Then Arden looked at Clarissa, eyes narrowing. "Stop trying to deflect the conversation."

And he was right. Clever Clarissa.

"Don't you think we should move this into privacy?"

A new voice. Hawk looked behind Arden and saw that Con had come into the inn. And that a bunch of villagers were sucking in every word.

Con was standing at the door to a small room. Hawk took Clarissa in there, feeling something sizzle and die.

Con had come in pursuit and somehow managed to be close. Being in the area, he'd sought a bed with his friend, which must have been interesting when it turned out to be a night of *accouchement*. Now they were discovered, and surely Con's steady eyes were disappointed.

Perhaps worried, too. About the role he'd have to play?

Second at a duel? He wouldn't let it come to that.

If only, though, he'd seized the moment to tell Clarissa the truth.

Arden strode in, and Con closed the door. "Want to explain, Hawk?" He stayed close to Arden. A show of support, or readiness to control violent impulses?

Clarissa replied before Hawk could. "We're eloping, Lord Amleigh. What need of explanation?"

"Why would be a start," Arden said.

Silence fell, and then Clarissa looked at Hawk. "Tell him why." She was clearly confident that he could.

Hawk smiled wryly, and looked at Con rather than Arden, seeing the firm resolve of an executioner. It wasn't a matter of Rogues versus the Georges for Con. It was simply the right thing to do.

Slippery slopes. From right to wrong as well as from virtue to sin.

"Why, Hawk?" Con asked. It wasn't a repetitive demand for an answer, but an opening offered so that he could tell Clarissa rather than have someone else do it.

So he turned to her and put the noose around his own neck.

Chapter Twenty-four

〜

"Because," he said, "if I try to marry you in the ordinary way, you won't do it."

She blinked at him. "I won't?"

"You won't." It was Arden's voice, cold and relentless.

Her eyes flicked to him, then back to Hawk, and she smiled slightly, as if any impediment was a laughing matter. "Tell me, then. It can't be as bad as you think."

"It is, Falcon." He took a last breath and kicked away the stool. "My father was born a Gaspard. You may not know, but that was Lord Deveril's family name. After much effort, he has managed to establish his claim to be the next Lord Deveril. And I, of course, am his heir."

In a way it sounded silly put into words. No hanging matter at all. Just a name, as Van had said.

But it was more than a name.

And just at the name, she paled. *"Deveril!"*

"Which means," said Arden moving to her side, as if protecting her from him, damn it, "you would have one day been Lady Deveril."

The tense he used neatly put an end to all hope, and when Arden put his arm around her, she did not resist. She did, however, stammer, "But . . ." confusion in her eyes.

"As you see," the marquess continued, his eyes suggesting that he was talking to a slug, "this raises questions about Major Hawkinville's attentions all along."

"Luce," said Con quietly, moving between them. "There's more to this than that."

"Is there?" Arden asked, his eyes still on Hawk.

"Yes." Everyone else in the room spoke at once, and the shock of it broke the tension. Clarissa laughed, then bit her lip, eyes still shadowed by shock and uncertainty. She pulled free of Arden, but made no move closer to Hawk.

This had snatched away her elusive beauty. All he wanted in life was to make Clarissa beautiful, each and every day, and yet by his actions he had doubtless thrown away the chance.

He spoke to her alone, without hope. "My father thought he should have inherited Deveril's wealth along with the title, and he spent in expectation of it. That's where the debt came from. I sought you out looking for evidence that you were involved in Deveril's murder because then the will would be overturned and the new viscount—my father—would inherit the money."

"You thought me a murderer! I suppose in some ways I should be flattered."

"Clarissa . . ."

But her hand covered her mouth. "I've just given you the evidence."

"You have?" Arden asked, sharply.

"I told him everything. Just as he planned."

"No!" Hawk exclaimed, but there seemed nothing left to pin hopes to except honesty. "At the beginning, yes."

"Do I have to slap you with my gloves?" Arden asked coldly. "I'd have to burn them afterward."

"Not now!" Hawk commanded, aware of Clarissa's sudden pallor. "Con—"

He put his hand on her arm to push her toward Con, but she twitched away. "Don't try and get rid of me! Don't you dare! Any of you. I'm not a child." She whirled on Arden. "You are not to fight over me."

"You have no say in this."

"I demand a say. I insist on it." When Arden stayed tight-lipped and resolute, she said, "If you duel him, I'll shoot you."

"Clarissa," said Hawk, wanting to laugh and cry at once. "I'm sure you don't know how."

"It can't be so hard as all that." She stared at him, eyes brimming with tears. "You said it was an honorable act for someone to kill Deveril. How could you even think of destroying people over it? Even for Hawkinville."

"I didn't."

"Then what drove you?"

"The will," he snapped. "Forgery is hardly cloaked with honor, Clarissa, no matter how you care to deceive yourself."

She stared at him and the elusive truth dawned even as she whirled to face Arden.

"It was a *forgery*?" She laughed. "Of course it was. How very stupid I've been. Deveril—Deveril!—leaving me all his money. He'd have rather left it to the Crown, or scattered it in the streets if it comes to that." She suddenly struck out at the marquess with both fists, pummeling him.

Arden stepped back, and before Hawk could reach her, he grasped her wrists and spun her to face him. "Hit him if you're feeling violent. He's the villain of the piece."

She staggered forward, weeping, and Hawk caught her, held her for a precious moment. "*I* have committed no crime."

Except breaking a heart.

"Abduction, for a start," Arden said.

"Stop." Con took Clarissa from Hawk, keeping an arm around her. She wasn't crying, but she seemed ready to collapse. "There'll be no duel," Con said, in an officer's unquestionable voice, "and no violence." Then he looked at Arden with a frown. "I gather criminal acts are not to be shared among the Rogues these days."

The marquess looked to be at the end of his tether. "Not lightly, no. And you came back from Waterloo in a bad way. We weren't about to add to your burdens."

Con pulled a face and sat Clarissa in a chair. He went

to his haunches in front of her. "What do you want to do?"

She looked at him, pallid, then up at Hawk. "I want to arrange to give the money to the new Lord Deveril."

Arden took a step toward her. "Don't be foolish."

Without looking, Con put a hand out to stop him. "It will be as Clarissa wishes."

"On Hawkinville's side, I see," said Arden coldly.

Con was steady as a rock. "It is Clarissa's choice. That has been decided."

It seemed to stop Arden's fight, but he said, "Perhaps she'll see sense when the shock's worn off."

"Do I have any say?" Hawk interrupted.

They all looked at him, but he spoke to Clarissa. "Hawkinville only needs some of the money—"

"Damn your eyes!" Arden exploded. "How much filthy money do you need?"

Hawk faced him. "Legally, the money belongs to my father. But twenty thousand pounds will suffice."

The arrogant disdain was designed to annihilate. "I will provide it for you on agreement that you leave Clarissa in peace."

There was nothing left but icy invulnerability. "Within the week?" Hawk inquired.

"Within the week."

Clarissa started to say something, but Arden overrode her. "We can discuss your situation later. Come along now. Beth will want to take care of you."

"But the baby . . ."

"Is not enough to tax my Amazon." He turned to Con, acting as if Hawk was not there. "Coming?"

"No. I'll deal with Hawk."

"He can't be allowed to harm Blanche."

"He won't."

"Of course I won't," Hawk snapped. Arden had drawn Clarissa to her feet, but she looked stricken still. "Clarissa, you don't have to go."

It was a faint hope, and her blankness denied it. She made no protest as the marquess took her out of the room, but then she suddenly stopped.

Hawk watched in faint beating hope as she turned back. She pulled off the two rings and put them on a table against the wall. And then she was gone.

Hawk was left with Con and could collapse into a chair and put his head in his hands. "I've known battles that have been easier."

"I'm sure you have."

"She was innocent," Hawk said, to himself as much as to Con. "All along, she was completely innocent."

And thus his treatment of her had been atrocious from first moment to now. He'd hunted down a sheltered young woman who'd been forced into an engagement with a depraved man. She'd been abused, terrified, threatened, and then witness to his bloody murder.

Arden was right. He deserved to be shot.

"You're not totally the villain, you know," Con said in a steadying voice.

Hawk looked up. "Oh, please, explain why not."

"You can't let Slade rape Hawk in the Vale."

"So I rape Clarissa instead."

"I am sure you did not."

Hawk sighed. "No, but I've used her shamefully."

"Last night was unwise, but understandable. And you planned to marry her." Con smiled a little. "If you wish, you can lay most of it at the Rogues' door. We came up with the forgery."

"You weren't even there."

"All the same."

"Ah," said Hawk, suddenly wracked by a weariness he hadn't felt since Waterloo, since after Waterloo with the chaos and the wounded and the mounds and sweeps of bodies and body parts so that victory, for the moment, was valueless. So one only wanted to turn back time for a few brief days to restore life and joy to the thousands of dead, and to their families still to hear the news, and then change history so that such battles never happened again.

Events, however, are written in ink the moment they occur, and cannot be erased.

"In that case," Hawk said, standing and beginning to

pull together what was left of his life, "can I ask you to deal with Arden about this? A duel, though I can understand his feelings, would serve no one. You can assure him that I will do nothing to endanger Mrs. Hardcastle or anyone else involved in Deveril's death. For the sake of Hawk in the Vale, however, I must take his money. In strict honor, I should not let the matter of the forgery go."

Con rubbed his chin thoughtfully. "Nicholas arrived at Somerford Court yesterday. You know who I mean? Nicholas Delaney? Apparently his Aunt Arabella summoned him to Brighton."

"Arabella Hurstman? Good God, a Rogue dragon as well. I was doomed."

"I'm afraid so, but since she was largely kept in the dark, I think the doom will fall on us. But when Van explained about the Deveril title, we agreed immediately that the money had been improperly redirected."

A crack of laughter escaped Hawk. "Now that's a way to describe forgery. And a damn good forgery, too."

"But of course," said Con with a smile. "You have to understand that everyone, including Deveril himself, thought he was heirless. The money was going to buy the Regent another gold plate or two, and without money, Clarissa's situation was desperate. You may not know, but Nicholas has an interest in that money. It was originally gathered by a woman called Thérèse Bellaire—" Con must have caught a reaction. "That name means something?"

"Oh, yes," said Hawk with another laugh. The debacle was beginning to take on an absurd humor. "I recruited Delaney for that job. He must be enjoying this turn of the wheel."

"Not particularly. But at least I don't need to dance around the details. The Bellaire woman gathered the money from Bonapartist supporters. She was supposed to take it to France to be ready for Napoleon's return. Instead she planned a new life in America. Nicholas distracted her sufficiently that Deveril was able to steal it."

"Gad. And she didn't kill him then and there?"

"She was, as I said, distracted. And by then, England was not safe for her. But Nicholas could hardly be happy leaving that money with a man like Deveril. When Clarissa's affair erupted, it was simply too good a chance to pass up."

Still swimming in lunatic humor, Hawk asked, "I wonder what happened to Thérèse Bellaire? She managed to work her way back into Napoleon's inner circle, you know, but Waterloo must have ended her hopes."

"I pray that's true. I'm sure she's never forgotten or forgiven any of this. I remember her. Honeyed poison. But the forgery was done under the assumption that no one had a better claim. Right is on your father's side and the money should be his. We agree on that, but Clarissa's situation makes matters difficult."

Hawk sighed. "I don't want all the money, Con."

"Fifty fifty," Con suggested.

Hawk laughed. "I see. You were sent here with power to negotiate, were you? How does Delaney plan to get around her guardian and trustees?"

"The Rogues can raise that much money until Clarissa comes of age. If she insists on having it all, so be it."

Hawk pressed his hands to his face. "On what's left of my honor, I'd not take a penny if it weren't for the people of Hawk in the Vale."

"I know that."

He pulled himself together. "I need the twenty, and I have to take a bit more for Gaspard Hall. Not for the place itself, and certainly not for my father, but for the people there. Something needs to be done to correct the decades of neglect. The Deveril tenants are probably the most innocent victims of all. But I want Clarissa to have the rest. Try to persuade her of that."

Con nodded. "She may not be willing to take anything now."

"I wish to heaven I'd never let that slip, but I didn't know— I should have known. She should have the money, but if she's difficult, point out that if the Devil's Heiress turns suddenly poor it would raise awkward questions."

They were talking so calmly of the future. The future with Hawkinville, perhaps even with his father at Gaspard Hall.

But a future without Clarissa.

Unendurable, except that like a soldier with a shattered leg, he had no choice but to endure the amputation and then—if that was God's choice—limp on.

"Are you all right?" Con asked.

With Con he could let the exasperation show. "No, of course not! I'm stuck in hell. Some of it is my own fault, but most of it isn't. It's my father's, and Slade's, and Deveril's, and your damned Rogues'. It's like being under the control of an insane and inept commanding officer who sends his men marching straight into a battery of enemy guns. And there's nothing, absolutely nothing, one can do but march."

Con, who had doubtless been in that situation, pulled a face. "What will you do now?"

"March back to Hawk in the Vale and arrange to pay off Slade. What else?"

Con nodded. "Nicholas would probably like to talk to you about this."

Hawk wanted nothing to do with the man, but he would go where the insanity sent him. "We didn't part on good terms back in '14, and I'm not sure I'm in the mood to be conciliating."

"He'll cope."

Hawk looked around and picked up the rings. "I knew my mother's ring was a bad omen." He put them in his pocket, then turned to go. But he stopped. "Dammit. I need to write to her."

He had to hunt down the innkeeper to get paper, pen, and ink—a slightly bosky innkeeper, who gave him a very suspicious look. Then he went back to the bedroom, out of Con's sight, though he didn't suppose his friend would be able to tell anything from simply looking at him as he wrote.

A wounded animal seeking a hole in which to lick its wounds.

There was no lasting privacy in any of this, however.

It was going to have to be acted out on an open stage. Could he mitigate things for her?

Writing was part of his expertise. Writing clearly, precisely, and succinctly so the recipient would understand the information or instruction without delay. Now, the blank sheet of paper was as daunting as a well-armed garrison, impossible to conquer.

He shrugged and dipped the rather unpromising pen. No words were going to create a miracle here, but he could not ride away without at least expressing himself clearly.

Honestly.

Yes, at this point at least he had honesty, with all its sharp tangs.

My dear Clarissa . . .

Then he wished he'd said "Falcon." No, it was better as it was. Or perhaps he should have written "Miss Greystone."

Perhaps he had better be more careful, or less particular. He'd been able to acquire only one sheet of paper, and he could hardly keep Con waiting for hours as he tried to form a miracle. He must also phrase this so it would not cause disaster if it fell into the wrong hands.

> *My dear Clarissa,*
>
> *Please read this letter to the end. I understand how you must feel, but you will not, I believe, find anything maudlin or embarrassing here.*
>
> *I wish to outline first what I have proposed to deal with our situation. Please believe that I sincerely wish only the best for you, but that I also have others to consider. You said that you had fallen in love with Hawk in the Vale,· and I hope therefore that you will not mind providing money to dispose of the odious Slade.*
>
> *In addition, there will be a small sum to begin the restoration of the Deveril estate, which has suffered greatly, through no fault of the people there.*
>
> *The rest is yours. At your majority, you will be*

*able to dispose of it as you will, but I hope you will
feel able to enjoy it.*

*As for our personal affairs, I cannot apologize for
everything, since I was striving to protect the innocents who would be harmed by Slade, but I do truly
regret ever thinking less than the best of you. I
should have known, as soon as I knew you, that you
were always beyond reproach.*

He paused, knowing he should sign it there, but unable
to forgo a little gesture toward hope. And also, maybe,
to salve her hurts. He knew, like a deep wound, that her
fragile confidence would be cracked. Pray God, not
shattered.

*Perhaps I will sound maudlin here, so by all
means cease to read if you wish. The necessary part
is over. I give you my word, my dear Falcon, that
as I once promised, I have never flattered you. My
delight in you—*

Hawk halted to contemplate a tense. Whoever would
have thought that tenses could be so crucial?

*My delight in you has been real, my admiration
of you deep and true. I am, alas, cursed with a future
as Lord Deveril, but perhaps that fate will not arrive
for many years, and perhaps it will seem less appalling by that time. Perhaps, too, you will one day be
able to forgive my many deceptions and trust me
enough to venture into the wilderness again with me.*

He paused again, wanting to write "I will wait," but
he knew that might place a burden on her, and above
all, he wanted to preserve her precious, hard-won freedom. And so, in the end, he merely signed it, "Hawk."

He resisted the urge to reread it, which would lead
him to want to rewrite it, he was sure. He folded it with
his usual precise edges, then realized he had no means

to seal it. It didn't matter. Con wouldn't read it—and what matter if he did?

He looked once at the room, at the disordered bed with the slight, telltale splash of blood, and a lifetime's worth of memories. Constantly, constantly, like a manic millstone, his mind ground round and round, seeking things he could have changed, paths he could have logically taken.

He shrugged and went back downstairs to where his friend patiently waited.

Perhaps still his friend, though he wasn't sure he deserved it.

"You always were the steadiest of us," he said as he passed over the letter.

"Someone had to try to steer us away from disaster. But I'm not doing very well by my friends, am I? Dare, Van, you—"

"Dare was not your fault. War is a temperamental bitch who gives no care to good or bad, justice or injustice. Look at De Lancey, killed by a ricocheting cannonball by my side, almost at the end of the battle. There was no point to it. And it could have hit me, or even Wellington, as easily."

"I know. But I've been too wrapped up in myself."

Hawk gripped his arm. "Perhaps none of us came out of Waterloo with anything in reserve for the other. We just chose different ways of hiding it."

Con's gray eyes searched him. "Will you be all right?"

"Of course. I certainly have plenty of work to do."

"Including saving Clarissa's reputation. You were seen racing out of the village."

Hawk grimaced. "Damn. I'll come up with something."

After a moment, Con clasped hands. "I'll take care of Clarissa for you. I have a horse in the stables here. Take it. I'll see you in Hawk in the Vale."

Con left, and Hawk took a moment to steady himself. The mill was still grinding, and probably would do so for the rest of his life, but even if it came up with the most brilliant solution, it was too damn late.

Chapter Twenty-five

~

Lord Arden had apparently ridden to the village—simply to accept the congratulations of the people gathered at the inn. To return, he commandeered Hawk and Clarissa's gig. She was slightly amused by seeing his lordly magnificence in such a lowly vehicle pulled by the placid cob. Only slightly, however, for she did not have the heart for humor of any kind.

She was trying very hard not to think about all that had happened, all she had learned, but it surrounded her like a chill wind, or an overcast day.

Hartwell. Thank God there was somewhere to go now, some haven. It had been a haven before. Beth had taken her there a few days after Deveril's death, and it was there she had made decisions about the future. If they could be called decisions. All she had wanted then was a place to hide.

She did not let the bitter laugh escape. She'd thought that she'd grown so strong, so brave, so able to deal with life, but here she was, rushing back to a safe place, and she could no more stay here this time than last.

Last year Beth had invited her to live with her, at Hartwell and elsewhere. Clarissa would have been safe inside the de Vaux family, but she had not wanted to be anywhere near the marquess, who had blacked Beth's eye.

As they rolled along the country lane, she glanced at

him, realizing that she felt differently now. Though she'd been stupid, gullible, and weak about Hawk, she had changed over the past year. She understood more about emotions, about control, and about how easily strong emotions could explode control.

She had hit Arden. A feeble hit, but only because she was feeble. If she'd been able she might have knocked him to the ground.

In an uncontrolled moment Hawk had shattered a gate, and he had not believed that his beloved had been with another man.

"I'm sorry for what I said back there, Lord Arden. As you guessed, I was deflecting the conversation."

"Next time choose another weapon."

She pulled a face. They had never been on good terms. She had indirectly caused his violent moment, and guilty people blame others if they can. Even so, he'd worked hard and taken risks for her, and she knew he would continue to do so. It was nothing to do with her, but all to do with Beth, whom he loved.

That was the point.

She understood now what Beth had been trying to tell her last year, that the love was true and deep, and that therefore he would make sure that such lack of control never, ever happened again.

"Beth won't be happy if we're at odds, my lord," she said. "And even if she's weller than she should be, I'm sure tranquility is good for a new mother."

He did glance at her then. "Her tranquility would be undisturbed if you'd behaved properly."

She swallowed an instinctive retort. "Yes, you're right. I was foolish. But . . . I didn't want to lose heaven, you see."

She bit her lip, determined not to cry. Now she certainly had lost heaven in all its aspects—both Hawk and Hawkinville. It had probably all been an imaginary heaven, anyway, but for a little while it had felt astonishingly real, as if it could, truly, be for her.

Lord Arden reached over and gently squeezed her hand. He was gloved, but still it was the most human contact she remembered with him. "My instinct is to tear Hawkinville limb from limb, but it's not so long since I did questionable things. I have some sympathy for him, pressured by the needs of his family and his land."

"So do I."

He glanced at her again, clearly expecting more, but she couldn't speak it. Deep inside she felt raw, where trust had been uprooted from her. Did Hawk want her now that he could have the money regardless? Last night she would have laughed at doubt, but now, swirling in the awareness of deception, it ate at her.

If he protested on his knees that he loved her, would it be pity, or obligation?

And then there was the problem of Lord Deveril. It should be a little thing, but it simply wasn't.

Deveril!

It was as if a ghoul had risen from the grave to drool all over her.

Lord Arden turned the gig between open gates and into the short drive through lovely gardens to the house. Hartwell was what people called a cottage ornée. It looked like a thatched village cottage, only grown to three times the size. Clarissa couldn't help comparing its pretty perfection unfavorably with Hawkinville Manor, which was real even to its warped beams and uneven floors.

Beth had joked that Hartwell was a bucolic toy for the wealthy aristrocracy rather like Queen Marie Antoinette's "farm" at Le Petit Triannon, but Clarissa knew Beth loved it, probably because it was home to her and the man she loved.

She'd told Hawk that she would live with him in love anywhere. And it had been true.

As Lord Arden turned the gig down a side drive toward the stables at the side, she swallowed tears. She was not going to turn into a wailing fool over this. She'd lost her virtue, her beloved, her heavenly home, and her fortune all in one day, but crying wouldn't bring any of it back.

She went into the house with the marquess somewhat

nervously, however. She was not so strong as to ignore what Beth would think of her adventures. They were still more teacher and student, and she had always been awed by Beth's intelligence and strong will.

When they found that Beth was asleep, she was as relieved as the marquess.

"And thank heavens for that," Lord Arden muttered. He looked at Clarissa, and she saw that he hadn't a notion what to do with her. Beneath the gloss and the highly trained ability to be the Heir to the Dukedom under the most trying circumstances, he was, quite simply, exhausted.

She was astonished to feel a need to pat him on the shoulder and tell him to go and have a nice rest. She settled for saying, "I know the house, my lord, so you may feel easy leaving me to my own devices for a while."

His look was, if anything, kind. "I'm sorry, Clarissa. I can say he's not worth it, but at this moment you won't believe that."

"This certainly isn't how I want things to be." But she looked him in the eye. "I wouldn't give up the past few weeks, Lord Arden, even had I known it would bring me here."

He reached out and touched her cheek. "I know that feeling. You have friends, Clarissa. You will be happy again soon."

"I'm ruined, you know," she said, wondering if he didn't quite understand.

"No, you're not," he said with a smile. "Just a little more experienced. You know Beth wouldn't disapprove of experience. Ask the servants for anything you need. Amleigh will be here soon, I have no doubt."

He'd made her laugh, and she watched him go upstairs, astonished by a touch of affection. Truly her experience seemed to have stretched her mind in some way, giving her glimpses of subtleties and, more important, understanding.

What to do?

She should be hungry, but she was sure food would

choke her. She probably should ask to borrow a dress of Beth's. They were, or had been, much of a size.

Perhaps she should write to Miss Hurstman, or even to the duke. Would the duke have to know about this?

In the end, aimlessly, she drifted out into the garden, wandering down to the river, where ducks busily paddled and dipped under the surface for food.

In her mind she was immediately back at another house on another river.

With Hawk in Hawkinville.

She sat down on the grass to think, to try to see what had really happened.

Hawk had gone to Cheltenham to find a criminal. She thought back over that day, tried to see it through his eyes. He must have been telling the truth when he said he changed his mind then. She'd been the most unlikely villain.

He'd drawn her to Brighton so he could dig for more evidence. She remembered wryly the number of times their talk had turned to London and Deveril, and the things she'd let slip.

The knife in the tent.

He was good. Very good.

But had the connection, the friendship, the passion, all been artifice?

What about the wilderness? That she would swear was real.

Ah. She remembered the splintered gate, and was suddenly sure that yes, it had all been real. Hawk would not lose control like that as a stratagem.

And last night. Surely there had been nothing false about last night.

But what did she really know about these things? He'd planned to marry her for her money and so he would have wanted her bound by passion.

And love.

And trust.

She grimaced at the way she'd babbled about perfection and honesty and trust. And told him everything.

She could only pray that he'd told the truth, that he had what he wanted. That Blanche would be safe.

She watched the river, thinking stupidly that it must be much easier to be a duck.

She heard footsteps and turned, thinking it would be the marquess, hoping against hope that it would be Hawk.

It was Lord Amleigh.

"There are suddenly a lot of titled gentlemen in my life," she said, and it was silly.

He smiled and dropped to the grass by her side, dark-haired, square-chinned, and steady-eyed. "Just me and Arden, isn't it?"

"And Lord Vandeimen."

"And, indirectly, Lord Deveril." He was still smiling, but there was something in his eyes that made demands of her. "Perhaps if you called me Con it would simplify your life."

"You're his friend. Have you come to ask me to forget it all?"

"I'm a Rogue, too, remember, and you are the one person who least deserves to suffer. Everything will be exactly as you wish."

She laughed, hiding her face against her skirt, into the deceptively simple cream muslin gown that she had chosen yesterday morning with such hopes and dreams, and that now held only stains, and memories.

"That does assume that I know my own wishes."

"You will, but perhaps not now. I know that at the moment it probably seems urgent, but it will all wait."

She turned her head sideways to look at him, this virtual stranger who was so intimately linked with her affairs. "But will the world wait—before condemning me?"

"The world won't know. Who's to tell them?"

Strange to think about that. Not the Rogues. Not Hawk, or Lord Vandeimen or Lord Amleigh. Althea? Hardly. Lord Trevor? Miss Hurstman would cut his nose off.

"The village of Hawk in the Vale?" she asked.

"Hawk will deal with them. He's gone back there."

She studied him. "You trust him."

"With my life and all I hold dear." After a moment he added, "That doesn't mean he's without faults."

She looked forward at the river. "So I can return to Brighton, and assemblies, and parties. It seems completely impossible, you know."

"I know. But life goes on. He sent a letter and asked that you read it."

She sat up and took the folded paper, but she wasn't sure she wanted to read it.

"It doesn't have to be now, if you don't want. But I think you should, when you're ready to."

Clarissa looked at the folded sheet. There was nothing on the outside, not even her name. There'd been no need of name or direction, of course, but it struck her as very Hawkish to be so precise about the necessities.

It was also, she realized, folded in half and then in three with impressive precision. Every angle was exact, every edge in line. How distressing it must be to a man of such discipline and order to be thrown into such discord.

She looked at his friend. "Is he all right?"

"No more than you."

"I'm in love with him, so even more than I want him, I want to make everything perfect for him. But I'm not sure what that perfect would be, and I am sure that I mustn't . . . melt myself into him for his comfort and pleasure."

"An extraordinary way of putting it, but I know what you mean. I don't have any wisdom to offer." After a moment he said, "I'm not even sure there is any wisdom when it comes to the heart, except the old nostrum that time heals. It heals, but healing is not always without scars, or even deformities."

She stared at him. "I'm certainly not being treated as a silly child, am I?"

"Do you wish to be?"

"Doesn't everyone wish to be, sometimes?"

"There you have an excellent point." He opened his arms, and she went into them. It was fatherly, or perhaps

brotherly. She, who had never had father or brother interested in holding her.

She remembered that after Deveril's death, Nicholas
Delaney had held her in the same way. But none of these
men, even if full to brimming with goodwill, could solve
her dilemmas for her.

"I suppose I have to return," she said. "To Brighton."

"Certainly Miss Hurstman will want to see you safe."

"Miss Hurstman is a Rogue." She said it firmly but
without resentment.

"No, she's not. She's a Rogue's aunt. Lord Middlethorpe's aunt, to be precise. If you think she's on our
side against you, you don't know her very well. She's a
fierce defender of women in any practical way. There'll
be skin lost over our mismanagement of this."

She pulled free of his arms to look at him. "She didn't
know any of this?"

"Not unless she's a fortune-teller. Nicholas asked her
to take you on because he thought you needed special
help to win your place in society. That's all."

"But she wrote to him. Reporting, I assume."

"Ah, that. She wrote demanding his presence. She has
an encyclopedic knowledge of society that exceeds
Hawk's. As soon as he appeared she remembered that
his father had been born a Gaspard, and that Gaspard
was the Deveril family name. It rang enough of an alarm
bell for her to send for him, but not enough of one to
take any action. She had no idea—probably still
doesn't—that Hawk's father has the title now."

"Then I'd like to go back there." She stood up and
brushed off her hopeless skirt. "Life goes on, but it
hardly seems possible."

Like a claw scratching at the back of her mind, she
wondered what she would do if she was with child. All
very well for Lord Arden to brush off her ruin, but a
swelling belly would be a very obvious sign of experience.

Would that mean that she'd have to marry Hawk?

He'd argued with her about just this. About her changing her mind, being with child.

Had he really tried to resist? Or had that simply been more cunning on his part?

She wanted him too much to make sense. Wanting was not the guide.

A child can want to grasp the fire, an adult want to throw away a fortune on cards.

Something popped up from the jumble of her mind. "You mentioned fortune-telling. . . . It's tugging at something . . . oh, Mrs. Rowland!"

He frowned slightly. "The woman in the village with the invalid husband?"

"Yes, I felt as if I knew her, but now I see she reminds me of that fortune-teller in Brighton. Madame Mystique."

Who had talked about the money not really being hers, and death if she did not tell the truth. She'd told the truth, but she still felt half dead.

"What is it? Are you faint?"

"No." She couldn't deal with another stir of the pot. "I think I need to eat something. And probably borrow a clean gown. Con," she added as a mark of appreciation for his kindness.

He smiled. "Come along, then." They began to walk back to the peaceful house.

Most people would prefer Hartwell, with its picturesque charms around a thoroughly modern and convenient interior.

But Clarissa knew that Hawkinville still held her heart.

Chapter Twenty-six

Hawk rode south almost by compass, driven by duty alone. It might be pleasant, in fact, to become lost. He'd looked into some cases of people who simply disappeared. Perhaps they too found themselves in a dead spot of life and went away. Went anywhere so long as it was not here.

He might collide with Van by pure accident on this journey, but that encounter could not be avoided. It really didn't matter when. It mattered whether Van, like Con, could hold on to old bonds in spite of present insanity, but he couldn't affect that.

He could affect Clarissa's reputation, and he put his mind to that.

He made Hawk in the Vale without incident, and saw everyone in the village turn to stare.

The Misses Weatherby popped out of their house, agape. Good.

Grimly amused, Hawk touched his hat. "Good evening, ladies."

They gaped even more, and he waited for them to frame a question.

But Slade marched out between his ridiculous pillars right up to his saddle. "Where's your impetuous bride, Major? Fled to warmer arms?"

Rage surged. Barely resisting the urge to kick the man's teeth in, Hawk put his crop beneath Slade's wattly chin and raised it. "One more word, and I will thrash you. My father's folly is to blame more than your greed, but you are very unwelcome here, sir. And your comments about a lady can only be attributed to a vulgar mind."

As if breaking a spell, Slade dashed away the crop and stepped back, puce with choler. "Lady?" he spat, then stopped. "May we know where the charming Miss Greystone is, Major?"

Very well. Slade would do, and the Weatherbys were all ears.

"It's none of your business, Slade, but she heard that her dear friend the Marchioness of Arden was in childbed and wished to be with her. As you said, she is somewhat impetuous."

Slade opened, then shut, his mouth. "And the happy event?" he inquired with a disbelieving sneer.

"A son. The heir to Belcraven, born just before dawn."

He heard the Misses Weatherby twittering, as women always did at these events, and of course at the slight vicarious connection to the birth of such an august child.

The birth was just the kind of incontrovertible fact that could glue together almost any lie.

Slade was certainly believing it.

"And the money?" he asked stiffly.

Hawk permitted himself a disdainful sneer. "Will be yours, sir, before the due date. I must thank you for being so obliging to my family."

With that, he turned his horse toward the manor, which apparently would survive, along with the heart of Hawk in the Vale. At the moment, he felt no satisfaction. He did not dismiss the value of preserving the village, but he did not dismiss the cost, either.

As he dismounted in the courtyard the scent of roses met him—sickeningly. He left the horse to the groom and strode swiftly inside.

"George? Where's your bride?"

His father stood in the doorway to the back parlor, leaning on a stick.

"Isn't it more a case of where's the money?"

"Definitely, definitely. You have it? If so, we can start planning the celebration."

"Go to the devil," Hawk snapped, then quickly reined in his temper before it drove him into something else to be ashamed of. "I have the money to pay off Slade, but there is no extra, my lord."

"There is always more money, my boy! I thought a fête similar to that one Vandeimen threw for his wedding. But more regal. Full dress. A procession—"

Hawk turned to go up the stairs. "You will, of course, do exactly as you wish, sir. I have no interest in it."

"Damn your eyes! And where is your bride, eh? Lost her already?"

Hawk paused on the landing. "Precisely, sir."

He entered his room tempted to sink into the darkness, but he had done this for a cause, and the cause went on. He opened his campaign desk. The familiar paper and pens swept him back to his other life. He thought there might even be a trace of smoke and powder trapped in the wood.

Why had the skills that had carried him through challenging and even torturous tasks in the army failed him here?

He picked up the flattened pistol ball that had been his constant reminder that blind luck played a huge part in fate. Perhaps this time his luck had run out.

But, no, that wasn't it. In the army he'd usually worked toward a single imperative. He'd had no personal stake, and a good part of his skill had been in blocking out all distractions of fact or sentiment.

In fact, this campaign was a resounding success.

Hawkinville was safe.

He deserved a medal.

He wrote a Spartan letter to Arden thanking him for his assistance and requesting that he arrange for the money to be available at his Brighton bank before the end of the month. Then, with distaste, he wrote a note to Slade requesting the name of the institution where his money should be deposited.

He went downstairs and sent a servant off with it.

And that, pretty well, was that.

All that was left was the rest of his life.

He walked out of the house at the back, and down to the river, but the ducks must have been enjoying some other part of the water, and heavy clouds were drifting between the earth and the sun. It seemed symbolic, but he knew the sun would shine another day and the ducks would return.

Only Clarissa would be perpetually absent.

Was there any chance that she would relent once the shock wore off? He couldn't bear to hope. If he did, he thought he would be frozen in time, waiting.

He heard a footstep and turned.

Van's fist caught him hard on the jaw and flung him backward into the river.

He sat up spluttering, hand to his throbbing jaw, tasting blood from the inside of his cheek. Van waited, icy.

"If you hit me again," Hawk said, "I'll have to fight back."

"You think you can win?"

"Would anyone win?"

Van glared at him, but the ice was cracking a little. "What's this claptrap about Clarissa going to Lady Arden's lying-in?"

Hawk decided he could probably stand up without having to kill Van and did so. "As a story it can hold if not challenged too strongly."

That was a hint, and he saw Van take it.

"What did happen?"

His boots were full of water. "I tried to elope. I evaded pursuit, but made the mistake of staying the night in Arden's home village."

A crack of laughter escaped Van. "Wellington would have your guts!"

"The thought has occurred to me. I forgot, I assume, that I was at war."

The ducks chose that moment to scoot quacking along the river, perhaps drawn by the splash. One duckling scuttled over to peck at his boots.

Hawk looked down contemplatively. "It seems to be my day for being attacked by animals."

"Are you referring to me?"

Hawk smiled slightly. "Is a demon an animal?"

With a shake of his head, Van stuck out his hand. Hawk took it and climbed out of the river to drip on the bank.

"What happened?" Van demanded. "The whole truth."

"I'm not going to add pneumonia to my other follies. Come inside and I'll tell you as I change."

Hawk discarded his boots by the back door and left wet prints as he padded along the flagstoned corridor and up the stairs. "Mind your head," he said as he went into his room.

Van ducked just in time, then flung himself into the big leather chair with old familiarity. The three of them had rarely chosen the manor over Steynings or the Court, but they had spent some time here, mostly in this room.

"You gave me your word that you wouldn't ruin Clarissa."

Hawk stripped, piling his sodden clothes in his washbasin to spare the wooden floors. "I said, if I remember, that I would not ruin her that day." He kept a careful eye on Van's fists. "I did not mean to be specious, but as it happens, I kept to the letter of my promise."

"And yesterday?"

"And yesterday, I did not." He toweled himself dry. "We were, however, on our way to our wedding. Except that we were stopped."

"By Arden. You don't seem to have been bruised before now."

"My golden tongue."

"Against *Arden*, when he found you bedding a woman he has to regard as being within his protection?"

"We weren't bedding at that moment," Hawk pointed out, pulling clean clothes out of drawers. "And," he added, "Con was there. And Clarissa."

"Didn't want to create a fuss in front of her?"

"Couldn't get through her would be more exact. This was before she realized the truth, of course." He pulled on his breeches, fastened them, and sat down. "She had no idea the will was a forgery, Van. No idea at all."

Van looked at him for a moment, unusually thoughtful. "What now?"

"Now I pay off Slade with Arden's money. It must be pleasant to be able to afford such lordly gestures, and it seems the Rogues wish to arrange to cover it." He explained the arrangements.

"But what of your father? He accosted me in the hall, chortling about outranking me. And going on about a grand fête to beat my wedding celebration."

Hawk sighed. "I deserve a penance, and I certainly have one."

After a moment, Van said, "At least you're free of that Mrs. Rowland. She packed her household into Old Matt's cart yesterday and headed away."

The part of him that was still the Hawk stirred at that. "Do we know why?"

"Not that I know. The general feeling is, good riddance."

"I agree, but I meant to visit her poor husband in case something could be done for him."

"I tried a few weeks back. I forced it as far as a glimpse into his room. I think he's done for. Haggard and frail. I gather there was a dreadful blow to the head."

"Poor man." But at the moment Hawk couldn't feel strongly about it. He couldn't feel very much of anything except loss and pain.

"Do you love her?" Van asked.

Instinctive defense almost had him denying it. "Yes, but it's completely impossible. Apart from my behavior, can you imagine her here with my father insisting on being Lord Deveriled at every turn, and complaining endlessly of not enjoying his true splendor at Gaspard Hall?"

"But her money . . . ?"

"The clear impression is that she would rather eat glass than take a penny of stolen money, and knowing Clarissa, I'm sure she'll stick to her guns."

Hawk couldn't speak of her without becoming maudlin. He surged to his feet and put on his shirt. He couldn't be bothered to go further than that. "Convey my apologies to Maria. What of Miss Trist?"

"Maria and Lord Trevor returned her to Brighton, I understand. Doubtless not looking forward to explaining the situation to Miss Hurstman." Van rose too. "Nicholas Delaney is here, by the way. Staying at the Court with his wife and child. I suspect he'll want a word with you, too."

"So Con said. I'm sure I have enough unmarked skin to go around. Are you off for Brighton, since Maria's there?"

"Yes. Will you be coming in?"

"What for?"

Van grimaced, gripped his arm for a moment, then left.

Hawk went to his window to contemplate ducklings.

Clarissa, dressed in one of Beth's simpler gowns, was attempting to consume a bowl of soup in a spare bedroom while waiting for Con to return with a carriage. She'd suggested that they use the gig, but he'd insisted that she have something better for the journey to Brighton.

The soup was a tasty mix of chicken broth and vegetables, and doubtless nourishing, but she was having trouble finishing it. Tears prickled around her eyes almost constantly, and Hawk's letter was a sharp-edged presence in her pocket.

After a rap, the door opened and Beth came in.

Clarissa leaped to her feet. "Beth, you shouldn't be up!"

"Don't you start pestering me," Beth said, sitting at the table. "Sit down. Eat."

"You look very well," Clarissa said, and Beth did. She was in a loose dressing gown with her hair in one long plait, but she looked much the same as always.

"I am well. It went easily, and I have done considerable research. There is no reason for women to lie around for days or even weeks after a healthy birth. Such a practice quite likely encourages debility. That and lack of fresh air and exercise during pregnancy. I walked at least a mile every day."

Clarissa chuckled, and some of the sodden sadness lifted. "And the baby?"

Beth's face lit up. "Perfect, of course. You must come and see him when you're finished."

Clarissa had no reluctance about abandoning the soup. "I'm finished. I can't wait."

Beth beamed and led the way down the corridor to the nursery. "This is next door to our bedchamber," she said softly, as a maid rose from a chair by the cradle to curtsy.

She led the way over to the grand gilded cradle swathed in blue satin. Inside, a tiny swaddled baby slept. To Clarissa he looked rather grumpy, but she whispered that he was beautiful.

Beth picked him up, and the tiny mouth opened and shut a few times, but then the baby stilled again. She carried him into the bedroom and shut the door. "It's ridiculous, but I feel as if I am stealing him," she said to Clarissa. "He has a staff of three, and that was only after a battle royal. Lucien can't imagine why he shouldn't have his own liveried footman! I have had to be very firm to have time to myself with him."

Clarissa smiled. "He's only eight hours old and you're already at war."

"I've been establishing the rules for months, but they still must be implemented." She grinned, however, as she sat down in a rocking chair, her baby in her arms.

Once settled, she gave Clarissa a clear look. "Now, tell me everything."

"Won't we wake the baby?"

"Not unless you plan to shriek. Anyway," she said, looking down at her child, "I won't mind if he wakes. He has the most beautiful huge blue eyes. I'm feeding him, you know. It's a bit sore at the moment, but it's wonderful." She touched the baby's cheek, and he made little sucking movements but didn't wake.

Clarissa was sure Beth didn't really want to hear about the distressing debacle. But then Beth looked up, all schoolteacher. "Out with it, Clarissa. What have you been up to?"

By the end of the story the baby had awakened, squawked a little, and been put to the breast, with some winces. Beth had told her to keep telling her tale.

Now she asked, "What is your intention now?"

"Not to take any of that money. I'm resolved on that. I still can't believe the Rogues would steal."

She thought that Beth was wincing at the suckling, but then she said, "It was my idea, actually. Forging the will."

"Yours!" Clarissa exclaimed, close enough to a shriek for the baby to jerk off the breast and cry. By the time Beth had him soothed and on the other breast, Clarissa was calm again. Astonished, but calm.

"Why?"

"Why not? Everyone said Deveril had no heir. You needed money. I was afraid even Lucien wouldn't be able to stop your parents from selling you in some way or another."

"But it's a crime."

Beth pulled a laughing face. "I must be of a criminal inclination, then. I even took part in the planting of the will at Deveril's house. Blanche and I acted the part of whores."

Clarissa gaped, and Beth chuckled. "Lucien was dumbfounded too. I wore a black wig, lashings of crude face paint, and a bodice that just barely covered the essentials."

"Dumbfounded" summed it up, especially since Beth seemed to be recalling a delightful memory.

"Do you think I should keep the money, then?"

Beth sobered. "It is more complicated now, isn't it? There is a new Lord Deveril, and without our interference he would have inherited it all." She considered Clarissa. "I am not clear how you regard Major Hawkinville at this time."

"Probably because I'm not clear either. My heart says one thing. My mind shouts warnings. We were warned often enough at school about the seductive wiles of rascals and the susceptible female heart."

"True," said Beth, but with a rather mysterious smile. "But it's as much a mistake to expect perfection from a man as it is to tumble into the power of a rake. After all, can we offer perfection? Do we want to have to try?"

"Heaven forbid. He wrote me a letter."

"What did it say?"

"I haven't read it yet."

"There's no need to make a hasty decision, my dear, but reading the letter might be a good start."

The door opened then and Lord Arden walked in. He halted, and looked almost embarrassed, perhaps because he was in an open-necked shirt and pantaloons and nothing else. Not even stockings and shoes.

But then he looked at his wife and the baby, and Clarissa saw that nothing else mattered.

As he went over to Beth, she slipped out of the room, certain of one thing. She wanted that one day. To be a new mother with the miracle of a child and a husband who looked at her and the child as Lord Arden had looked.

And she wanted it to be Hawk.

She went back to her cold soup to read his letter, then cooled the soup some more with tears. Neat, crisp folds and neat, crisp phrases, but then those poignant perhapses.

Or were they simply the pragmatic analysis of the Hawk's mind?

If only she had some mystical gift that would detect the truth in another person's heart.

Chapter Twenty-seven

~

The trip by carriage took a lot less time than the wandering journey that had carried Clarissa and Hawk to the fateful village. Con, wonderful man, did not attempt conversation, but eventually she weakened and asked him about Hawk.

His look was thoughtful, but he talked. She saw their childhood from another angle. The bond was still there, and the fun, but they were shaded by Con's exasperation with his wilder friends. Lord Vandeimen, it was clear, had always been given to extremes, inclined to act first, think second. Hawk, on the other hand, had thought too much, but relished challenges. He had also lacked a happy home.

She learned more about his parents. Though Con was moderate in his expressions, it was clear that he despised Squire Hawkinville and merely pitied his wife.

"She was hard done to," he said, "but it was her own folly. Everyone in the village agrees that she was a plain woman past any blush of youth. Would the sudden appearance of a handsome gallant protesting adoration not stir a warning?"

He clearly had no idea how his words hit home to her.

"He must have been very convincing," she said.

"Such men usually are. When the truth dawned, she would have been wiser to make the best of it."

"Why? To make it easier for him?"

He looked at her. "That was her attitude, I'm sure. But she only made matters bitter for herself, her child, and everyone around her. There was no changing it."

"And she couldn't even leave," Clarissa said. "It was her home." And perhaps she, too, had loved Hawkinville.

Con said, "It's made Hawk somewhat cold. Not truly cold, but guarded in his emotions. And he's never had a high opinion of marriage."

Clarissa was aware of the letter in her pocket. Guarded, perhaps, but not well. And not cold. And he wanted marriage.

Could it all be false?

She didn't think so.

Con called for the carriage to stop, and she saw they were at a crossroads. "We can turn off here for Hawk in the Vale," he said.

"No."

She wasn't ready yet. She was determined to be thoughtful about this.

"I was thinking more that we could go to my home, to Somerford Court. We don't even have to go through the village to get to it from here. Nicholas Delaney is there, and I'm sure he'd like to speak to you. We can send a note to Miss Hurstman and go on to Brighton tomorrow."

Clarissa was certainly in no rush to return to Brighton. "Why not? I wouldn't mind a word with him, either."

The Court was almost as charming as Hawkinville Manor, though centuries younger, but Clarissa was past caring about such things. Con's wife, mother, and sister were welcoming—Con's wife insisted on being Susan— but it couldn't touch her distraction. Nothing in the world seemed real except her and Hawk and her dilemma.

And stopping where he was mere minutes away had not been a good idea.

Nicholas Delaney took one look at her and suggested that they talk, but ordered a wine posset for her. As she went with him into a small sitting room, she said, "I'm not hungry."

"You need to eat. You can't fight well on an empty stomach."

"I'm likely to fight you. This is all your fault."

"If you wish, but I think the blame can be well spread around. There's nothing so weak as 'I meant well,' but in this everyone meant well, Clarissa."

"Not Hawk. Hawk wanted my money. I'm not touching it." That should shake his complacency.

"As you wish, of course," he said. "I'm sure Miss Hurstman can find you a position pandering to a not-too-tyrannical old lady."

She picked up a china figurine and hurled it at him.

He caught it. "It would be foolish to be wantonly poor, Clarissa, and no one has a greater right to that money than you."

"What about Hawk's father?" She made herself say it. "The new Lord Deveril."

"Only by the most precise letter of the law." He put the figurine on a small table. "Sit down, and I'll tell you where that money came from."

She sat, her revivifying anger sagging like a pricked bladder. "From Lord Deveril's unpleasant businesses, I assume."

"He might have increased it a bit that way, but even vice is not quite so profitable in a short time."

Clarissa listened in amazement to a story of treason, embezzlement, and pure theft.

"Then the money belongs to the people this woman got it from. Except," she added thoughtfully, "they would hardly want to claim it, would they?"

"They could be found. Thérèse happily gave up a list of their names once she had no more use for them. In the end the government settled for letting them know that they were known. Many of them fled the country, and I don't think those that remain would want to be reminded of their folly."

"The Crown, then."

"The Regent would love it. It would buy him some trinket or other. But by what excuse can the money be given to the Crown?"

She was arguing for the sake of arguing, because she was angry with them all. "When I'm twenty-one, I can do with it as I wish."

"Of course. I arranged it that way. In retrospect, that was an indulgence. It apparently gave Hawkinville reason to doubt the will." He smiled. "It does seem unfair that women at twenty-one are considered infantile, when men at the same age are given control of their affairs."

"That sounds like Mary Wollstonecraft."

"She made some good points."

There was a knock on the door, and a maid came in with the steaming posset. When she'd left, Clarissa decided not to be infantile. She sat at a small table and dipped in her spoon.

Cream, eggs, sugar, and wine. After a few mouthfuls she did begin to feel less miserable. "This will have me drunk."

He sat across the table from her. "Probably why it's excellent for the suffering invalid. There are times when a little inebriation helps."

She looked at him. "What do you want me to do?"

He shook his head. "I have put you in charge of your own destiny."

She took more of the posset, and the wine untangled some of her sorest knots.

"I'm afraid of making a fool of myself."

"We all are, most of the time."

She glanced up. "For life? How does anyone make choices?"

"Of marriage partners? If people worried too much about making the perfect choice, the human race would die out."

"Not necessarily," she pointed out, and he laughed.

"True, but it would be a chaotic system. Marriage brings order to the most disorderly of human affairs."

"But there are many bitter, corroding marriages. Hawk's parents, for example. And mine."

"True fondness, goodwill, and common sense can get us over most hurdles."

She spooned up the last of the sweet liquid, and the

wine probably gave her courage to ask a personal question. "Is that what your marriage is like?"

He laughed. "Oh, no. My marriage is one of complete insanity. But I recommend it to you, too. It's called love."

Love.

"Perhaps I should see Hawk," she said, a warm spiral beginning to envelop her in betraying delight.

But Delaney shook his head. "I think we'll wait an hour or so to see if that's only the wine talking." He rose. "Meanwhile, come and meet my insanity. Eleanor, and my daughter, Arabel."

As they went to the door he said, "Would you be able to call me Nicholas?"

"In what circumstances?" she teased.

"Damned tenses. I would like it if you would call me Nicholas. I think you are by way of being an honorary Rogue."

Con, and Nicholas. New friends. And her acceptance of it was something to do with Hawk, and with Lord Arden.

"Nicholas," she said, but she added with a giggle, "I'm not sure I can call Lord Arden Lucien, though."

"Definitely the wine," he said, guiding her out of the room. "The number of people to call Arden Lucien is small. If not for the Rogues it might be down to one—his mother."

"And Beth, surely."

"Perhaps."

She understood. Without the Rogues, Lord Arden might not be the sort of husband Beth would call by his first name. He might be the sort who expressed every sour emotion with his fists.

"Perhaps I should call Hawk George," she said. "Less predatory. But then he wouldn't call me Falcon."

Nicholas shook his head. "We must definitely wait an hour."

Eleanor Delaney was a handsome woman with a rooted tranquility that Clarissa admired. Of course, it must be easy to be tranquil with a husband such as Nicholas. Clarissa was sure he had given her no trouble, told her no lies.

Arabel was a charming toddler in a short pink dress showing lace-trimmed pantalettes. Her chestnut curls were cut short, and she was playing with a cat that Clarissa recognized.

"Jetta!"

The cat reacted to the name, or perhaps to her. Whichever, Clarissa certainly received a cold stare. Lord above, was a cat capable of fixing blame for the loss of its hero?

"It was thought to be in danger from the manor dogs, so I brought it up here." Nicholas swooped up his daughter and carried her, laughing, over to be introduced. Clarissa saw identical sherry-gold eyes.

Arabel smiled with unhesitating acceptance. " 'Lo!"

"Not the beginning of an ode," said Nicholas, "but her greeting."

The child turned to him, beaming, to say, " 'Lo! 'Lo! 'Lo!" But then she said, "Papa. Love Papa."

Clarissa almost felt she should look away as Nicholas kissed his daughter's nose and said, "I love you too, cherub."

Insanity.

Love.

Heaven.

But then Arabel turned to her and stretched out. Astonished, Clarissa took the child and duly admired the wooden doll clutched in one fist. Nicholas went to talk to Eleanor, and the child didn't turn to look.

What blithe confidence in love that was, that never doubted, or feared the loss of it. Would she ever feel that way?

Then Arabel squirmed to get down and led the way back to the cat and some other toys. Clarissa sat on the carpet and played, discovering one certainty.

She wanted a child.

She wanted to be married to Hawk and have Hawk's children, but if that didn't happen, she wanted to be a mother. A married mother.

She tried to imagine being married to someone else.

It didn't seem possible, but time must have an effect on that. What was the difference between a wild passion and an eternal love?

Easier by far to play with the child than to tussle with adult problems.

But then Mrs. Delaney insisted that it was bedtime. When she came to pick up her daughter, she said, "I understand that you are a Rogue now. I hope you will call me Eleanor."

Clarissa scrambled to her feet, not quite so comfortable with this informality, but she agreed.

"And if you want a woman to talk to," Eleanor Delaney said, "I am a good listener. No hand at good advice, you understand, but we can often work these things out for ourselves once we start, can't we?"

She carried the child away, and Clarissa glanced at the clock.

"Still half an hour to go," Nicholas said.

She pulled a face, but said, "Then I think I'll walk in the garden and talk to myself."

She expected a comment, but he only said, "By all means—if you promise not to sneak down to the village."

She glared, but the thought hadn't occurred to her. It was a very little time to wait, and she knew it was wise to see if her forgiveness seeped away with the effects of the posset.

When she left the room, the cat came with her. She looked down. "I thought I was the enemy."

The cat merely waited. Perhaps the clever animal had decided she was the key to Hawk. It would be nice if true.

The Somerford Court gardens were pleasant, though rather formal. She crossed a lawn and wandered down a yew-lined path, greeted by a gardener busy keeping the hedges trim. It was a warm but heavy evening. Even the birds were quiet. Apart from the *snick, snick, snick* of the gardener's shears, it was soundless.

She came to a round fishpond dotted with water lilies and sat on the stone edge to trail her hand in the water.

A fat carp came to nibble, then swam away, disappointed. Jetta crouched on the rim, also disappointed.

No food.

No fortune.

Her slightly inebriated mind didn't want to focus, not even on talking over her problem with herself.

She looked around, but nothing offered wisdom or inspiration. The pond sat in the middle of a hedge-lined square, with four neat flower beds set with bushes in the center and lined with low white flowers. It struck her as amusing that Hawk of the neatly folded note had the lush, willful garden, while Con owned such precision.

Both had been formed by previous generations, however.

Each side of the square hedge had an opening leading to another path. None of them invited.

Then a figure crossed over one of those paths. A maid in dark clothing with a large bundle. And Jetta rose to hiss.

Clarissa looked at the cat. "Another rival for Hawk's affections?" But the cat was simply twitching its tail restlessly.

Clarissa frowned at it. "Now you have me twitchy." She scooped it up and went down the path to catch another glimpse. The woman was far ahead, going briskly about her business, which was probably to take laundry to the village. Jetta gave another, almost huffy, hiss; the woman turned right and was out of sight.

Clarissa turned back toward the house, but something about the woman was on her mind now. She hurried in a direction that should provide another view, giving thanks for the straight lines of the garden. She came to the abrupt end of the garden, with countryside before her.

The woman was already across a pasture and climbing a stile, bundle under her arm, to follow a footpath along the edge of a harvested field toward the village. It wasn't a servant. It was that Mrs. Rowland.

"Still don't approve?" she muttered to the tense cat. "Misfortune turns some people miserable, you know.

And see, she has to take in laundry to put food on the table."

Or she might be stealing. An unfair thought about the poor woman, who'd shown no sign of furtiveness, but Clarissa decided she had to tell someone. She turned back to the now rather distant house.

Somerford Court was a rambling place, and when she eventually entered, she found herself near the kitchens. She stopped in there, faced by half a dozen female servants who didn't know who she was, and feeling very foolish.

"I'm Miss Greystone. A guest."

Then Jetta leaped down and was immediately the center of attention. "Wonderful mouser, it is," said the woman who was probably the cook, smiling. "Can we help you, miss?"

Clarissa felt that she had been properly introduced. She almost didn't want to spoil it by saying anything, but she made herself speak.

"I just saw someone in the garden. I think it was Mrs. Rowland, from the village. Does she take in laundry, or mending, perhaps?"

And what business is it of yours? she could imagine the servants saying.

"Her?" said the cook. "Not likely. She has been here now and then, to speak to her ladyship—the Dowager Lady Amleigh, that is. Begging, if you ask me, for all her airs. But not today, miss."

Protesting that would do no good. Perhaps she should speak to the dowager.

She left the kitchen and headed toward the front of the house. The Court, however, was the sort of rambling place built in stages, where no corridor went in a straight line. She was beginning to think she'd have to call for help, but then she tentatively opened a door and found herself in the front hall.

Now what? Her alarm about Mrs. Rowland was beginning to seem very silly, but she decided she would find the dowager.

At the moment the house was as sleepy as the gardens,

but she'd seen a bellpull in the small room where she'd talked with Nicholas. She was heading there when Nicholas came out of another room. "Ah, your hour's up," he said, smiling.

If she'd wanted to block her decisions from her mind, she'd certainly succeeded. For the past little while she hadn't thought of Hawk at all. Perhaps that was why her mind had eagerly clutched the little mystery.

Now that the idea was back, it pushed out all others. "I still want to see him," she said.

"Very well—"

"Nicholas!" They both turned to see Eleanor racing down the stairs, white-faced. "I can't find Arabel!"

Nicholas caught her in his arms. "She likes to hide—"

"We've searched her room. The ones nearby. I've called." She turned, searching the hall. "Arabel! Arabel!"

He pulled her back into his arms. "Hush. She can't have come down here. We'll get everyone to search."

Con and Susan had emerged from the room where Nicholas had been. They immediately went off to set all the servants to the search, inside and out, and a message was sent to the village for extra people.

The Delaneys hurried upstairs, calling their daughter's name. Clarissa raced after them, caught up in the alarm at the thought of that sweet child perhaps stuck in a chest, or having tumbled down some stairs.

It was only upstairs, wondering helplessly where to look, that the thought struck. It was too ridiculous to bother Nicholas with, so she ran in search of Con, finding him in the front hall marshaling affairs. Quickly, she told him about Mrs. Rowland.

"You're sure it was she?"

"Mostly," she said, less sure by the moment. She almost said, "Jetta hissed," but that would make her seem a complete idiot.

"But she was carrying something?"

"I thought it was laundry. Or mending."

But then his eyes sharpened. "Didn't you mention her earlier? That she reminded you of someone?"

"Of the fortune-teller." But then she inhaled with

shock. "She talked about Rogues. And she gave me Nicholas's initials!" She quickly sketched that encounter.

"Who could be interested in Clarissa's money and in the Rogues?"

Clarissa turned to see Hawk there, hat, crop, and gloves in hand. Their eyes met in a sudden collision of need and problems.

Con said, "Madame Thérèse Bellaire." But then he added, "It's insanity. Why would she even be in England?" He was already turning to run upstairs, however. "We have to tell Nicholas. Dear God . . ."

Clarissa and Hawk ran after him.

They found the Delaneys opening and shutting drawers and armoires that had to have been searched before.

Con told them, and they both turned impossibly paler.

"Thérèse," Nicholas said. "Please, God, no."

Eleanor clutched his arm, and then they were wrapped with each other. Clarissa remembered that Madame Bellaire was the woman who had gathered the money, then lost it to Deveril. She'd thought when Nicholas told her that there was more to the story.

If only she had pursued. Or done *something*.

"We have to follow it up," said Nicholas, coming back to life. To Clarissa he said, "Which way did you see her go?"

"Down to the village." She described it exactly.

Before she could say she was sorry, Hawk said, "That path splits three ways. And I doubt she took the village one. She moved her whole household out at crack of dawn."

"Where?" Nicholas asked.

"No one knows, and we won't until Old Matt returns to say where he took his cartload. Madame Mystique must have some base in Brighton, but there's no saying she's returned there. If it is she." He added, looking at Clarissa, "Fortune-tellers can be uncanny."

"I know! I'm not sure of anything."

Clarissa could almost feel Nicholas's need to rush off, but he looked at Hawk. "I'm in no state to think, Hawkinville. I gather this is your forte. Will you take command?"

Clarissa saw a touch of color on Hawk's cheeks. She remembered then that he and Nicholas could be seen as on opposite sides in respect to her. All that was unimportant now.

"Of course," Hawk, said. "I'm sure you want to do something, however. Why not follow the route Clarissa described? Look for clues or people who saw the woman. Take a couple of Con's grooms to follow other routes when it splits."

Nicholas hugged his wife and left. Susan went to hold Eleanor's hand.

Hawk turned to Con. "I'd like you to head for Brighton by the most direct route, looking for the Frenchwoman or Old Matt. If you get there without a trace, find Madame Mystique's establishment and check it out. Take a couple of armed grooms—and be careful."

"Aye-aye, sir," said Con ironically, but without resentment, and hurried out.

The salute brought a slight smile to Hawk's lips.

"Shouldn't someone check Mrs. Rowland's place here?" Clarissa asked.

"Yes, I'll do that. It won't take long, and it needs a careful eye. I'll see if my father knows anything about the woman, too. He was mightily upset to hear of her leaving."

He turned to go, but Clarissa grabbed his sleeve. She wasn't sure what to say except that she had to say something. "Find her."

He looked at her with deep darkness, then touched her cheek. "If it is humanly possible—"

Then in a black streak, Jetta leaped in to sit on his boots, as if trying to pin him down. Clarissa wondered for a mad moment whether the cat knew he was going into danger. He picked it up and moved it, and strode out. After a shake, Jetta strode after him. There was no other word for it. Clarissa felt as if he had a guard.

But then she turned back and saw Eleanor's face. "I'm sorry. I should have gone after her."

But Eleanor shook her head. "She would have killed you. Or taken you with her if she could."

"Then I should have raised the alarm! Immediately."

"Why?" Eleanor had lost all that placid calm, but she came to take Clarissa's hands. "Why should you imagine anything so extreme? Life would be impossible if we all jumped to such conclusions every time we saw something out of the ordinary."

"But," Clarissa said bitterly, "I should have learned from experience. Everyone who has anything to do with me ends up in disaster."

Eleanor gathered her into her arms. "No, no, my dear. Everyone who has anything to do with Thérèse Bellaire ends up in disaster. Really," she added, with a touch of unsteady humor, "Napoleon would have been well advised to wring her neck."

Chapter Twenty-eight

~

The women continued the search for a while—Clarissa even ran out to the fishpond in case the child had escaped the house and drowned—but no one's heart was in it. They were all sure that Arabel had been stolen away.

Clarissa took a moment in the garden to let out her tears, and she felt better for it, if drained. But, oh, the thought of that sweet, trusting infant, who seemed innocent of anything but adoring kindness, in the hands of "Mrs. Rowland"! If only she'd not acted sensibly for once. If only she'd been impetuous, and pursued. Perhaps she might at least be with the child and able to protect and comfort her.

The only "if only" that mattered now, however, was if only she could do something to speed up the child's safe return.

She returned to the house and discovered that Hawk also had returned and taken over Con's study for what could only be called a command post. She entered to find that he'd set the women to work, even the dowager and Con's sister.

A map was spread on the desk, and Hawk was studying paths and roads under the eye of a watchful cat. Eleanor was taking notes and seemed much steadier. Everyone else seemed to be drawing. Clarissa soon gathered that they were drawing rough sketches of routes, with churches, houses, streams, and such as markers.

She was given a piece of paper, and Eleanor read off some details for her.

"We're going to send out riders along all these routes," Eleanor said. "It will cover everything from here to a five-mile radius." She glanced at Hawk. "He is very meticulous, isn't he?"

Clarissa looked at him too. "He has that reputation." She couldn't help adoring him for his control and discipline. Knowing him, she realized that inside he was probably as achingly worried and anxious as they all were, but he was intent on his goal. Rescue.

He said something to Eleanor, looking up, and his eyes found Clarissa. Something flashed there—a need, she hoped—but immediately it was controlled. "The Henfield road goes through two tollgates," he said to Eleanor. "The second should be far enough. The river blocks any roundabout route. Who has that one?"

Eleanor looked at her list. "Susan." She went to relay the instructions to Susan, who was using the deep windowsill to work on.

Then Nicholas returned, looking exhausted but better somehow for racing around. She realized that Hawk had sent him for exactly that reason, and had probably put Eleanor to work to help her, too. So many threads in his fingers, each one to be done perfectly, because failure was impossible.

Then the maps were finished, the waiting grooms summoned, instructed with crisp precision, and sent off.

"They can be back within the hour," said Hawk, but he glanced out of the window at the overcast sky. "If the weather holds." He looked at Nicholas. "The woman may have gone to Brighton, but it might be too obvious. What do you want to do?"

"Ride hell-bent for Brighton, of course," said Nicholas. "Or to London. Or to the Styx to bargain with Charon—" He stopped himself. "We will wait until the riders return, and hope there's a clear path. It would be worse, after all, to go in the wrong direction entirely."

"Then we must eat," Hawk said. "Susan?"

Susan left, and everyone moved restlessly, waiting for something that could not come for a while.

"If Con finds anything along the road," Hawk said, "he'll send back word. What's the woman like? From all I've heard of her, devious but not stupid."

Nicholas rubbed his hands over his face. "No, not stupid. But she can be foolish. She prides herself on her arcane plans, but then gets lost in them. Certainly following a straight line is unlikely to find her. You're going about it the right way. Spin a web."

Now that the immediate work was done, Eleanor Delaney had sunk into a chair, staring into nowhere. Nicholas went to her.

Clarissa turned to look out of the window. Evening was beginning to mute the day. Realistically speaking, it was no more terrible for the child to be in the hands of a madwoman at night, but it felt as though it was.

Hawk came to stand nearby. She knew it even before she looked.

"Is she mad?" she asked.

"Probably not. But there's a kind of madness that thinks only of itself. All controls to do with decency or humanity are lost, and only the desires and pleasures of the person matter. I suspect she is that sort of woman. What do you think?"

"I think of her with her children."

He put out a hand to her, then stopped it, lowered it. She did not protest. There was no place in this for them, for the tangles and dilemmas still to be sorted out.

Susan returned, followed by maids with trays holding tea, wine, and plates of hastily made sandwiches. Certainly, thought Clarissa, sitting down to dinner would be macabre. The maids left, and everyone was busy for a moment, pouring, passing, taking plates. But then stillness settled.

"Eat," Hawk said. "You can get it down if you try, and strength is needed. And don't get drunk."

After a moment, Nicholas put down his wineglass and

picked up a sandwich. Eleanor was drinking tea, but she started to eat too.

Hawk ate two sandwiches, but he seemed to be thinking throughout the meal. Then he said, "The most likely situation is that the Bellaire woman has taken the child to hold for ransom. I gather she has reason of sorts to think that Clarissa's money is hers. My father was under the illusion that she was going to marry him as soon as she was widowed. No illusion, actually. That doubtless was her plan once he had the money. I suspect I was her hunting dog, sent to sniff out the villains. An interesting mind. I assume that my elopement told her the plan was dead—so we have this."

Nicholas put down his food. "But we only arrived yesterday. This has to have been an impulse. Had she no other device? It is unlike her."

"She prefers multiple plans?"

"She adores them."

"Mrs. Rowland had two children," Hawk said, "a boy and a girl. Are they hers?"

Nicholas laughed. "Thérèse? Impossible to imagine, and two years ago she boasted of the perfection of her body, unmarked by birth. Good God, has she kidnapped others?"

"Or adopted, to be fair. She's been here for months with them. A strange ploy if she took them for money. No," Hawk said.

He picked up Jetta and stroked the cat as if it helped him think. "I suspect the children were simply disguise. Perhaps poor Rowland was too. Intriguing, really. She must have been left in a very difficult situation after Waterloo. Stranded in Belgium, without her powerful protectors, and thinking of her money in England. If she found a wounded officer and persuaded him to claim her as his common-law wife—perhaps in exchange for nursing him—and acquired a couple of the stray orphans that always wander after battle, she would have an excellent cover for a Frenchwoman to enter England."

"You sound as if you're falling under her spell."

Hawk looked at Nicholas. "I'll wring her neck if need

be. It's often necessary to enter into the mind of villains to decide what they will do. And villains rarely see themselves that way. They see themselves as clever, as entitled to what they seize, as justified in the evil that they do. You're right about her having some other plan. Knowing what it is would be useful, but the main point is that she will demand money. A great deal of money and in short order. Can you raise it?"

Clarissa stood. "I wish I could give her all of mine! I don't want it. She was right when she said it was poisoned."

"But you can't get it in a day or two," Hawk said, as if the money was of no importance to him. "Arden offered me twenty thousand, so I assume he can put his hands on that quickly."

"The Rogues," said Nicholas, suddenly alert.

But then pounding feet had them all turning to the door. It burst open, and a panting groom raced in. He looked around the crowded room in confusion. "Sirs, letter from his lordship!"

Hawk took it and opened it. It contained another sealed paper. "She went through the Preston toll," he said, reading. "A woman fitting her description in a fast carriage. Bold. And, even bolder," he added. He looked at Nicholas. "The woman paid the tollkeeper to give this letter to anyone who asked." He held it out. "It's addressed to you, but of course Con read it."

Nicholas was already reading. "She wants a hundred thousand pounds before eight o'clock tomorrow evening." He gave it to Eleanor.

"Impossible," gasped the dowager Lady Amleigh.

"And she has her other string," Nicholas carried on, looking strangely stunned. "She claims to have Dare."

Clarissa looked around in confusion. Hawk said, "It's not possible—" But then he breathed, "Lieutenant Rowland." He cursed, which, given the presence of ladies, showed how deeply shocked he was.

"She wouldn't lie," Nicholas said. "It has to be true. Pray God it doesn't make Con do something wild. We have to go."

"Yes, of course." But Hawk held up a hand. "What of the money? We have to think now how to raise it." But then he looked at Nicholas. "If it's Dare, he's in bad shape. Van saw him briefly. He thought he was dying."

"We get him and Arabel back," said Nicholas flatly. "By all means, let's think how to get the money. If Thérèse can be easily found in Brighton, Con and Vandeimen will do it."

Hawk sat at the desk and put a clean sheet of paper in front of him. "You have all I can raise, but it's precious little, even with jewels included. Arden's twenty thousand, of course."

Clarissa bit her lip, thinking what that meant for Hawk in the Vale, but there was no choice.

The dowager suddenly stood and took off her rings and a brooch, putting them on the desk. "I'll go and get my jewel box."

Con's wife and sister did the same. Eleanor said, "Everything I have with me, of course. But most is back in Somerset. There's not time, is there?"

Nicholas took her hand. "We can try. But there are those closer. Arden," he said to Hawk. "He's good for more. Beth has diamonds worth a good part of the amount."

Clarissa had seen Beth's diamonds. They were part of the ducal estate and not really Lord Arden's to give, but she knew he would.

"Leander's probably in Somerset, but we'll send to his Sussex estate in case. Francis. Hal's in Brighton, but he has little. I think Stephen's in London. If there are ways of raising money, he'll find it. We have to contact the Yeovils too."

"Dare's parents?" Hawk said. "Yes, of course. Though he may not be a pretty sight."

"If he's alive, do you think that matters?"

"No." Hawk added the name.

The two Lady Amleighs and Helen Somerford returned and put jewel boxes on the table, Clarissa didn't think the contents would be worth a vast sum, but they would be treasured pieces given up in this cause.

"I have some jewelry in Brighton lent me by the Duke of Belcraven," she said. "You can have that. When I come of age," she added firmly, "Deveril's money will go to repay all these debts. I am determined on it."

She said it looking at Hawk, afraid of objection, but he nodded. "I hope to get through this without paying a penny, and with the woman locked up for her crimes."

"Not wise."

They all looked at Nicholas. "We really don't want Thérèse on trial. She knows or guesses far too much. I'm sure she's counting on that. Of course, if she harms Arabel in any way, I will kill her. I hope she's counting on that, too."

The first grooms began to return with their pointless reports on their routes. They were sent to eat while Nicholas wrote letters to the Rogues and the Yeovils, asking for the money and jewels, and a message to his home in Somerset instructing a trusted servant to bring the contents of his safe.

Clarissa couldn't help thinking that some lucky highwaymen might make the strike of their lives.

"Where shall we ask that it be sent?" Nicholas asked.

After a moment, Hawk said, "Van's house in Brighton," and gave the address. Once the letters were on their way, he said, "And now we can go. She's gone to ground in Brighton, but by God, there has to be a way to find her."

Clarissa, Eleanor, and Susan jammed into the Amleigh phaeton, Eleanor driving, the gentlemen on horseback. Again Jetta insisted on riding with Hawk, sitting upright in front of him.

"She'll fall off at speed," Clarissa said.

"I doubt it," said Nicholas, his horse sidling impatiently, doubtless a reflection of the rider. "The Chinese trained cats to ride into war exactly like that. They would leap at opponents and blind them."

Clarissa shivered at the thought, but all in all, the more protectors Hawk had, the better.

Then they were off. Five grooms not needed for other duties rode with them. Heads turned as the speeding cavalcade whipped past. Clarissa could only think of all the people with small problems, all the parents whose children were safe.

In a short while Nicholas drew alongside to tell Eleanor he was riding ahead, and she gave him her blessing.

"If I were any rider at all, I'd go with him. It is so *intolerable* not to be racing to do something, no matter how futile." She cracked her whip, and the horses picked up pace as the sun set sulkily behind heavy clouds.

Chapter Twenty-nine

~

Brighton. Clarissa remembered entering Brighton a short while before, full of nerves and hope. How different now, with so much at stake. How trivial all her earlier anxieties seemed. The past hours of stress had scoured away her uncertainties about Hawk. In this uncertain world, what did twenty, forty, sixty years matter?

Carpe diem, for indeed, one could not know what the morrow would bring.

The sunlight had almost gone by the time they entered Lord Vandeimen's house, finding the Vandeimens there, along with Con and Nicholas. Con seemed afire with new purpose, and it was all to do with Lord Darius.

"Madame Mystique has a house on Ship Street," he said, "but it seems deserted. I hesitated to break in."

"Good," Hawk said. "We can't be precipitous. We risk triggering her to do something undesirable. No sign of Old Matt?"

Clarissa had to think who that was. Oh, the carter who had transported Lieutenant Rowland and the children.

No, she corrected. He'd transported Lord Darius Debenham and the poor waifs picked up from who-knew-where and subjected to Thérèse Bellaire's cold heart for a year. She desperately regretted returning the children, but couldn't see how she and Hawk could have done anything else.

"Not on the road," Con said. "I've sent the grooms

to check on all the inns and taverns. He likes a drink. But how do we search all Brighton?"

"Meticulously," said Hawk with a hint of a self-mocking smile.

"We don't have enough people to comb thousands of households!"

There was a rap on the door and they all turned. They were all, Clarissa realized, still standing in the narrow hall.

The nearest person opened the door—Susan.

Blanche and Major Beaumont came in. Blanche went straight to Eleanor and put a bundle in her hands. "Lucien's necklace is the most valuable piece, but I've put in some stage trumpery too. Perhaps she won't have time to study it."

"Good idea," said Nicholas. "Maria, which jewelers here are most likely to keep paste for people to wear?"

Everyone flowed into the front parlor and soon Maria had a list, but it was too late to visit jewelers today.

"We have to do something," said Eleanor fiercely, desperately. "Dear heaven, if she's awake, she will be so frightened!" Nicholas went to her, but he was haggard with the same need.

"We try to find her," Hawk said steadily. "Maria, may I have some of your servants?"

"Of course! Which ones?"

"A few who are Brighton born and bred."

She hurried out and soon returned with a maid, a sturdy young man, and a frightened-looking boy, whose eyes seemed to be trying to go all ways at once.

"Listen carefully," Hawk said in a clipped, military voice. "We need to find a woman in Brighton. The main thing is that she is French. She was last seen looking sallow and dressed in black, but she may have changed. She's slim, dark-eyed, and about thirty. She will probably have one or three young children with her. We're also looking for a very sick officer, who might go by the name Lieutenant Rowland. The last person is a carter called Old Matt. Old Matt Fagg. He might simply be drunk in one of the taverns. All three people are somewhere in

Brighton. You are to alert as many people as possible—children too—that anyone who brings me news of where any of these people are will receive ten guineas."

The maid and groom came to sharp attention. The lad gaped. That was probably his yearly wage.

"What's more, if any of these people are found by anyone, you three will each receive ten guineas for yourself. Mind, though, everyone is to be careful. We only want to know where she is. We do not want her disturbed. Do you understand?"

All three nodded, though "dazzled" might have better described their state than "comprehending."

"Do you have any questions?"

The lad said, "Ten guineas, sir?"

"Yes."

The three servants backed out, but then Clarissa heard one set of running footsteps. She was sure they were the boy's.

"I do hope no one will get hurt," she said.

"You wouldn't make a general, love."

It slipped out and they looked at one another.

"I have this constant urge," said Nicholas, pacing the room, "to go and search the streets. It's irrational."

"But perfectly reasonable," Hawk said. "Waiting—and watching—are always the hardest parts."

Clarissa guessed that he referred to his army career.

"What about Madame Mystique's house?" she asked.

"She might try to hide in open view?" Hawk asked. "I doubt it. It would be a trap. But it certainly should be checked. Who's best at housebreaking?"

"I've done it," said Nicholas with a wry smile, "but I wouldn't say it's a skill of mine."

"I'll do it, then," said Hawk, picking up a satchel he'd brought and taking out a ring of strange-looking keys.

"You must have had an interesting war," Nicholas remarked.

"That's one way of looking at it. As I pointed out recently, however, it was nothing so dramatic as chasing down spies. More a question of checking out warehouses."

Clarissa remembered, and knew he'd said it deliberately, as a kind of connection.

He took Nicholas with him, as a kindness, she was sure, and Jetta by necessity, but they were soon back to say that the house was deserted and no clue could be found there. "Except traces of opium," Hawk said. "So she probably does have Lord Darius and the children drugged."

"It can be so dangerous," Eleanor whispered. "I've never given her it. Not even for teething."

The door suddenly opened and Miss Hurstman stood there. "Ha!" she exclaimed, fixing Clarissa with a dragon's eye. "Maria, I told you to tell me if she turned up." But then she looked around. "What's the matter?"

Nicholas went and took her hands. "Thérèse Bellaire has kidnapped Arabel."

Miss Hurstman, who Clarissa had thought was made of pure steel, went sickly sallow and sat down with a thump. "Oh, heaven help the poor angel!"

Clarissa thought the woman might cry, but then she stiffened. "I assume you men are dealing with it?"

"As best we can," said Hawk dryly.

A knock on the door brought the maidservant who'd been sent out to search. "I found the carter, sir!" she declared, flushed with excitement as if this was a treasure hunt. For her, Clarissa supposed, it was. "At Mrs. Purbeck's lodging house, sir, but dead drunk. Really drunk. She thinks he's drunk uncut brandy, sir, for there was a half-anker nearby."

Maria gave the woman her ten guineas and told her to go and find a way to bring the unconscious man here.

"Uncut brandy?" she asked when the maid was gone.

"Smugglers ship it double strength in small casks," Susan said. "It saves space. Then it's watered to the right proof over here. There's many a man drunk himself to death sneaking a bit from a smuggler's cask."

Clarissa had learned that Susan was from the coast of Devon. Did all people there know such details?

After that, it was merely a question of waiting. Old Matt was trundled over in a handcart and put to bed in the kitchen, but it was clear he would not wake soon—and perhaps not at all.

The Delaneys left to go up to the room prepared for them.

Clarissa realized that she would have to return to Broad Street. Foolishly, she didn't want to leave Hawk, and she didn't want to leave the center of the action in case some miracle should occur.

But then, after a short interval, the other two servants straggled in to say that no one seemed to have seen a trace of the Frenchwoman, or the invalid officer. Hawk gave the lad and the man their ten guineas anyway, and rubbed a hand over his face.

"She can't have hidden that thoroughly. It's not possible."

"Unless it's a blind," Con said, "and she's not in Brighton at all."

Hawk considered it, but then shook his head. "She wants her money, and this is the place she appointed. I'm missing something. We all need sleep."

Clarissa couldn't imagine how anyone could sleep, but Miss Hurstman rose, a very subdued Miss Hurstman. Clarissa realized that there hadn't been a word about her elopement. It was a very minor thing.

She turned to Hawk. Minor or not, it seemed strange to leave without something meaningful between them. "Can you sleep?" she asked. Good heavens, it had been only last night that they'd slept together.

It was Lord Vandeimen who answered. "He can sleep through anything when he decides he needs it. We thought it would be a nice nostalgic touch to share quarters before Waterloo. We didn't realize then what kind of work Hawk really did. Con, Dare, and I couldn't get a moment's rest for the coming and going. Hawk, on the other hand, would suddenly stop, lie down, and go to sleep, telling whoever was there to take messages."

Hawk winced. "Was it as bad as that?"

"Yes." But then Lord Vandeimen added, "We wouldn't have missed it, all the same. I hope to God it is Dare, and we can save him."

Hawk picked up a pen from the table, turning it restlessly in his fingers. "He came to speak to me that last night. He was leaving for the Duchess of Richmond's ball. You two had already gone to your regiments, and I was busy, but Wellington wanted as many officers as possible there to keep up appearances.

"He came into my room and said he wanted to thank me. I asked what for, of course. Probably rather shortly. I was busy, and his gadfly antics in the past weeks hadn't endeared him to me. He gestured at all the papers in that way he had that made it seem that he took nothing seriously. 'Oh, for all this, I suppose,' he said. 'An excellent education in the complexities of military affairs.' Then he said that if he lived, he planned to take a seat in Parliament and work to improve army administration.

"I suddenly took him more seriously, and I worried. Men do get a premonition of death. I asked him, but he shrugged and said something about it being reasonable to consider death on the eve of battle. Flippantly, in his usual way. Then he asked me to take care of you, Con, and I realized that most of his gadfly japes had been a deliberate attempt to carry you through the waiting time."

Con's mouth was tight with suppressed tears. "But he's alive. And we'll find him and make him well again."

"Yes, we will. I didn't look after you, Con, but we'll get Dare back, so he can berate me about it."

Clarissa couldn't be cautious or discreet. She went over to Hawk and pulled his head down for a gentle kiss. "Tomorrow is the battle, but I will be by your side."

He cradled her head for a moment, his eyes telling her what she knew, that there was a great deal to be said but that this was not the time. Then he kissed her back and said, "Sleep well."

She nodded and left with Miss Hurstman.

She arrived back at Broad Street exhausted from an astonishing few days, but not ready for sleep. She wandered into the front parlor.

To find Althea in the arms of a dashing gentleman.

"Althea!" Clarissa gasped, absurdly shocked.

Althea and the man broke apart, both red-faced and appalled.

Miss Hurstman let out a crack of laughter. "It's as well I don't plan a career as a chaperon. I'm clearly a total loss at it. You, sir—who are you, and what are you doing? Oh, forget that. It's clear what you're doing."

The man had struggled to his feet and was pulling his waistcoat down. He was not a young gallant, but he was a fine figure of a man, with short, curly hair, a handsome face, and good broad shoulders. Althea leaped up and stood beside him in a protective posture that Clarissa recognized.

How on earth had Althea got to this point with this man with her none the wiser? She'd never seen him before.

The man tugged on his cravat, then said, "I am extremely sorry. Carried away, you see. But Miss Trist and I have just agreed to marry."

"Very nice," said Miss Hurstman. "But who are you?"

"The name's Verrall," he said, swallowing. "I do have Miss Trist's father's permission."

Clarissa gaped. This was Althea's hoary widower?

He stood straighter, chin set. "I thought I was prepared to wait while Althea had her holiday here, but her letters began to worry me." He turned to Althea. "I hope you don't mind your father sharing them with me, my dear?"

Althea shook her head, blushing beautifully.

"I did not like to push my suit too strongly, but I became convinced that it would be folly to delay with so many handsome gallants around. So here I am."

"So here you are," Miss Hurstman said. "Excellent, but there's no bed for you here, Mr. Verrall, so off you go. You can return in the morning."

Mr. Verrall took his leave, not even daring to take a final kiss under Miss Hurstman's eye. Despite everything that had happened, Clarissa felt like giggling, and she was truly delighted for her friend's happiness. Incidentals like age didn't matter. Only trust and love.

But then Althea obviously gathered her wits. "But you, Clarissa. We heard . . . Maria Vandeimen said . . ."

Clarissa made a decision. "Oh, that was all a misunderstanding." She used the excuse Hawk had apparently spread around. "I went to attend Beth Arden's lying-in."

"You, an unmarried lady!" Althea gasped.

"I was always somewhat rash, Althea, you know that. Come up to bed."

She glanced at Miss Hurstman and saw that the woman understood. There was no point in disturbing Althea's happiness with a crisis she could not help with.

It was dark in the small space, and windowless, but a tight grille in the door let in glimmers from a lamp some distance away. A swaying lamp.

Lord Darius Debenham lay propped up on the narrow bed, watching the two older children play with their food. Exactly that. There was bread here. They'd eaten some, then molded bits into little animals with practiced skill. So few proper toys they'd had.

They spoke in whispers. They always spoke in whispers, probably because Thérèse Bellaire had punished them if they didn't.

Thérèse Bellaire. The whore who had tormented Nicholas for fun. She would have no sweet ending planned. They were to die here, and he couldn't do a damn thing about it except pray.

And keep the children at peace as long as he could.

He gently touched the hair of the one cuddled against him. Thérèse had said she was Arabel, Nicholas's child. He'd last seen her as a baby, but in the uncertain light he thought she had Nicholas's eyes. Dear God, what he must be suffering.

And there wasn't a damn thing he could do to help.

Little Arabel had awakened crying and had called for her mama and papa, but she'd calmed. Lord knows why. He couldn't think he was a sight to soothe a child. Perhaps it was Delphie and Pierre, who'd hovered, whispering their comforts and their admonitions to be quiet.

So she was quiet, but she stayed close by his side, and

the trust pierced him when it was so misplaced. The child might well be stronger than he was. He'd made himself eat some of the food left here, but when had he eaten before that? Food had no savor for him, no importance.

His recent life seemed like pictures glimpsed in darkness. She'd said it had been a year. A year! That he'd been close to death.

He remembered the battle, but not whatever disaster had ended it for him. A bullet in the side and a hoof in the head, she'd said. Certainly he had headaches. He could remember the pain so fierce that he'd welcomed the drug, begged for it.

But had it been a year?

And had he really believed he was another man? He couldn't think clearly about it all, but he remembered a time when everything had been blank. He'd welcomed the facts she put in his memory, meaningless though they had been. When he'd begun to doubt, there had been the children. If he wasn't Rowland, they weren't his. So they weren't his.

How could he save them?

Did he want to be saved?

He looked at his bony, quivering hand.

He thought of his parents, his friends. He thought of them finding him like this, a weak husk of a man, already shaking with the need of the stuff in the bottle she'd left.

Perhaps he'd be better dead. But he had to stay alive to take care of the children.

He ached for the laudanum, but she'd left only a spoonful, maybe less. A calculated torment. He didn't need it badly enough yet. She'd given him a lot before she moved him here. Enough for deep dreams, enough for thought. But all he had was in that bottle. Once that was gone, it was gone, and the need would tear him apart. He couldn't let the children see that.

He would kill himself first. It would be kinder.

If he had the strength.

He looked at the bottle again, could almost smell the bitter liquid through the glass. He started to sweat, belly aching.

No. Not yet.

They needed to escape.

He would have laughed if he'd had the energy. He could hardly walk. He'd checked the space, crawling, sweating, and aching every inch of the way. When he'd tried to stand, his legs had buckled under him. Delphie and Pierre had helped him back to the bed.

The door was solid and locked. If he could smash out the tiny grille, not even Delphie could escape through it. And he'd be hard-pressed to gather the strength to pick up the damn bottle and pull out the stopper!

Delphie scrambled to her feet and came over to him, holding the rough doll he'd made for her one day. It was just sticks and rags, but it had been the best he could do. It was their secret, always carefully hidden.

"Mariette's arm is broken, Papa," she whispered in French.

He looked at it as she climbed up beside him. "I can't fix it now, sweetheart. There's no need to whisper. She's gone."

Delphie looked up at him with huge eyes. "I like to whisper."

He held her close as weak tears escaped.

Delphie looked at Arabel, then put the doll into her hand. "You can have her for a little while."

Arabel doubtless didn't understand French, but she clutched Mariette as if the doll could take her back to her loving home.

Dare leaned his head back and did the only thing he still could. He prayed.

When Clarissa woke the next morning she was thrust abruptly back into the horrific situation. She sat up, wondering where the poor children had spent the night. She looked at the window and realized it was raining. That seemed suitable. This was the day of battle. Presumably at some point Thérèse Bellaire would tell them where to send the money. The money Clarissa prayed had been coming in through the night.

Then she would tell them where the prisoners were.

If Hawk hadn't found them beforehand.

Althea stirred and smiled, clearly full of more pleasant thoughts. "Clarissa," she said, turning sober and sitting up, "would you mind very much if I returned with Mr. Verrall to Bucklestead St. Stephens? He can't be away long, you see, because of the children. And . . . and I want to go home. I'm very sorry, but I don't like Brighton very much."

Clarissa took her hands. "Of course you must go. But all the way with only Mr. Verrall?"

She was teasing somewhat, but Althea flushed. "I'm sure he can be trusted."

"Ah," said Clarissa, "but a chaperon is not to keep the wolves away. It's to keep the ladies from leaping into the jaws of the wolves."

"Clarissa!" gasped Althea. But then she colored even more. "I know what you mean. But," she added, "it's not like that with Mr. Verrall and me yet, and I'm sure I can trust him to be a gentleman."

Clarissa smiled and kissed her. "I'm sure you'll be very happy, no matter what happens."

They both climbed out of bed, and Althea asked, "What of you and the major? It all seemed so strange."

Clarissa didn't want to lie. She looked at Althea and said, "I'm not sure you want to know."

Althea blushed again. "Perhaps I don't. But are you going to marry him?"

"Oh, yes," Clarissa said. "I'm sure I am."

As soon as she was dressed, she hurried downstairs and told Miss Hurstman about Althea's plans, and that she herself was going over to the Vandeimens' house. She was braced for battle, but Miss Hurstman nodded. "I'll come over myself when Althea's on her way. Take the footman, though. Just in case."

So Clarissa was escorted all the way, astonished that she had never considered that she might be in danger. After all, she was the one who was technically in possession of Thérèse Bellaire's money.

She arrived without incident, however, to find that

wealth had poured in, but that nothing new had turned up to tell them where the hostages were.

There was a heavy sack of jewels. Some were Blanche's theatrical pieces, but most were real. A great deal of it had come from Lord Arden, including, originally, what Blanche had referred to as Lucien's necklace, which was a ridiculously gaudy piece with huge stones in many colors; it had to be worth thousands.

Clarissa smiled at the friendly, understanding love that had given the White Dove something she would never wear but something that would amuse her, and keep her if she ever fell into need.

A strongbox had come from someone in London, and more from Lord Middlethorpe in Hampshire. Clarissa looked at it all, remembering with some satisfaction that all these people would be paid back from her money.

But then she realized that would mean that Hawk would lose Hawkinville. She could bear that, but she ached for the poor people there, and she knew the pain must be ten times worse for him. Ignoring the presence of all the others, she went to where he sat, clearly furious at himself for not being able to solve the problems single-handedly. Jetta was curled at his feet. Tentatively, Clarissa put her hand on his shoulder.

He started and looked up, then covered her hand with his. "Where do we stand?"

She smiled. She too wanted this clear. "On our own two feet? I suppose that should be four. I meant what I said about using my money to pay everyone back. Even if they resist."

He turned to face her. "I know. It's all right."

"What about Hawkinville?"

"That's not all right, but if it's the price, I'll pay it."

She raised his hand and kissed it. "If you happen to have a ring, I'd be proud to wear it."

He stood, smiling, and produced it, slid it on her finger.

She smiled back at him, not teary at all, but firmly happy that things were right. About this, at least.

"And now," she said, "please solve all our problems, sir."

He groaned, but said, "I don't expect always to do miracles, but in this case I feel that I've missed something."

She sat down beside him. "What if I go over it? She snatched the baby from the Court and brought it to Brighton. Lord Darius and the children had already been brought here by Old Matt. I assume he hasn't said anything?"

"He's dead, love. The alcohol killed him."

It sent a chill through her. One death could so easily be followed by more.

He took her hand. "She might not have meant to kill him."

"But she didn't care, did she?"

"No," he admitted. "She didn't care."

She pulled her mind straight and tried to help him again. "She sent a note . . ."

But he said, "Wait! Smuggler's brandy! Smugglers," he said to the room at large. "Of course! She's linked up with smugglers. She's on a boat."

The room suddenly buzzed, and Susan said, "I know smuggling."

"Do you know any smugglers here?" Hawk asked.

She pulled a face. "No, but my father's name will count."

Even more interesting, thought Clarissa. But she was fizzing with excitement, too.

"Go out and see what you can learn. Con—"

"Of course I'm going with her."

The two men shared a look, then laughed.

The Amleighs left and Hawk paced. "She's on a boat, ready to take off for the Continent as soon as she has the money. I'll go odds she has her hostages on the boat too. No, not on the same boat—on another boat. We need to check the fishermen as well as the smugglers. They're not always the same thing. Van? And see what there is that we can hire. We need to be on the water."

Lord Vandeimen left, and Hawk looked around the room. "I wonder if anyone but Susan knows how to handle a boat."

"She's a smuggler?" Clarissa asked tentatively.

"Just closely connected," said Hawk with a smile that was partly excitement. "We've cut through her lines at last. We'll have this all tight by evening."

Time returned to creeping in halting steps. Clarissa kept thinking of the children, wondering if they were still drugged—which would be dangerous—or frightened, or hungry. If they were on a boat, were they safe or could they fall overboard and drown? Were there rats?

She knew it must be much worse for the Delaneys, but they seemed to have found a stoic calm as they waited.

Con and Susan returned first. "I made contact eventually," Susan said. "I had to persuade Con to go away. He has far too much of a military look about him. I put the word out and offered a reward, but no one would say anything directly. They'll send word here if there's anything."

"Can you sail a fishing boat?" Hawk asked.

"Of course," she said, as if it were the most common thing.

"We weren't all raised by the sea, you know. With any luck, Van has found us a boat. We need to be on the water this evening when the payment is made." He looked out of the window at the sea, choppy and gray on this miserable day. There were plenty of boats bobbing at anchor. Clarissa wondered which ones held the villain and the hostages, and what would happen if they searched them all.

Disaster, probably.

Then Lord Vandeimen returned. "The *Pretty Anna*," he said, eyes bright. "I can point it out."

"We've hired it?" Hawk asked.

"No. We've hired the *Seahorse*. The *Pretty Anna* is probably where Dare and the children are. The young man who owns it has been acting strange recently. Not going out fishing on good days, disappearing now and then. Talking about traveling. Yesterday he talked to one man about selling the *Pretty Anna* to him."

"Show us."

Everyone crowded to the window, and Lord Vandeimen pointed out one small boat among many, but that one had the dull glimmer of a lantern, showing that someone must be on board.

"Can we go?" Eleanor asked. "Now?"

But there was a new knock on the door. There seemed to be a confusion of footsteps, then the door opened. "A message for Mr. Delaney," the footman announced, the paper on a silver tray.

Nicholas strode over to take it.

"And," intoned the footman, "there's a man at the back door asking after Lady Amleigh."

Susan rushed out, pushing the footman out of the way. Someone shut the door on him. Everyone looked at Nicholas.

"She must have caught wind of our tack. It's the *Pretty Anna*, now, with whatever valuables we have. No promise of telling us where the hostages are." He looked at Clarissa. "You and I are to take the ransom, dressed in only the lightest clothes."

"Clarissa?" said Hawk. "That's not acceptable."

"I agree," said Nicholas. "I'll go alone."

"No. If she wants me, I have to go. We can't risk the children."

"She probably has no intention of telling us where they are," Hawk said. "And with luck, we can find them with the other boat."

"Luck is not acceptable."

"Use some sense! She'll probably take you as a new hostage."

"I'd die first," said Nicholas.

"So you'd be dead. What good would that be?"

Silence crackled.

Clarissa put her hands on his arm. "Hawk, I have to go. With or without your blessing."

He glared at her, but then brought himself under control. "All right. I go with Susan. I'm a strong swimmer. If we can close, I can swim over."

"You'll need weapons," Nicholas said.

Hawk's knife appeared in his hand.

Nicholas said, "I have something similar upstairs. But Clarissa could do with one too."

Clarissa shook her head. "I can't use a knife on someone."

"You can if you have to."

"I'll get something from the kitchen," Maria said and hurried away.

Susan came in, bright with excitement. "We've got her! She's paying Sam Pilcher to take her to France. He has a fast cutter he claims can outrun the navy. He was taken with her charms, but he's beginning to wonder."

"Is she on the boat now?" Nicholas asked.

"No. He's just been sent word that she'll be there in the hour. But," she added, "he swears there's no one else on the boat now. He'll take someone of ours out there to capture her."

"I'll go," said Lord Vandeimen, clearly itching for action.

"And I," said Major Beaumont.

Susan went out with them to introduce them. Clarissa heard her instructing them not to act like military men.

"So," said Hawk, "she has them on the *Pretty Anna*. She'll plan to take the money there, then probably be rowed over to the other ship. Susan can block that as soon as we have the hostages. I don't think it will be so easy."

"She'll take Arabel with her," Nicholas suggested.

"It's possible. You have to kill her, you know. She's a viper. You can't take her to court, and if she gets away you'll never know when she'll be back, more vengeful than before."

"You can't doubt I will if necessary."

Maria came back with a handful of knives. "Cook's in tears."

The note specified that Clarissa was to wear only a dress—no spencer or cloak. Nicholas was to be in breeches and shirt. Few places to hide weapons. No place to hide a pistol.

Soon Clarissa had a narrow knife tucked down her gown in front of her corset, carefully pinned in place in a kind of sheath. The heavy linen protected her from the blade, but she could feel it, hard and unnatural.

"I still don't think I could use it," she said to Hawk, who had put it there without a hint that he found it arousing.

He looked at her, all officer. "Don't let her hurt you without a fight. Go for the face. She's vain. For the eyes with your fingers and nails. If this works properly, however, I'll be there to take care of you."

He kissed her fiercely and left with Con and Susan for the *Seahorse*. Clarissa saw Jetta streak to catch up and hoped the cat truly was descended from an ancient Chinese warrior line.

Nicholas had two knives tucked away. They gathered the money and jewels into a heavy leather bag.

"We'll delay a little," he said to Clarissa. "Give the others time. But we can't wait too long. All right?"

Clarissa felt the electricity of fear, and wasn't sure if it was bad or good. "Yes. I suffer terribly from impatience, though. I want to get on with it."

"Let's go, then." He went to kiss his wife.

As he swept Clarissa out of the room, however, she saw the expression on Eleanor Delaney's face. She looked as if she feared that she would never see her husband again.

Chapter Thirty

~

The rain was a weary drizzle, soft but chill. They crossed the deserted Parade to the seafront, then headed right. "Now that we're out here there's no need to hurry. She's probably watching through a telescope, and if she sees we're doing the right things, it will be all right."

Clarissa scanned the choppy gray sea for Hawk and Susan, but there were so many boats, and she couldn't even tell if most of them were moving or not.

"Why did Eleanor look so very frightened?" she asked. "Did she think we're to be murdered?" She was proud of her level tone.

Nicholas looked at her. "It's old history. I got on a boat with Thérèse Bellaire once before and she didn't see me for six months. She thought I was dead. We're on a basis of truth, aren't we? The truth is that Thérèse might want me dead, but she certainly wants to taunt me, to finally prove that she can win. I don't think she wishes you harm. I think she wants a witness, and she'll be as unpleasant, as lewd, as she can be. I'm sorry."

"It's not your fault."

"Who can say? If I'd had the sense not to dally with her so many years ago . . . Hawk was right, though. If necessary, don't hesitate to hurt her."

He stopped and looked out to sea. "That's the *Pretty*

Anna, and there's our boat." He pointed to a dinghy tied up at a wooden jetty.

"All details taken care of," she said, and they hurried in that direction.

Clarissa shivered. In part it was because the rain had soaked her light dress, and the breeze was cold. It was also because of that waiting boat, because they were walking a path created by the evil Madame Bellaire.

She scanned the water again and saw no other boat swooping in. Of course it was too soon.

Their footsteps rattled on the uneven planks of the jetty, and then they were above the boat, a rough wooden ladder leading down.

"Can you manage it?" Nicholas asked.

"I'll have to, won't I?"

"I'll go first," he said, and climbed nimbly down with the bag of loot.

Clarissa took a deep breath and eased herself over onto the ladder. "Give thanks," she said, "that Miss Mallory's School for Ladies believes in physical exercise and womanly strength."

The ladder was rough beneath her hands, and the wind swirled, seeming to snatch at her, making her skirts snag on rough edges. She went steadily down, letting the fine cotton rip if it had to. Another dress ruined.

At the bottom, Nicholas gripped her waist and eased her into the swaying, bouncing boat. He settled her on one bench, then took the other and swung the oars over the water.

She clung to the sides, feeling sure it would tip with the next wave. "I've never been in a boat before."

"There are worse things," he said with a smile, and started to pull.

"I can't swim, either." The boat bucked, and she held on tighter, determined not to scream. Were they making any progress against this rough water? And how was everyone else? The children. Lord Darius. Hawk.

From above, the sea had seemed choppy. From down here, the waves seemed huge.

"Hawk said he would *swim* in this?"

"He'll be all right," Nicholas said, rowing in an easy rhythm. "He said he is a strong swimmer, and I don't think he's the boastful type."

A wave slapped and drenched her hand. They were getting nearer to the *Pretty Anna*, but not quickly enough for her. A viper waited, and perhaps a test of courage, but it looked so much more solid than this swaying, bouncing little boat.

Nicholas's drenched shirt clung to his body, a body, she noted, as well made as Hawk's. It pleased her, but it didn't excite her. Please, God, let Hawk be safe. Please, God, let them save the children and Lord Darius.

Please, if that's what it takes, let the Frenchwoman have the jewels and money, and go. Go far, far away. She knew Hawk wanted her stopped, but Clarissa was with Nicholas in simply wanting this over.

"Do you see anything?" Nicholas asked.

Clarissa snapped out of her thoughts and looked at the boat, twenty feet away. "No sign of anyone."

"Keep looking."

She scanned the simple boat with the small shedlike room and a tall mast. A lantern bobbed, but the vessel looked completely empty. If Nicholas was right that Thérèse Bellaire wanted to gloat, she had to be there somewhere.

Their boat jarred against the *Anna*, and Nicholas tied it up close to a ladder. "I'd better go first," he said.

"No," said a familiar French voice. "The girl first, with the ransom."

Clarissa started to shake and tried desperately not to. After a shared look with Nicholas, she put the satchel across her chest and gripped the ladder. It was harder going up than down. She felt heavy, and her hands were aching with cold. She made it, though, and scrambled over the top to tumble awkwardly onto the deck.

She struggled to her feet. "I'm here," she said, wishing her voice didn't shake. "With the money."

She heard a sound and whirled, but it was only Nicholas beside her.

"Thérèse?" he said, sounding completely at ease. "At your service, as always."

A woman ducked out of the small covered area. She wore an encompassing cloak, but Clarissa could hardly believe it was Mrs. Rowland. The skin was clear, and even glowing in the chilly air. The eyes seemed huge, the lips full and red. In a chilling way, she was very beautiful.

"Nicky, darling," she said. And he'd been right. She was gloating. Clarissa fought a desperate battle not to look around for the *Seahorse,* which carried Susan and Hawk.

The woman stepped a little closer, and a man emerged behind her. A handsome man. Young, but tall and strong, and with a pistol in his hand.

"These the ones, then?" he said in a local accent. "The ones who stole your money?"

"Yes," she purred. "But they have returned part of it, so we need not be too harsh. Come forward, my dear, and give me the bag."

Clarissa shrugged it off so it was in her hands, then walked forward. She suspected what was going to happen here. When she got close, the man would grab her and Nicholas would be at the woman's mercy.

She dropped the bag on the deck a few feet from the Frenchwoman's feet.

The dark eyes narrowed. "Bring it to me."

"Why? That's it. Take it and go."

"If you don't bring it to me, I will not tell you where the children are, where Lord Darius Debenham is."

"Do I care?" Clarissa asked, drawing on experience of the most silly, heartless schoolgirls she'd ever known. "You're taking my money. You say it's yours, but it's mine, and you're stealing it."

The young man started to speak, and Thérèse hissed at him to be silent. "It is *mine.* I worked hard for that money, and you did nothing. Nothing! You didn't even kill Deveril. Now pick up that bag and bring it to me."

"Make me."

Thérèse smiled. "Samuel, shoot the man."

The young man blanched, but his pistol rose.

Clarissa snatched up the bag from the deck.

"That's better," said Thérèse. "You see, it does not pay to fight me. You cannot win. Bring it here."

Clarissa walked forward as slowly as she dared, willing Hawk to appear. She was about to put the bag into the Frenchwoman's hand, when the man said, "Here! What're you doing?"

Clarissa turned to see that Nicholas had unfastened the flap in his breeches and was undoing the drawers beneath. "This is what you want, Thérèse, isn't it?"

The Frenchwoman seemed transfixed. Not by the sight—Clarissa could tell that—but by satisfaction. "Yes. Strip."

Nicholas continued to unfasten his clothing, slowly, seductively. Clarissa realized she was gaping and looked quickly at the young man. He was red-faced. He suddenly jerked the pistol up and aimed it.

Clarissa swung the heavy bag and knocked the weapon flying into the sea.

Samuel howled and rushed at her. She dodged, fell, and quite by accident slipped behind Madame Bellaire so he ran into her.

He howled again, staggering back. Clarissa saw blood.

"Oaf!" the Frenchwoman spat, a bloodstained knife in her hand.

Nicholas had a knife out too, and Clarissa saw a boat sweeping close, sails full. It looked as if it was going to crash into them. Not with the children surely here!

She scrambled up and ran for the shed, but she was grabbed and hauled back. She saw the knife in Madame Bellaire's hand and knew she should be terrified. She thought she heard someone bellow, "Clarissa!"

Hawk.

Go for the eyes. She scratched the woman's face as hard as she could.

The Frenchwoman shrieked and Clarissa was free. She ran, but tripped over the bag of treasure.

Then Madame Bellaire was coming at her again, livid scratches on her face, a face ugly with furious hate.

Nicholas was running forward, but the man Samuel, blood still streaming down his side, threw himself at him.

It all seemed slow, but Clarissa did the only thing she could. She threw the bag.

It hit the woman, staggering her, then fell, spilling gold and jewels.

Madame Bellaire froze for a moment, staring at it. Clarissa fumbled for her knife, catching it on every edge, it seemed, as she struggled to get it free.

Then something jarred the boat, and Hawk landed on the deck. He grabbed the woman's arm, but she twisted, knife lunging. A black shape flew through the air at her face, and she screamed.

Hawk tore the spitting cat away, trapped the woman in his arms, turned her . . .

And threw her, suddenly limp, over the side.

When he turned back, the knife was gone.

It wasn't quiet. The wind rattled the assorted bits of the boat, and the waves slapped hard at the sides. But the people were silent, even the young man, Samuel, who'd been fighting Nicholas in the cause of the woman who had stabbed him.

"What have you done with her?" he cried, and staggered over to look out at the sea.

Hawk and Nicholas looked at each other.

"She was beautiful to me once," Nicholas said, fastening his clothing. "But thank you."

Samuel was weeping.

But then a faint voice cried, "Papa!" and Nicholas ran for the shed that must contain the steps.

Clarissa watched in a daze as the Amleighs climbed over the side of the boat. They must have rowed over. Susan began to do things to the boat, but her husband raced below.

Clarissa looked at Hawk.

He said, "Yes, I killed her. I'm sorry if that upsets you."

"I'll grow accustomed."

He pulled her into his arms. "God, love, I pray not!"

They clung together as things happened around them,

and then Nicholas was on deck, a wan child clinging to him, and the boat was under one sail and moving carefully toward the jetty.

Con brought the other two children up, and they huddled close to each other, but Clarissa separated from Hawk and sat down to hold out her arms. After a moment they came forward. Hawk sat beside her, and soon Delphie was in her lap, Pierre in Hawk's.

"Mrs. Rowland," Hawk said gently to them in French, and their eyes dilated. "She is dead. She will not return."

The two children looked at each other, and the boy said, "Papa?"

Clarissa bit her lip.

"Your papa will be fine," Hawk said, but he gave Clarissa a helpless look.

She mouthed, "Perhaps we can take care of them?"

He smiled and nodded.

The boat bumped gently against the dock, and Hawk and Clarissa scrambled off, each with a child. She, for one, was deeply grateful for a solid surface beneath her feet. Eleanor was already there, and Nicholas put Arabel into her shaking arms, then held her close. Blanche wrapped a cloak around them both.

Major Beaumont and Lord Vandeimen ran up and helped carry Lord Darius gently off the boat. Though it took three men, it was clear that he weighed little.

The children pulled away from Clarissa and Hawk's arms and pressed close, whispering, "Papa, Papa," and he touched them with his trembling hands, telling them in French that it would be all right. That all these people were their friends. That he would make sure they were all right.

A black cat wound around from Hawk to child to child . . .

And Clarissa wept. She wept for love, and courage, and trust, and hope. She wept for weariness, cold, and death. She wept in Hawk's arms as he led her away from horror, back to the Vandeimens' house.

And the Duke and Duchess of Yeovil were there.

At the sight of her son, the duchess half fainted, and

then crawled to him. The duke was pale and trembling, but he helped her to sit up, and gripped his son's hand. Delphie and Pierre were tucked close to Lord Darius, as if they'd never leave. Clarissa didn't think they would accept any other home, or that Lord Darius would easily let them go.

She heard him struggle to say, "It's opium, Mama. I'm addicted to opium," and his mother say that it was all right, that he was home now, and she would make sure it was all right.

Clarissa turned to Hawk. "We're home now," she said. "And I believe it will be all right."

"You have my solemn vow on it, my love. Marry me, Falcon."

"Of course."

Heaven suddenly seemed possible, but it was rather alarming, even so, when a knock on the door produced the Duke and Duchess of Belcraven. Slim, cool, and elegant, the duke raised his quizzing glass and looked at her. "I hear alarming things of you, young lady."

Clarissa couldn't help it. She curtsied and said, "Probably all true. I'm delighted you're here, your grace. You'll make it easy for me to marry Major Hawkinville as soon as possible."

"I gather that is a necessity."

"Completely," she said. The duchess laughed and came over to hug her.

The duke's lips twitched, and he looked around. "From the general tone, I assume the valuable items I've brought are not necessary. The Rogues rule the day again?"

"And the Georges," said Hawk, stepping forward to bow. "You doubtless have misgivings, your grace, but I hope you will consent to our marriage. I will do my best to make her happy."

"As I will do my best to ensure that you do, sir. And my best is very formidable indeed. In moments, I wish to see you to discuss the marriage contract." He then went over to talk to the Yeovils and congratulate them on the return of their son.

The legal discussion did not take place in moments. A doctor was summoned for Lord Darius, and rooms were arranged for the Yeovils at the Old Ship. Once the doctor assured the duke and duchess that it was safe, they all left, Lord Darius on a stretcher, two waifs attached. Clarissa recognized that Delphie and Pierre had chosen their own home. Surprisingly, Jetta had too. She leaped onto the stretcher but eyed the children, as if they were her new charges.

All who had been on the water were damp and went to change. Clarissa hated to leave, even for a moment, but Hawk escorted her back to Broad Street for a dry dress, and then brought her and a relieved Miss Hurstman back. Althea and Mr. Verrall had apparently only just left. Clarissa chose to wear the cream-and-rust dress she had worn that first day on the Steyne, the one with the deep fringe. She grinned at Hawk, and raised the skirt a little to show more of her striped stockings.

He shook his head, but his eyes sent another message.

She could wait. Now all was certain, she could wait to lie again with him naked in bed.

Back at the Vandeimens' they found everyone in the riotous high spirits of relief. The ladies were adorning themselves with the jewelry, real and fake. Clarissa acquired a tiara, and Miss Hurstman didn't complain when Nicholas pinned a gaudy brooch onto her plain gown. She had Arabel in her arms by then, and the child, beginning to blossom again, reached for it with delight.

Nicholas laughed and gave his daughter Blanche's necklace, which met with her rapturous approval. Clarissa noted a shadow on him at times, however, and remembered him saying, "She was beautiful to me, once."

She knew the death would not rest easily upon Hawk, either, though it could not be the first time he had killed. It was his way, she was sure, to deal with such problems by himself, but in time it would be her blessing to share them with him.

Then they all sat at the dinner table, with candlelight shooting fire from thousands of pounds' worth of jewelry.

Hawk rose again, however, and raised his glass. "To friends," he said, "old and new. May we never fail."

Everyone drank the toast, and then Nicholas stood to propose one. "To the Rogues, who in the end, at least, never fail. Dare will be whole again."

Con rose to add to it. "With the help of the Georges." He grinned. "An interesting alliance, wouldn't you say?"

"The world is doubtless tipping on its axis," murmured the Duke of Belcraven, but with a smile, and he drank the toast along with everyone else. He even proposed one himself—a slightly naughty one about marriage, which made his duchess blush.

By the time the dinner was over, the duke remarked that no one was in a state to draw up legal agreements, and made an appointment the next day at the Old Ship, where he, too, had rooms. Clarissa insisted on being present. He gave in in the end, but insisted on seeing Clarissa and Miss Hurstman back to Broad Street.

"We'll have no more impropriety, Clarissa," he said on leaving her there.

She just smiled. "I will try, your grace, though I'm not sure it is in my nature."

She slept deeply and late, awakening to an extraordinary sense of calm—like the calm of the sea on a perfect day, all the power of the oceans still beneath it. She breakfasted with Miss Hurstman and told her the details she'd missed. Miss Hurstman was astonished to find that she'd been regarded as a warder, but rather amused that she'd been thought to be part of a wicked plot.

Hawk came to escort Clarissa to the Old Ship. They strolled along the Marine Parade, by a calm sea touched to blue by the sky and sunshine.

"Do you think summer is here at last?" she asked.

"*Carpe diem,*" he replied with a grin.

She smiled back. "I promised the duke to try to behave. We can marry soon, can't we?"

"Today would not be too soon for me, love."

"Or me. But, Hawk, I would like a village wedding like Maria had. Is it possible?"

He took her hand and kissed it. "I would give you the stars if I could. A village wedding is surely possible."

They entered the hotel in perfect harmony, but Clarissa found that she had to fight to give him enough for his father to fully restore Gaspard Hall.

"Think of it from my point of view," she said. "I want our home to ourselves. If we give your father enough money, perhaps he'll leave immediately to take up the work."

"An excellent point. Hawkinville," said the duke, "consider it settled. In strict legality, all the money should go to your father. If you present difficulties, I may make it so."

Hawk rolled his eyes, but surrendered. "The rest of the money is Clarissa's, however. I want it retained under her control. Once free of debt, the manor will provide for us."

Clarissa didn't argue except to say, "You know I will spend some on our comforts and pleasures. But I do want to use most of it for charity. It has a dark history. I thought perhaps a charity school in Slade's house."

Hawk laughed. "A wonderful idea! He'll doubtless have to sell it to us cheap as well."

"So?" Clarissa asked Hawk. "When do we marry? I am ready to fly."

"It is for the lady to say, but the license will take a few days."

"A week, then, if all can be arranged."

He stood, bringing her to her feet. "It will all be arranged with Hawkish perfection. To do it, though, and to retain my sanity, I'm going to leave." Ignoring the duke, he kissed her. "We have no need to seize the day, love. We have the promise of perfect tomorrows."

"Alliteration?" she murmured, and he winced.

Hawk walked out of the dark church into sunshine, and into a shower of grain and flowers thrown by his boisterous villagers. Everyone smiled at a wedding, but he could see that these smiles reflected delight of an extraordinary degree. Not only was the Young Squire—

as they'd decided to call him—married, but the Old Squire had already gone. His father had leased a house near to Gaspard Hall and left without a hint of regret.

The village was free of Slade, too, and the threat they'd all sensed from him. His house would soon be Clarissa's to do with as she wished. The most important repairs to the cottages were already in hand, which was also providing necessary work.

He looked at his bride, glowing with her own perfect happiness as the villagers welcomed her as one of their own. He said a prayer to be worthy, to be able to create the happiness neither of them had ever truly known. It should be easy. She'd had her modiste recreate the simple cream dress that had marked their adventures, and she was wearing a similar hat and fichu. He could hardly wait to strip it off her, in the manor, which sat contentedly waiting, open-windowed in the sun.

He turned from that—it would wait—to accept the congratulations of Van and Con. Susan was definitely with child, and now Maria had hope. It was possible that Clarissa would also have a child in nine months. A new threesome to run wild around the area.

Unable to bear to be apart, he retrieved his bride from among beaming villagers and drew her in for a kiss.

"Give thanks," he said, wondering how soon he could sweep her laughing into his arms and carry her upstairs to a bed covered with smooth sheets fresh from hanging in the sun. "We have hope of heaven."

"Alliteration!" Clarissa pointed out, with a twinkle in her eye that told him her thoughts were perfectly in accord with his.

Enough! He picked her up and spun her around and around. Then, "Enjoy the feast!" he called, and ran for their home.

Author's Note

~

I hope you have enjoyed the three linked stories about the Georges. If you picked up *The Devil's Heiress* first and want to catch up on Van and Con's stories, they are still available because they came out just a few months ago.

Van's story is "The Demon's Mistress" in a collection called *In Praise of Younger Men*. Con's story is *The Dragon's Bride*. The are all from this publisher, Signet.

As for the Rogues, the books about them are not all so easy to find, but the first two have recently been reissued. They are *An Arranged Marriage* (Nicholas and Eleanor) and *An Unwilling Bride* (Lucien and Beth).

You can find a full, annotated booklist on my Web site, www.poboxes.com/jobev.

You will also find there some pictures of places in the books, including Brighton, which I visited recently to brush up my memory, and background information about my books.

Steyne, by the way, is pronounced Steen. Van's estate of Steynings is my invention, and I pronounce it Stainings, but there is a village in Sussex called Steyning, and they pronounce it Stenning. Ah, English. So illogical. Take your pick!

I enjoy hearing from my readers. You can e-mail me at jobev@poboxes.com, or mail me c/o Meg Ruley, The Rotrosen Agency, 318 East 51st Street, New York, NY 10022. An SASE is appreciated to help with the cost of a reply.

Dear Reader:

I hope you've enjoyed reading this adventure of the Company of Rogues.

I love these men, and I've had fun writing about them over the past thirty years. (Yes, really! My first Rogues novel was the first book I ever finished. It just took a while to get it right and sell it.)

The adventure started for them when they were schoolboys at Harrow. Boys' schools were rough places in those days and an enterprising lad called Nicholas Delaney gathered a group for mutual support—one for all and all for one—forging a bond that lasted into adulthood.

They're a mixed bunch because Nicholas chose the outsiders, the unusual, and the ones who needed protection most. For example, we have Miles Cavanagh, an Irish rebel, and Lucien de Vaux, Marquess of Arden, haughty heir to a dukedom. Leander Knollis was the suave son of a diplomat, who scarcely knew England at all, and quiet Francis Haile, Viscount Middlethrope, arrived at school grieving his recently dead father. Despite their variety, the Rogues are consistent in honor. Whatever their natures, they serve their country in Parliament, on the battlefield, or by tending the land, because that's what heroes do.

For me as an author, their differences have been a joy, because each Rogue has fallen into a different kind of adventure. Or perhaps I should say, they have run into a different kind of woman, seemingly designed to test their limits. A tempestuous ward. A Regency-era feminist. A woman trained in the erotic arts. A poet's widow who's fed up with being seen as the perfect "angel bride." (Want to guess which Rogue above gets which?)

All things come to an end, however, and they are nearly all settled in matrimony. *The Rogue's Return*, on sale in March 2006, will be followed by Lord Darius Debenham's story in 2007, completing the series.

However, there will be books about friends and relatives, all in the same "world." The Company of Rogues series (including some spin-offs*) is as follows: *An Arranged Marriage* (Nicholas), *An Unwilling Bride* (Lucien), *Christmas Angel* (Leander), *Forbidden* (Francis), *Dangerous Joy* (Miles), *The Dragon's Bride* (Con), *The Devil's Heiress**, *Hazard**, *St. Raven**, *Skylark* (Stephen), *The Rogue's Return* (Simon).

I hope you enjoy them all.

All best wishes,
Jo

Hazard

The sheltered daughter of a duke, Lady Anne Peckworth has always been a perfect lady, even when jilted. Twice. Now, however, she's angry, and she's angry at the single most reckless, most irresponsible, most irresistible man she's ever known, Race de Vere. Race has invaded her orderly world like a pirate, tempting her to the edge and beyond. He leads her into impropriety, into wickedness, and then into the most dangerous step of all—the adventure that could win or lose her everything in one hazardous night.

"Engaging. . . . Fans will appreciate the spicy chemistry between [Anne] and Race."   *—Publishers Weekly*

"Fans of Jo Beverley's Company of Rogues series will truly enjoy this delightful adventure."   *—Booklist*

St. Raven

Cressida Mandeville agrees to Lord Crofton's vile proposal, but secretly she has other plans. She will trick the loathsome man, find her father's hidden wealth, and save the family from ruin. All goes well, until a daring highwayman, Tristan Tregallows, Duke of St. Raven, stops their carriage, whirls Cressida up onto his dark horse, and demands a kiss. When St. Raven discovers Cressida is on a quest, he knows he must become her partner and protector. But he doesn't expect the dangers to his heart.

"Beverley's delicious, well-crafted, and wickedly captivating romance is a surefire winner."   *—Romantic Times*

"A well-crafted story and an ultimately very satisfying romance."   *—The Romance Reader*

Skylark

Once she was Mrs. Hal Gardeyne, the darling Lady Skylark of London society, but now she's a terrified mother. Hal's death has made young Harry heir to her father-in-law's title and estates, and she fears Harry's uncle wants those prizes enough to commit murder. Then a mysterious letter that could change everything arrives. Is there a long-lost heir to the Caldford estate? Laura must uncover the answers even if it means turning to Sir Stephen Ball—a man whose heart she broke years before. Together, Stephen and Laura must discover the truth despite the dangerous obstacles in their path. Will they be able to overcome their enemies before the passion that has reignited between them sweeps them both away?

"Beverley is a master who sets the tone for a wickedly sensual romance."   —*Romantic Times*

"The story is told with charm and wit, with narrative limited to the pertinent, and plenty of lively and meaningful dialogue."   —Romance Reviews Today

COMING IN MARCH 2006

The Rogue's Return

After years living in the New World of Canada, Simon St. Bride is ready to return to aristocratic life in England. But his plans are delayed by a duel and a young woman he feels honor bound to marry, even though his family is unlikely to welcome her. And despite her seeming innocence, Jane Otterburn is hesitant to speak of her enigmatic past. Then treachery strikes their world. As Simon and Jane fight side by side against enemies and fate—on land and sea—he discovers a wife beyond price and a passion beyond measure. But will the truth about Jane tear their love asunder?